THE END GAME

dhtreichler

Prelude: The Mountain

Everything changed the night of Barak Obama's first presidential inauguration. Even though he had nothing to do with the events I experienced that night, he would as things progressed. I've tried hard to forget what happened, but I can't. Nothing had prepared me. Not my time in the Army, law school; not even my training with the FBI.

It all started that January night in Dallas. Something was gnawing at me as I pulled over. The rusted black Honda Civic I'd liberated from the city impound stopped at the curb just down the street from the target house. I had a bad feeling about the mission. I remembered Sergeant Dean telling me more than once in combat that I needed to listen to the bells in the back of my head. I don't like those bells. Never did.

Maybe they bothered me because I associated them with Mom's funeral. That was the hardest day of my life. I never wanted to feel like that again. The place Mom lit up when I heard her voice is empty now. She had a way of making me feel special I've rarely experienced since. She passed on a rainy September night in '04, the victim of a drunken driver. I've filled up the empty space with all the feelings I couldn't face and slammed the door shut. Keeping that door closed gets me through most days.

On the night of the raid the bells in my head weren't sad, but they were persistent. Things didn't feel right, but I couldn't figure out why. I'd done the work-up and plan. I knew it was right. The M-4 carbine lay across my lap but I didn't touch it .... not yet.

When I snapped down the night vision goggles on my helmet the target became clear. A small wood-sided white house. In this part of

Walnut Hill Lane in Dallas nearly every house looked the same. I'd been in more than my share. I could practically predict the floor plan.

In the front yard a broken tricycle sat on patchy grass surrounded by low-growing shrubbery; holly berry, or something. I knew the shrubs would be razor sharp. I'd have to be careful. The live oaks that grew everywhere in this part of the world hadn't missed this house. Three mature beauties stood in the yard. So the house had been here a while. From what I knew of the residents, they hadn't.

I'd been on dozens of these operations and was getting sick of the younger FBI agents telling me the time had come to find a rocking chair. I thought the reason Bud Myers still sent me out was to provide adult supervision. I also made sure nothing went wrong. Something was satisfying about joining the Bureau later in life, after ten years of military service. I was older than the others, but time in the Bureau was what counted despite my experience, the preference for youth prevailed.

These young guys all seemed to think they could act on their own. I had to pull them aside and show pictures of my first partner who thought so, too. Davis's recklessness was the only reason I wasn't in the picture. Dumb move by my partner, but he saved my life.

Sitting next to me was Alene Oliviera. She was wearing the same uniform but without the helmet or weapon. She wouldn't be coming in to the house until everything was over. She was younger than me and a whole lot better looking. But at the time I didn't really notice – well, maybe I did, but I shouldn't have. Anyway, she worked for the Justice Department. A lawyer, just like me. She was brilliant, a Brazilian zest for life and on a rocket trajectory to the top. She'd gone to Harvard, which I could forgive as a Yale man, but not forget. Everyone has momentary lapses. But then she went back there for law school, so she clearly lacked good judgment.

Alene was working what they called interagency cooperation. She was supposed to be writing some kind of report. I could never figure out why my mission was selected for her first-hand observation. I'd not heard that she was covering any other missions in Dallas. Maybe I was just lucky. Not likely. She was looking for something; I just didn't know what. Right now she was an observer; along for the ride, or so I was told.

She was nervous about something, too.

"Confess?" I asked her.

"Agent Carr?" Alene abandoned her private thoughts.

"Your perfume. Is it Confess?"

"Obsession, why?"

"Lexie, my girlfriend, wears Confess. Smells the same."

I watched a late model white van marked Jefferson Plumbing and Heating pass by. It slowed down in the middle of the street, just beyond the target house. The back door swung open. Eight black suited and armor vested Dallas Police and Drug Enforcement Agency agents piled out, each with a helmet, night vision goggles and an M-4 automatic weapon. The M-4 was the weapon of choice these days. For a close engagement I preferred the AR-15s that the Army Special Forces used, particularly when it had an M203 grenade launcher attached.

I picked up the M-4. "Show time," I remarked. Alene vaguely acknowledged me. She had asked some question about changing tactics and the need to adapt to what the other side was doing. I was still thinking about it as I slid out, but had to put it aside now that we were moving on the target. I refocused and stayed back to let the Dallas Police and DEA guys take the lead. They got paid for going in first. As FBI I was supposed to identify the bad guys, set the trap and investigate the crime scene to bring in the evidence to put the scum bags in jail. I hated that these dealers sold dope to kids. I knew most of them grew up poor. If I were in their position with no education and no future would I do what they did, I sometimes wondered? I hoped not.

Before I'd left the office I scanned the assignment list from DEA, just to be sure. No Lexie. Lexie Jones and I had known each other for about five years. We had been living together for the last three. She had an impish smile, emerald eyes, dark red hair and a freckled face. We'd met in an argument over jurisdiction. As a Drug Enforcement Administration field team supervisor she thought she owned my evidence on a bust we'd both been assigned by our individual agencies. She had a way of getting what she wanted, but I'd won on that occasion. Losing an argument must have made me a challenge for her, but she never let on. I think she finally agreed to move in with me to make sure I'd never win another dispute. She completely owned me and I adored her.

For some reason my fears about this assignment had haunted me for a couple of days. I didn't want her anywhere near this mission. She'd noticed my tension when I left the apartment earlier and said I seemed unusually quiet. I jokingly invited her to join me just so she wouldn't. She smiled as I left.

I adjusted my body armor. Thirty five pounds of ceramic plates designed to stop most shots to my body. The weight just slowed me down and I hated it.

I fell in behind the team. The lead DPD officer, carrying a breaching ram, went to the door and knocked, "Police, we have a warrant. Open up."

Automatic weapon fire from the inside burst through the door.

The impact lifted the officer up off his feet, threw him into the two agents behind.

The armor I so detested saved his life. He dropped the breaching ram and rolled to his left. The automatic fire from inside started coming from everywhere.

One of the agents took a round to the side of his head. He didn't move again.

I dove to the ground wishing I had that AR-15 with the grenade launcher. I crawled over to a window and brought up my M-4. Even with my night vision goggles I couldn't see anyone through the glass.

Bullets kicked up dirt around me.

Two rounds hit the back plates on my armored vest. The force shot through me even though the bullets didn't.

The agent to my left opened fire. I copied him. The firing from the window stopped. *Dead or laying a trap?* I hadn't reached the age of forty two by making assumptions in a fire fight. I'd left the Army to prolong my life. Here I was back in the middle of cordite and lead. *Bad career choice, Carr,* I thought as I rose and raced forward, crouched low with my weapon up.

Through a window, before bullets took it out, I checked what I thought to be the living room. One man was down inside, but no one else.

The holly berry bushes stood between me and the window. I was careful not to snag my pants and climbed through into the room.

A gunman appeared in the doorway. Two rounds struck my chest throwing me back against the wall.

That damn armor saved my life … again. Dazed, I returned fire.

My first shot spun him around. I hoped it wasn't lethal so I could question him.

I got my wish. Two more bullets lodged into my armor leaving me breathless and no choice. I returned fire.

A single head shot. He collapsed to the floor, unmoving.

I hated taking a life. Every time I did it, I hoped I'd never have to again. I took his rifle, slung it over my shoulder and moved out into the hallway.

The new lead agent burst through the front door. The men in the kitchen opened fire giving me a clear view of their positions. I did my best to wound them, but three returned my fire. I had to pull back, partially. Two shots took down one gunman.

Another gunman shot at the lead agent as he came rushing in. I saw a tossed smoke grenade, as if in slow motion. I pulled back and heard the explosion. I rushed the kitchen before the gunmen looked up and saw the downed agent out of the corner of my eye. The body armor hadn't saved him this time. Trailing agents were in the doorway, but I was now in the kitchen standing over the three remaining bad guys. They lay down their weapons. I kicked them away.

There, near the door I discovered a mountain of clear plastic bags of white powder. About a ton, or so it seemed. I'd never seen so much cocaine in one place before.

I'd uncovered a first tier link to Los Zetas cartel. My research had identified this site as important, but I had no idea this house would be the main distribution point in the entire Dallas area. I'd hoped I could get those I took into custody to talk. This much cocaine meant we were a whole lot higher in their organization than I'd expected. Our raid also meant they'd shift operations quickly.

As the other agents entered, each stopped in disbelief of the amount of coke.

I left the DEA agents with the suspects and went up to clear the rooms on the second floor. I discovered stashes of automatic weapons, handguns and boxes of bullets sufficient to hold off a small army. *Why hadn't they used these weapons?* My team had surprised the defenders, I thought. *But they were prepared when we got to the door.* I thought otherwise. *They'd been expecting someone. One of the other cartels maybe?*

Back in the kitchen, the cocaine mountain seemed smaller.

"That it? Just nine men to protect all this?" I asked the young DEA agent.

"Looks like it, sir." A Mississippi man.

The other agents didn't look as clean cut. *Mississippi must be an office puke, and the rest field agents. The others probably distracted the guard while they removed what they wanted of the drugs and secured their bonuses, in gym bags in the van.*

"This your first Op?" I asked Mississippi.

One of the long haired agents came back in. I knew him by sight. His name was Prescott Anderson. "Scott" Anderson had a law degree from the University of Chicago and someone upstairs liked him. He got the plumb assignments and was on his way to a big job at the Agency. At least that was the rumor.

"Good work, Agent Carr. These scumbags weren't even on our radar. How'd the FBI figure this one out?" Anderson asked.

I heard the sound of a step behind me. I looked around to find Alene standing there. Just then the gunmen in the corner snuck a pistol from his boot and got a shot off. Mississippi went down with a neck wound.

The gunman sighted in on Alene. I stepped between them. The second shot burned in my left arm as I dove at him, knocking him over. We wrestled for his weapon.

I jammed my thumb behind the trigger and ripped the gun away.

Anderson shot the gunman in the head, even though mine was only inches away.

When the gunman collapsed I glanced around to make sure Alene was okay. She was, staring at me as if she'd not yet understood how close she'd come to death. Relieved that she was fine and the struggle was over, my emotion soon turned to anger. I wasn't happy to lose someone who could have given us information. I was furious that Anderson could have easily shot me in the head instead of the gunman.

I thought most DEA agents only wanted to eliminate a piece of the problem rather than solve it. *Kill every last one of them,* seemed to be their philosophy.

As an investigator I shot to kill only as a last resort. Getting information from a dead person was difficult. I censored myself, offered a grudging "Thanks," instead.

I turned to Alene, who now seemed in a state of shock. "You okay?"

She nodded, fixated on the dead gunman who had wanted to kill her.

Since no one else reacted, I went to apply first aid to the wounded young agent. "You'll be fine. Just a scratch." The wound was serious, but no sense alarming the kid.

Alene came over to help. I pressed a handkerchief against his neck wound and told him to apply pressure to slow the bleeding. Alene noticed the blood dripping from my left arm. "You're wounded," sounded more like an observation than a question. I could tell she was still in shock. "You saved my life. He would have killed me."

"He wasn't playin' favorites. He'd have killed all of us if he could." I responded through the pain in my arm. I'd have to get a tourniquet on soon.

"You saved my life." Alene repeated.

"Yes, ma'am." I didn't know what else to say.

Mississippi needed medical attention. On a battlefield you always triaged the patients and got those most in need the attention first. That was Mississippi.

"I fucked up, didn't I?" The young agent asked.

"It's your first time out. You'll get better."

I removed a shoelace and tried unsuccessfully to tie it around my arm. Alene came out of shock. She took over for me, pulling tight so the blood flow stopped and then knotted it. I wondered where she'd learned first aid but didn't ask.

"Or I'll get dead." The young agent looked at me to judge my response.

"You took this bullet for me?" Alene asked, touching my arm.

"Sometimes that's the only way." I responded.

"Why would you do that? Take a bullet for me?"

"You're worth it." I smiled at her and returned my attention to Mississippi. I knew he was looking for reassurance. "My daddy always told me that who I am is determined by what I do. You've got a lot of life ahead of you, agent. You'll be fine."

"Have you done what your daddy wanted you to?"

I looked away, nibbling at a painful subject. "I'm a long way from where anyone thought I'd be, particularly my daddy. The world's not the place we grew up in, an' that can lead us to do things we never thought we'd do."

"Will God forgive us for killing people? Just for breaking a law?"

I heard an echo from my past. "I hope so." I answered for both of us.

Seeing that she'd stemmed the blood flow from my arm and that the young agent was apparently going to be okay, Alene rose and went over to the mountain of drugs. Anderson came back into the room. "Carr. Hank tells me you knew her. "The question was out of context, but just the way Anderson asked sent chills through me. "Who?"

"Agent Jones. They just took her body out. She didn't make it."

I was stunned. I didn't believe him. *She couldn't be here. What was he talking about?*

"Not Lexie." I whispered.

"Afraid so." Anderson confirmed.

"She wasn't on the roster." I protested.

"She added herself this morning. She always got what she wanted."

As the reality sank in, I slammed the door to my heart shut for the second time, sealing away five years of happiness for the lifetime of guilt and regret ahead.

The Devil

A week after the cocaine raid in Dallas Adrian Flores, the graying mayor of the small village of Santa Rosa, Mexico, worked too late for his own good. The day had been long. The clock on the wall over the door to his tiny office approached six pm. He noticed, through the open door, that young Graciela, the village clerk, had started to gather her things. She was leaving to pick up her baby from her mother. Then she would go home to fix dinner for her husband, Guillermo, by seven, as she always did. Her husband had a job on the reconstruction of the bridge that washed out in the spring flooding. Adrian remembered the bridge replacement as another of the unexpected expenses for the village that made balancing this year's budget so difficult.

Mayor Flores heard the door to the village hall open, but he couldn't see who came in. He did notice Graciela step back, seemingly afraid.

"Senior Mayor," she called with both a question and a warning in her voice.

Adrian found five strangers, dressed as peasants, crowding in to his office. Each carried an automatic weapon. The shortest man brandished his handgun in the Mayor's face. *Jose Dominguez.* Adrian had seen his picture. *An up and comer in the Zetas.* Two of the men took Adrian by the arms nearly lifting him off his feet. They led him through the outer office, and then roughly pushed him out into the street.

A crowd had already formed. Adrian saw their fear. This wasn't the first time a cartel had come to his town. Usually they roughed people up and gave them a stern warning. He heard Graciela come out of the village hall behind him. Dominguez pushed her down on the ground. Adrian tried to help her up, but another of the gunmen barred his path. Graciela got up on her own, and the men turned their attention to Adrian.

Dominguez spoke first, "You are the Mayor?"

Adrian nodded, without looking at the questioner so much as all of the others. Ten men now. All armed. He recognized only Dominguez.

"Do you know who we are? Why we are here?"

Mayor Flores, shook his head as he looked around at the villagers he knew so well. Hector, the grocer, was his best friend. Hector wouldn't look at Adrian. Not a good sign. He realized the villagers were all inside the perimeter of the gunmen. *They'd been herded here at gunpoint. This won't end with threats.*

The violence had been increasing. He thought about the police department over in San Ynez. Every officer had resigned and moved away. The Police Chief's family had been murdered by the cartels. The cartel hadn't injured anyone else. They'd simply killed every member of the Chief's family. The Chief left town the next day and hadn't been heard from since.

Mayor Flores thought of his wife who passed on two years earlier. He was relieved she wasn't here. They never had children, even though that had been an eternal hope. He had an illegitimate daughter, Angelica, but no one knew about her. He intended to keep her safe. Far away in Matamoros.

The village where everyone knew everyone else had never needed a police force. The Village Justice always took care of anything that needed to be settled.

"You're helping the Juarez cartel," Dominguez made the accusation.

"I know nothing of cartels." Mayor Flores replied flatly. He glanced at the villagers who all seemed as confused, except Roberto, the son of the mechanic at the one service garage in town. Roberto looked around, but didn't seem to meet anyone's eyes.

"You lie. We know they store their weapons, here, in this village. We know they change couriers, here. We know you protect them."

"Why would anyone want to change couriers here? We are nowhere of importance," the Mayor asked, trying not to sound disrespectful.

No response.

Adrian had a duty to end the threat and get his villagers home safely. "You must have the wrong village. No one here helps any cartel. We scratch out a living. No one lives in a big house. No one wants to get involved in your business. We just want to be left alone." His protest had no effect.

The sun was setting. Adrian no longer needed to squint to see some of the men. The heat began to lessen and people became more active .... usually. But everyone remained motionless, waiting to see what came next. The villagers were looking to him, the Mayor, to resolve the situation.

Adrian heard the distant honking of car horns. Graciela spoke up, "Our team must have won. The soccer game was this afternoon."

The crowd stirred. Nervous glances exchanged. Faint smiles of pride appeared. The home team had won a championship, even if only the regional league. Adrian realized this was a dangerous turn of events. If the gunmen thought the villagers weren't being compliant to their wishes the situation could get ugly, fast.

The sound of vehicles came closer. "Our school children. They won the championship. Please just let them enjoy their celebration," the Mayor said with due subservience.

The gunmen closed on the circle of townsmen. The Zetas hid their weapons so they wouldn't be visible from the oncoming vehicles. The first truck came into view. Adrian recognized young Jose, the widowed dressmaker's son. He sat in the back waving a banner from the school. Jose shouted in English, "We won! We won! We are the champions, my friend!" picking up on the song by Queen.

Other vehicles followed, blowing their horns, players and fans leaning out of open windows. All shouted their delight. "It's been a long time," the Mayor noted with a mixture of regret and pride.

Adrian studied the young leader's eyes. Dominguez's Zetas were warring with the Juarez cartel for control of the area. Both claimed primacy. He'd had brushes with both in the past, but this seemed more dangerous than any of those earlier encounters. He'd been able to steer a middle ground, to keep everyone safe. But apparently Roberto had done something to tip the balance. Adrian felt sorry for the mechanic's son suspecting Dominguez already knew Roberto was helping the Juarez cartel. Adrian resigned himself that nothing could be done to stop what would happen next.

The vehicles passed through the square, the last shouts of pride and triumph faded into the distance. The young men and fans of the team went on to broadcast their triumph. *The Zetas were at least respectful of some traditions*, Adrian thought.

Dominguez motioned to a white pickup truck parked just off the square. The driver pulled up behind his leader. Everyone in the square tried to see into the truck. Large stones filled the back. Dominguez picked up one from the pile "You'll carry out our vengeance. Whoever's responsible for the Juarez cartel's operations here will die. You'll stone him with these." He held up the stone for everyone to see.

The Mayor didn't want to start a witch hunt amongst the villagers. "Who's responsible?" he asked Dominguez.

To his surprise, the young leader responded, "You're responsible.

You know and protect him." Dominguez cast the first stone hitting the Mayor on the forehead. A stunned Adrian took a step back.

The other gunmen took large rocks from the truck. They handed a stone to each of the villagers. The Mayor looked on with dismay and astonishment. His mind raced, but he couldn't think of anything to do. He realized Dominguez planned the stoning.

When everyone had a stone, the cartel members stood back. "You'll stone your mayor to death or die in his place," Dominguez said. "Throw your stones now or die."

Adrian tried to protest, but before he could get the words out a stone knocked the wind out of him. Looking up he realized only Roberto had cast a stone.

"So you think he should die for your sins?" Dominguez asked Roberto.

"He's old. I have much to live for." Roberto answered defiantly.

Dominguez looked Roberto in the eye. Roberto couldn't hold his gaze. "You have a guilty conscience. You shall die." Dominguez fired a single shot into Roberto's forehead. The bullet passed through his skull, exploding out the back, covering those behind in his blood and brains. People tried to move away from the gore. The gunmen grabbed them and pulled them back. Roberto slumped to the ground.

The Mayor stepped forward to stop the leader. He was too late.

Dominguez looked at the Mayor. "You knew he was the one, but you said nothing." Dominguez turned to the villagers, "Either cast those stones or die."

Adrian couldn't let the Zetas force his neighbors to take a life. Everything was getting out of hand. "Kill me if you must, but don't put my blood on their hands."

Hector, the grocer, dropped his stone first. Those in the front row followed. Adrian tried to stop them but was forced to watch as the gunmen shot the front row of villagers, one by one. *Always in the forehead.* The next row of villagers threw their stones at the gunmen. The ducking cartel members responded with a blizzard of bullets. But the gunmen didn't stop there, shooting every single villager, except the Mayor, Graciela and a little boy. The Mayor recognized Pepe as the seven year old son of Hector the grocer, who'd been the first to drop his stone. Pepe's dead father now lay in a pool of blood next to the boy. Pepe's eyes were wide with fear.

Graciela had gone into shock. So many of the villagers she spent her whole life with lay dead on the ground. Each had an impossible choice to make: stone their friend to death or be killed themselves. Adrian knew that not one of the villagers could have killed him. Killing a friend wasn't in them; just as he couldn't give up Roberto.

Dominguez watched as the gunmen put a final kill shot into each of the villagers lying on the ground, man, woman and child as if an everyday event. The Mayor closed his eyes. *They're innocent. They don't deserve to die because of a gang dispute.*

Dominguez turned to the Mayor. "Two of you will die."

Adrian Flores knew he'd be one. But the other was another impossible choice: A young mother with a child waiting, or a child himself with a lifetime before him. "Why two? Why not just me?"

Adrian studied Dominguez. He couldn't have been more than twenty years old. *About the age of Graciela. Someone's child. He must have some feelings for others.* The young leader didn't look at the Mayor. Instead, he checked the other gunmen. Adrian realized Dominguez didn't have full control of the gang, but led only because someone higher up had appointed him. The Mayor had heard the rumors that the Zetas had a sponsor somewhere. Was Dominguez sponsored? Even if he was, he still had to have the support of the gang for his decisions or they might not back him. So the young Zeta leader was hostage to the mob. Adrian thought that not a good thing.

"That's just the way it is. I only need one of you to tell the story of what happened here today. And that person must be the most credible."

The Mayor didn't back down, "And who's that?"

Dominguez looked at Graciela. Adrian thought she didn't appear to understand the discussion. She didn't seem to comprehend the implications for her.

"She has a baby," Adrian had to make the decision clear. "Less than a year, now. Her husband …" but the young cartel leader cut him off.

"I don't care. She will die. She's only a woman. No one will believe what she has to say." She absorbed the impact of the first bullet from Dominguez and remained standing. But the other gunmen followed with nine more shots, throwing her backwards. Graciela's expression seemed to call to her child, that she wouldn't be coming home.

Adrian snapped. He knew he was already dead, so nothing made any difference. He flew at Dominguez, launched himself into the younger man. The Mayor took him to the ground, came up on top, choked Dominguez until other hands pulled him off. Those hands held him tight. The Zeta leader rose apparently still feeling the choke. Dominguez tried to clear his throat, but found he had trouble speaking. Adrian smiled, knowing he'd had some effect upon this demon. He regretted not being able to take a life.

Dominguez nodded to the men who held the Mayor. One released Adrian's right arm. Only a moment passed before a closed fist knocked Adrian Flores, Mayor of Santa Rosa to the ground. The punch dazed him. Not more than a few seconds passed before the first stone bounced off his skull. Adrian tried to get up but then the rain of stones began, inflicted agony across his body. Several cartel members zeroed in on his skull. Stone after stone struck him. But it took him a long time to die.

Two Years Later: Christmas Cards

Two years had passed without Lexie as my source of happiness. I sat in the administrative hearing room of the boxy modern J. Edgar Hoover building on Pennsylvania Avenue in Washington. My supervisor, Bud Myers, younger by probably a decade, sat next to me at the table, clearly unhappy to be here. I didn't know why Bud was sweating. He was just the Dallas office Special Agent-in-Charge and not the one on the hot seat. But then again, whatever the administrative law judge decided Bud would have to implement. I knew the charges against me were serious. Any one could put me out of the Bureau. Several could land me in jail. Frankly, I didn't care because everything I had done was all payback....for Lexie.

All I could surmise was that Lexie wanted to protect me at the cocaine bust. She'd replaced the DEA team lead with herself and not told me. Apparently my tension at home told her volumes about the danger. I sat here because after Lexie's death I really didn't give a shit about much of anything except killing anyone who moved drugs. The one exception had been a brief interlude with Dr. Isabel Stanhope during the Avian Flu Pandemic a year earlier. That was on one of my cooling down periods where the Bureau gave me a shit assignment that no one thought would lead to anything just so I wouldn't end up killing anyone for a while. The assignment turned out to be a major event that probably delayed the inevitable until Isabel moved to New York knowing I wouldn't follow. But maybe I did have friends in the right places because we were disrupting things sufficiently that no one wanted me to stop. Based on how few Christmas cards I received I knew not many wanted to be associated with me. I was surly most of the time I wasn't brooding. I got to sleep most nights through alcohol induced fatigue.

I wondered why the walls of hearing rooms always had wood paneling. I thought of my father's knotty pine lined den back on the Triple C Ranch near Waco. Dad spent a lot of time there. He didn't like us kids bothering him when doing the books. It seemed to me that he really went there to hide out from our mother. That happened a lot in the thin years when we didn't have much money. And no money seemed to be most of the time.

The administrative law judge, a woman of probably fifty years, carried the weight accumulated over those years both on her body frame and in her dour demeanor. She entered the room, sat across the table from us. The supporting cast of a thousand, or so it seemed to me, came in and took up their positions to prepare for the execution.

I leaned over and whispered to Bud, "Where is it?"

"What?" he whispered back.

"The guillotine. Must be somewhere around here."

The judge pounded her gavel once to let us know she was ready. "Agent James Carr. I have read in detail the case presented. I'm prepared to render my decisions. You've been provided a copy of this documentation. You've been advised that you should seek counsel. You've refused, citing that you're a member of the bar in Dallas County, Texas, although I see you've never practiced. It says you put yourself through college and law school after your service to your country. Since you've not practiced, I'm once again advising you that it's your right to be represented by counsel. Do you still wish to represent yourself in this matter?"

"Yes, your honor."

"Very well then. As to the charges that you recklessly endangered the lives of other agents in your conduct of assigned missions on seventeen different occasions over the last twenty-four months, I find you not guilty. Agent Carr, as an aside, it was very clear to me that you continually put yourself in grave danger while performing your duties.

But from reading the reports closely it was evident to me that no other agents were seriously endangered by your behavior. In fact, you may have saved the lives of other agents on at least five of those occasions. You get no special commendation given the circumstances."

I nodded and breathed for the first time since the gavel was struck. Would my luck hold up or was this just the throw away before they went on to send me to jail for the rest of my unnatural life? One down and two more to go.

"As to the charges that you unnecessarily employed deadly force in the conduct of thirty-four missions…" This was the big one. This one could put me behind bars. "I find you …" She seemed to check with herself that she was satisfied. "Not guilty."

I relaxed, but only a little. Things were going to be all right. I wasn't going to prison unless some god I didn't worship was just having fun with me.

"I'm entering into the record that each affidavit was contradictory. In no instance was tangible evidence provided to establish that you ever fired first. No irrefutable evidence was provided to establish that you were not defending yourself, another agent or law enforcement officer, or civilian. I feel compelled to give you the benefit of the doubt in this matter. But I'm also a student of statistics. The incidence of death on missions you were on is significantly higher than for the Bureau as a whole. It's also significantly higher than for missions you were on in the twenty-four months before the period in question. The facts of this matter cause us all great concern. I've instructed that a note of caution be put into your personnel file."

Two of the three charges dismissed with a note of reprimand. Looked like I might live to fight another day, only carrying a much heavier collar around my neck. One more. I glanced again at Bud who perspired heavily even though it was snowing outside. Bud seemed frozen, fearing the final outcome and its impact on his career.

"As to the final charges against you, disregard of direct orders. In this instance the evidence is clear. You were, on thirteen occasions, given specific instructions by your supervisor that you didn't adhere to in the conduct of the missions assigned. Mitigating circumstances were noted on each. You successfully brought felons to justice each time. And while the evidence isn't clear as to whether your disregard of instructions was the reason for your success, the end result was you ended dangerous situations. It's also noted that you have a military record of high commendation before joining the Bureau. There's something to be said for experience over procedure, but I can't base my decision on your experience alone. I find myself in a difficult spot. I can't ignore your infractions. I also can't assess a severe penalty. Given the facts, I find you guilty of insubordination, but with mitigating circumstances. I'm directing that a reprimand be placed in your personnel file, that you be fined a total of five thousand dollars and be placed on administrative leave for two weeks without pay."

So much for my meteoric rise to the top. Brought down by the laser rays of insubordination. What would Lexie have said about all this? She'd probably have said, *'No one is ever successful by making only the necessary mistakes.'*

I missed Lexie more than ever.

As I stood I noticed Alene Oliviera leaving the room. She nodded to me. I returned the nod. I hadn't noticed her earlier, but then I'd been a bit busy. I'd heard she prosecuted several agents who'd removed the cocaine from my Dallas raid. Was she here to see if I'd be found guilty as well? Or was she here to make sure I wasn't? Once she'd left I wondered again at her presence.

Two Months Later: The Rose Garden

President of the United States Barak Obama didn't like being alone. He often felt that way these past three years, even though constantly in the company of advisors and staff. Today he felt overcome by the knowledge that his term was coming to an end with no guarantee of another. He knew he might be judged by what he accomplished now.

Obama had arrived with plans and momentum. Most plans hadn't been implemented, not for lack of trying. The momentum had shifted. He felt the disappointment even more than the millions who put him in office.

He ran his hands through his once jet black but now short silvery hair and walked with his head down through the Rose Garden. He didn't notice the bright sea of new blossoms surrounding him. Eric Holder, the Attorney General, trailed a half step behind along with Chief of Staff, Walter Josephson, and Alene Oliviera, now Director of the National Drug Intelligence Center within the Department of Justice.

Obama wanted to get away from the Oval office. The high pitched sound of the white noise used to obscure his communications bothered him more and more. He asked the National Security Agency to find a way to minimize the sound since it caused his headaches. NSA never found a satisfactory solution. The headaches only got worse the longer he stayed in office.

He tried to wrap his mind around the problem Eric brought, but couldn't concentrate. He'd always been good at controlling his feelings, stuffing them deep inside to a place where they wouldn't get in the way of the decisions he needed to make.

As the time remaining in his term clicked down, Obama felt a paralysis he'd never known before. The easy decisions became less clear cut, less comfortable. And he began to question whether his vision remained achievable.

"Mister President. The Ambassador from Mexico has arrived." Genevieve, his administrative assistant, called out in her French accent. Obama knew she accentuated her pronunciation when she wanted to get his attention, as she did now.

Eric stared at Obama, clearly waiting for some response to the dilemma he brought. *And now the Ambassador.* Obama felt the knot tighten in his stomach. He needed to get to the gym and work out. He used to play basketball to clear his head. If only he could find time to think things through now. But days where his time was his own were gone. His days now consisted of briefing papers on pending decisions.

Others did the analysis for him. He was usually offered a set of alternatives with a recommendation and rationale. Policy didn't come from him, but from experts he brought to his team. And all too often he found himself simply taking their recommendations. *Not enough time to check things out personally. Not enough time to talk to people. No time to really understand the issues and how the solutions would play out.*

"Sorry Eric, a lot going on right now."

"As always, sir." Eric sounded impatient.

Obama hated giving an excuse for not making a decision. "You're right, Judge Gray is the right man for the top DEA position. Put in the paperwork."

"Could we have him start immediately, sir? The position's been vacant for eleven months. Not that Brooks isn't doing a good job, but we need to move Brooks out as quickly as possible."

Obama remembered the question he wanted to ask, "Why?"

"His brother-in-law has a recent felony drug conviction. Brooks self-disclosed."

Obama asked the one question that kept coming up when drugs were involved. "What drug?"

"Marijuana." Eric seemed embarrassed.

Obama had shared his opinion about the criminalization of weed with the Attorney General. He felt the enforcement was too random. And yet the prisons were full of drug offenders. He knew that four out of five were in for possession, not dealing. In his heart he knew the law needed to change, but he felt powerless to convince Congress to do anything about the problem. And now a good man was being passed over for an important position. All because of an indiscretion by someone who wasn't even immediate family. "So we keep making the cartels rich. And we can't even promote a good man."

"I'm afraid so, sir."

Obama heard the helplessness in Eric's voice.

As they started back towards the Oval Office Obama thought about the other heads of the drug hydra. He'd just read the report of the Commission on Drug Related Violence. The report was grim. The situation south of the border was getting worse. He knew he had to take action, but felt the recommendations were weak and probably wouldn't have much effect. He needed to do something more, but what? He had no idea. He skipped ahead to the next meeting. "What am I supposed to tell the Ambassador about the drug Intelligence he's asking for?"

"It's difficult when whatever we give them seems to end up in the hands of the cartels. Too much of what we're getting implicates the source. When we give the Intel to the Mexicans, the source ends up dead," Eric explained.

"You've been making the same argument since the beginning. How do we get their government useful Intel?"

Alene spoke up for the first time. "Sir, if we convince them to hand pick a rapid reaction team where we can embed folks from our side at the last minute, maybe we can find a way. Intel only gets shared with a small team and used immediately. Our team doesn't officially exist so the Mexicans claim full credit for their successes. We're just along for the ride, but we ensure success with our Intel and special operators backing up a law enforcement team."

Holder shook his head. "No good. We need to control the team and the Intel. Joint missions with the Mexican Army just won't work if they have to lead."

Even though Holder was her boss, Alene pushed back. "It's their country, Eric. Mexicans have to solve the problem. We can help, but if we don't let them lead, at some point we'll have no choice but to send in troops to restore order. Is that what you want?"

"We put covert people into nearly every country of interest. Why not let the Army lead this? They have lots of experience from the Middle East wars."

"Mexico's a law enforcement issue, not a military one." She argued.

"Shows how little you really understand what's going on."

Alene held her ground. "We don't want a war on our border."

"We already have one." Eric responded watching the President.

Obama waved his hand to stop the discussion. They were both right. He looked directly at Alene. "I'll put the Ambassador off, but you need to be back here in a week with a solid plan.

Merger

Jose Dominguez may have been younger and a foot shorter than Ruben Castillo, but he had a nastier temperament. Castillo, pock marked face, dark hair and non-descript clothes, looked older than his thirty-two years. Dominguez knew Castillo had spent most of his life doing whatever he was told. He'd been told to kill, rape and steal anything of value from anyone who stood in the way of the cartel, his cartel. The Zetas had always been Castillo's. Even when he delivered product and picked up cash in a Monterrey neighborhood at fourteen, Los Zetas was his cartel.

Dominguez talked with Castillo often. They'd become close in a way that only two men without conscience could. He knew Castillo liked his position in the world, because it made him feel successful. In the vacuum caused by his predecessor's demise, Castillo assumed the role as leader of the Zetas. He had a small group ready to do anything he ordered. A larger group stood ready to do whatever Castillo's small team handed down. Most of the latter knew Castillo's name, but only a handful like Dominguez had ever actually met him.

Dominguez knew Castillo kept access limited to survive. No one could know his location from day-to-day. He feared someone would give him up. Someone would hand him over to the authorities. Whoever did would live on some island for the rest of his short life. The turncoat's life would be short because whoever gave up a Zeta leader would become an example to make sure no one else ever dared do the same. Dominguez, however, had a plan.

Bernard Villareal wasn't much older than Castillo. He had gray hair and bloodshot brown eyes. Villareal sat across from Castillo. Villareal believed he led the Beltran Leyva cartel. Beltan Leyva was one of the smaller cartels, but in a prime spot in the drug routes. Dominguez knew not everyone agreed to Villareal's leadership. Beltran Leyva had been killed in a shoot-out with the Army. Several others had stood up to try to lead the remnants of his organization, and Bernard Villareal won the competition, sort of. A few others ran small groups still affiliated with the cartel. They didn't recognize Villareal as the supreme leader, just one of many now. Villareal made no secret of his intention to consolidate power.

Seven others joined the meeting, although only Castillo and Villareal talked. Castillo summarized where he thought they were. "We have to think differently if we hope to survive. We go our separate ways and the Army will eventually pick us off one-by-one. Together we can stand up to anything the Army throws at us."

Villareal didn't buy any of Castillo's arguments. "How can I trust you? You're as bad as the Army. You kill my men when we show up at the same place. You don't treat us like brothers; you treat us like the scum that you are."

Castillo's eyes flared, but his voice didn't reveal emotion. "We've been in competition for years. Many unpleasant things have transpired between us. However, I'm offering you an opportunity to be a full partner in our efforts. You'll be honored and respected for what you contribute. You'll make more money than you've ever made, even in the most lucrative days."

Villareal shook his head, "Bullshit. There isn't enough for all of us anymore. You'll get rich and we'll die for it."

"And how many millions made it into your bank account last year?" Castillo challenged, "You'll never see a million in your account again unless you join us."

"And what happens if we don't?" Villareal asked as if suspecting the answer.

Castillo didn't flinch, having expected the question. "Nothing."

Villareal couldn't suppress his surprise, "Nothing? You go your way and we go ours? You own one part of Mexico and we own another?"

Castillo smiled, "I didn't say that. What I said is I can see us walking out of here with no agreement. So nothing's happened, except you've rejected our offer of partnership."

"And what happens if we don't have an agreement?"

Castillo maintained that smile, "We kill every one of you. As I said, Mexico can't support all of us. Either you're with us or against us. You join us and we share what we take. If you're against us, then I'm duty bound to hunt down every one of your men. We'll continue until not a single one of you survives."

Villareal didn't respond.

Castillo waited. Dominguez suspected that Castillo knew time was short and wanted to make sure he didn't have to watch his back if Villareal agreed.

"Why should the Beltran Leyva cartel join the Zetas? We've been here much longer than you. I have more judges and politicians on my payroll. What do I have to gain by joining you rather than the other way around?"

Dominguez saw that Castillo's amused expression made Villareal uncomfortable. "Okay. We join you and what happens? We have to get permission?" Castillo asked

"Sounds like what you just offered me." Villareal responded.

Castillo let his annoyance out. "No, no, no. That's not what I said. We make you full partners. You get a share of everything we do. As others come into the fold there should be more deals to share with more of us all operating as Zetas."

"But there are already fewer deals. You just said so yourself. " Villareal challenged.

"Right now, yes, but we'll find other sources of revenue. We aren't just drug dealers. We're purveyors of illegal opportunity. We'll provide whatever someone will pay for. The more we offer the more money will come our way."

Villareal nodded, but Dominguez could tell he wasn't convinced.

"So how does this all work? We have so many men and you have so many men. We share based on the number of men we bring to the table? Is that how it works? Or is it based on the number of pesos we bring in? We do fifty percent of the revenues we get to keep fifty percent? I don't understand the deal here."

Dominguez realized Castillo hesitated because he hadn't really thought this part through. "We'll negotiate."

"Based on whose men take the deal down?"

"If you wish."

Villareal saw a loophole, "So we go do a deal together. Your guys kill all mine before the deal is done. I get nothing. Is that how this works?"

"No way. We're a team now. Your men are as important as mine. I said we can't expect we'll all eat if we don't join forces. But once your men are Zetas, we're brothers. We watch out for each other. We make sure we get our due and set up the next deal. We supply you weapons you can't get. There's honor amongst thieves, especially the Zetas."

Villareal stood. "I hear words, but I don't see anything that tells me I can trust you. We're not going to do this deal. We agree on territory and that's it. You stay out of ours and we stay out of yours. Any deal we originate's ours. Anything you put together is yours. Just like before."

Castillo nodded once and slowly rose to his feet. Villareal rose with him. Dominguez had moved behind Villareal. Dominguez held a hypodermic needle. Faster than anyone could react, Dominguez plunged the needle into Villareal's carotid artery, injecting the contents.

Castillo watched as Dominguez released Villareal, letting him slump to the floor, the needle still in his neck. "Generally a perfect partnership consists of only one leader. There's only one leader, now. Does anyone here think he shouldn't be part of the Zetas?"

Dominguez watched as the remaining Beltran Leyva cartel leaders moved their hands to show no intent or threat. Each one nodded agreement… eventually.

The Bandy Rooster

Alene Oliviera was an enigma to Barak Obama. Why did she suppress her natural Brazilian beauty? No makeup and earth tone clothes without accessories. Shoulder length hair full of luster hinted at what she hid. She engaged him with her sparkling emerald eyes and her brilliant mind. He thought she didn't want anything to detract from what she had to say.

He heard she was different outside of the professional arena.

"You seem preoccupied, sir. Should I reschedule?" she asked. He shifted, "No." He smiled at her, "If there's only one thing I've learned about this job, there's never a second chance. No time for do overs or delays."

He remembered why he was so taken by this woman. She pointed things out his staff never would. Most of his staff had empires built on sand constantly shifting. She, on the other hand, had no empire, assiduously avoided castles and said what was obvious to her, but not necessarily to him. She regularly disagreed with Eric, intelligently pointing out alternative, but logical conclusions to their discussions. As Obama had seen, their discussions sometimes became heated, but he knew each was a professional disagreement. He wondered if he could get her to switch places with Walter Josephson, who sat next to her? Barak Obama was afraid that Josephson was looking beyond their remaining time in office since a second term was far from assured. He had seemed more disengaged lately, preoccupied with personal things. He needed Josephson to keep the team focused. But that fleeting thought passed when he realized that bringing Alene to the White House might shatter her objectivity. She'd then fall into the quicksand of power and privilege.

He looked at her. A reserved smile appeared and he thought he must look guilty. "Have you worked out your differences with Eric?"

"We're on the same page, sir. We were just reading from different paragraphs."

"Can't have that, Alene. Neither of you'll succeed if you're not aligned. Drug violence poisons our relations with Mexico. Violence undermines their future as a nation. The Zetas have upset the balance and there are more and more threads from them into our country. Our current policies just aren't working. You have good ideas and I want you to handle this. But so far I'm not seeing results, only territorial skirmishes."

"Yes, sir."

"Walter, I want an assessment done on what it'll take to stabilize the situation south of the border. Full range of options. Should be interagency. I want Donilon doing the final." Tom Donilon was Obama's National Security Advisor. "He needs to pull it together and put his spin on it. Alene's the staff lead and will actually do the writing. Yes, Alene, I want you to write it personally, not your staff. If you're going to own the effort I want you to really understand what it will take to get it done."

"Due date, Mister President?" Walter asked.

"Thirty days. We don't have much time."

"It'll be superficial, sir." Walter observed. "Can't properly…"

"You don't understand, Walter. We've got agencies around here with nothing but data: FBI, DEA, ATF, State, National Security, Border Patrol, National Guard, the various state police organizations along the border. If you ask me we have too many people collecting data and not enough actually doing something about the problem. That's why we're going at this a different way. Alene'll lead the program, but I want the effort very clearly defined before we start."

"Yes, sir. Thirty days."

Obama saw Alene's face brighten, as if she'd been dreading a dismissal of her idea. He'd seen a lot of dread of dismissal in his staff. People would begin leaving soon if he didn't give them a sense of opportunity and accomplishment. Why was he so curt? He needed to think about that.

She smiled. Another thing he liked about her was that she didn't talk just to hear herself. He realized she was modeling the behavior she wanted him to adopt. Listen first, confirm and question second, then reserve your opinions. Had he really expressed so many by now that everyone knew where he stood on every issue?

Back to her question. "Anyway, your charge is to cut through all the conflicting priorities. I need you to make sense of not only what's going on, but what we should be doing as opposed to what we are doing."

She studied Obama in a way that made him uncomfortable. He felt as if she was peering into his soul and not particularly liking what she saw.

"Can a non-existent team to help the Mexicans be an option or does everything have to be open?" Alene asked.

Obama didn't like the implication. He knew nonexistent organizations had gotten many a president in trouble in the past. But what they were doing clearly wasn't helping end the violence. "All options are to be examined, Alene."

"Will I get to hand-pick my own team? Even if they don't have pristine records?"

"I expect you to get the job done. How you do it's up to you. Just don't plant any bombs I can't handle."

She seemed at peace. "I appreciate the opportunity, sir."

Obama pushed a button on his intercom, "Genevieve, please send in Hillary and Eric." Hillary Clinton was the force of nature Secretary of State.

As the latest guests joined them Obama continued. "All right. The Mexican Ambassador's joining us momentarily. We have to convince him to ask us to work with his Army."

"Mister President, Ambassador Arturo Sarukhan Casamitjana of Mexico." Genevieve announced. Once the Ambassador entered, she closed the door behind the bandy rooster of a man who walked into the oval office as if he owned it.

"Mr. President. The President of all the Mexican peoples sends his greetings."

Obama rose but remained behind his desk. "Ambassador Sarukhan. How are you, my friend?"

As they shook hands, Obama saw deep lines around the eyes of this man he had come to know well. The spark and fire had diminished. Something bothered his friend. He could see it was serious.

"Muy bien."

Obama watched the Ambassador study him in turn. He saw he wasn't coming out favorably either.

Walter, Eric, Hillary and Alene also rose to greet the Ambassador, but the greetings were a mere formality. They weren't the show here and acted their part.

"I hope your family's well, Mister President?"

"They are. Thank you."

"Mister President I am here to make a plea. We must cooperate more closely on transnational drug movements."

"How do we achieve that, Mr. Ambassador?"

"If you'd but provide the drug related intelligence your many agencies gather, we'd end the scourge upon my nation. We need nothing more."

"Except a few Blackhawks." Obama was aware of a Mexican request for a dozen such aircraft.

The Ambassador smiled. "That too. But intelligence is the key. Who is where, what are they planning?"

Obama came out from behind his desk and leaned against it. "You haven't and can't safeguard our sources. Until you do, we can't provide the requested information."

"But you have to understand, the Mexican people must take back our country. No other solution will work in the long term."

"I do understand. But the last time we provided you with intelligence our sources were killed within days. We can't let that happen again."

"Without the intelligence we can't succeed."

"Then, how would you propose we work with your forces?"

Arturo Sarukhan Casamitjana, considered the conundrum. He felt constrained in his response. "US forces cannot come into Mexico to conduct operations."

"I agree with you, but we want to find a way to work with your Army. Maybe some of our folks can participate in select missions where we guide your forces without revealing our sources or even the fact that we are involved."

The bandy rooster politician looked curiously at Obama, wrestling with something. "We can't accept Americans killing Mexicans, even if they are cartel. Such events would evoke two centuries of fears."

"What if our effort's led by law enforcement officers from our Department of Justice?" Obama gestured toward Eric. "We have a long history of cooperation."

Obama noted how quickly the Ambassador responded, as if he'd been expecting such a suggestion. "The law enforcement organizations share limited Intel to solve individual cases. Not the same."

Barak Obama wondered if someone had prepared the Ambassador for the conversation. "Our proposal gives you the ability to use our Intel without compromising the source." Obama let him sit for a moment.

Sarukhan came back unexpectedly, "I don't know how we could permit your people to participate in our missions. Such an approach would attack our sovereignty."

"Then you'll do it without our Intel. I won't sacrifice one more person."

Abruptly Sarukhan rose to his feet. "I'll discuss it with my president, but frankly I don't see a clear path forward. My president asked me to once again request that you close your borders to gun trafficking. Automatic weapons from the US continue to kill thousands of my countrymen. It must stop, and only you can stop it."

"I appreciate your willingness to discuss this with your president." Obama rose and offered his hand. He ignored the final shot, a continuing point of contention between them. Both knew the political lobby against an automatic weapons ban wasn't something Obama would take on. An assault weapons fight could poison the well for his party for decades. Sarukhan shook the hand of the US President, but left unhappy.

An Invitation

The next day was Saturday. My cell phone buzzed even though I generally shut it off. In fact, I had to search around to find it since I usually left it on the kitchen table. *Aha! The bathroom.*

"Yes?"

"Agent Carr?" A woman's voice.

"Yes."

"Are you on a land line?"

"Who is this?"

"Are you on a land line?" came across more insistent and not particularly friendly. The voice was familiar but I couldn't place it.

"No."

"Please go to your office and wait for a call in exactly sixty minutes… That will be eleven-thirteen your time."

"It's Saturday."

"It's important."

"Yes ma'am."

Fifty-seven minutes later, when the phone rang at my desk in the

Federal office building at 1100 Commerce Street in downtown Dallas, I was taking a bite of a chicken taco. In passing I thought of Dr. Isabel Stanhope, the Center for Disease Control researcher who wouldn't be too happy with my choice of meal. We had a close encounter during the Avian Flu Pandemic a year before. She needed to save the world from further pandemics, and I only wanted to stop drug trafficking. She'd gone on to the World Health Organization. I went back to find revenge against those who'd taken Lexie from me.

"Who is this?"

"Alene Oliviera."

Alene was linked to what had become the most painful day of my life. I didn't want to talk with her. I let the silence go on until she continued.

"I recently recommended you for an important job. I had strong indications that I shouldn't, but now have reluctant clearance to talk with you. It's highly sensitive and that's why the secure communications."

I was unaware of anyone's interest in me other than to see me leave the Bureau. *What was this all about?* "Go on."

"You don't sound particularly interested."

"Listen Miss Oliviera. Even my supervisor doesn't send me a Christmas card. If you check you'll find I was recently reprimanded for insubordination. I'm not your man."

"I have the Administrative Law Judges' decision in front of me. Reads like an impressive resume, at least for what I need."

I had no idea what she was talking about. Generally when new teams were being set up scuttlebutt circulated. But in this case nothing. "You assemblin' the dirty dozen?"

"No. I need someone who doesn't particularly like the cartels."

No hesitation on my part. "Count me in."

"You haven't heard me out. There's more to this than just going around killing those who are selling drugs."

"No need. Anything that disrupts the cartels, I'm all for it." My voice was calm but my emotions weren't, remembering Lexie as she'd been when she last smiled at me.

The silence grew. Alene must be trying to decide whether I was right for her mission or not. I assumed she was leaning toward the latter.

If I wanted to be on her team I better come up with a good reason for her to continue this discussion. I played the card I'd hoped to avoid, and it came out in a voice I hardly recognized. "You were there."

Her voice was distant, "I remember. You saved my life."

I thought I now understood why she offered the job, maybe to repay me for taking that bullet. But if I were a loose-cannon I'd never get it. And I knew a lot of people thought of me exactly in those terms. "Then what's the job?"

"Director of Ops for a special task force."

Curious. Again no scuttlebutt. "And what does this task force do, exactly?"

"I can't tell you at the moment."

Her reluctance gave me pause. "So why me?"

"Truthfully, lots of people are saying you're not the right person."

She must have disagreed. "What do you think?"

"I'm withholding judgment. I've seen what you can do.

Everything you've done since says you're not the guy, unless you look at those same events through a different lens. I'm trying to understand which view of the events is correct. You're the right guy only if your head's screwed on right."

She'd found the problem. "How do I convince you, one way or the other?"

"I'm asking you to do the next mission right. No excessive force, no endangering of agents."

I looked out of the small window in my office. "So my next time out's an audition. I do it your way and you'll take me. Otherwise I'm out."

"Pretty much." She didn't sugar coat the situation.

"Okay. Got it." I hung up and sat there totally empty for a long time, staring out the window, but not seeing the building across the street or anything except Lexie's smile.

The Audition

After my no expenses paid vacation on the Bureau I was blessed with all the shit assignments. I thought I'd never get a chance to prove to Alene I could do a mission right. Bud wasn't about to let me anywhere near the bad guys for some reason. I must have been in another cooling down period, until Bud needed a victory to send back to Washington. One of my assignments in particular seemed a waste of time. I'd been put on a stake out at a place with a curious name: The Montezuma Produce and Chinese Laundry Company. We had a tip about something of interest going on there, but the informant had disappeared and then turned up dead in a hotel room in Santa Fe. No one had any specific information and we didn't even know what the something of interest might be. We really had very little to go on. I didn't know how much longer we'd chase this particular ghost.

In early evening I was on my way to the stake out. I stopped at a red light. A shit-brown Chevy, maybe ten years old, with Hispanic passengers pulled up beside me. That was unremarkable. The barrel of an automatic weapon pointing at me wasn't. I dropped down on the seat just before a spray of bullets blew through the windows.

Still lying down, I punched the gas pedal to the metal, praying for no cross traffic. My Honda slowly gathered speed and ultimately raced, as much as a Honda could race, down Malcolm X Boulevard past the Jack-in-the-Box where I had dinner the night before. The Chevy was in pursuit. I turned right onto Grand Avenue.

Nearing the entrance onto South Central Expressway I slowed.

I waited…

…and waited…

…and waited some more…

The Chevy was practically in my trunk when …

... I cut in front of an oncoming Tahoe…

…that spun out of control to avoid hitting me …

I headed up the ramp.

The spinning car snarled traffic for a minute or so.

But as I merged into traffic my rear view mirror showed the Chevy roaring up the entrance ramp.

I played maps in my head.

The Honda served the purpose of being inconspicuous. However a stock Honda was no match for even an old Chevy on an open road.

I weaved in and out of the other cars to keep out of a direct line of fire. Yet as I approached the Hatcher Street exit I saw the Chevy gaining on me. A moment later the back windshield disintegrated into thousands of tiny fragments.

I was out of options and took the ramp down, not even slowing.

A hard left turn onto Hatcher miraculously escaped any oncoming traffic.

The eighth precinct offices were three blocks down Hatcher. I chose the police station as my destination, expecting no rational person would follow me there.

I slid into the motor pool, spinning 180 degrees to bleed off forward motion.

The Chevy came right in after me, smashed into the Honda and pushed it into a parked Dodge Charger I'd worked hard to miss.

The passenger in the front seat of the Chevy sprayed the Honda with automatic weapon fire, blowing out the remaining glass.

I crawled across the seat, opened the door and worked my way away from the Chevy and its occupants.

Bullets searched for me, but collided with the parked vehicles.

I kept low and made a run for the precinct house door. Bullets lodged into the masonry right behind me.

I launched myself at the door, let myself in and then pulled the metal door shut.

Only a moment later the door burst open behind me.

As I dove for a side corridor, a hail of bullets kicked up plaster and paint on the wall at the end of the main hallway.

I found a sergeant in his office. "Shooters. Where's the armory?"

"Who are you?" The astonished Sergeant asked.

I flashed my badge, "FBI. Help me!"

The Sergeant led me down a hallway and made a left turn removing a key from his pocket as we walked.

A moment later the armory door swung open.

I found racks of assault rifles, shot guns, and Glocks.

I looked at his name plate, 'Sergeant Adams'.

Adams looked at me for only a moment, "Here, put this on so everyone'll know you're with us."

He handed me a kevlar-reinforced armor plated black vest with DPD in white letters on the back. I slipped it on.

"Flash bangs?" I asked.

The Sergeant shook his head, "Got smoke grenades."

"Bring 'em." I confirmed and slammed a magazine home on the M-4 assault weapon I'd selected since my weapon of choice wasn't among the options.

I slid as many 30 round magazines as I could into my pockets and belt. Sergeant Adams followed me back to the corridor. We heard the continued firing coming from the direction of the hallway ahead. I raced across the cross hallway leaving Adams on the near side.

One of the assailants came out of an office.

Adams took him down with two shots.

His shooting confirmed the pattern.

Don't waste bullets.

Tap. Shot, shot. Two bullets at a time and no more.

Sergeant Adams and I advanced on the assailants. "How many are there?" the Sergeant whispered.

"A car full. Didn't get a chance to count noses."

I motioned to Adams to check the office where I saw a uniformed patrolman lying on the floor, blood slowly oozing from behind his head.

The Sergeant came back into the hall in time to see more officers peek around the corner with their weapons.

He motioned with his hand to join us. Three officers with automatic weapons came out into the hallway.

"He's FBI," Adams offered.

One of the officers asked, "What's happening?"

"They're after me." I said. "I'll explain once we disarm 'em and get 'em into custody."

The same officer asked the others, "Any of you recognize him?" he gestured to the gunman on the floor.

Each shook his head.

We started advancing toward the main corridor.

I motioned for Adams to cross over to the other side past the cross corridor.

He did, just in front of a flood of bullets adding their mark on the end wall.

"Guess we know where most of the bad guys are, anyway." I said to the remaining three officers as I motioned to Adams to check the offices on the other side of the hallway.

All four of us watched as Adams checked one office at a time. When he came to the last one, a torrent of shots came out of the door. Adams leaned in with a tap, tap and ended the fight.

I peeked around the corner.

Four men, all carrying automatic weapons were in sight.

Tap, tap and back.

A moment later I saw them enter different offices on both sides of the hallway.

Tap, tap and back.

I turned to the three officers. "One of you cross over and help pin down the two on this side. The rest of you, stay here and pin down the two across the hall. Suggest you use smoke to flush 'em out."

I motioned for the last officer to follow me. "What's your name?"

"Swiatko, sir. Justin Swiatko."

I nodded recognition. "We're going around. See if we can cut off escape."

"What about cross fire?" One of the remaining officers asked.

"Don't worry, we know where you are and if you have to shoot, do it."

Swiatko trailed me as I raced down the hallway, turned right this time and came into the lobby. Several officers waited with weapons drawn. I put up my hand to stop them from shooting me, "FBI. We need a SWAT team here. Four, maybe five armed men in the wing. They've shot at least one officer, maybe more."

I didn't stop to watch what happened next. Swiatko followed me out the front door. "What's the plan?"

"We need to set up to stop them from coming out the back door. How many people work in that hallway? I think I saw at least five."

Swiatko had to think a moment, "Fifteen, maybe. But probably not many would have been in this time of day."

We came to the gate to the motor pool. I crouched down to check out the Chevy.

No driver evident, but he might be somewhere in the area, preparing for a getaway.

I signaled to Swiatko to go left.

I quickly covered the short distance, searched for the driver, scanned for any movement that would indicate where he might be.

Nothing.

The driver might have gone in with the others, I thought. *They might just go out the front door. If they do, the driver will probably come this way, anyway.*

Swiatko kept moving, crouched low, weapon at the ready.

I moved away from him, following the perimeter when suddenly the door I previously had entered burst open. Smoke from a grenade poured out.

One gunman emerged from the white vapor. Three others backed out behind him. Each held a hostage, shielding the gunmen from the officers in the hallway.

The first gunman out noticed motion and took out officer Swiatko using a long burst from his weapon.

I kept the gunmen under surveillance while my mind raced, looking for alternatives. I couldn't think of any.

The first gunman looked for a vehicle with open doors.

He found one, got inside and hotwired the start.

I rose up, tap, tap, and took him out.

The windows on the car I stood behind burst out with the shots from the remaining three gunmen, who still held their hostages.

I moved quickly to another vantage point, towards the street, *box 'em in.*

One of the gunmen yelled, Hispanic accent, "We know who you are. We're gonna kill your family and everyone you know. This isn't a warning. This is the beginning."

I didn't know what to make of his warning so I sighted in on one of the men as he dragged his hostage with him toward a van parked near the entrance. The hostage was Sergeant Adams. I hesitated. No clear shot.

The gunman opened the door on the back, stepped in and took Adams with him. The other two dragged their hostages to the van as well.

Again, no clear shot. I was beginning to think I had underestimated these guys. The gunmen seemed wild in their approach, but clearly knew what they were doing.

As the door slid closed, I stood up.

Tap, adjust aim, tap and the tires on the driver's side went flat.

The van started up and moved forward, flat tires notwithstanding.

I raced towards the vehicle. A non-hostage face appeared in the passenger seat.

I sighted in on the run and fired.

The man slumped over. Adams drove with a gun to his head. He watched me.

Which ones were the gunmen?

I only had a split second to decide.

I saw a laser scope paint my forehead just as I sighted in on the gunman standing behind Adams.

Adams braked hard causing the front of the van to dip.

Tap, tap.

The windshield shattered, shots entering and exiting simultaneously.

The force of two bullets slammed into my left side, lifted me off my feet, spun me around and dropped me to the ground face down.

A moment passed before I realized I wasn't dead. But then the pain from the bullets slamming into my armored vest reminded me I was alive and still needed to deal with the threat in the van. The vest I so detested wearing had saved me once more.

I rose slowly, shaking off the pain, turned into a kneeling position and raised my M-4. As my vision cleared I saw the two officers in the back wrestling with the remaining gunman. I quickly approached the van, aiming through the remains of the windshield.

The gunman pushed a hostage forward just enough to raise his weapon towards me but in doing so also revealed his forehead.

Tap, tap.

The sudden silence unnerved me.

I stepped closer. Sergeant Adams had been shot in the back of the head. His brave action in slamming on the brakes probably saved my life but took his. The sudden vehicle motion threw off the gunman's shots so they struck armor rather than my head.

One gunman lay slumped across the transmission. Another, displaying two prominent bullet holes in his forehead slumped back in the left side back seat.

The final gunman lay on the floor.

The two hostages came out of the van, stepping aside so I could react to anyone who might make a move.

There was no need. Regret swept over me. I wanted one of them alive to find out what the fight was about. Why would they take on a whole precinct house to get to me? My job wasn't to kill anyone, but to discover the truth and act on what I learned. I'd failed my basic mission. I'd prevented more of the officers giving their lives, but that wasn't enough. Worst of all I'd no idea why the attack had taken place.

One of the officers, visibly shaken, looked at me. "I thought we were done when he took you down."

I looked at the flattened bullets lodged in my tactical vest, and, still dazed, handed the M-4 to the officer. "Guess I won't need to re-qualify on this now,"

I realized I'd probably blown the audition for Alene Oliviera's job. *Oh well,* a life of shit assignments wasn't such a bad prospect, given I was still trying to figure out if I was alive or a walking ghost.

Fateful Decision

Alene received a call from Eric to tell her about the precinct shooting.

"It's time for you to move on. I know you thought there was something special about him, but he was responsible for four of the six kills and more Dallas cops were killed than bad guys. Doesn't sound like someone who's in control." Eric summarized.

Alene was surprised by the incident and Eric's conclusion. She wasn't ready to simply move on after waiting for Agent Carr to prove himself. "Those all the facts you have?" she finally decided was the best defense.

"Do I need any more?"

"I'd hope you'd do more diligence if someone made an accusation against me."

"Accusation?" She heard the surprise in Eric's voice.

"You have alleged events, with no facts other than people are dead. For me to simply write off Agent Carr without learning the facts is not how I operate and I hope it's not how you do."

Eric must not have been used to subordinates pushing back as strongly as Alene did in this instance. "Are you saying I've rushed to judgment?"

"Sounds that way unless you bring forth a whole lot of facts you haven't shared."

His response was quieter. "That's all I have."

"In that case I'm flying to Dallas tomorrow to investigate. I intend to get the facts of this incident and then I'll report my decision to you. If the situation is as you have characterized there's no doubt I'll offer the position to Agent Brooks. He has a good record at DEA even though he was tarnished by the arrest of his brother-in-law. I've confirmed he was totally unaware of the situation and backed jail time after the brother-in-law's arrest. But if the facts are not as you suggest, I will offer the position to Agent Carr and will get on with things."

"Fair enough."

Alene knew she'd pushed Eric about as far as she could on Agent Carr. It had moved beyond a feeling for her. The investigation was necessary for her not to lose face. Had she agreed to give up on Carr, it would have been an admission that she'd made a poor decision. Sure she knew it was a lot better to admit a mistake and move on than to go down fighting for something that was a lost cause. And she knew that Eric thought Carr was a lost cause. That was why she had to throw out the bone that she would move on to his choice if she couldn't prove her case.

The problem was she had no facts at the moment other than what Eric had detailed. Those facts didn't bode well for Agent Carr. Four kills equaled the largest number from a single mission in the case against him by Internal Affairs. Eric had said something about the shooting taking place in a precinct house. What was Carr doing at a precinct house in the first place? Why was he the one to make four kills when there had to be many more Dallas cops than FBI agents?

The more she thought about the brief description she'd had from Eric, the more things didn't add up for her. She decided to call Bud Myers and gather as much information as possible. She'd found Myers to not be particularly forthcoming, and in fact, he seemed to be unwilling to talk freely about Carr. She'd seen his performance at the administrative hearings. If she'd not known better she would have thought he was the subject of the hearing. He should be able to at least give her some direction about who was involved and who else she could talk to in order to gather the facts.

"Special Agent Myers, This is Alene Oliviera at Justice, how are you today?"

"I thought you'd be calling," was his response.

Not even a greeting. This won't be very informative, Alene thought.

"Why is that?"

"The shooting. Agent Carr."

Bud's not going to give me details so might as well get a few names and just move on. "What can you tell me about the situation?"

"Obviously I wasn't there, so everything I can tell you is second hand."

"But factual." She pushed back. She didn't want opinions or speculation. Wouldn't help her cause with Eric.

"Oh, absolutely."

Alene waited, but Bud didn't continue. "So?"

"There was a shooting at the eighth precinct. The perpetrators were all killed in the engagement. We're assisting the DPD in the investigation. Obviously since several officers were killed, they took the lead. We haven't been able to determine whether there was any interstate or international involvement yet, so we're proceeding as if it's a local jurisdiction event."

Special Agent Myers always seemed to be focused on things other than what she wanted to know. "What was Agent Carr doing at the precinct house?"

"His statement said he was pursued there by the perpetrators under fire."

"Do you have any corroboration?"

"We have reports from motorists detailing a pursuit occurred at the time he indicates and that shots were fired at his vehicle during the pursuit. The cars described match both the one he was driving and the one the perpetrators arrived in at the precinct."

"Any indications that he returned fire?"

"No reports of such." Bud confirmed

"How do you know the cars matched?"

"The vehicles are still in the motor pool."

She was confused, "Why would the cars be in the motor pool?"

"Agent Carr drove into the motor pool expecting the perpetrators wouldn't follow. Unfortunately for a whole lot of folks they did, crashing into his car and preventing his escape."

Alene was relieved the facts suggested a situation very different from what Eric had inferred. But she needed more to support the actions she wanted to take than just a verbal report from Special Agent Myers.

The Call

A week passed. I wracked my brain trying to understand why I'd become a target of some very unpleasant folks. Their national origin made me think the answer had something to do with one or more of the busts I'd been responsible for. But which one? How'd my name surface? How'd they even know who I was? I wasn't being observed as far as I could tell, and I could usually tell. I kept asking myself the question but didn't come up with a satisfactory answer.

I'd gone back to my routine of looking for opportunities to disrupt the cartel activity, although after the precinct shootings Bud had me on an even shorter leash while the internal investigation continued. I guessed the people above me couldn't figure out if I'd somehow incited the incident or been the intended victim. I had no doubts.

I concluded I'd never hear from Alene, when she called.

"Is anything easy with you?"

I recognized her voice instantly. "I hope not."

"What happened?"

I didn't think she really wanted the answer, so I gave her the cliff notes. "Sergeant Adams gave his life to give me a chance to save the others. That's what I did."

"You always this black and white?"

"No. Usually I don't answer questions like yours."

"Then why did you?" She sounded more annoyed than curious.

"Because you believe in me. And there aren't many left who do."

"What makes you think I believe in you?" She seemed surprised by my statement.

"If you didn't, you never would have called."

"Don't make any assumptions. I'm going to be in Dallas tomorrow and I want to meet with you. Eric's pushing another candidate. A safer candidate, given your record."

"Eric is?"

"The Attorney General. Solid citizen, but he has his own way of looking at things."

I was surprised at her honesty. "So this the final test?"

"And it's pass or fail.

The Test

When Alene walked into Stephen Pyles' Restaurant in downtown Dallas every head turned to look at this beautiful woman. I'd forgotten; maybe because every time I looked at her I relived the raid where Lexie died.

She shook my hand and came close enough that her perfume invoked memories. She wore a perfume that smelled like Lexie's. Obsession as I recalled. The loss of Lexie overwhelmed me for a minute, but I had to close the door quickly and get my head back into this meeting. We were taken right to our table in the back. I have to admit I couldn't stop looking at Alene. She noticed but said nothing.

Small talk and ordering filled the first few minutes, but once done I had to say something. "I need to thank you." I began.

She shook her head.

"No, really. You've been there on some of the worst days of my life and you've not been scared off."

She reflected on something, then, "Am I going to have trouble with you?"

About fifteen responses flew through my mind before I settled on the one I thought she'd find acceptable, but she didn't let me respond. "Stop right there. If you can't give me your first response, I don't want to hear it. I need you to be open and honest and not bullshit me, not give me half-truths, not shade things so you think I'll be able to accept your version of the truth. If this is how you're going to be then let's just have dinner."

I stood up, pushed my chair in and watched her eyes. They half closed and she looked away.

I waited, then pulled the chair out and sat down again. "Every time I look at you I see someone else. Working for you will probably be the hardest thing I've ever done because you remind me so much of Lexie Jones. And yet I want the job you're offering. It'll give me a chance, I expect, tell me if I'm wrong, to hurt those who took her from me more than what I've been doin'. It's that simple for me."

She ran her hand through her long dark hair, which was very distracting, but I refocused and waited. "Eric says it's time to move on with another candidate."

"I understand he wants to follow the safe path."

"He's a politician, he has to think of low risk."

"And you're not?"

"Seven dead police officers and six bad guys. Not a good ratio. I still don't understand. Who was involved? Why did they try to kill you? Why did they kill those policemen? I don't know why you went to the precinct in the first place. I need to know your side of things before …"

I waited a moment, but she didn't finish the thought. *She was about to decide against me. I wasn't in a position of strength. If the answer came out wrong the evening was over. Maybe shit assignments would be better.* Her emerald eyes kept bringing up Lexie's lopsided smile. I had to push Lexie out of my head, but no time. "You've read the report, I'm sure. You know I have no idea who they were or why they opened fire on me. Could have been the stake out. Could have been that raid we were on together or one of a thousand cases I've worked. The chase … was all about self-preservation. The precinct was an expectation on my part. I thought whoever was after me wouldn't follow me in there. I was wrong and not for the first or last time that day."

"What else were you wrong about?" The tone of voice and line of questioning made me sure she was just going through the motions now.

"I thought I could take them alive."

Something seemed to change in her demeanor. "I thought you were out to kill every last one of them. I mean with your history and background." There was something different in this question. Not antagonistic, more like she was surprised.

I formed a hunch about where she was going and played it. "Look, I've been a lot of things, but none of them are me now. I had a job to do back then. I did it the best way I could. People counted on me for their lives. I'm not in the Army anymore. I'm trying as hard as I can to be someone who people depend on, like I was then, but in a different way. And all this business, with Lexie and all … Well, no road in life is straight."

She reflected on my response in silence, and then re-engaged my eyes. "What do you want out of life?"

I said the first thing I thought of, "I want to stop looking in the rear view mirror."

"Meaning?"

"I want to be the kid I was twenty-five years ago, when I left the Triple C Ranch. I want to have life be whatever I can make of it. There were no limits then, no boundaries I couldn't overcome. I want life to be simple again. Not so hard."

"But life isn't simple. We live in a complex world of shades of grey and no clear right or wrong. What we believe today is wrong or irrelevant by tomorrow's standards. That's what makes what we do so hard. A single change of national sentiment and our political landscape shifts one hundred and eighty degrees."

I heard what she said, but disagreed. "We have to enforce the laws as they exist today and not try to anticipate what life could be. That's not what they pay us to do."

"Then why have you killed so many drug dealers?" This was the key question.

"I'm an investigator. I can't question a dead man. I kill only to save lives."

"Come on, Agent Carr. I read the report. You're a statistical anomaly. You've killed a lot more people in the last two years than you did in the two years before. You have a note of caution in your file. Normally your career would be over. So why should I believe the situation in the precinct wasn't exactly the same as all the others in the last two years?"

She'd gone to the heart of the problem. The result was the same as all the others, even though my motivation was exactly the opposite. How could I convince her? And already I was taking too long to respond. "Because you asked me to do it differently. I told you I wanted the job and why. They would have killed the hostages. I couldn't let them and I couldn't let them get away. As I saw it, I had no choice, even though it resulted in everything I wanted to avoid. Why would I kill four men when what I wanted more than anything else was to show I could do it right? Besides, I wanted to find out why they were trying to kill me. I'm sitting here without any idea why. I have no idea as to whether I have to worry about another attack or not. Did I kill everyone involved or are others getting ready to kill me as we sit here? I don't know. And I have no way of finding out. By killing them, I've ended up exactly where I don't want to be."

The test was apparently over as the waiter came, took our orders and she changed the topic. We talked about the food and the wine, discovering she was an aficionado; about books we had read recently, discovering we liked several of the same authors, and we talked about the political situation which just baffled both of us. I found we had a lot in common. I would never have suspected we did. I concentrated hard to look into her emerald eyes and focus on her, not Lexie. Her perfume made it seem as if Lexie were sitting next to me, but I had to keep her at a distance and not acknowledge her.

Alene gave no hint of what she'd decided. I assumed her decision wasn't favorable when she didn't order coffee or desert. She excused herself saying she had a lot of work to do, a day of meetings coming up and a late flight back.

The New Kid

A week later I found myself on the 44th floor faux wood panel offices of the Joint Task Force. Alene, now assigned to the Dallas office, laid out the mission for the twelve members of the Rapid Response team present. "Agent Carr was responsible for shutting down the main route through Dallas a couple years ago. Brilliant analysis and inspired team work led to recovery of almost a ton of cocaine. His effort significantly disrupted the flow of drugs. It's exactly the kind of missions we expect to undertake. Detect, identify and disrupt. As Ops Director for our Team, Jim will be planning the missions and coordinating your efforts. You will give him your full cooperation."

She'd gone to the Hatcher Street precinct and spoken to nearly everyone there the day of the shootings. The desk sergeant told me her whole demeanor changed when she looked at the shot up Honda, the van the perpetrators tried to escape in and the vest with two bullets still in place. Whatever they told her convinced her to offer me the job.

We were in a small conference room just off the sparsely decorated offices in Bryan Tower in downtown Dallas. The commercial office building seemed to be a strange location for offices of a law enforcement organization. Still, if security was what the Task Force was looking for, Bryan Tower qualified. Security cameras everywhere. Badge readers to get in, guard in the lobby. High floor levels.

One of the first things I learned was the offices of the Federal Narcotics Joint Task Force were also affectionately known as the "Joint." Since Alene's Rapid Reaction Team wasn't intended to show up in any directories of Federal agencies, we needed to become part of something already in existence. The Joint Task Force was a remnant of the post 9/11 attempt to break down barriers between Federal agencies. The original collaborating agencies were the Drug Enforcement Agency and Alcohol, Tobacco, Firearms and Explosives, also known as ATF. As needed, representatives of other Federal, state and local agencies would join from time-to-time to run specific operations. The other agencies seldom stayed long. With the arrival of the Rapid Reaction Team, a broader representation would exist for as long as our team stayed intact. From the first moments a resentment of our special status began brewing among the old hands. I needed to understand why.

As I wandered down the hall, one office building looked pretty much like any other. That is, until I walked into the bull pen. From the floor to ceiling windows I could see the entire cityscape of Dallas for miles. The view caught me by surprise. I was disoriented, touching the wall for balance. I stared for a moment. A telescope in one corner trained on a specific location caught my attention.

I noticed a familiar face, Tom Strickland. Actually I knew his partner at the Dallas Police Department, Willy Graves, better than Tom. We'd worked a number of cases together. As detectives the two were about as good as you'd find in Dallas. "Hey, Tom," I said. "You just get here? Where's Willy?"

Tom turned, saw the face attached to my voice and stood up. "Agent Carr, I presume?" He shook my hand. "Willy's not coming. Got on an undercover assignment. He's been working it for a while. You know Willy. He doesn't like change."

I was disappointed. Tom and Willy were better as a team than either was alone. I was only going to get half of what I hoped would be my eyes and ears on the street. "Need someone who can put the pieces together like with those Arabs last year."

Tom played something in his mind's eye. "Willy took the credit."

"He did, as usual. But as usual, I'm sure he didn't do shit." I joked.

Tom's smile told me all I needed to know. "Willy's like my brother. We still eat Mexican every Friday over in South Oak Cliff when he's not undercover. But Willy's gotta be responsible for Willy at some point. Don't ya think?"

"Makes sense. Since Miss Oliviera…"

"You mean the Assistant Attorney General?" Tom threw me off my stride since I didn't know she'd been promoted.

"Yes. She's given me authority to set up the team and get you started. What I need you to do is to get a handle on the info from our brothers here."

"Already started. Amazing how much duplication between DEA and ATF."

"Let's see if we can avoid that and just use what they have."

Tom nodded. I spotted Alene entering her office and excused myself.

The Border

The C130J medium lift transport rolled to a stop at the El Paso Airport. A swarm of Tahoes, Explorers and Suburbans quickly surrounded the aircraft. Tom Strickland and I were among the first down the ramp, having been volunteered by Alene to assist the Army. We wore body armor vests and carried a knapsack bag each. We piled into a waiting vehicle. In all, nearly fifty federal officers and agents came off the aircraft. We headed toward the Intel Fusion Center at Ft. Bliss.

We were taken to a large room with floor to ceiling monitors on the walls and workstations. We were greeted by an Army Special Forces team led by a tall young Colonel by the name of Mark Blum. Ramrod straight posture, short cropped hair and a starched camouflage uniform informed us he was a professional. His profession was killing anyone who threatened the national interests of the United States. He stood surrounded by a small group of special operators. I looked at the weapons they carried and didn't recognize a single one.

"Listen up. We got a situation goin' on just across the stream here that's of grave concern." Blum's Virginia accent was strong. "Los Zetas has attacked the main garrison outside Ciudad Juarez, pinnin' the Mexican Army in their barracks. With the Army unable to respond, a killing spree between the Zetas and the Juarez cartel's in progress. You're here to monitor the situation and advise of any action that needs to be taken to protect the lives and property of American citizens. We're not here to help the Mexicans. What's going on over there's their problem. Now, I need to tell you since you're sitting less than a half mile from the border, you're the first line of defense if there's any kind of incursion here. We'll back you up, but without Presidential authority we can't mobilize more than this advisory group. The President won't authorize further efforts because he doesn't want to incite an incident. Is that clear?"

"You have any training for this?" Tom gestured at the equipment before us.

"Guess when the world's goin' to hell in a hand basket you don't need trainin'. You only need volunteers." I observed.

Sergeant Jackson, tall and from Detroit from his accent greeted us.

"Okay Sergeant. How do we use these here toys?"

He smiled. I thought I wouldn't want to be on the other side of a fight with him.

"That's what I was hoping you'd ask."

Opportunity

The street fighting had lessened. Juan Dominguez checked his team. Most were just tired, but a few had wounds that needed attention. He was already down seven men. He hated to lose the good ones and it always seemed the ones he lost were the ones who were aggressive and would go right after the *sicarios*. Seven men gone. He'd have to start recruiting again in a few days. He'd need some time to regroup and let his men get some time with their families after this week. Killing whole families made his men realize theirs were vulnerable. His men needed time with their families just to reconnect. He thought it strange that men who killed for a living needed to connect with family. Maybe they valued that which they took from others more. He never felt that way, never went home and never even thought about his mother or father. They disagreed with his chosen profession. They had kicked him out when Dominguez was only twelve. He'd not been home since.

As his team moved on the home of one of the area captains Dominguez had a déjà vu moment. The house was on the Southside in a neighborhood of very small homes. The house looked much like the one he'd grown up in, even though his family spent little time there. His father and mother went back and forth to the US to get work. What got his attention was the baseball glove on the front step. It was a catcher's mitt. That was the position he'd played with the other kids in his neighborhood. He'd been a good catcher. He knew the pitches, even though most of the kids could only throw a fast ball or a change-up, which was really a slower fast ball, but they'd try to throw it high and let it drop through the strike zone to fool the batter. The problem was not many batters were fooled. If they fouled the fast ball the dropping slow ball would be coming.

Dominguez loved baseball, even though most of his friends

preferred futball or soccer as it was known in the US. Dominguez had been uncoordinated for a long time growing up. He never could get the control he needed to play futball. But he'd always been strong and could hit a pitched ball further than any of the other kids his age. He was also fast and could play outfield. However, once he played catcher and controlled how the game was played he was hooked. He was all about leading and controlling things. That was why he wanted to catch, even though he hated having to sit down on his haunches throughout the game.

The glove on the doorstep kept his attention. He went through the motions of sending his team off into their positions. They intended to kill the occupant of this particular house. Dominguez's goal was to disrupt the Juarez cartel distribution in this city as much as possible. Wipe out the leaders so Zetas could come in afterwards and take over. This particular captain had an important territory. He needed to gain this foothold. This captain was important in shipping cocaine across the border. He'd also been increasingly handling meth amphetamines. Meth was the growth part of the trade. Dominguez wanted to control the growth.

His men were now in position. He expected the captain was aware they were here. Dominguez hadn't made any particular effort to conceal what he was doing. He wanted to see what would happen. Would the Juarez captain summons others to come help him? Would he attack Dominguez's men and try to drive them off? Or would he simply wait until Dominguez's men came in after him and try to pick them off one at a time?

Dominguez gave him about ten minutes to see if anyone was coming to the rescue. No one appeared. So it was down to one of two probabilities. He sent the second team around back so he could attack from two directions at the same time.

He gave the signal. The two teams advanced as one, hitting the front and back doors at the same moment. They were through almost instantly.

Ten men entered.

Ten shots were fired.

The building exploded, knocking Dominguez off his feet.

Momentarily stunned, he looked about blankly, then realized it was a trap. He motioned to those who were covering the teams that had gone in to come with him to check things out. As he crossed the front doorstep, he reached down and picked up the catcher's mitt, tucked it under his arm. He sharpened his senses to see what had happened inside the house that seemed so familiar.

The explosion had killed all of his men, including some he'd come to trust implicitly. He was now down seventeen men. The whole day was turning into a disaster, even though he'd achieved his objective of killing key Juarez captains. And then the first bullets came in.

"Ambush!" he screamed at his men. Moving to the openings where windows had been before the explosion, his remaining men began to return fire. How many were there? He spotted a half dozen from just this vantage point. Probably the same number waited for him on the other side of the house.

Dominguez raised his AK-47 and picked off two of the sicarios. They weren't well trained and he felt better about the trap he'd walked into. He got up and walked back into the house looking for the body of the captain they'd come to kill. The man wasn't there. The Juarez captain was outside leading the attack on him. The fact he'd let someone turn the tables made him mad. He went back to the door and yelled, "Cover."

He waited only a moment for his men to lay down a blizzard of shots. He stepped out the door picking out the first of the four remaining *sicarios* he'd spotted earlier, dropped him, turned to the next, repeated his dead aim shot and then the third, who'd been hit by a shot from one of his men. Dominguez started walking around the house to his right, picking out the *sicarios*, aiming and taking each out with a single shot. By the time he'd circled the house and returned to the front door the shooting had stopped and his men were coming out of the house.

"Which one's the captain?" Dominguez asked Pablo, his lone remaining team leader.

"Tell you in a minute."

"Over here," came the call from one of his team who was out checking faces and recovering weapons, ammunition and money from those they'd killed.

Pablo looked at the catcher's mitt under Dominguez's arm. "On your way to a game?"

Dominguez had remembered the mitt, found it where he'd dropped it and put it on. "Fits." Memories of games he'd played passed through his mind. Feelings of happiness and good feelings came back. During his childhood he knew most of his feelings were about how poor his family was. He was looked down upon by most of the kids as a little guy whose parents couldn't even buy him a good glove. "Think I'll keep it."

Pablo wasn't happy. "Think we need to call it quits for today. There aren't enough of us left to take on the next target."

Dominguez looked around, figuring if there was a glove there must be a ball somewhere. "Find me the ball."

"What?"

"The ball. I want the ball and then we're going to take out the next objective. We don't go home until we're done or dead. It's that simple."

Pablo got the message. "Find him the baseball. Then change your clips. Need full ammo 'cause we got one more before we head out of here."

One of his men found a baseball and tossed it to Dominguez, who caught it with the catcher's mitt. He stood feeling the ball in his hand and the mitt on the other. He felt the same power he had in those childhood games. He also felt like he couldn't lose, just like in those games.

Retribution

I watched a gun fight on a Ciudad Juarez street on my monitor. I asked Specialist Richards, who was sitting to my right, if he knew where the fight was taking place. He pointed to a small map in the upper right corner of my screen.

"Southwest sector. You know Juarez?"

I shook my head.

"Neither do I, but bet I could find my way around from all the time I been looking at things over there."

Tom leaned over, "Is what we're seeing what's happening now?"

"Afraid so," was all I could think to say.

"And this is going on just across the river?"

"Unless these sensors are someplace other than where they told us."

I watched as a small group of gunmen advanced on a house. I saw the fight wouldn't last long, even though whoever was in the house might make a valiant effort to defend it. I watched a flanking group working their way around to the back. I thought the fight would be over shortly, as soon as the flanking group stormed the house.

I looked up at Sergeant Jackson, "And we're supposed to let them just kill and not do a thing?"

"We saw it all the time in Iraq and Afghanistan, Sir. Just the nature of war."

I thought about the nature of war. I wondered if the killing across the Rio Grande was indeed a war or just a street gang that had grown up. If a street gang, the violence should be a police matter and not a military action. I figured the US government had decided the conflict had military implications by the fact that Sergeant Jackson and his compatriots were here.

I turned back to observe the incident. Today must not have been a happy time for the poor person living in the house I observed. I didn't know how I felt. I knew I was watching a street fight between two gangs who were distributing drugs. The gangs were battling over turf. Their battle shouldn't have been of particular interest to anyone other than the Mexican police.

But then again, normally I'd be trying to arrest both gangs and take them off the streets. So I should be happy the gangs were taking care of at least half of the problem by themselves. But I couldn't settle. I hated watching as one gang ran roughshod over the other. I knew at the end of the day there'd be fewer bad guys and fewer kids in the US would be getting their drug of choice. But the fact is those kids would still get their drug of choice, just not from the same source. And probably at a higher price.

Bad guys were dying. But they were people. Why would anyone feel good about someone dying?

I watched as the armed men consolidated their position at the rear of the house. The men seemed to be taking their time in mounting the assault. I looked up at the clock and realized I'd been watching the assault unfold for almost an hour now. And then as if on cue, I saw the men at the rear of the house move as another group approached the front door. In a moment the assaulters were inside. I couldn't hear a sound, but my mind filled in the shots.

I flashed back to the man in the van at the Dallas precinct looking over the shoulder of Sergeant Adams. I should have died. I miraculously survived because of Sergeant Adams. I still felt guilty that he died to save me and his fellow officers.

I shook off the memory, and looked back up at the screen. The building exploded. "Jeesus Christ," was all I could say.

"What??" Tom asked and came over to look at my screen. Specialist Richards did the same.

The men who had been waiting outside rushed in. Then more men appeared surrounding the house. The attackers were inside the remains and suddenly I could see an ambush had been sprung on the attackers.

"Who the fuck is he?" Tom asked pointing at one man who came out of the building, clearly firing on the ambushers. I wondered how long he'd survive, but he circled the house, firing at his attackers. By the time he completed a sweep around the house it appeared that the attackers had either died or fled. I'd never seen someone who literally dared his attackers to kill him and survived.

A whole bunch of men had made the ultimate sacrifice, not to preserve justice, but because they sold drugs. Someone else had an advantage in the gang wars in Mexico. I didn't know who or why, but I decided after watching the death of *sicarios* on both sides I needed to know a whole lot more than I did.

"What's going on?" Tom asked.

"There's a lot of money on the table. They're tryin' to make sure they get their share." I tried to decide what I wanted to watch next. I knew I had to keep watching, but it had become increasingly difficult to do so. People were dying for real and I could only sit back and watch.

"Just keep telling yourself it's a sovereignty issue." Tom said. I didn't buy this.

"What if one of those who died was your kid? Would you just watch?"

"People are supposed to respect the law. A few might not and that's why we're here. But what we're watching just doesn't make any sense to me. It's open and blatant gang murder."

Richards spoke up, "We could take them out with the Predator, sir."

I regarded him as if he was a Martian. "I thought we couldn't even watch."

"We can't watch US citizens. Predators can take out authorized targets."

I looked at Richards for a long time, then at his screen. The soldier could see things I couldn't. The image moved, following a road, peering into yards.

"You're sayin' we could stop the killing if the Mexican government gave us permission?" I finally asked.

"They gave us permission in Afghanistan and Pakistan. We found the targets and the government let us take 'em out. That is, until we unfortunately took out some civilians as well. If we can figure out how to make the strikes more surgical we could end the conflict real quick."

I thought about what the young man said. "Anyone ask for permission?"

"From what I hear, we've asked and been told to stay out.

Claustrophobia

Alene was unsettled. She should have been working on her progress report to Eric on the first hundred days. Of course she wasn't there yet and most of the time so far had been spent on planning and getting the key personnel on board. But most of those tasks were now behind her. Eric was comfortable with the plans. But something wasn't right and she couldn't put her finger on what.

She went to the window wall of her eleventh floor apartment in downtown Dallas. Her view to the right overlooked the American Airlines Center where the professional basketball and hockey teams played. Victory Plaza was directly across the street and the rental agent had told her on July 4th and New Year's Eve fireworks lit up the sky right outside her window. She was looking forward to being there for both of those events. Only lately she'd been feeling the claustrophobia that had haunted her since losing her parents. The holidays had been the few times when she felt close to them. They would take time out from their busy lives twice a year to share experiences with her. She had been in nearly every capital city of Europe on one New Year's Eve or another. In nearly all, fireworks of one sort or another ushered in the New Year.

On each July 4th, her parents would take her to a different American historic site. Together they would research what had happened there that had contributed to the development of the U.S. as a world power. She thought it was little wonder that she did well in school, because on those annual treks she learned first-hand what made America great. She met people who she stayed in touch with over the years. She saw the context of things she read about. She was able to visualize things her teachers discussed, while for most of the other students they were abstract concepts.

She missed her parents, even though most of the year they had been cold and aloof. They tried to make up for the passage of time with those holiday trips. Her main objective had always been to make her mother laugh during the first hours of the first day. If she could set the tone with them they were much more engaged with her. She fought for that time because it only came twice a year. The situation had made her fearless about relationships. But she'd met so few people whom she felt strongly enough about to fight for. Why was that? What made her so solitary? Did she really prefer to be this way or had she decided that someone else needed to fight for her? Only one man had ever fought for her attention and affections.

When first on her own after her parent's accident, she had willingly gone with anyone who paid attention to her because she felt she needed someone. None had treated her well. But in each instance she had felt less alone for at least a little while. The women she befriended used her to attract guys. But as soon as they got into relationships became too busy for her. Eventually she came to regret any involvement and simply wouldn't connect with anyone outside of work. That made the isolation worse. She had to cram all of her connections into her work day and the people with whom she worked. With one brief interlude, that had been her fate now for far too long.

The problem was how to change her situation. She really had no idea because she had no easy way to meet someone having no friends to begin with. People meet people through other people. So how could she start? She knew she had to meet someone outside of work. Meet someone who would introduce her to other people.

She thought again about Agent Carr stepping between her and probable death. The fact that he hadn't asked for anything, simply made the sacrifice for her, remained the mystery that kept bringing him back into her consciousness. What had it been, about two years between the shooting and the administrative hearing where she next saw him? Her near death kept haunting her. Yet he never tried to exploit what he must have known to be a debt she owed to him. Even when she called him about the Ops job, his first reaction was to remind her that he wasn't going to get a Christmas card even from his supervisor. She liked his sense of humor. She wondered if his humor was Texan or something particular to him. Maybe his frequent lapse into Texan speech patterns was what intrigued her. She knew he was a chameleon. If he wanted to be authoritative he sounded like so many lawyers she'd met from Yale and Harvard. But most of the time he seemed to want her to underestimate him. Other times he seemed to approach people so they would accept him as an equal. Just another guy. Why would he keep changing his approach? Had he learned to do so from someone? Or did he have to fight for acceptance much the way she had while working her way up the Justice Department ladder?

She realized she felt the same loneliness in Agent Carr that she felt. They were both drifters. Was her perception of his unhappiness what drew her to him? She wanted to say no. She was too professional to let someone's personal situation influence her. Or was she? Where did she draw the line between being too involved in the lives of others and not being involved enough? She'd tended towards the latter. But somehow she'd violated her distance rules when it came to Agent Carr. She decided she'd done enough for him. It was time to stop all the nonsense of trying to repay him. He was just another guy, wasn't he?

She gazed off into the distance of the Dallas night time sky. She looked at the airplanes lining up to land at DFW airport in the distance, headlights in the sky as she'd heard Jim refer to them. Jim? Why was she letting herself think of him as Jim? He was Agent Carr. Keep the distance. Keep the relationship professional. She didn't want to open up, even though she felt him struggle to maintain the professional distance too.

Then she let her internal defenses down for a moment. She was sending Jim off on missions from which he might not come back; probably wouldn't come back if the Zetas figured out what her team was doing. Sure he would be embedded with a Mexican Army team. He was supposed to stay in the rear to share Intel. But she knew Jim was incapable of standing back when others were going into the fray. She'd watched him at the cocaine raid go right into the lion's den, leading the charge that brought the mission to a quick conclusion. She knew he'd never stay back when the bullets began to fly. His being first into the fray was the only reason she was still alive.

Now that she knew what was unsettling her, she could fix the problem. And then she realized she couldn't. She had to send him off to do what he did best. Lead the teams and engage the enemy so quickly and so violently that they'd have no chance. His propensity to do so was what led to the administrative hearing. She counted on him bringing those same qualities to the missions he would run for her. Together they'd be successful, as long as he didn't get himself killed. How could she save him and at the same time carry out their mission? She didn't know.

Connection

When I arrived at the Joint, my head was pounding with a flashback to the Dallas Precinct shootings. I couldn't focus. I went to see Tom, his morning McDonald's coffee in hand. "That your report?"

Tom returned from his apparent trance, "Yeah. Couldn't sleep last night."

"Mind if you just add my name and save me a mornin' of boredom?"

"For a hamburger today, I'll gladly pay you Tuesday."

Knowing the Popeye cartoon reference I responded, "You're a gentleman and scholar."

Tom returned to reading his draft. "And I only use the Queen's English. Hope you don't mind."

"You been to London town?" I inquired, having never been.

"Yeah, couple of years ago. Invited by the Yard to observe a drug trafficking case. We raided a safe house, but we didn't get anything like what you did, when was that? Two or three years ago?" Tom added my name and sent the report.

I suddenly made a connection. "Was the attempted hit on me because of the cocaine raid? It was a long time ago."

"Unless your name came up in a fortune cookie. The cartel boys got long memories. Particularly when you deprive them of a lot of money."

Tom's comment triggered a recollection. One of the gunmen at the precinct shooting said something about the attempted hit on me not being the end, but the beginning. I had the urge to call home to the Triple C Ranch, something I rarely did since I'd been on the outs with brother Bill. Dad wanted to pay for my college after I returned from the Army. Bill said the Ranch couldn't afford it and he was managing the Ranch.

I had a sinking feeling in my stomach. *What if whoever came after me knows where I live? Not here in Dallas, but my family. Where I came from. Why didn't I think of this before?* I called the memorized number, "Hello? Janice? It's Jim."

I heard tension and caution in her voice, "Oh, hi."

"Janice? Everything okay?" I was even more worried given the tentative tone to her voice, one I'd never heard before. Seemed she wasn't sure she was glad I'd called.

"Heavens no. Bill's out milkin' and Dad's out plantin' the Brussels sprouts. Other than that, everythin's fine."

I knew they had no milking cows and my father hated Brussels sprouts. "You got company? Unwelcome company?"

"That's right. Hope you can come see us real soon."

I felt my heart skip a beat. I knew my family was in trouble, but I needed to know more. "I'll call the Sheriff over in Waco."

"You know I've always been able to feed an army."

"You got lots of company."

"Seems like weeks."

The line went dead.

I called the Sheriff's office. They'd have someone check on the ranch when they could. They were understaffed and it might take a while. The next call went to an old friend, Adam Bates at the Texas Parks and Wildlife Commission.

"Officer Bates, can I help you?"

I never felt happier to hear Adam's voice and never dreaded so much what my friend might tell me. "Adam, Carr. You got a bird up near Lake Whitney?"

"Agent Carr. Got another kidnap for me to track for you?"

"This one's closer to home. Need someone to fly over my brother's ranch."

"Missing cattle?" Adam's voice changed knowing he couldn't do a personal favor.

I shook my head even though Adam couldn't see what I was doing. "I think he has some unwelcome company."

"Anyone I know?" Adam seemed tentative, trying to understand the situation.

I could only imagine who might be there. "For your sake, I hope not."

The tone of Adam's voice changed. Apparently he understood the reason for the call wasn't primarily personal. "Not over the lake, but can be there in about… fifteen minutes." I heard Adam talking on the radio and then come back on the phone. "All set. I'll let you know what he finds."

"Great." I let the phone drop back in the cradle and raced to my old red Porsche parked in the garage across Federal Boulevard from Bryan Tower and the Joint offices. In a matter of minutes I flew down I-35 toward Waco and Lake Whitney. My destination was almost two hours away … except in a Porsche.

Headlong Homecoming

Adam called before I even got out of Dallas. The pilot reported several white Suburbans or Tahoes in the driveway. Nothing else seemed unusual. I had no idea if Bill had a Suburban or Tahoe, but several white ones didn't make sense and would be impossible to find without plate numbers.

Forty-five minutes later I passed into Hillsboro near the outlet mall. I didn't remember the speed trap on the interstate until a highway patrol car came out of his hiding spot. As much as I wanted to just keep on going I decided to stop. A red Porsche was a magnet for policemen looking to raise revenue for their cash-strapped municipalities. I was doing a little over the speed limit.

I pulled over and jumped out racing back to the blonde, fresh faced patrolman, who looked at me with sheer terror in his eyes. He got out of the car to meet me.

"Afternoon, do ..."

I stuck my credentials under the patrolman's nose. "You've got to be the sorriest excuse for a highway patrolman I've ever met. What's your name?" I looked at his badge, "Peterson?"

The highway patrolman scanned my FBI credential and must have realized he was in trouble. "Sorry..."

"I need you to follow me, Patrolman Peterson," I growled

"Why, sir?"

I recognized the fear in the young patrolman's voice. "Because some folks, not so far away, have some very unwelcome company."

The young patrolman finally got what I was saying, "FBI? Holy crap."

"God damn it Peterson, keep up." I ran back to the Porsche. I gunned my engine, leaving the young patrolman warding off flying gravel from my tires and scrambling to get back to his cruiser.

Farm-to-Market Road 22 came up about ten minutes later. The Porsche raced over the familiar undulating terrain toward the far side of Lake Whitney where the Carr ranch ran between Farm-to-Market Road 56 and the lake. I'd had lots of time to remember on the way. The Triple C, as my family's ranch was known, had graced the Texas countryside for over a century. When the Carr family bought the land near the turn of the twentieth century, a lake hadn't entered the minds of my great grandfather or the local government officials. But in 1944, my grandfather had been one of the ranchers who asked for help in controlling the annual flooding of the Brazos River. He continued to lose cattle in those annual floods. He wanted something done; not realizing the result would be a need to sell off half of his land to the county. Nor did he realize he'd end up with a near mile long mud beachfront without any sand.

All ancient history as far as I was concerned. I just remembered the gorgeous views and vistas from the farmhouse. I'd been raised on the Triple C. My brother Bill continued to live there when I moved away after high school. My younger sister Tess left two years after me. Dad turned the ranch over to Bill and Janice when Mom passed on.

At Mom's funeral I didn't say a word to Bill. I realized, as I raced toward home, that I had no idea how Bill, to whom I'd been so close when we were young kids, had coped with the loss of our mother. And now Dad lived with Bill and Janice. So Bill made sure Dad was taken care of. Maybe the ranch wasn't such a great deal for Bill after all.

I couldn't see the patrolman in my rear view mirror. Apparently I'd lost him somewhere along the way. I slowed down, looking around for any clues as to what might have been going on when I talked with Janice.

Janice was the best-looking girl in my class. Bill had come out of nowhere and plucked her away from me. Throughout middle school and high school, I always thought I'd figure out a way to be with Janice. Even told Bill how I felt about her.

I'd never forgiven Bill for asking her to the Senior Prom, when I'd told him I was going to ask her to the Junior Prom that year. In Lake Whitney, Texas there weren't many opportunities to socialize with the girls except in school and at church. So I couldn't claim I'd had a relationship with her first. Besides, Janice didn't even seem to know I was alive once Bill started paying attention to her. I told myself she made her choice. I needed to accept the situation. But still I couldn't forgive Bill, who knew how much she meant to me.

Dad tried to explain what had happened. As a shy person, Bill would have trouble doing anything other than ranching. Apparently Janice was happy being a ranch wife, probably because it was the only life she'd known. Bill would succeed on the ranch, Dad had said, 'because the cattle have to listen to him, whether they agree with him or not.' I didn't have the limits Bill did, Dad went on. I didn't need a ranch to guarantee my success. I could find my own. He also told me that from what he'd seen of Janice, she wouldn't be comfortable with the kind of life I might lead. I never realized until that moment, blasting over the rolling Farm-to-Market roads, heading back to the source of all my childhood memories, that Dad knew me better then, than I knew myself.

I turned off onto the dirt road that snaked down to the lake and my childhood home. I thought of the hot summers spent at the lake after the ranch chores were done. And then the phone conversation with Janice played back in my mind one more time.. The dread in me rose.

No Place Like Home

Triple C ranch was for Caleb Carter Carr, my great grandfather. He'd bought the land from old man Whitney. Most of the land under the lake had been owned by my family, but had originally been owned by the infamous Whitneys, so the lake had been named after them not us. I didn't lose any sleep over the slight, but the naming reminded me justice didn't always prevail in the plains and hill country of North Texas. Beyond the lake view, I saw smoke. I knew the smoke came from the main house.

The smoke could only mean one thing. The threat made by the gunman outside the Dallas precinct had been real. I feared for Bill, Janice, and Dad, sure something bad had happened to them. The tension drained from me. My foot on the gas pedal relaxed. I really didn't want to know what had happened since the call only a few hours ago. The fire hadn't started yet when Adam Bates' pilot had flown over.

I began steeling myself for what I'd find. By the time I turned into the drive, I didn't want to proceed the last half mile.

The fire was evident through the smoke. The main house had nearly burned to the ground, even though surrounded by fire trucks. Hoses from the tankers sprayed water to try to save some remnants of my youth, but I knew the result wouldn't be worth the struggle. And with the loss of the house, all the roots I had to this land, to this place, to this lake and the people who once made this a home for our family also ceased to exist.

I felt hollow, as if every childhood memory I'd been keeping inside all those years had suddenly evaporated. Everything that represented me as a child and young man seemed to have taken flight. I never thought a simple wood frame house could have such impact. I felt as if I were approaching nothingness, a vacuum of sorts, one of the soul.

Anger made me breathless. Someone had taken my childhood. Someone sought to destroy the memories of my youth, of my innocence, of my emergence as an independent being capable of making a difference in the world. Someone had decided to strike a blow against me, to remove something from the earth precious to me and few others. Destroying my family home had to be aimed at me, but Bill, Janice and Dad were now homeless and I feared much worse.

The Scene of the Crime

Only the Sheriff and firemen were at the scene. None of them had seen Bill, Janice or Dad. But they'd not yet been able to enter the remains of the house. I called Bud in the Dallas FBI office, explained what had happened, and asked if he'd send an investigation team down. Bud agreed when I tied the fire to the Dallas Precinct shootings on which the Bureau was cooperating with the Dallas Police. He said he'd call Alene for me and let her know what happened and that he was coordinating the investigation. I still didn't know the fates of Bill, Janice or Dad.

Lon Rogers, my FBI partner, arrived with five others about three hours later. By then the fire had burned itself out and firemen were making their first ginger forays into the glowing remnants. The firemen moved slowly as if swimming against a current.

"I am truly sorry about this, Jim." Lon said in his proper and precise English accent, adopted after he went to university in London. "What do you think happened?"

I put my arm around his shoulder and drew him in close. "Wish I knew."

"Bud requested we look at these events from the angle of the precinct shootings."

I looked down at the ground. "I wouldn't rule out anything at this point."

Lon turned away and asked his team to get started. I knew that regardless of my feelings, the investigation and law enforcement response couldn't be my concern, officially. Lon would keep me informed. I'd be questioned as often as necessary. But I wouldn't be allowed to participate in the actual apprehension of the suspects when the time arrived. I fully understood all the reasons why. But in reality I'd very different ideas about what would happen. How I'd exact my punishment upon those who stole my home from me, our family and those who spent time with us here.

Lon turned back to me. "When Bud told me about your call I volunteered."

"I wouldn't want anyone else to lead this investigation," I truly meant what I said. I'd worked with Lon long enough to know him to be a thorough professional who'd continue to turn over clues until he found every piece of relevant evidence. I also knew Lon would keep me informed throughout the process, regardless of what he found.

I looked up. Alene stood in the driveway looking bewildered. I left Lon and approached her. "You didn't have to come."

She reached out to touch my shoulder. "I wanted to. What happened?"

"Bud give you the overview?"

She nodded. "Your family?"

I choked up and had trouble speaking. "Don't know. They haven't been able to walk through as yet. Thank you for coming. It means a lot to me." I touched her arm gently and she looked into my eyes. I thought she wanted to know how the events were changing me and what that meant for her.

I led her over to Lon, "Let me introduce you to the FBI team Bud sent."

After brief intros, Lon seemed to be thinking I was the lucky one working for a woman as striking as Alene, but he remained professional and quickly returned to the task at hand. "What did your sister-in-law, Janice say that alerted you?" Lon watched my face closely as he asked the first in what would be a series of painful questions.

One of the firemen yelled, "Found one."

Without thinking or feeling I started walking toward the fireman. A deputy sheriff intercepted me carrying a pair of big rubber boots. "You'll need these to go in there."

Stopping long enough to pull the boots on, I stepped through what was once a door. A memory flashed of opening the door when Janice came to the house for the first time. But she came to see Bill, not me. All the feelings of betrayal rushed back. I turned around and moved into what had been the living room. I remembered arguments with Bill. Then the day Dad told me Bill would be getting the ranch and I needed to start thinking about what I wanted to do with my life.

By the time I reached the body, the fireman had moved on. I tried to place where I was in the house. This would have been the kitchen. I remembered where the phone would have been. I looked at the now unrecognizable body, its flesh burned off. Janice.

I felt nauseous and could feel something behind that wall around my heart kicking and screaming to be let out. Janice was my first love, even though platonic and from afar. She was the woman who came between me and my brother, but that didn't mean I loved her any less. And now she was gone. Why'd someone have to take her life? She was a fun person with a mischievous side, always laughed at even the worst jokes. She loved my brother fiercely. I'd seen that close up. She'd stand beside him even if doing so meant her life, which ultimately she'd surrendered, but for me, not Bill.

I was responsible. I couldn't make up for what had happened. Not now. I couldn't do anything. And here lay her remains. I'd never be able to forgive myself. I'd never stop searching for whoever was responsible.

Kneeling down to get a better look, I discovered what appeared to be two small holes in her forehead. Tap, tap. Whoever killed her had been professionally trained; maybe a soldier. Janice had been killed before the fire. Probably right after I talked with her. Her killer had used her to get to me. Was her killer sending a message to a single FBI agent? I knew the killing and fire had to be risky for whoever burned down the ranch. Someone was sending a clear warning that had to be aimed at a wider audience. The killers were trying to say they wouldn't stop, ever. Anyone who opposed them would die and their families would perish.

I understood the tactic. Tamerlane and Alexander were famous for killing whole families. The only difference seemed to be that after killing everyone, those warlords tended to marry the daughters of the now dead leaders as a gesture of peace. In this case I didn't expect to get any invitations to a wedding.

"We got another one over here," the fireman called out.

I said a brief prayer for Janice's soul and moved on to the next body. This was Bill, no question. He'd been nicknamed the Moose. A big guy, he played left guard on the offensive line of the high school football team. In another of our many contrasts, I remained agile and quick, a quarterback, starting as a sophomore when Bill was a junior. Bill protected me on the football field that year. But Bill hadn't protected my heart. As close as we'd been when we were kids, everything changed. I knew I'd miss him terribly. I regretted I could no longer offer him forgiveness.

I saw the two holes in his forehead. Tap, tap. Close range. No question. The gunmen must have separated Janice from Bill in their final moments. The fireman called out, "Got another." I dreaded this most of all for I had to believe Dad had been in the house, as much as I hoped he'd been elsewhere.

I realized Janice must have thought about what to say for a long time. With the message the precinct shooters delivered, I would arrive in only a matter of time. How long had the men been holding Bill, Janice and Dad hostage? Maybe Lon could tell.

I said a final prayer for Bill, remembering only the feelings about the good times we shared and reluctantly went to the third body. Not Dad, the body was too small. The body looked like someone about five foot six. Dad had been over six foot. This person was small and fine boned, Dad had been big boned and rugged from all the years of working a farm. With Bill's size people had often described me as the runt of the litter until Tess was born. Tess and I took after our mother. Bill had never tired of telling me I was more like a woman than a man. As a result I'd occasionally feigned being gay and telling Bill I really did love him, which always got a reaction.

I saw no bullet holes in the head on this third corpse. Maybe Bill had somehow taken out one of the attackers, but doing so hadn't been enough to stop the men from their plan. I wondered if they'd killed Bill immediately afterwards, or if the men kept him alive until after Janice spoke to me. If they hadn't, Janice must not have known when we spoke. With the fire, I'd probably never know.

But what about Dad? I found no evidence those responsible had taken him, but I kept remembering Janice's reference to Brussels sprouts. I could only assume she was telling me he hated being captive to these men. They'd be waiting for me to try to find him. But how could I? I didn't have any idea who might have taken him. There were multiple cartels and who knew how many different gangs that could have been involved. I had found nothing to give me a starting point. I had to hope someone made a mistake or left a clue I could follow.

Moonlight

For the next several hours Alene sat with me in my Porsche while the firemen continued to put out the fire and Lon's team gathered clues.

"You were close to your family?" She asked.

I nodded without elaborating. "Older brother and younger sister. It was just us and hundreds of acres to tend."

"I saw cattle coming in."

"About a thousand head at the peak, but couldn't sustain that many. We just didn't have the money or help to manage."

"I couldn't imagine growing up like this. I was an only child, although my parents generally thought they didn't have any. I always wanted a brother or sister or both, but my parents didn't want me to have either. They thought I was too disruptive to their lives. More of me would have been impossible." She laughed, but I could feel regret and loneliness underlying.

"Where are your parents now?"

She looked down at her hands, steeled herself and finally looked directly at me. "They died in an auto accident in Brazil on my twentieth birthday. I was in college and they'd gone home to visit both families."

"In Brazil? So they weren't US?"

Alene nodded. "They were both born in Rio and came to Washington with the company that employed my father. I was born here."

"Why didn't you go home after they died?"

"This was the only home I knew, even without them here. I'd visited Rio and met my relatives, but I didn't know them. This was where I belonged."

"Must have been hard for you, in college and all on your own."

She smiled a lopsided smile just like one I'd seen so often in Lexie. I had to get past the resemblances. "I know lots of people who say college was just the greatest experience of their lives. I learned a lot, but I wouldn't do it again. I had way too much to deal with back then."

I saw that I'd misjudged her. Life hadn't been easy for Alene Oliviera. But I wasn't able to respond with the smoke still rising from the ashes of my childhood.

"Must have been hard in the lean times." She said.

"Some of the best times were when we had nothing except each other." I responded. "Life was simple when we had to rely on ourselves to have enough to eat. We pulled together more. We were thankful for what each of us did to help the whole family."

"I envy that closeness." Made me think she'd not been that close to her parents. I stayed quiet to let her say more but she didn't. I wanted to know more about her, she was there to help me cope with what had happened, not become closer as coworkers. But I felt closer just the same.

Shortly after she left the remains of Bill and Janice were removed. I spent the next two hours with the firemen going through the rubble. I looked for anything that might help Lon and the investigations team. I turned over everything I found to Lon.

The moon was full. I lingered, sifting through the ashes of the house. Lon and the team prepared to leave for their hotel, over on the interstate. I had to get back to the Joint the next day while Lon and the team continued their work. Only three bodies were found. I had no idea what happened to Dad. I kept playing the conversation with Janice over and over in my mind. Was she telling me they'd already taken him away? Was she trying to tell me where I'd find him?

Lon put his hand on my shoulder. "I believe we've done about all we can tonight. I'll bring the team back at dawn to finish." He led the investigators back to the black Tahoe. I felt a compulsion to walk through one more time, even though moonlight had never been the best way to spot anything.

About twenty minutes later I saw a reflection in the moonlight. A bullet casing. The killers had been careful to remove the casings from the scene, but now I had one. I picked up the casing with a handkerchief, lifted by the rim around the base, then carefully wrapped up and put it into my pocket.

I looked out over the lake; bright moonlight cast shimmering reflections on the waters. This was the first time I'd returned to the Triple C in many years. I knew I'd never return again, for nothing here remained of value to me now. The ranch belonged to Bill and Janice. The land would go to their son, Dan, a junior oil and gas attorney in Fort Worth. Dan had no interest in raising cattle and ranching. He skedaddled off the farm as soon as he could, just as I had, but for a totally different reason. Dan didn't want to be a rancher; I did.

I called Dan to inform him of the death of his parents. He was shocked. He took a while to respond to me. With the late hour he decided to come down in the morning.

As I settled into my Porsche and began the journey back to Dallas, I wondered: *Why did fate twist things? Why had I found myself in law enforcement? All I ever wanted was to be a rancher like Dad. Now my nephew, who couldn't care less about ranching, would inherit the one thing I'd wanted all of my life.*

My mind still reeled from the events of the day. I needed to know who was responsible. Then I'd decide how best to retaliate. The only clues I had pointed in a single direction: the cartels. But I wouldn't close off other possibilities. The last thing I wanted to do was start a war with someone with unlimited resources and more guns than the FBI. But on the other hand, if a cartel did this to get at me, they wouldn't stop.

Somehow a cartel had my name. Someone apparently knew a lot I didn't want him to know. So how'd that person come by my information? Access remained the most puzzling question since my records with the FBI were closely guarded. *How could someone know?*

Night Rider

The roads were deserted until I turned up onto the interstate. Here I found an occasional car or truck. I knew I could kick my speed up ten to fifteen miles per hour over the speed limit and not have a problem. I felt no need to hurry home. I wanted the extra time on the road to help me think.

I knew I'd have difficulty sleeping; the images of the charred bodies and remains of the ranch were fresh in my mind. I had to keep pushing horrific thoughts of what must have been their last living moments out of my head. But when the freeing of my subconscious started, once I finally got to bed, I knew those images would come again.

As I approached Hillsboro, a highway patrol car came out near the place from which I'd lured Patrolman Peterson. The officer never appeared at the ranch. *No surprise, the man seemed totally inept.* Peterson had probably returned to his lair, spotted my red Porsche on the return trip, and wanted to find out why I didn't wait for him. At the point where Peterson stopped me, still not knowing for sure what was happening at the Triple C, I hadn't intended to wait for anyone.

I let the memory fade and slowed to let the cruiser catch up. I pulled over to the side of the highway. According to procedure the cruiser stopped behind me, but the officer didn't input the license data I knew to be the standard procedure. Instead he came out of the door. I watched in my rear-view mirrors. The patrolman walked up beside my car with his hand on his revolver. I hadn't been speeding, hadn't been driving erratically.

As the patrolman came up alongside, I lowered the window. I

kept the engine running just in case. The patrolman pulled the strap that held his weapon in place. His action violated policy. He had his handgun ready to be used. The traffic stop wasn't what it seemed. I checked his face. Latino. Bells were ringing loud in the back of my head.

"Evening Officer." I held my identification in my right hand, even though I had to cross my body to show him. When the gun started out of the holster, I was ready, having unlatched the car door with my left hand…

… I slammed the door into the patrolman…

… reached through the window with my right hand to seize the revolver by the barrel and twisted the weapon away.

As if by reflex I came out of my car, holding the weapon and closing the distance between the patrolman and myself. "Who the fuck are you? Why are you trying to kill me?" I had the Latino by the front of his uniform and the revolver in his face.

"No hable Ingles." The patrolman pleaded scared to death.

"Bullshit. You speak as well as I do. Who sent you?"

"No hable!"

Pulling the patrolman over to his vehicle, I confirmed whether the patrol car was real. I opened the back door, pushed the patrolman in and closed the door behind him.

At the driver's side, I reached through the window, picked up the microphone and called in. "This is FBI Agent Carr. I have a gentleman in custody who's driving one of your vehicles. He claims he doesn't speak English. Think you could send an assist team? I'm about three miles north of Hillsboro on I-35 toward Dallas."

The dispatch must not have understood, "Who's on this frequency?"

"This is FBI Agent Carr. I work out of the Dallas office. I have a gentleman wearing one of your uniforms. He has a name plate of Martinez and claims he doesn't *hable Ingles*. However, he just pulled his service revolver on me and I was forced to disarm him. If I were a bettin' man .... which I ain't by the way.... I'd say he had something to do with the triple homicide that just occurred at the Triple C."

"Who's on this frequency?"

"You ain't listenin' real good. You got a problem and need to get someone out here. I may be forced to tie this idiot up, stick him in your trunk and leave him for your mornin' shift."

I saw headlights coming toward me, and realized I was exposed. I thought I'd better just leave. I could outrun anyone in my Porsche, but I hesitated. Doing so went against my training. Interrogate and learn what I can. Don't give up on a source.

I slid into the driver's seat of the patrol car, closing the door behind me. A vehicle approached and I ducked.

A white pickup truck probably on the way home.

"Agent Carr? Is that your name?" a different voice came on the radio.

"Yes. Who's this?"

"Sergeant Ted York, I'm the Hillsborough night supervisor. What's the situation?"

"You missin' a cruiser and a patrolman? I got the cruiser, but not sure who's wearin' your monkey suit."

"Three miles north of Hillsborough?"

I saw distant lights and had a real bad feeling. "Yeah an' I'm feelin' like a sittin' duck out here. You got anybody in the neighborhood?"

"Ten minutes. Stay put."

"No comprende, amigo, where you at, I'm comin' your way."

I put the cruiser into drive and pulled into the lane. The oncoming lights continued to grow larger. I accelerated.

"We're in Hillsborough near the outlet mall, just off the highway." The voice said. "Take the next exit, and come on back south. I'll give you directions from there."

I sped up, trying to put some distance between myself and the approaching headlights, but the lights continued to grow larger. I was already driving over eighty miles per hour.

I saw the flashes an instant before the back window shattered.

I ducked down but kept my head up enough to see the road as I floored the cruiser.

The heavy cruiser didn't respond to more gas. The lights continued to grow. More bullets buffeted the cruiser, taking out the windshield as well and spraying my face with sharp glass shards.

With the wind and blood running into my eyes I made out the exit. I had to decide whether taking the ramp would help my escape or slow me down.

Making a move toward the exit first, I spun the wheel in the opposite direction…

… fish tailed across the lane hoping not to roll … and hit the median with tires chewing at the grass, trying to reverse the forward momentum.

I pulled back up on the pavement and hurtled south, picking up speed.

I watched the rear view mirror for the shooter's car. No lights.

Only a moment of relief before more bullets hit the cruiser.

Someone was following, but had turned off his headlights so I wouldn't see the car until too late.

I juked the cruiser back and forth, trying to make myself less of a sitting duck.

But the bullets continued to impact.

I saw flashing red lights come up onto the highway from the Hillsborough entrance ramp. The patrol car headed north as I came south.

One of the bullets struck the rear passenger side tire.

The car swerved ...

The rear end came around...

... and the car and I went into a roll that flipped us over three times, taking us off the highway and landing on the car's driver side.

I felt more bullets buffet the car again...

... and then stop.

Sirens approached.

From what I could tell the patrol car crossed the median as I had and came back.

I released my seat belt, fell onto the door, and crawled out the broken windshield, cutting myself again in the process. Once outside I stood up, waited for my equilibrium to return before taking steps.

The patrol car approached. I walked to the rear window, looked inside. Officer Martinez lay crumpled onto the down side door. I couldn't see him very well, but his stillness didn't bode well.

Two officers exited the new cruiser, "You Agent Carr?" The first asked.

I looked for my identification. "Yeah, my ID must be with my car, up a ways and on the other side. The Porsche."

The fact I didn't have ID put the Officer on his guard, "Okay, but we'll need to see it when we take you back there."

"No problem. You know Patrolman Martinez?"

The second patrolman looked over the bullet-riddled, dented cruiser. "Sarge ain't gonna like this one bit."

The first patrolman responded, "Yeah, he works out of our barracks."

"Well, tell me if this is him." I brought the patrolman over to the back windshield and let him lean in with his flashlight. I watched as he felt the man's neck and withdrew trying to avoid the broken glass.

"Never seen him. This the guy who pulled his weapon on you? What were you doin'?"

"Comin' from a murder."

The driver came closer, "The Triple C? What happened?"

"Don't know for sure, but somebody's out here drivin' 'round with their lights out, shootin' up highway patrol cars. So I suggest we bring our friend along, go back to your barracks and call for more help. This ain't nearly over yet."

A Marked Man

I met Alene in her office the next morning. She listened carefully to my description of the events after she left the Triple C. "So somebody has my car, and my FBI credentials." I said.

"We'll have to deal with your credentials." She penned a note to herself.

"Must be related to the precinct shooting. But I still don't know who was behind it or why they want to kill me and my family."

"Think this has compromised your ability to do your job?" she went right to her issue, one I hadn't even considered.

"Hell no." I knew I came across too strong, but she wanted me unfiltered, so she was seeing me raw. "Look, I know you're worried about me getting out of control. I brought that on myself. But as I said before, I just need you to believe in me and I'll make you glad you gave me the chance."

Alene grimaced. "Send me the funeral arrangements, I want to come." Her request caught me by surprise.

Her phone rang. Alene's administrative assistant, Jan called through the open door. "Eric on line one."

As she picked up the phone she nodded toward the door, "I need to take the call, but I want to talk some more about what's happened to you. Yes, Eric." A short silence as she listened. I rose to leave. "That's right. What do you need from me?"

Quest for Clues

I found Nick, the FBI computer wizard who'd been attached to the Task Force. He must have been in his late twenties, but looked fifteen. Maybe the way he dressed created that image, like he was a skateboarder. They let him grow his hair long, and he had a peach fuzz goatee. As I approached Nick's desk, I wondered if he used an eyebrow pencil in the morning to make his beard look darker. By the end of the day the goatee seemed almost invisible again.

As always, Nick appeared engrossed in something on his computer screen when I approached him. "Nick."

No response.

I grabbed his earphone wire and gave a yank. I heard heavy metal music. Nick looked up as if in a daze. "Hey! That's my personal space, Carr. What's the deal?"

I sat down next to the space cadet. "The deal is I've got real work for you for a change." I removed the shell casing from my pocket, and held it up. "I need a name and address, if there's a print."

Nick thought for a minute, "That hasn't come in through evidence."

"No, and it won't until you give me the name and address."

Nick puzzled, probably thinking I was asking him to break procedure.

"You get shot up again, Alene's going to be asking questions."

"I get shot up, I won't be telling anyone anything, now will I?"

Nick continued to stare at the shell casing, "Where'd you get it?"

"My brother's place. If there's a print it belongs to someone who was there." I saw Nick had heard about what happened and now considered the whole chain of events.

"So you're asking me to break a rule so you can break some more rules."

"That depends on what you find, Mister Wizard."

Nick looked at me earnestly now. I knew the kid fancied himself a genius of sorts. He could do things with the FBI systems no one else could. I'd been surprised the Bureau gave him up to Alene's Rapid Reaction Team. Everyone went to him with the hardest problems. Lon told me he'd heard Nick hacked a bureau database. The Bureau banished him to teach him a lesson. And now I sat here asking him to continue his rogue behavior.

"So why me? It's a simple lift and check the database. You could do it."

I shook my head, "I suspect any print would belong to a person with military training, and most likely not US military."

I saw the fires of a challenge begin to glow in Nick's eyes. "So I hack a whole bunch of foreign military personnel files until I make a match?"

I nodded.

The fire in his eyes burned brightly. "Where do I start?"

"Mexico."

Bait

The same night I looked out the window of my apartment and saw the moonlight illuminate the stakeout team on the street. The second team was based in an apartment building across the street. I felt like bait, and I was. Since everyone expected someone to try to kill me again, I'd been forced to slow down my planning for an expedition to Mexico.

As expected, Nick came up with a name and an old address. The fingerprint belonged to one Miguel Hernandez Anjel. He was thirty-three years old, or there about. Nick couldn't find more on him. He'd apparently disappeared.

I moved back into the room and turned off the light so as not to be quite so exposed. I called Lon from my land line.

"What have you found out?"

I heard Lon take a deep breath as if this would be a difficult conversation. "Whoever killed your family was well trained. The killers swept it clean, made sure tire tracks were from commodity tires on millions of cars, wore shoes purchased in any mall in America, and used inflammatory liquids sold in any gas station."

"Does that mean you're at a dead end?"

"We have bits and pieces, nothing more."

"So you finished out there?"

"The team came back at noon today. Not much more we can do there. We're starting to work on the highway patrol car tomorrow. Maybe we can get lucky on the weapon."

"Thanks. Let me know how it goes."

I hung up and wondered when I would learn the real story. The call had been almost word for word what Lon and I rehearsed before I left the Joint. I didn't like being bait. From what I had seen, the people I had to worry about were professionals. They wouldn't walk into an obvious trap. I had to be most concerned about the time I'd normally be least concerned about my safety. So I decided the last thing they'd expect of me would be to take a walk, particularly with the heat over one hundred degrees. I changed into a dark colored t-shirt, jeans and running shoes and slipped down the stairwell to the garage.

I stopped short. My red Porsche was parked in its normal space. A moment passed before the situation sank in. I took off running at full speed ... away from my prized possession.

The explosion ripped through the garage.

The force of the expanding gasses threw me headlong outward, hitting face down on the concrete drive.

I took the skin off my chin and embedded pebbles into the palms of both hands.

I landed clear of the building, stunned for a moment.

The apartment building began to creak and groan.

I heard a popping signifying the shearing of bolts, followed by twisting of metal, and then the fracturing of concrete.

The building collapsed with a dull roar into the parking garage beneath.

Dust poured out of the structure. The sounds of automobile alarms blared. After a moment of stillness, I heard voices from within the rubble.

I found my cell phone about ten feet from where I landed and called 9-1-1. "There's prob'ly fifty people or more in there." I shouted, not realizing I was doing so, because my hearing had been affected by the blast.

The stakeout teams arrived and joined me in pulling apart the rubble. We carried the living and the dead out to the street. We worked side-by-side through the night.

Only once did I wonder if someone was watching. If they had me in their sights, so be it. People were badly injured. I had to help. I couldn't hide. I wouldn't hide. I intended to carry the fight to whoever was trying to kill me. I just had to figure out how.

Cocktail

About four am a cab dropped me at a cheap drive-in motel known as the Sleep Inn in Lakeside for what remained of the night. This motel had to be about the last place anyone would look for me. I was filthy from pulling broken cement and steel beams off of people. My clothes were ripped and covered with dust. I wanted to shower. I was wired and exhausted from the events. I didn't know if I could sleep.

Alene appeared at the check in. She surprised me, making me think of Lexie. I missed her all over again. I had no idea how Alene knew where I was. She silently waited for me to finish signing in and accompanied me to the room.

"Should have been watching for your car," she started, sounding regretful.

"Not your fault. I was the one who was stupid."

"A Yale man admitting he acted less than diligently? Unheard of. Particularly admitting it to a Harvard grad." She kidded me and I needed something to get me out of the funk I was in.

I looked into her eyes and had to catch my breath. She had Lexie's eyes, right down to the same questioning look. With Lexie I always wondered if she were looking to see what kind of person I was deep down inside. Would I disappoint her? Would I always stand beside her? Alene's look was different, but no less piercing and questioning. I had to get past my memories before I could respond. And my response was feeble. "Even Yale men are prone to momentary lapses."

"I'll note that for posterity." She smiled at my mock anguished look. "Anything I can do for you tonight?"

I had to discount the obvious second interpretation of her question. I checked her out, realizing she was much more attractive than I'd been admitting to myself. I think she noticed, but said nothing. "Got something to knock me out for the night? Goin' to be hard to sleep with all that's happened."

"Take tomorrow off. I need you to get refocused on the Zetas and not yourself. I know that'll be hard, but I'm sure you can do it."

"I'll be in as soon as I get something suitable to wear."

"That all you have left?" she seemed to realize.

"Yeah, but I'll go see my bud Ron Sall. Owns a men's store, Sall Stearns."

She looked at my torn and dusty jeans and t-shirt, "Probably a good idea. Come see me when you get in. Some things are brewing. We need to chat."

"I hate to be a burden on you. Particularly when you had to go to bat for me."

She reached out and squeezed my hand, "I'm glad I could be here for you." Her smile was genuine. I got lost looking at it. I thanked her for coming, and watched as she drove away in her late model black BMW.

As soon as I sat down in my room weariness settled over me. I pulled off my shoes, letting each drop to the floor with a thud. My clothes trailed behind me into the bathroom. I turned on the shower. My muscles ached. The hot water poured over me. But as much as I tried to relax in the spray, I didn't feel the normal release. I couldn't relax because I knew I was still in danger. I would be until I killed every last person responsible for taking my family away from me. I'd start with Miguel Hernandez Anjel, and see where he took me.

I thought I heard a sound like a glass shattering. I peeked out of the shower. Flames filled my room. The flames came up from the floor. I noticed a hole in the window where a brick preceded a Molotov cocktail, setting nearly everything on fire.

I bolted from the shower…

Raced for the bed…

Pulled the blankets off …

Tried my best to smother the fire while keeping low and below the window.

The flames burned a hole in the blanket.

I snatched the pillows and finally smothered the fire.

I lay on the floor, pulled on the dirty clothes over my still wet sweaty body.

I found my secure cell and called the watch team.

No answer.

Not a good sign.

I entered the number for the backup team.

No answer.

I could only think of one person who could help me now.

I hit the speed-dial to reach Lon. "This is Mister Rodgers, welcome to my neighborhood." he said jovially.

"Lon. Jim. Got big time trouble."

Twenty minutes later I walked out of the hotel in a Dallas Patrolman's uniform and entered a waiting black and white squad car.

Patrolman Ken Boerner, the driver, radioed in: "Car one thirteen, wheels up. What do we know?"

"We have four dead officers, both watch teams," came back across the radio. All I could hear in my mind was, 'tap, tap.'

Embarrassed

Ruben Castillo stared at Jose Dominguez from behind the massive oak desk in his elaborately paneled and expensively furnished Ciudad Victoria home office. The bright rays from the late afternoon sun caused him to squint just enough to make his face seem even more intense than normal. As he watched he saw something he'd not seen in a while. Dominguez seemed uncomfortable. Dominguez's discomfort made Castillo happy. Castillo knew if Dominguez was uncomfortable he'd take action to resolve the cause of his unhappiness. Castillo had seen Dominguez do so many times. Now he needed to send a strong message.

"The Messenger failed me. You said he'd take care of this FBI agent. But he still lives. Please explain to me why this FBI agent still lives?"

Castillo watched Dominguez shift his position before responding. "The Messenger has a different plan."

"A different plan? Are you telling me he intends to let this man live even though I gave orders to kill him?"

"The Messenger will kill him, have no doubt. He understands your personal vendetta against this agent. But he knows you wish to make a statement."

"Yes, anyone who fucks with Ruben Castillo's a dead man. How ambiguous can that be? How hard is it for the Messenger to deliver my message?"

Castillo watched Dominguez wrestle with how to respond. "You want to clear the path for distribution in the US. These are the people trying to stop us. If we take the battle to all of them early, as you said you wished, we buy time."

"Fuck all that. I want this one man dead and I want him dead today. Now. This very minute. Do you understand me?"

"He is dead. And after this last week he knows he's dead."

Castillo nearly came across the desk, "Stop bullshitting me. The only message that went out this last week is either we are inept or this agent is the luckiest man alive. I don't want to send either. I don't like being embarrassed. That's exactly what the Messenger has done. He's embarrassed me in front of the Zetas, the other cartels, the Army and my family. He made the Americans think we can't even kill one fucking FBI agent. I want this done. Do you understand?"

"I understand, but you don't. This man's death will occur. His death will happen soon. But when it happens, the message will be unmistakable and fitting."

Castillo snorted, "I didn't ask the Messenger to grow a brain. I gave him a direct fucking order. Has he carried it out? No! There are no points for style. Dead is dead. It's unmistakable as you point out. I don't give a fuck about fitting. Just get it done, even if you have to kill this man yourself."

"What do you lose by being patient?"

"You better see to it that the messenger gets this done. He better not do anything else before I attend a funeral and laugh at the grave of this man."

Dominguez didn't respond.

Shrink Wrapped

The next morning Alene hung up with Eric as Jim came into her office. She wondered what he was thinking since he avoided eye contact. She followed his gaze and thought he was probably thinking about the lack of personal effects, probably thinking she didn't expect to stay with this project long.

When Jim finally looked at her, he seemed to be embarrassed. Alene looked down where he'd glanced and noticed her blouse was unbuttoned. She wore a minimalist bra and knew Jim could see nearly everything. Alene wondered at Jim's embarrassment. So many men would have simply enjoyed the view. He was trying so hard not to succumb to her charms. She leaned forward, buttoning as she did.

Alene had been trying to figure out how to help Jim with the loss of his family. She probably should have given him more time off, but knew she'd have to name an acting Ops Director if she did. Eric was all over her about getting a mission going. After several sleepless nights trying to decide how best to approach him, she'd come to a simple answer. Ask him. "Do you want to go back to your day job?"

He looked panic stricken. "I can help you better here than back schlepping stake outs for Bud. I've got my head together now. We want the same results. But if you send me back; I can't help you."

Alene raised an eyebrow. "Would you really be content with seeing them brought to justice?"

"Yes." he lied. She knew he lied.

She wanted to help him, but she didn't know if keeping him

engaged in the Rapid Response Force was the best way or not. She thought taking some of the pressure off might help him get his head together. The only thing she could think of was to make it very clear what she expected of him. If he wanted to persist she'd have to let him try. "I told you I understand about losing someone close to you. I know people handle loss differently. I need you to stay with the program. My program. We've had this talk before. I really don't want to take you off the team. But if you don't stay in bounds, you'll leave me no choice."

"Ah kin live with that." His best Texan accent, she realized he was blending.

"Two conditions." She saw he thought he was done, but not quite yet. "First, I think you may be suffering from post-traumatic stress."

"That doesn't make any sense to me," sounded hollow to her.

"I've noticed from time-to-time you seem distracted, not focused in on the discussion, like you're someplace else."

Jim thought about Alene's observation. "I'm planning out the next step. You know how women can multi-task? Well, I can't. So I have to get one thing straight in my mind before I go on to the next."

Alene smiled with him, "That's about the lamest excuse I've ever heard."

He laughed too, "No, it's true, I swear."

Now that she had him laughing was the right time. She slid a business card across her desk. Jim looked at the card but didn't pick it up. "Dr. Graham served in the Army and has a lot of experience dealing with the effects of stress."

"People trying to kill me isn't something I haven't dealt with before."

Alene knew about his army experience, "I also don't want you to stay in one place for more than a night or two." Alene went on. "I know it's going to be inconvenient but I don't want you to become a target."

"Like I'm not a target now??"

"You know what I mean," she responded, knowing she'd missed the point.

"Why not just let me stay at the homeless shelter? I'm sure I'd blend in there," he offered. She almost thought he was serious.

Her voice became all business again. "We can do better."

"Have you checked your budget recently?"

She didn't like being challenged on what she could or couldn't do. She was trying to help him and he didn't seem interested in taking her help.

"The homeless shelter will be a step up from what you can get authorized, I'm sure. Motel Six is a luxury stay for us when we're on the road," he continued.

Having thrown down a challenge, the humor left her eyes. "You may think I'm just a bureaucrat, but there are some things I can fix."

"I never thought of you as just a bureaucrat." Jim winked at Alene.

She wished she knew if he was only using her to get to the Zetas or whether he was really trying to help the team accomplish the larger goals. She couldn't tell which, and she didn't know how she felt about it either way.

The Garden Spot

Adam Bates was on the line. He'd taken a long time to track me down. I'd tossed my compromised cell phone and had a new number. "Carr, my eyes in the sky were up looking for the usual suspects, and …."

I was still trying to understand why Alene thought I had post-traumatic stress. I was sure simple survival instincts were taking over.

"…we discovered this landing strip. Amazing we've flown over it a thousand times and never noticed. Whoever put the strip there went to a lot of expense to make sure no one see's what's really there."

A landing strip. Could this have been where the Triple C murderers came across the border? "Where is this garden spot?"

"Between Artesia Wells and the Chaparral Wildlife Area. Probably fly in and out over the reserve. Not more than fifty miles from the border near Laredo. Had my pilot do some low level runs. Looks like the runway's active. They even built a hanger that looks just like any other barn, except for the door."

"Fifty miles? They're makin' the sanctuary zone along the border even wider." I mumbled more to myself than Adam who didn't ask about the comment. "As always, you're the pride of the Texas Fish and Wildlife Commission. Your contributions exceed your pay grade."

I could see his shrug in my mind's eye. "Glad someone understands 'cause no one here does."

Dan

Dan Carr was tall like Janice, had Bill's slow humor, but really didn't look much like either of them, at least not in my estimation. I'd taken time to have lunch with him in Fort Worth, even though an hour drive in mid-day. Longer in the evening rush hour. He chose the Petroleum Club because his firm had a membership there and the 39th floor vistas were comparable to Bryan Tower where we had our offices.

He sold off the cattle except the number needed to keep his tax exemption. He decided he would keep the land, at least for now. Said that as an oil and gas attorney he wanted to keep it in case the mineral rights might be worth something. I couldn't imagine the Triple C covered with oil or gas wells. But Dan clearly knew more about all that than I did.

When Dan finally got around to asking why his mother and father had been killed I answered the only way I could. "I don't know and I don't know where your Grandfather is either. But I won't stop until I know both answers."

Dan considered my answer. "Does Aunt Tess know?"

I nodded. "Spoke to her right afterwards."

"But she couldn't come for the funeral?"

"It's a long flight from India. Better that she not come back until we know why this all happened. Was it just something about the ranch, or does it have something to do with the family?"

Dan contemplated my answers as he nibbled at his dessert.

Tempering

That afternoon Alene and Jim were on her speaker phone with the DEA and ATF guys. Jim seemed distracted to her, but she wasn't quite sure why. Was it PTSD or was it something else he was working, like what had happened to his father?

Alene plugged back into the conversation when DEA said they should lead. "Jim was the source of the lead, why do you think DEA should handle it? You have no proof that it's anything other than a farmer who's keeping a plane in his barn." Alene was trying to make the case.

"Miss Oliviera, DEA handles hundreds of situations just like this every day. The best thing you all can do is just go back to doin' whatever it is your team does and let the experts do their thing." Ron Christman, was the DEA agent on the phone.

"Ron is it?"

"Yes ma'am."

"Who do you work for?"

"Joe Huntsman, the agent in charge of the Dallas office."

"Ron, I work for the Attorney General and was selected for this job by the President. I think that puts me up a little higher on the pecking order here." She wasn't kind to poor Ron Christman.

"That's all nice, Miss Oliviera, but you're not in my hierarchy. I gotta job to do and so do you. You want to come into my territory and do my job, you go back and ask the Attorney General for my job. I bet he won't let you do it 'cause you ain't got the experience and years in the field I have. So until I get a direct order from someone in my hierarchy tellin' me to do it differently, DEA will lead the investigation."

Alene thought about all the interagency cooperation she had tried to foster in one of her prior roles, realized it wasn't working. Jim interrupted, "Ron, I don't want to speak for Miss Oliviera, but I think we can work something out here that'll satisfy everyone. We have a mission to perform just as you do. Ours may seem unimportant to you 'cause you only got one thing to worry about. We have a lot more on our plate. So I'd suggest we pool our resources. You can lead the investigation and any tactical stuff we end up having to do. But because there may be more than just narcotics involved we want ATF and some of our folks working the investigation as partners."

Alene frowned at Jim, couldn't understand why he was caving in to Christman's stupid demand when she needed a victory, but she didn't interrupt.

"Just so long as you do it my way. I don't like being second guessed."

"Nor do I. We don't need credit for this, but we need to learn everything we can about what they're doin' and how they're doin' it. So no holdin' back and no restriction on access and participation."

Christman sounded annoyed but resigned. "I don't like to work that way, but I'll get my ass chewed if I say no and probably have to do it anyway."

"So we're agreed on how to handle this?" Alene asked frostily.

"Yeah, I can live with it." Christman signed off.

Alene hung up. "Why'd you let him get away with being disrespectful?" She was angry with Jim.

"Because we're going to need him and the other guys at his level at some point. Better to not piss them off. Let them win the throw away deals so we can win the ones that are really important to us down the road."

Not good enough. "You made me look weak, and this is exactly the kind of mission we're supposed to lead. Cross border, cross agency, drugs, firearms, explosives."

"No, I made you look reasonable, like someone who he can work with when he needs to and when we need to. He doesn't think any less of you. He can't now that he knows the President's backing you up. That's why he caved on our participation."

"You're supposed to back me up. You didn't." She was still angry and not understanding why Jim didn't lay down a gauntlet when she had.

"Is Christman going to write your performance review?"

She frowned, "Of course not."

"That's where you're wrong. Christman will talk with everyone about the bitch at the Task force, but he got what he needed to do his job. That description will get around, even to the Attorney General. The feedback will be that you've got your head screwed on right, not just using your position to get what you want when there are competing objectives."

"Your description's naive. That's not how the world works." She was challenging Jim and somehow herself at the same time.

"In a large organization, like the government or the Army for that matter, performance evaluations are always based on the relationships. Are you helping people do their job or are you part of the problem? Everyone knows who makes things happen. Everyone knows who's out there layin' it all on the line every day. You may make the absolute best briefing charts in the world, but when it comes down to who's going to move into the top chair? It's always the one with the broadest support and you don't get that by being a bitch."

Alene twitched at the second use of bitch. She'd been called that before and it had taken a long time to get past. "You've referred to me as a bitch twice now. Is that how you see me?"

Jim had to refrain from saying the first thing that came to his mind and Alene noticed. "Obviously you do." She answered for him.

"On the contrary. If you were a bitch you'd have never even considered me for this job. You'd have gone the political route and put in the guy Eric wanted. A bitch is someone who doesn't care about anyone but herself. I've seen enough of you to know that doesn't describe you. Through everything that's happened to me and with my family you've been there when you didn't have to be."

She thought about Jim's answer, "Then how would you describe me."

"Gorgeous," slipped out before he could catch it. Jim was embarrassed now and had to figure out how to get out of the box.

She smiled at him, "You're not supposed to notice, and besides I'm talking professionally."

"Smart ...committed, engaged, fair, thoughtful..."

"Not tough, arrogant, hard to read?"

Jim hesitated, processing the words she'd used. "Someone describe you that way?"

She grimaced, reliving the prosecution of the cocaine theft from Jim's raid she'd have rather not lived the first time.

"If that description was accurate then, it's not now."

She was pulled back into the moment, smelling Bob's cologne on

Jim again. She'd meant to say something to him about it a long time ago, but she felt awkward asking a man to change his scent. "Think you could change your fragrance?"

"My fragrance?"

"Yes."

"It really that bad?" Jim acted like he tried to remember what it smelled like.

"It's just distracting for me." She studied his reaction. He didn't know what to make of Alene's request and it was evident from his expression.

"Sure. Any requests?"

A haunted smile and shake of her head was all she'd give him.

In the Garden Spot

The garden spot seemed an apt description for the airfield Adam's pilot recognized. The barn was tucked into a tree line and looked like any other barn, probably newer than most, but the door caught my attention almost immediately. The door was not only large enough for a tractor, the purpose of most barn doors, but this one could easily accommodate a twin engine aircraft. I expected a King Air or similar size plane. Drugs don't take up a lot of space. They could carry a lot in a twin engine plane. What concerned me, more than anything else, was that the cartels may be planning on carrying something other than just a big bag of money back.

Helicopters dropped off the twenty or so Federal agents just after sunset. The helicopters ensured no vehicle tracks coming in or out that might give away our presence. The barn sat on the edge of a pasture area, which doubled as the landing strip. The roadway remained all dirt.

Ron Christman seemed large and in charge, as I'd heard others describe people who micromanaged things. Christman had the whole site laid out in grids and assigned agents to certain positions. He even assigned certain weapons to people as if he had the whole battle sequence laid out in his head. If he did, then he'd not shared the battle plan with anyone.

Looking up I knew there was a nearly full moon, but a drifting fog obscured it for the most part. I wondered if whoever was after me had somehow managed to follow me out to this garden spot. Were my pursuers hiding in ambush? And even so would anything happen tonight? We didn't have any intelligence on when something might happen here, but the investigation showed the property was owned by

Sheila Gillette, who paid cash for the land and the barn construction. She was reputed to be living with a man with a Hispanic surname no one could remember. Cash payment alone raised enough questions that the team intended to stay here until something happened.

I knew the Intel bubbas back in the agency had high level profiles that gave a lot of information about the top people supposedly behind all of the violence. The street level captains remained a mystery. The captains brought in the drugs and arms fueling the violence. Our mission was to learn more about the next tier. Find the captains and work our way back up the chain to the bigger bosses with incontrovertible evidence.

Tom Strickland sighted in the M110 semiautomatic sniper rifle Christman assigned to him. "He would pick the one weapon I'm out of qual on," Tom grumbled

"You wanna trade?" I asked. I had a standard issue M-4A1 semi-automatic rifle. The effective range was 5-600 meters, while Tom's weapon had a rated accuracy of 800. Since the hanger/barn was about 750 meters from where Christman placed us, I would protect Tom, who'd pick off any of the perpetrators that happened to be in violent disagreement with the notion of spending the rest of their productive lives in prison.

Tom looked at the M-4A1, must have realized the limited range was a handicap and shook his head, "A Chay Tac .408 would make all the difference."

I knew he was thinking he was working the limits of the range on the M110 and wished he had the Chay Tac with much greater range and a better fit for this kind of mission. He went back to sighting in, preparing like the rest of us for what was about to come.

Arrival

About one-fifteen in the morning the fog became denser and began to settle over the airfield. The fog created a ghostly nightscape illuminated by the bright moonlight. The scrubby pines stood silent sentinels on the borders of the main field. The fog seemed to glow in places. In others the fog seemed almost non-existent, as though holes in cheesecloth covering the landscape. The effect was beautiful and mysterious. I knew the fog wouldn't help if something actually happened.

While I mused on the fog I became aware of the sound of an engine in the distance. At first I couldn't tell whether the sound came from a car or truck or an aircraft. As I listened the engine sounded more like a land vehicle. Not one, several. I heard a click on the radio telling everyone to be ready. Sure enough, within a few minutes five black GMC Denali Sport Utility Vehicles drove into the area next to the barn. The Denali's drove without headlights. The SUVs were coming when the moon was still nearly full, to have enough light by which to see. The fog must have upset those plans, but the SUVs didn't drive like the fog was a problem. As the men came out of the vehicles, I noticed the drivers wore night vision goggles. The goggles explained why the darkness and fog didn't bother the drivers. The goggles were enhanced vision models, issued by the military.

Two of the men went to the barn and opened the doors. All five Denali SUVs drove into the barn. Then the door rattled shut from inside. Five men took up positions around the barn. The guards carried weapons looking remarkably like the one I held.

The hardest part was about to begin. Twenty or so agents; spread out, all in hiding, not making a movement or sound while they waited. If we revealed our presence the aircraft with the evidence would never land. I expected we'd find boxes of weapons unloaded in the barn. And I feared when we sprung the trap, the cargo might come into play. I hoped not. I wanted this to be a peaceful bust. But I estimated there were already more of them than us waiting for the next move.

An Extreme Swap Meet

At 2:10 am I heard another sound in the garden spot, this time from the sky. At first I couldn't locate the source in the fog. When the sound reached one of the cheesecloth holes I saw a twin engine aircraft, illuminated in the night-time sky. The aircraft looked like an older Cessna King Air. Another indicator that this wouldn't be a peaceful bust. The size of the aircraft meant they were willing to risk greater probability of detection to carry back a sizeable load. So the five Denali SUVs almost certainly contained the one thing the cartels were all looking for: advanced weapons.

I felt certain we were in the middle of a swap meet of an extreme kind. Weapons for drugs. The distributors north of the border were more connected to their suppliers than in the past. Ours would be an important bust. Hopefully we'd slow the northward movement of violence, if only for a while. The bust would drive some folks back underground who were apparently feeling relatively secure in the transactions they carried out.

On the other hand, if a sanctuary zone existed on the US side, pretty much controlled by the cartels, and the garden spot was in the zone, then the fight could get ugly real quick.

I watched as the Cessna approached the pasture and made an unassisted landing in the dark. The pilot was good. Another indication the cartels were spending heavily to get the best of what they needed. The job of the Rapid Reaction Force would continue to grow more and more difficult.

I heard, before I saw, the doors to the barn/hanger open from inside as the aircraft approached. The drug runners intended to do the exchange inside the barn with the doors closed. They wouldn't be observed either by people on the ground or by any kind of aerial surveillance, including satellites. Adam Bates was right. Someone thought this site out very carefully. Someone had invested a considerable sum of money to make sure transfers would go off smoothly.

The aircraft approached the hanger and drove directly into the building. The doors closed behind the aircraft. The sound of the engines died.

I didn't know if Ron Christman had foreseen how the events would play out, but he must have thought he had the Zetas in his trap. He called out with a megaphone. "There's a joint Federal team surrounding your position. Lay down your weapons and come out, one at a time, with your hands raised above your head."

The perimeter guards knelt down to make themselves smaller targets. They raised their weapons and pulled down their night vision goggles, looking for the source of the megaphone message. They waited, apparently for instructions. Everyone on our side stayed put, waiting for a signal or response.

"Got your target?" I whispered to Tom, who grunted in response.

The perimeter guards got whatever message they waited for. The armed men opened fire. I heard bullets hitting the trees around us. I couldn't be sure if the guards had picked me out. They may have been shooting at general areas where men could hide.

Tom squeezed off his first shot. I saw the guard closest to us go down. Two more did as well at about the same time from other agents with sniper rifles. Tom moved his weapon to bring a second guard into his sights. His target lay down prone to reduce his profile. Apparently all three of our snipers targeted him because after their shots he didn't move. This left only one guard, still firing a continuous stream of bullets, probably without any specific target in mind. Tom took aim, but in only a moment the guard's weapon jammed. "Overheated the barrel." Tom muttered. "No discipline."

The guard threw down his weapon, held up his hands above his head and rose.

Christman repeated his demand. "You're surrounded by Federal agents. Your guards are down. Come peacefully."

Christman evidently thought he'd won the test of wills. The doors slowly slid open. Christman came out of his hiding spot carrying the bullhorn. He was riddled with bullets from multiple shooters somewhere in the barn.

In a moment the five SUVs roared out of the barn, racing toward the trees and underbrush concealing agents. The vehicles purposefully ran over Ron Christman. Concentrated gun fire from our team didn't have any evident effect on the Denalis.

"Armored." I observed to Tom who took aim at one of the shooters back in the hanger.

Tom got the shot off. He moved his aim to find another target inside the barn. Suddenly the back of his head exploded from the force of the speeding sniper bullet that ended his life.

I stared at Tom, not sure that what I saw was real. The shots around me finally cut through the fog of horror that settled over me. Something in the back of my head warned me I was as much of a target as Tom had been, just standing there.

I crouched down behind the tree I'd been standing next to. Looking around I attempted to clear my head and get back into the struggle continuing all around me. Tom. He was shot. I needed to check him.

Trying to stay low I slid in next to Tom so the sniper who shot him wouldn't see me. Tom showed no vital signs. So I picked up his sniper rifle and 7.65mm ammo. I moved away from Tom's spot, sure I was in someone's sight.

From a new covered position I used the thermal sniper sight to look into the barn/hanger. I saw snipers in the back of the building, evidently watching for flashes. They returned fire to each location.

I didn't want to use Tom's sniper rifle, too many memories. I had to shut them down. I moved to my left. Someone had to disable the vehicles. I removed a grenade from my web belt. Christman had told me I didn't need the grenades. But then again he'd already been proven wrong on his battle plan and paid the price. I knew most of the team was overpowered. I was one of the few who'd brought along my own ordinance. I wished I had a rocket propelled grenade launcher, but no such luck. I had to disable the vehicles the hard way. I pulled the pin on a grenade and rolled it into the path of the oncoming Denali. I hoped to blow off a wheel.

The first grenade rolled too far under before exploding, but apparently threw shrapnel into the transmission. The vehicle ground to a halt. Only one person sat in the vehicle. The thick glass windows didn't permit him to shoot. The Denalis were trying to run down the Task Force, I figured, flush us out and let the shooters back in the barn take us out. The process was inefficient, but since we didn't understand what was going on, effective.

A second Denali came over to try to find the source of the weapon that disabled the first vehicle. I timed the second grenade better.

The explosion blew off the driver's side wheel, which rolled away. The Denali dropped down to the left plowing into the ground for a short distance.

I heard the Cessna engines start up. Crates still sat on the floor of the barn/hanger. I didn't want to, but in the confusion of the circling Denalis I reluctantly used Tom's sniper rifle. In rapid fire I took out two snipers in the barn. Knowing they were looking for muzzle flashes, I rolled to my left to make sure others didn't find me the way they found Tom. Using the immobile Denalis as a barrier, I began to spray sniper shells into the aircraft cockpit. I thought one shot hit the pilot, but couldn't be entirely sure.

I whispered into my radio, "Snipers, get the aircraft, pilot, co-pilot, whoever moves. The rest of you concentrate fire on the snipers in the back of the barn."

I fired shot after shot into the cockpit, taking out the windshield. Then I peppered the aircraft where the fuel tanks should have been. The hope was to at least cause leaks to prevent the plane from making it all the way home.

Someone apparently observed my muzzle blasts. My position became compromised. A shot came in barely missing me. I rolled to the left and came up shooting. I gained my feet and zig zagged to the two disabled Denalis. I saw the remaining three Denalis flushing agents out of hiding. Several agents were taken down by the shooters in the barn. The drivers of the Denalis were talking on cell phones, probably giving the shooters positions. I had to move and set up again.

But then I got a different idea. I appeared to pull the pin on one of my remaining grenades, raced toward one Denali, letting the driver see the grenade.

I bent down as if rolling the grenade under the driver, then ran away.

The driver was out of the vehicle in a flash. I turned and wounded, but didn't kill him. Disarming the man, I handcuffed him to the door handle on the vehicle.

"You can't." The man said to me in heavily accented English.

"Why not?" I responded.

"Because they kill me."

I felt no sympathy. "Should have thought of that before you got into drugs."

"Tell you all I know, you let me go."

"Problem is you don't know shit."

"No, no. I know much."

Yeah, right. I started to walk away. "*Amigo,* I know where guns."

I turned to him, still not believing. "Tell me."

The driver looked around, trying to assess, I felt sure, whether telling would save him from the certain death of being handcuffed to the vehicle door.

The driver must have known he was about to cross a line from which there was no return. Once he told us what he knew he could never go home. He pulled on a ski mask. I thought to make sure no one from the cartel side could identify him specifically. This man wanted to protect his family.

"Cedenos. Buy guns for Army. Some come to us."

I listened, not making sense of his answer, "Which Cedenos?"

A bullet took him down. Great! Was it someone on my side who just woke up and thought he was saving me? Or had the cartel started killing their own? But then a third possibility occurred to me. Was it someone on my side who didn't want someone from the cartels giving me information? I couldn't be sure of the truth.

Moving away, I left behind the answers that would never come.

A Denali raced across the space between me and the now three disabled units. I stepped out and revealed myself to the driver, throwing a grenade. The driver bailed, just as I expected. One of the task force members cut him down. I raced across the open space, picked up the grenade, which still had the pin in place, and leapt into the armored vehicle. I drove it along a tree line. Several of the joint team got in.

I turned toward the barn in time to see the aircraft rev up and pull out. The pilot headed for the open field and the runway. I had apparently failed to prevent the escape, even after dropping shot after shot into the cabin. Maybe the leaks would make the plane crash or at least shorten its range.

Flooring the Denali wasn't like taking the same action in my old Porsche. The Denali took a long time to gather momentum. The slowness of response gave the Cessna a chance to get out of the barn. The pilot headed for the grassy airstrip. I pursued him anyway, hoping to close the distance. I wanted to get in front of the plane before the pilot became airborne.

A U.S. helicopter came into view, a Huey. I thought the Huey must have been one of those that dropped us off earlier. Not a gunship like an Apache; the helicopter couldn't turn the whole situation around by itself. What the Huey did do, however, was head for the Cessna as the plane taxied out onto the airstrip. My team in the Denali remained in hot pursuit.

The Huey intercepted the Cessna as the plane began to take off. The helicopter pilot flew over the Cessna at the same speed, holding the aircraft down on the ground. The Huey pilot simply wouldn't permit the airplane to become airborne. The Cessna tried to lift off as we pulled up alongside in the Denali. The helicopter remained just above.

A tree line at the end of the field suddenly loomed large. The Cessna didn't appear able to rise above the trees, but was now going too fast to stop. The Denali couldn't keep up and we fell back.

The Huey pilot pulled up enough to skim over the tree line. The Cessna pilot counted on him doing so. He followed the Huey up, backed off his airspeed a tad to fall behind the helicopter, rising just high enough to clear the trees, bank to the left and separate.

The Cessna quickly maneuvered away from the Huey, gaining enough altitude and airspeed to clear the tree lines, but stay low enough to evade the border radar.

Disappointed, I turned focus to the men at the back of the barn. I had an assault team in the vehicle. We raced back across the open field.

I drove the Denali into the back of the barn. As the door behind me opened, bullets began to bounce off of our vehicle. But now the advantage had shifted. Our men with M-4s took out the cartel shooters from close range. We were close enough to overcome the advantage of precision shooting from the remaining cartel snipers and gunmen. I tossed my last grenade over the Denali to take out the shooters on the other side of the vehicle. The explosion changed the balance of the engagement.

I'd changed the equation, taken the initiative. But the Cessna was on its way back to Mexico. I couldn't stop him.

The drivers of the last vehicle took to the field to try to escape, but the second Huey had returned and paced him as he headed away from the scene.

The first Huey returned to pick us up. As we did our assessment, I counted five cartel members in custody. Thirty-three bodies lay in and around the barn. Of the original twenty agents, only six of us were still active.

I was angry. Too many died. Tom died. I had no idea how to explain what happened to his wife. I had even less idea how to explain his death to his partner on the Dallas PD, Willy Graves, who'd been like a brother to Tom. I didn't know what I was going to do with the fact another person I'd gotten to know and like was dead and I was still walking around. Dr. Isabel Stanhope, from the Centers for Disease Control who Willy Graves dubbed 'The Bug Lady' during the Pandemic said something about death following her around. I understood for the first time. Death wasn't only following me, but seemed to have gotten me into its sights. Only so far death was proving to be a bad shot. Anyone close was likely to take my bullet.

Still feeling numb, I watched the first Huey carrying the wounded agents lift into the sky. The second Huey returned. The pilot told me he'd followed the Denali into a roadblock about a mile away. The driver was in custody. As we loaded the remaining gunmen I thought of Alene. I wondered how to explain what went wrong and why so many of us died. How to explain why the Cessna had gotten away. I expected she'd blame me, even though this wasn't under my command. I knew she counted on me to make everything come out right.

Post Mortem

The next afternoon Alene sat across from Jim and Miguel "Mike" Garrido, who, with the demise of Ron Christman, became the senior DEA member of the Joint Task Force. Mike and Jim had jointly filed a report.

Alene had just listened to Mike's summary. "Okay, now that we have the official report, what really happened out there?"

Mike answered first. "We weren't prepared for the sophistication of their weapons or tactics."

Alene tried to put his response into the context of the report they'd filed with her. Something was missing. "What do you mean?"

"Up-armored vehicles for one. We were lucky they didn't have the ability to fire back. They'll make sure they do next time." Jim responded.

"How?" Alene couldn't conceive of armored vehicles in a law enforcement situation.

"Probably some kind of sunroof with a pop up plate to protect the shooter." Jim surmised.

"Without Jim's hand grenades, I doubt we could have prevailed." Mike added.

"We were outnumbered, they had vehicles to run us down and flush us out. They killed our trained snipers by tracing the muzzle flashes. They were good and they're only going to get better." Jim added and then paused. "So we got trouble in River City. And I for one don't intend to go up against them again without more firepower than we had."

Alene thought about their comments for an uncomfortably long time. She was afraid the type of violence was already spiraling beyond what Eric and Justice would let her and her team handle. The type of engagement they were describing was just too dangerous for light weapons, even the type that the Special Weapons and Tactics boys used. She was afraid Eric would shut down the team and hand the problem over to the Army. The Mexicans were using Army troops to engage the Zetas and other cartels. She had a sinking feeling that she'd lose control and have to sit back and watch others try to address the problem. "Sounds like you think this is more military action than law enforcement."

"We just fought a paramilitary force." Mike observed. "I agree with Jim. Not sure I'd want to face them again without a few more tricks in the kit bag."

Alene stopped at the term paramilitary. She knew the FBI Academy was working with new technology to train agents to handle paramilitary involvements. She'd have to do some research. She made a note to herself.

"What kind of Intel did we get from the survivors?" Jim asked.

"Definitely Zetas. Appears this one was the personal handiwork of Juan Dominguez, reputed to be the number two. Oh, and your driver's tip about Cedenos isn't credible." She said.

Jim gestured to stop her. "I've given that comment a fair amount of thought. He was … scared … shitless. Thought he was gonna die if I didn't do somethin' for him. The Cendenos tie to the American Army doesn't make any sense, I agree. But what if he was talkin' 'bout somebody else's army? Nicaragua or Venezuela for instance. We're the ones assuming he was talkin' about the US."

Alene nodded seeing the logic Jim was following. She was pleased he was trying to understand the range of possibilities and not just throwing the problem over the wall to someone else to figure out. "Worth checking into."

"Already started." Jim responded. "What happened to the aircraft?"

"The pilot was good." Alene began, "But we got him just before he went across the border. Understand we had to shoot holes into his wing tanks. Used helos to force him down. He took out one of our Hueys, but the other got his rudder, so he couldn't maneuver. Quite an air battle, from what I'm told."

"Who was the pilot?" Mike asked.

"American. Used to fly for Air America. CIA ties and all that. But just another mercenary as far as we're concerned."

Jim seemed to react to something from his past. "If the pilot had CIA ties, is there something going on between our side and the Zetas?"

"No." She frowned not really sure.

"If there's a back channel we need to know about it. Otherwise we'll never come out on the winning side." Jim pushed back.

"No back channels. We don't talk with the Zetas. They're a criminal element, not freedom fighters we use to undermine an unfriendly government."

"I'm sure you think Justice has your back on what the CIA might or might not be doing, but my experience in the Army was I never assumed anything. The CIA would use anyone against anyone to achieve whatever geopolitical aims they were charged with. I absolutely won't lose team members because a CIA operative decides he wants to get brownie points by having the Zetas take out the body guards of some minister who was making life difficult for some political objective of our government. I have firsthand experience with the CIA on more than one black op I've been on." Jim filled in the missing pieces to his response.

"We still need to enlarge our roster of weapons if we're going to tangle with them again." Mike was apparently uncomfortable about the CIA discussion.

Alene tried to decide how to proceed. She had one thought about the academy, but it was only one. She heard the request, knew the consequences if she turned it down. But she also didn't want to encourage a spiral by trying to stay one step ahead of the Zetas on weapons and tactics. "The President expects us to handle this without declaring war. We need to keep the encounters from escalating. Get them back into a box we can manage."

Jim cut her off, "Are you waitin' for this to become personal before you act? At what point does what happened become real? We lost good men out there. A lot of good men, trained to do what was necessary. And still they died."

Alene looked at Jim for a moment. How would she feel if she said no to their request and Jim was killed next time out? If he hadn't brought his own ordinance at the Garden Spot, Mike was of the opinion they may have all been killed. There had to be another way. "Maybe we need to work earlier in the food chain. Avoid the armed conflict." She suggested, wanting a confirmation.

"About the only way I can see that happenin' would be to kill the crops before the drugs ever get into the distribution chain." Mike offered. "I know our guys have been paying farmers to grow other crops in some of the South American countries."

"I see the reports. We've done a good job but not really even put a dent into the total supply. We have to rely on the governments of small countries. Their police and army get bought off. We give the police money and Intel about where to look. Even with the subsidies to plant alternative cash crops we just never get there." She mused.

"We're playin' a chess game and the game won't be over until the King dies. Everyone else along the way's ready to give his life to protect the King. Don't you see? We can't avoid gettin' bloody."

Alene didn't like the recommendation Jim spelled out. She began to run her fingers through her hair unconsciously. She had to make a choice. She would discuss with Eric and some of the DEA and ATF guys. Whatever they did would have to be a coordinated response to have the desired effect. For her to go nuclear when everyone else was using pop guns would create a ripple effect she and they wouldn't be able to control. Finally she looked up and saw Jim studying her with a curious expression she'd not seen before. "Mike, what do you think?"

He responded without emotion, "Ma'am, they already killed most of my cousins in Mexico, because they were cops and wouldn't take the payoffs. My Uncle was a judge and they killed him and his wife. I can never go back. I'm a marked man down there because I'm US DEA and the Zetas know who I am. So, yes, Agent Carr and I look at this pretty much the same way."

Alene looked at Mike Garrido with a new respect.

Dealing

After the meeting Alene walked back towards my office with me. She apparently wanted to talk but not in her office. "How are you doing?" She asked.

Was this part of a continuing assessment of whether I was going to explode on her or was she looking for something else? I shrugged.

"How was your meeting with Dr. Graham?"

"She sent you a report."

Alene looked at me closely, "I'm looking for your take."

I stopped walking and turned toward her, which was always hard, encountering those emerald eyes and her perfume that so reminded me of Lexie. Every time, I had to push the pain back behind the door and restart my brain. "She's a nice lady."

"You probably say that about your mother."

"My mother died in '04. Drunk driver."

Alene pulled inward. I'd stuck a nerve remembering her parents had died in a car accident. But she didn't let me back her off. "I'm sorry. But I need to know."

Pushed into the corner I had to respond. I knew she wouldn't let me massage my answer. "She told me I don't deal with my feelings."

"And?"

"She thinks I need to start."

"Was killing those cartel gunmen how you deal with things?" came hard.

"Which time?" I regretted my unfiltered response, since it sounded flippant.

As I expected she reacted negatively. "Look Jim. We're on the same team here. You're carrying a heavy emotional burden and I'm dropping a heavy work load on you. I've got to know if it's going to work, or am I putting you in a no win situation?"

"Have I ever not succeeded?"

She didn't even hesitate. "There was that French class back at Yale."

She had me. An eight o'clock class in my freshman year, what can I say? "You really checked me out."

"I've been watching you do the same," came dead pan, but with a hint of a smile.

I answered her quietly. "Lexie had emerald eyes. Every time I look at you it hurts and still I can't stop looking at you."

I don't think she had any idea what I'd been dealing with just being with her. She looked down for a long time and then toward the windows at the end of the hallway. She looked back at me. Her eyes were the darkest green I'd ever seen, almost black. "I'd never connected that about Agent Jones. I'm usually good at details."

"You never met her."

"How do we get past my resemblance and your reaction?" There was a new level of familiarity in her voice I hadn't heard before.

"It's my problem, not yours. I'm here to help you get the job done."

She looked down again. She was trying to work through my denying her an opportunity to fix the situation and I couldn't imagine why. She nodded. "How can I help you deal with everything?"

My immediate response was, "Just believe in me. I won't disappoint you."

She studied me. I wouldn't break eye contact, even though she seemed to be peering right through me. I don't know what she saw or what she thought about. She made a decision and simply said, "You certainly don't make it easy for me."

"Tell me how I can?" I responded not sure what she wanted to tell me.

She looked at me as if she hadn't expected my question and struggled for an answer. I thought she was going to say something and evidently changed her mind. She finally settled on: "You need to keep your appointments with Dr. Graham."

I should have expected her response but hadn't. "That part of my probation?"

"You help both of us if you do."

I was surprised she looked at the situation as help 'us'. At least she was evidently thinking about an 'us' just as I was. That alone made the conversation worthwhile. "Anything else?" I knew she was about to leave and I didn't want her to.

"I need you to go back to being the person you were two years ago, before the cocaine raid, before you decided to take on the cartels all by yourself."

"I had to make sure no one else would lose the most important person in their life in another drug raid." I said truthfully, and I saw she understood.

She studied me, making a decision I was sure. But she wouldn't voice her thoughts. I watched her walk away from me. For the first time I actually saw Alene not Lexie.

Intelligence

Barak Obama, finished his daily intelligence briefing, thinking some would say the world was going to hell in a hand basket. He wasn't quite sure, but he thought events certainly were living up to the old Chinese curse of 'May you live in interesting times.' In the small conference room just off the Oval Office he looked across the table to Hillary Clinton his Secretary of State.

"What's your Ambassador to Mexico saying these days?"

The petite Secretary removed a single sheet of paper from her portfolio. She slid it across the table to him. He quickly scanned the report. The document was a State Department warning stating that all visitors to Mexico needed to proceed with utmost caution. Random acts of violence were possible all along the border and in several of the Mexican states that fed the drug trail. Kidnappings had been taking place and increasing instances of mass killings had been observed.

"The Maquiladoras are no longer safe for American companies." He said. "Tourism's off because of safety concerns. Mexicans are spilling across the borders looking for work and safety for their families. Resulting increases put pressure on our social services and schools. The results hurt our economy."

Hillary smiled, "It's nice to know you read the briefs. But there's one fact you haven't considered."

"And that is?" he was surprised he'd missed something.

"The other effect of the drug trade on the Mexican economy."

She had his interest now.

"Go on."

"The legitimate Mexican economy is about one trillion US dollars. Ten percent is the estimated average profit creating an economic impact of 100 billion dollars."

"Great. A lesson in international economics. What else do you have for me?"

Hillary smiled at the dismissal and continued on. "Estimated value of the illegal drug trade is somewhere around 40 billion US dollars. However, its profitability is thought to be ninety percent. That makes the economic impact of the drug trade in Mexico 36 billion US dollars. Nearly one third of the rest of the economy."

He was amazed. "So what are you saying?"

"Ending the drug trade could send the economy into a free fall. You need to tread lightly. The unintended consequences might be unmanageable."

Her argument didn't resonate. *Why?* "Columbia took control of its drug problem and didn't bankrupt the country."

"Different situation. Columbia had Pablo Escobar, who pretty much ran the whole drug trade. He kept most of the profits for himself. In Mexico, there are many more cartels, many more people involved. The value of the trade is huge in comparison."

He had to ask the question that instantly came to mind. "Are you saying we should ignore the thousands who are being murdered?"

Hillary spoke solemnly. "In Mexico, people want a better life. The better life for a lot of folks currently comes from the illegal drug trade. The government allows different factions to fight to control the money that makes the better life possible. We simply watch from across the border. We do little to help end the violence. The Mexican government is totally overwhelmed by the task. The firepower of the cartels and the corruption that runs throughout the police is beyond them. Without our help, they can't stop the violence. Because of the economic impact, they don't want our help to end it."

"I'm getting mixed messages from you," he observed.

"We have multiple objectives. From a human rights point of view we can't condone the violence taking innocent lives. From an immigration control point of view we can't continue to let our border be so porous that millions come across illegally. From an economic point of view we should be supporting efforts to jump start the legitimate Mexican economy. We want people to have the opportunity to find good legal jobs at home. From a US budgetary point of view we can't let illegal immigrants continue to flood our social services and educational system. Because of the language barrier, they're more expensive to educate. We also find they have a tendency to drop out of school and then clog our courts and jails. In fact, we're seeing an increase in violence related to the drug trade on this side of the border because of the drop outs. Drop outs here often have relatives across the border involved in drugs."

"You're saying the different impacts are all related, all negative for both Mexicans and Americans. And yet you just cautioned me that anything we do might actually bring resistance because of the negative economic impact."

Hillary responded glumly, "In a nutshell, yes."

He leaned back in his chair. "So what should I do?"

"Whatever you do will have negative consequences for one or more of our national policy objectives. You'll have to choose which ones."

Graves' Revenge

I was more than surprised when the bulky Willy Graves wandered into the Joint. He came right to my office. I looked up from my desk and asked, "Willy?"

"It's your fault. You take my partner and you let him get himself killed. So whattam I supposed to do here? You convince him to come help you. Told me you said he was the one who nailed them Arabs on that bomb deal. Next thing I know he's dead."

I shook Willy's hand. "I'm real sorry about Tom."

I saw the red in his eyes. He couldn't talk about losing his partner.

"So what's the deal here? I get my ass drafted. Next thing I know they're telling me I hafta baby sit some fuckin' Fed named Carr. What kinda shit is this? I mean I know you what? Maybe five years or something? No biggie as far as I'm concerned. But then they tell me Tom reported to you and you let him bite it. So whattam I supposed to think here? You know? Am I next? Are you a jinx or what?"

His question made me think for a moment. What if he was right? What if I was a jinx? People were dying all around me. "Tom was doin' what Tom needed to do. That's about all I can say."

"Sounds like the prick. He always made me look like the slacker I am." Willy seemed to reflect on their many assignments together. Or maybe all the Mexican dinners they shared on Friday nights. Willy seemed to come out of his reverie, looked at me with sorrowful eyes and seemed to tune in. "You know I would have come just for Tom. It's payback time."

"The situation's a little more complicated. This isn't a couple of guys and a one-time deal. This is a whole bunch of different armies fighting over a lot of money."

"Yeah? So how do we make them pay for Strickland?"

"Not sure you can. This is more about how do we stop them from comin' across the border. We need to make sure they don't kill innocent folks over here the way they're doin' south of the Rio Grande."

He shrugged. "I'm not into all that greater good bullshit."

I had to keep Willy focused on the right things. "I understand. But as you get comfortable with what we're doin', you'll get with the program."

"Don't blow smoke up my ass. I'm here for one reason. Let's leave it there."

I was glad to have Willy on board, but I needed to get him there and quickly. "First thing I need some help with is a search of the tactics they've been employin'. Until recently their approach was all a guns in the street kinda thing. But they changed. Remember the car bombs in Ciudad Juarez and Monterrey? First Improvised Explosive Devices. This's all startin' to look like the Middle East. So search through and let me know what you find."

"Yeah, I can do a search for you." Willy didn't seem too focused. I worried he would be a loose cannon for some time. But then I realized if people knew what I was doing they'd probably think the same about me. Oh great, two cops pushing each other for revenge. Sounded like a great way to keep a lid on things.

Crossing the Rubicon

Dominguez was uncomfortable. And as always when finding himself in such a state, he looked for the opportunity. He and Castillo were at Castillo's Ciudad Victoria house where they often met to discuss opportunities and problems. Always in that order. Always just the two of them first, then they'd decide who else to bring in. Dominguez thought Castillo had a weakness since he could only trust one person at a time. Lucky for Dominguez he was the current person. But he also knew Castillo could change his mind over night. Usually when Castillo changed his mind the unlucky person was found dead within twenty-four hours. The pattern was established. Dominguez had no illusions that the current situation would last forever. In fact, he had plans to make sure the situation wouldn't. However, Castillo's plans and his didn't align.

"Leaders don't take shit from nobody." When Castillo talked trash Dominguez knew he was particularly agitated. Normally Castillo invoked his Yale education to impress. When he went street, someone had really gotten under his skin. Castillo was more reckless than usual. When in such a mood he needed to lean on Dominguez's particular skill sets more than he liked. Those skills led to brutally efficient killing.

"This isn't personal." Dominguez observed.

"Maybe not to you, but you don't sit in this chair." And to emphasize the point Castillo poked his index finger down on the arm of the chair in which he sat. "We got a half-billion dollar payment due and if we don't deliver you know what will happen."

Dominguez frowned, returned to the problem. "You've crossed some threshold. Something triggered the banker's response. You must have asked for too much."

"Bullshit. They can pay." Castillo shot back.

"Sure they can pay, but you could have asked for less and probably gotten it without any push back. I just think you must have gone up too much and they couldn't hide the payment amount."

"They hide shit like this all the time. It's just part of the cost of doing business."

"I agree with you when you're talking a Mexican company. But they're American. They've got different rules. They have to disclose all kinds of things companies here don't. It's just different, that's all."

Castillo had evidently been listening more carefully than Dominguez expected. "What's really bothering you about my plan?"

Dominguez didn't want to answer, but he was boxed in. He had to. After a moment of silence he responded neutrally. "You go through with your plan and I'm the one who has to pick up the pieces. I don't like American scrutiny. They bring toys and shit that makes it harder for us to do what we do so well. Why bring scrutiny when we got alternatives."

Castillo smiled evidently thinking he had Dominguez in a place where he could whip him. "What are you afraid of? An official protest from the US Secretary of State to our Foreign Minister? That's all that ever happens."

"That's all you read about in the papers, but behind the scenes all kinds of things happen you aren't aware of."

"And you are."

"Yes." Dominguez answered.

"And how are you aware?"

"Let's just say I've been developing my sources and they're reliable."

"You're not going to tell me, are you?" Castillo clearly didn't like the direction the conversation was taking.

"I tell you about my sources and they're no longer mine."

Castillo's voice took on a threatening edge. "And why should that be a problem?"

"It's only a problem if more than one of us wants them to do something. They're willing to do what I ask. You start going direct they'll likely stop doing what I want and only do what you want."

"That's all bullshit. You've just got to figure out how to do what I want. This banker said he's not going to pay the new going rate. I expect you to follow my instructions exactly on how to change his mind. You will follow my instructions?"

Dominguez didn't mistake the implied threat. He knew he was already on thin ice because of the whole Messenger situation with the FBI agent. But he knew the plan for the FBI agent was solid and would be the lynch pin to his bigger plans. He had to buy time to let those plans play out. "Absolutely. Kidnap, rape, murder. Whatever you want. We're a full service cartel here."

Castillo's eyes became hooded. Dominguez knew he wasn't convincing. What to do? Dominguez took only a moment to recover, "You want to come along? See that we do exactly what you want?"

Castillo raised an eyebrow.

Serendipity

Alene called me into her office along with Willy the next morning. "I have instructions to send one of you to Mexico. Seems we received a request from the Mexican government to provide an assist on a kidnapping. Twenty year old daughter of a prominent banker in Mexico City who works for a US bank. So your old bosses thought since you're both taking Spanish lessons one of you ought to go."

Willy looked at me, "No hable Espanol, por favor."

Alene shook her head, "Don't sweat it Graves, I already decided I needed to send a grown up. So Jim, you have the pleasure of holding hands with the Federales for a couple of days. Here's your ticket." She slid the documents to the front of her desk.

Willy looked upset, "Then why'd you haul me in here too?"

Alene stood up in dismissal, "Because I'm required to inform your day job superiors that I discussed the mission with you and gave you an opportunity to volunteer."

"But you didn't do shit."

"You want to go instead of Carr?"

"Fuck no, but this ain't fair. I demand my rights as a Dallas detective to get equal respect from the FBI."

Alene didn't even wait for Willy to finish before escorting him to the door. "I think we're finished here. Carr …. wait a moment."

Willy stepped out and she closed the door.

"Your boyfriend coming to town and you need to get me out of the way?" I asked.

She wasn't happy with my question. "I don't have a boyfriend. And even if I did, that wouldn't be reason to send you out of town."

Another key piece of data. "I thought you wanted me to push hard to get the team ready." I didn't have a good feeling about this assignment. Seemed to me she was getting me out of the way for some reason I didn't understand. Had I screwed up? Did she think I wasn't up to the job? I felt the churn in my stomach and just knew the result wasn't going to work in my favor.

Alene anticipated my reaction. "You need to get out of Big D for a few days. Mexico City's probably the last place whoever's after you would look. I have some things going on in the background here that have to get resolved. By the time you get back we should know if we can accelerate or if we have to take a different tack. I think general preparations are far enough along that we won't lose any momentum if you're gone a couple days. Besides, the kidnapping's thought to be the work of the Zetas. Should give you some insights from the other side."

I understood her logic, but wasn't sure I agreed. Despite her assurances my stomach remained in a knot. Then I realized the trip could give me a chance to start looking for Hernandez-Anjul. Maybe a couple days in Mexico City wasn't such a bad idea.

1984

On the long American Airlines flight to Mexico City I tried to get comfortable. But jammed into a middle seat with the seat in front pressing into my knees, I couldn't. I used my alias of Bob Smith. Just in case someone looking for me might come across a passenger manifest. I didn't like hiding in plain sight. But I wanted to avoid being an open target.

I read the case file on the plane. The father had been the CEO of a Mexican bank before it merged with an American bank. The father was now the CEO of the new Mexican subsidiary. While the FBI didn't have direct authority in the case, Alene instructed me to lend assistance. Since the kidnapping appeared to be cartel related I understood Alene's willingness to have me get some time on the ground on the southern side of the Rio Grande. I just didn't buy time on the ground as the sole reason for my name coming out of the hat.

I'd never been to Mexico City, so was unprepared for the culture shock. Chaos was how I'd describe what I found. The infrastructure at first glance seemed to match that of major cities I'd visited around the world. In fact, some of the architecture was stunning. But nothing seemed to work as expected. Waits were long. Cab drivers didn't seem to know where anything was other than the major hotels and restaurants. People were perpetually unsettled, suspicious of even the smallest things. Undoubtedly they were trying to understand whether anyone posed a threat.

I planned to start asking questions casually to find out if anyone knew of the guy whose fingerprints Nick matched to the shell casing. Miguel Hernandez Anjul. I was curious as to what I could learn about him. Beyond that I hoped he wouldn't be expecting me. If I ran into Hernandez I might just get a chance to have a one-on-one discussion about Dad and other things. But I had to start with the reason I was sent, which was all about a kidnapped girl.

Sergeant Arturo Sanchez met me at the airport, holding a sign for Bob Smith. He looked bored. He was in his late twenties, listened to an iPod all of the time, even when I talked to him. He checked out his appearance in every reflective surface he could find, even the paint on the car he drove.

We got in the car, "How long you been a Federale?" I asked.

"Too long."

"Got to be a tough job at the moment."

Sergeant Sanchez glanced out of the corner of his eye, as if I were a Martian who landed just to plague his existence. "Better than some."

I heard reluctance to get into a conversation. "What's the latest on the case?"

"Same as yesterday."

"Okay. Let me recap what I know and maybe you can fill in some blanks."

Sergeant Sanchez glanced at me again, but didn't comment.

"It seems Sonja Arroyo, aged twenty, daughter of the Chairman of Bancomex, was kidnapped approximately a week ago. That correct?"

Sanchez nodded.

"And around eighteen hours ago, her father received a ransom demand for approximately $5 million US Dollars."

Sanchez thought for a moment as if calculating the exchange rate. "Approximately."

"Funds are to be transferred electronically to a bank account. The number will be provided by a phone call at two minutes prior to transmission. Not enough time to trace the account before transmission."

"FBI teach you anything other than memorization?" Sanchez asked.

"If the Bureau taught memorization it'd be a god-send." I responded, knowing I didn't have the respect of the Sergeant.

We rode the rest of the way in silence. I looked at the street. So much I observed surprised me. As we drove, I realized Mexico City had been beautiful. The city could still be considered such. The problem appeared to be safety. No matter how much some of the architecture wowed me, I felt this overriding sense that I needed to be on my guard. The sense wasn't so much what I saw, but a feeling Sanchez conveyed, along with the people at the airport, probably not consciously. But the air felt pregnant with caution. People appeared to have their guard up. I wondered if Mexico had become the society in George Orwell's novel, 1984.

Restless Energy

The Arroyo house occupied an entire city block. Ten foot masonry walls surrounded the main building. Closed circuit cameras were evident everywhere. An armed guard manned the entrance. Various obstructions limited access. I even had to wait for a metal barrier to be lowered.

Two more guards with automatic weapons stood behind barriers at the portico. The guards watched the arrival of the vehicle. Each kept his weapon at the ready. I wouldn't have been surprised to find the guards had me in their sights. And if these two didn't, two more I couldn't see probably did.

The butler opened the door to let us in. The house itself was magnificent. Dark stained hard woods, inlaid marble flooring and crystal chandeliers. "When was this house built?" I wondered aloud to the butler, who spoke surprisingly good English.

"1843 was the original structure." He told me. "What you see now was mostly built in 1893. The house was modernized in 1943 and again in 1993. So it's been a work in progress for many generations of the family."

"The same family?"

"Yes. The Arroyos were ranchers, who invested in the first railroads to Mexico City. They kept investing in new technologies over the decades. First steel to make train tracks. Then gas and oil as automobiles became prevalent. Banking, when their main bank demanded additional collateral for loans during the depression in the 1930s. They have always been an entrepreneurial lot, the Arroyos."

"Sounds like a matter of being in the right place at the right time." I mused.

"Actually their prosperity results from a restless energy. The family wanted to understand the methods of those whom they were dependent upon in their core businesses. In every case the Arroyos decided they could do what their partner did better. The Arroyos kept vertically integrating. Each time they cut their business partners loose."

"Seems to have worked well for them."

"Very well indeed." The butler led me into a parlor where the Federales were busy at work, monitoring communications and waiting for the next contact from the kidnappers.

A tall, young and muscular officer came across the room. He held out his hand, "Captain Morales, head of the investigation. You are agent Smith?"

"Bob Smith. Yes." I showed him my alternative ID. "I'm out of the Dallas office. Is Morales a common name in Mexico?"

The Federales officer inspected my badge. "Nearly as common as Smith in your country."

As I studied Morales he completed his detailed inspection and handed the badge back. He gestured to the room. "I'm sure you've seen this all before."

"Looks familiar, yes. Could you give me an update? Sergeant Sanchez was a bit vague on where things stand."

Morales seemed to puzzle on my comment for a moment, but let his question pass. "You're aware of the demand for ransom?"

"Yes. Approximately $5 million. That was when? On Tuesday?"

"Yes. The funds transfer is to take place tonight at 3:00 am."

"Why 3:00 am?"

"That was the time in the note."

"Banks aren't open then."

"Arroyo runs the bank. I'm sure they thought he could arrange a 3:00 am wire. Where the funds would arrive it would be normal banking hours. The kidnappers apparently wish to send the funds on immediately."

"London would be nine am, so they could be sending the funds as far as Jakarta in Indonesia and still get immediate funds."

Morales was curious, "You seem to know a great deal about banking."

I shrugged rather than confirm or deny his observation.

"When was your last contact with the kidnappers?"

"Tuesday, when the ransom note arrived."

"How did the Arroyos receive it?"

"Postal mail. Sent from a street mailbox picked up by the post office closest to the airport. No video surveillance or anything we could use to identify the sender."

"Prints on the letter?"

Morales shook his head.

"So no contact in two days. What else have you been able to learn?"

"Truthfully, nothing. Seems as if they don't exist. No one's come forward. None of our informants know anything. We have no leads."

"How was she kidnapped?" I asked.

"She played a football game, sorry, soccer to you Americans, at one of the major parks in Mexico City. When the game was over, her team loaded into cars to have a few *cervesas*. The team intended to celebrate a significant win in their league. She never arrived at the designated bar."

"And no one saw anything." I guessed.

The Captain shook his head.

"How long did she play in this league?" My questions just kept coming. He looked exasperated now.

"Futball is practically the national sport. Everyone plays."

"Did she have security?"

"Yes, but the driver hasn't been heard from or seen since she disappeared."

I gave him a short break to let him cool down. "The driver could have been involved with the plot." I suggested less forcefully.

"I think not. His family has served the Arroyos for generations."

"Sometimes familiarity breeds discontent. Especially when those he serves have everything and his family has nothing."

Morales became curt. He had run out of patience with me. "That is where you do not understand our culture. He is not a suspect."

I backed off. "All right. No contact in two days. Money to be wired tonight. What can the Bureau provide for you?"

He appeared pleased that my inquisition was over and he could get back to what he was doing before I interrupted his work. "I cannot think of anything. Our best people are here. I think we have prepared thoroughly. But please feel free to observe and comment."

I wandered about the room, looking at the books on the shelves, all in Spanish, and old. I looked at paintings of a much smaller and more elegant Mexico City. I looked at the pictures of the family. As the only daughter Sonja stood out amongst the three children. She looked much like her mother, bright eyes and smile. She had warmth to her appearance. The older son looked unhappy to me, as if he carried the cares of the world. The younger boy had a devilish look in his eye, as if he were plotting some mischief.

I recognized the wire-tap equipment. The Federales were using standard procedure, but something bothered me. I didn't detect an air of urgency, of working leads to try to head off the kidnappers. I thought the Federales had been through this situation many times before. With only money at stake, why get too excited? The girl would be returned unharmed, with another adventure to tell her soccer mates. The kidnappers would retire somewhere no one would find them.

I found a seat and watched the silent room. Everyone acted as if they had been given instructions to sit at their post and wait. When the call came in they'd respond as trained. Three a.m. was still several hours away. I didn't observe any communications between the Federales. Curious.

Willy's Worries

The Mexican adventure went off just as expected with just one glitch. The money was wired at 3:00 am thanks to the cooperation of Mr. Arroyo's bank. When the Federales arrived at the designated park to pick up Sonja Arroyo, there was no sign of her, nor had there been by the time I left to return. I offered to stay, but Captain Morales assured me they had the matter in hand and it was just a matter of time before her return.

Within an hour of landing in Dallas I got a call from Alene.

"You still at the airport?" her greeting didn't give me a warm feeling.

"Just cleared immigration."

"Do you have clean clothes with you?"

I had to think for a moment. "Yeah, if I'm eating donuts and taking notes on ransom calls."

"Go pick up some workout clothes and come back to DFW. I need you and Graves to take a little trip for me."

"Where to this time?" I really wasn't curious.

"El Paso. Seems our Army friends want some help checking out a tool they just bought. Think it can help in our efforts to disrupt things."

"Is their toy nuclear?" was the first thing to come to mind.

"Don't think so." Sounded like she actually thought about my question.

"Probably only a stop gap measure then."

"You can voice your opinions, but not until after you've given their system a chance." She warned me, probably knowing all too well that I wouldn't hide my opinion under a bushel basket.

"Why would the Army care about my opinion? Been out longer than I can remember."

"Justice Department's interested. One's at the FBI Academy at Quantico."

"Since the Justice Department has far more qualified folks than me using it, why's this a priority?"

"Ours is not to reason why…"

"You know I've been meanin' to talk to you about that."

"Colonel Blum will meet you at the airport if you text him your flight info."

"At least there'll be one friendly face there." I offered, not wanting my time with her to end, even if only on the phone.

"You consider him a friendly?" she seemed surprised.

"Relatively speaking when you compare him to a cartel leader."

"Never met one, not a helpful frame of reference. Eric's on my other line. Ciao."

She didn't give me a chance to say I'd rather not or learn anything more about her personally. And after the call I wondered why I was happy she'd called me, at the same time being disappointed that I wouldn't see her for a few more days.

Willy sat next to me. I wondered if I'd survive his harassment for a whole hour.

"I'm generally an upbeat kinda guy, you know?" Willy began. "But it seems the world went to shit when that camel jockey tried to blow up that god-damn office tower."

I tried to place what Willy was talking about, "What camel jockey?"

"Abu Salim. I called you on him. You never called me back. Now what was that all about? I've never done nothin' but give you 'xactly what you asked for."

I searched my memory, "Don't remember the name. Sorry."

"The undercover counter terrorism job I was workin' when you wanted me to come join your team with Strickland. I couldn't come 'cause I was tryin' to put the kid away before he hurt someone. Anyway, the kid thinks he's gonna blow up the Mercantile Bank building and be the next god-damn Osama. I had to make sure we caught him in the act so we could lock up his ass until camels rule the earth."

"Or they legalize prostitution." Willy use to round up hookers.

"Hey they did that some place in Europe, I hear. They call it the stop light district or some such shit."

"Red light and it's in Amsterdam."

"What's wrong with them people? Ain't they got no born again Christians keepin' their husbands in check?"

"Whatever. What's the moral of your story?"

Willy thought for a moment. "Oh yeah. The camel kid. Anyway, he thinks he's gonna blow up this bank buildin' an' he's never even been inside. I ask him why you want to blow up this god-damn building? And you know what he says?"

"No idea."

"He says because Jihad makes him do it. What the fuck is that? Is it like the devil made me do it? I don't get it. Anyway, we give him the phone an' tell him it'll detonate a truck bomb. At the appointed time he makes the call to trigger the bomb an' wham, bam, thank ya ma'am, we haul his ass off to jail."

"Okay. So again, what's the moral?"

"I'm comin' to that. Ever since our little sting on Abu Salem it seems everyone's a god-damn terrorist, you know? I mean we get put on this task force. We watch these gun battles in Mexico... All that shit that happened to you. It just seems someone has it out for us."

"For us? Like who are you includin'?"

Willy shrugged, "Like everyone. You, my brothers down at the Southside Precinct that got all shot up..."

Willy looked away. "Strickland…" He struggled for a moment. I knew what he was feeling. "It's all around us …. like …. air."

"You just lost me."

Willy faced me, "I'm just a simple minded cop. Everything's black and white, you spend your time with the hookers an' pimps an' drug dealers an' petty thieves. There ain't much white. You work mostly at night. You do your share of murders an' assaults, an' breakin' an' enterin'. You get to know the fences, the pushers, the innocent bystanders, who always seem to be around when somethin' happens. After while it dawns on you that they ain't so innocent. You know?"

"That why you're over helping me?"

"Naw. It ain't so bad. I got a lot of friends on the street. I got hope for some of them.... kids like Juan, the one you met. He's gonna be a photographer, did I tell you that? I got some of his work at my house. Even my old lady likes it. He'll do all right if he can just survive a couple more years in the 'hood."

"He won't if you keep pickin' him up and lettin' him go. The gangs know what you're doin'. If he's not talkin', you ain't pickin' him up. See what I mean?"

"Not a problem." sounded defensive enough to play for the Dallas Cowboys.

"Willy, I know you like the kid. You want to talk with him and keep him straight. But think of the position you're puttin' him in. Every time you talk to him, you mark him. Let him disappear. I'll bet one day you'll get an autographed picture in the mail and you'll know he made it."

Willy didn't like what I had to say, but didn't comment further.

"Okay, so back to Abu Salim."

"Who you put away."

"Right. Anyway, ever since him it seems we're in this us against them thing."

"What do you mean?"

"I mean..." I saw he wanted to reach for something. And that something seemed hard for him to express. Then his feelings all came tumbling out.

"I generally arrest one person at a time. One fucker who breaks a law. We say do some time, pay for your crime, an' we'll let you come back out to play."

I nodded.

"Suddenly the world's gone to shit. Everyone we go up against now has a gun or a hundred guns. No one has any hesitation about usin' 'em. It's like no one cares about the fact they're killin' another human bein'. It's all about money. If you don't have it you just take it from the guy who's making it over on the next street. A gun makes you king. Whatever you want is yours for the takin'. I know we're dealin' with drugs here, and that's the worst. Nobody has a conscience. It's like that's a requirement. You got a conscience, you can't be part of our cartel. What happened? What changed? I've never seen anything like what we're seein' now."

I sat quietly. I'd never seen anything like what we were seeing either; even when I worked organized crime. The cartel violence pushed way beyond what had been the norm and with no end in sight. I knew some Hispanic gentlemen would die for what they did to Bill and Janice. More would die if they'd harmed Dad. And deep down inside, I'd already admitted to myself I no longer expected to survive. What Willy described had become the new normal.

Dwelling on the situation did no good, "Well, you could always ask to go back to the streets, hasslin' the pimps and shakin' down the hookers to keep the morality on the Dallas streets in line with societal expectations."

Willy seemed nostalgic for a moment, "Yeah, the good old days, when lovin' was cheap and lyin' was easy."

"I'm sure many a Christian woman would love to have you back enforcin' things for 'em, while their husbands are visitin' the strip clubs by Bachman Lake."

"I probably know most of 'em by their first names." Willy observed.

I couldn't resist. "The husbands or the wives?"

"Actually both, but for different reasons."

I noted the sparkle in Willy's eyes again. The heaviness seemed to lift. "So is that why I never seem to be able to raise you at lunch time?"

Willy looked straight into my eyes, "My boys took out a drug house, last night."

The change of tone caught me by surprise. "Everything okay?"

"It was three fucking houses from where I live."

His work had come home with him only he wasn't even aware of the danger. He lived in his wife's old neighborhood, in the house where she grew up somewhere in Oak Cliff. When Willy described the location it seemed to me to be not too far from the Texas Theater where Lee Harvey Oswald was arrested after killing President Kennedy. "Transients?"

Willy shook his head, "Known those god-damn lettuce pickers for what? Goin' on five years. They weren't just passin' through. And you know what the worst part is?"

I was afraid to ask.

"They took out a god-damn arsenal. Automatic weapons, grenade launchers, enough fuckin' ammunition to kill everyone … for a mile. And my kids walk past that house every day on the way to school."

The way Willy spoke sent the same chill down my spine I felt when I saw the smoke rising over the Triple C. I couldn't find the words to respond.

"It's my family. They're comin' after my family. Everythin' that's happenin's gotta stop. First Strickland, and now my wife and kids. No place's safe until we take them all out. We've gotta take them off the streets .... now."

Willy turned away and didn't say another word for the rest of the flight.

The Best Defense

From the outside the building on a back Monterrey street looked like any other commercial building in this industrial neighborhood. But once inside, you found only a big burly guy with huge arms, slicked back hair and a pale young woman who tried to look prettier than she was behind a thick glass window. You simply slipped the required cash payment through the protected tray. Instantly the guy opened a door to let you into paradise. At least the club was paradise to the men who wanted forbidden pleasures.

On this night Ruben Castillo, surrounded by his lieutenants, sat at one of the dancer pits. The young woman, with no more than a few square inches of fabric covering her snow white skin, simulated copulation in syncopation with the music. Castillo liked to have meetings here because the distractions told him who was disciplined enough to ignore what was going on around them. Herbiberto kept glancing up. Castillo knew his shooter, as to referred to Herbiberto, liked the women and liked beating them even more. Castillo wondered if he could catch Herbiberto not listening.

"Fucking Guzman." Castillo said. "He must have given us up in Dallas. How else would they have known where to find us? I mean we were on a fucking back street in a residential neighborhood with cops for neighbors."

"Five years of work down the drain." Dominguez observed.

"Fucking right. How we going to make sure Guzman doesn't give us up again?"

Herbiberto volunteered. "We could tell the cops where to find his safe houses."

Good, Castillo thought, at least he's trying to listen.

Dominguez annoyed Castillo by responding before he could. "All that'd do is escalate the war. They'd retaliate and we'd be scrambling to find new safe houses. It's always dangerous when you're setting up new distribution. People see things and report what they see. Better to avoid warfare."

"We need to find another way to keep Guzman from turning us in ever again." Castillo wanted to focus on the problem he was concerned about.

"Why not take him out? He's history, anyway. We could take over his distribution and double in size overnight." Dominguez offered.

Castillo glanced around to see the reaction of the other lieutenants. Not many seemed to be in favor. He knew the Juarez cartel had hired mercenaries to provide their security. The mercenaries tended to be more difficult to buy off. He knew about mercenaries because he used to provide security for the Gulf cartel. "If Guzman were gone, would that put Raul Ramirez in charge?"

No one offered an opinion.

"Sometimes it's better to deal with the devil you know than to unleash one that may be worse." Castillo wanted to get back to his question.

"And sometimes it's better to decapitate your enemy." Dominguez challenged the dismissal. "Cripple them. Then we Zetas can take over the Juarez distribution. We'd get back to where we were before the PRI lost the presidency and the next government started the whole holocaust of cartel leadership."

"The Juarez cartel was one of the original four families, we weren't." Castillo reminded everyone.

"Exactly why we should want to take them over. We become one of the four families." Dominguez copied Castillo's style, which annoyed Castillo even more. He needed to pull the string on Dominguez's behavior and find out his motives.

"My young friend has the right idea, but it's not time. We aren't ready to take them on at the leadership level. They're still too strong. No one takes on a rhino when it's feeding. We should nip at the Juarez boys a little at a time. Weaken them. Sap their strength. Don't let the Rhino realize it's no longer as strong as it was. Let it go on thinking everything's fine. Soon they'll be where we can bring them down."

"Let's start taking bigger bites, then."

Castillo took Dominguez's comment as a direct challenge. "Only I say when we take bites or how big they'll be."

Simulation

Colonel Blum met Willy and me at The University of Texas at El Paso campus. It was stark and barren as the whole city seemed to me. Buildings were low, adobe-like without much vegetation to provide a break from the relentless sun. A curious place to house a simulator, I thought, until Blum reminded me that there were over thirty-five thousand soldiers at Ft. Bliss, the heart and soul of this community.

We entered one of the laboratories. What I found surprised me. We came into a large room with black walls and ceiling and indirect lighting. Centered was a matte black space frame about the size of a basketball court. Television monitors hung from the frame facing away at one end. Three rows of chairs faced the monitors. Small black and yellow boxes were mounted above the space frame looking down. In a corner sat a large computer rack and a desk with several smaller monitors, one man, working feverishly sat before them. Lockers stood up against the wall behind him, and two tables held what appeared to be M-4 assault rifles and Sig Sauer pistols. I didn't know what to make of what I'd found.

"You're going to be visually immersed into a virtual city." Blum told us, bringing my attention back from this incomprehensible device. "You'll physically move around in the virtual city as you do here; only the city will look like some other place. You'll be present in that world, not looking into it like through a window or TV screen, or using a joystick to move around like a video game."

Willy shook his head, "I don't get it."

"You have to get in it to get it, detective." Blum responded. "You'll work as a team. Your objective is to defeat an opposing force." The Colonel looked for comprehension. I showed it…sort of. "Over time, others will be immersed with you. Some will be real people, and others virtual. You won't be able to tell the difference. The virtual humans have roles, intentions, skill levels and reactions to the things you and the others with you will do."

The Colonel pointed at me. "If Agent Carr raises a weapon in there the virtual humans are likely to shoot first. If he says hello, they may come over and talk, unless their intention is to blow up Agent Carr. Then they might detonate an improvised explosive device, or pull the trigger on an explosive vest that kills Agent Carr and the wearer of the vest at the same time."

"What you're sayin' is we get into your toy there, and it's just like bein' here, but we're somewhere else?" Willie asked clueless.

"Other way around. You're physically here, but you see a different place where you'll be moving around."

"Who came up with this toy?" I asked

"The system was designed by a company named Motion Reality. They use a technology called motion capture. Computers create an avatar of you in the virtual space. You see a replica of your own body and everyone else in the system sees your avatar too. You're modeled exactly as you stand - same build, same size."

I knew kids and adults had been playing videogames for decades, ever since Pong. But the Colonel told us specifically what we were looking at was no video game. What else could it be? I thought of the teleport chamber on the Starship Enterprise, only a whole lot bigger. Was it possible that someone had actually built a place where you could go to seem to be somewhere else? I didn't know, but the device had a futuristic look. What went on under the space frame? Did the system really take you somewhere else? I didn't think so, unless the machine just teleported your consciousness. I was in over my head.

One of the systems operators, a UTEP graduate named Armando, came over carrying equipment for us. He helped me put on a backpack, placed markers for the cameras to track me on various parts of my body, and handed me the essential 3D goggles.

"I take it you're gonna suck me right into that there computer and the next thing I know I'm gonna be Tronned?" I asked.

"No. You stay in the physical world. You even move around like normal. But you'll be seeing the virtual world and feeling the effects of your actions there. Let's get you acclimated," Armando answered.

"Feel the effects?" I asked.

"These patches we put on your arms and legs conduct 100 volts of electricity. If you're wounded by someone's avatar or a virtual human the shock simulates the pain of the wound."

I wasn't sure I liked the idea of a hundred volts of electricity coursing through me.

"Okay, I need you to stand over here. Hold these handguns and stand still until I tell you it's okay to move." Armando moved back to the console. He pushed a button and all the cameras came on, bathing me in infra-red light.

"Gotcha. Okay. Detective, if you'd take the handguns from Agent Carr, and step right over where he was. Good, hold them out at an angle for me. That's it. Now stand still until I tell you it's okay to move."

I was surprised to see Alene enter the lab and approach Colonel Blum. I had mixed feelings. I didn't want her getting any ideas about participating in any ops we might do. This could be a bad precedent. The infra-red lights dimmed. "Gotcha." Armando took the handguns from Willy and handed replica M-4 assault weapons to each of us.

"Your system here a super arcade or some such shit?" Willy asked.

"It's a tactical trainer. We're more concerned with teaching you how to fight as a team than your individual shooting prowess. What we're going to do is take you to an automotive repair shop in Detroit. You'll start out with a simple building clearance. Move through the rooms, and look for hostiles or hostages. You need to make sure you know who's friendly and who's not. You'll see each other come into the virtual world wearing FBI uniforms. Anybody you encounter could be virtual or live. In the virtual world you can't tell the difference. But let me explain one thing". He pressed a button and I felt a shock on my arm. "You feel that you'll know you're wounded or dead." Another shock to a leg. "Leg wound." A sharp pain in my left arm. "Arm wound. As you can see there are real consequences if you get into a fight. I suggest you take it slow -- and remember: taking out a civilian results in an immediate after action review. So make sure you know what and who you're shooting at."

"So that's what a hundred volts feels like?" Willy asked no one in particular.

Alene came over to me. I watched her graceful movement and the sway of her breasts as she walked. "Blum's not impressed." She said. "Thinks you're not up to it. Could you prove him wrong for me? I need a victory. Someone's whispering to the President that our efforts aren't producing much."

A moment passed before I caught up to what she'd said. "Hold on a second." I was surprised Blum had made a snap judgment about me since I hadn't had a chance to show him anything. But the whispering to the President alarmed me. *Who was trying to undermine us? We hadn't had a chance to even establish ourselves*. I didn't want people saying Alene made a mistake taking me on, knowing such a mistake could affect her career as well as mine. "What does he mean not up to it? Damn, a critic and he doesn't even know me."

"Says he's seen thousands of guys go through training and he just doesn't think you and Detective Graves are right for this project. Thinks I should get someone a whole lot younger."

"Like the Wizard?"

She looked at me blankly.

"Nick. Our twenty something analyst."

She hesitated before responding, "More in the ballpark, yeah."

"Guess we need to prove him wrong."

Just before I pulled my goggles down, I saw Alene smile at me. I remembered the discussion with her about the test to see if this simulator could accelerate preparations for paramilitary operations. I thought Blum was trying to make the test into a referendum on me. I wondered if Blum knew anything about the whispering to the President? I needed to take this exercise seriously, but the device as described seemed like a game. I hadn't seen anything yet to change my impression.

The countdown started, three, two, one. I heard a click. A 3D virtual repair garage surrounded me. As I moved my head I saw the virtual room, not the college laboratory I'd been standing in. I looked to my right. Someone stood next to me. Same shape and size as Willy, only he wore a uniform, with the letters FBI on its back. "That you, Willy?"

"Ain't the ghost of Christmas past."

This might not be so bad. I took a step. It was just like walking into a real garage. With each step I got closer to things in the room. I walked into the adjacent garage bay and noticed movement on my left. A man ducked behind a grease barrel. My Army and FBI training kicked in. I was in this new world and responded automatically. I went down on one knee and covered the position of the man behind the barrel with my M-4. "Willy, over there."

"Where the fuck is there?"

"To your left."

"Oh, that you? I think you look better virtually."

We walked around a table with tools resting on top, approached the barrel, looking around the virtual garage at tire racks, a car lift, and a dingy office off to the right. Cars waited outside to be serviced. I began noticing details. Broken glass windows, the trash on the floor. I didn't see any people other than the man behind the grease barrel.

"Okay… he's the fucking FBI. Come out with your hands up." Willy called out.

The virtual man stood up. He held an AK-47 assault weapon pointed down.

"You mean all I gotta do is ask 'em politely?" Willy wondered aloud, but then the man raised his weapon and fired. I responded with a two shot burst to his mid-section. The man went down.

A momentary searing pain in my left arm. I froze for a moment, and then flashed back to the Dallas precinct motor pool. I was facing down the gunman in the truck. I saw the assault rifle pointed at my head. The red laser illuminated and painted my face. In my mind's eye I saw Sergeant Adams hit the brakes. My life was saved. I felt the bullets strike my armor plate.

Superimposed on the flashback, I felt all four pain points bringing me back into the virtual world. My goggles turned red.

I heard Willy shout, "God-damn."

Willy and I had been shot by another virtual human neither of us had seen, having focused only on the one.

Willy flipped his goggles up. "Re-set. They ain't gonna get away with that again."

Armando came over to me. "What happened, sir?"

I finally re-engaged, "Oh, sorry. Got distracted."

"Flash back?" Armando asked, "You replay a skirmish you been in?"

I hesitated.

"Not a problem, sir. Happens a lot the first time in. You'll get past the flashbacks in a bit. Anyone who's been in battle's subject to them. Just take it easy and we'll have you back in the fight in no time."

I wasn't going to take it easy and took the position to start the next exercise. Alene came out on the floor. I found myself watching her hair bounce, wondering if it smelled and felt as good as it looked.

"I can't tell you how important it is that we understand the true potential of this kind of training and mission rehearsal." She said. "If this device can accelerate the preparation of teams to fight the Zetas, that advantage will be a major shift in our ability to destroy them. I know you may be skeptical, but give it a chance."

"Yes, mother." Willy pulled his goggles down and moved to the starting point.

"We're taking you to a GOPLAT." Armando announced. Alene returned to stand next to Colonel Blum, who looked cool and dismissive.

"A what plat?" Willy asked.

Alene turned and looked at me with a look of concern. She knew I was watching her and not listening to Armando. She answered a question from Blum. I pulled my goggles down in preparation for the next scenario.

"Gas and Oil Platform. You'll come in on a helicopter. Dismount and do a search and clear. This time you're looking for a hostage....

The Whipped Puppy

The first hours in the simulator were awful. Every time I thought I had a scenario figured out something else caught me unaware. I saw Alene talking with Blum, who frequently shook his head. I was sure he was telling her I wasn't cutting it and she should send for Nick. I wasn't going to fail. I was determined to figure out how to survive and carry the fight. But every time I flashed back I lost contact with the virtual world and ended up wounded or dead.

About four o'clock I finally seemed to get the whole thing under control. The idea of a virtual world we walked through that had real consequences seemed to click for both Willy and me. When we got all the way through the first scenario alive and triumphant, we high fived and acted like a couple of kids who just won a football game. The tempo picked up, our shots improved and tactically we started covering each other better, moving in anticipation of where the bad guys would be. Blum stopped shaking his head, but I saw a lot of gestures towards me that I couldn't interpret. Alene stood next to him, unsmiling.

At nearly nine o'clock Willy and I headed to dinner with Alene. The simulator wasn't so bad, we felt. We could anticipate where threats might come from. We worked off each other. We used hand signals. We were becoming more instinctive about how we reacted to threats based on what each of us happened to see and we were seeing much more. My shot accuracy climbed.

"I think we finally redeemed ourselves." I told Willy.

"Speak for yourself. I'm a whipped puppy, here."

Alene scrolled through her email messages.

"You gonna put in my retirement papers?" I asked

She disengaged from what Lexie used to call the crackberry, because it seemed at the time I was addicted. The memory overwhelmed me. Alene seemed to notice my reaction, but probably had no idea what I reacted to. "Not today. I think there's hope, although Blum still thinks the jury's out."

"Big of him." Willy noted. "They put me back in tomorrow I'm likely to shoot the instructor. God-damn I'm tired. If my head drops into my steak, let me get a few?"

"Might even eat your steak too. I'm famished." I said.

"Where's the Carr-ism? Like I could eat a rattle snake in the middle of sheddin' its skin? You must be gettin' lazy there."

"Didn't know you were keeping up with my homilies. Might make you a Texan."

"A boy from Jersey? Not gonna happen."

Alene smiled at me. I returned an appreciative look and smile. She acknowledged the look but her expression quickly changed back to somber. She was working through something. I could tell it had to do with me. Having told me someone upstairs wasn't happy with the way things were going, as her Ops Director I'd be cited as the person responsible. What did she want me to know? Would she talk openly in front of Willy? I needed a one-on-one with her before she left in the morning. I'd actually been surprised to find she stayed the night.

Willy must have understood, "Since you two aren't consuming alcohol tonight, I'll be at the bar until they deliver my steak."

I turned to Alene, "So what's the problem?"

"ATF."

Alcohol, Tobacco, Firearms and Explosives Administration.

They were a sister agency and had been involved in the garden spot raid because of the suspected gun transfer. "What's the problem?"

"This one's going all the way up to Eric." *The Attorney General. Not good.*

"How can I help?"

"ATF let assault weapons be transported across the border, knowing they'd end up in the hands of the cartels. Intent was to trace the weapons back and figure out who was selling them. Problem was the weapons they let cross were used in a raid that killed a couple of our DEA agents. We've got hell to pay now, and the Mexicans are absolutely furious we were letting weapons cross without telling them what we were doing."

"If ATF was involved, how does that affect you?"

"ATF's in the penalty box as far as Mexico's concerned. President wants me to show the Mexican government Justice is serious about helping them, and not contributing to the problem."

"How do we do that?"

"He wants us to conduct a joint mission, without acknowledging our presence. And he wants us to do it now."

I heard the alarms going off in my head. I felt there was more than she was saying, but didn't want to put her on the spot. Maybe she couldn't say more. I didn't know. "Is that what this simulator training's all about?"

She gave me a barely perceptible nod. We weren't ready and it would be hard to accomplish what the President wanted.

I took a deep breath and made a judgment. "Remember the garden spot?"

"Of course."

"We weren't ready then and the mission almost came apart. We're not ready now. You willing to take the chance we might really screw the pooch?"

She looked away and bit her lip.

I waited a moment and then put my hand on hers. She looked back at me with red eyes. "I'll fix things. You put me in this position even though others warned you not to. Tell me when we have to be ready and we will be."

Alene stared at me for a moment. I held my breath, thinking of Lexie's green eyes. Maybe she saw my response, maybe not, but her voice was like a whisper. "Next week."

I wondered how the hell I'd ever be able to pull off getting ready in a week.

Lend Lease

I didn't sleep much, knowing Alene was down the hall and imagining things I shouldn't have. I also spent a little time wondering how Willy and I could be ready in a week, but not coming up with any answers. I wondered what I wasn't being told, imagining both the best and worst possibilities. Was I letting my growing awareness of Alene get in the way of listening to what she wasn't saying? Why was I here? Why had I been sent to Mexico City? Why wasn't she asking me to do the job she hired me for? What was this whole thing about Blum thinking I couldn't do whatever he was looking for? I didn't sleep much.

Alene joined us for breakfast. She announced she was staying through the morning meetings, and had a mid-day flight back to Dallas. I was unaware of any meetings, but what did I know? I drove us to Ft. Bliss instead of UTEP. At first I was angry, thinking we needed all the time in the simulator we could get. A meeting had to be a complete waste of time. I looked at Alene who simply said as if reading my mind, "Something happened yesterday. We all need to take a look."

We found ourselves back at the Interagency Intel Fusion Cell on the fort. Colonel Blum was talking with a group of men I didn't recognize. When the conversation ended the other men took seats at consoles around the room. They evidently operated the sensors and this center. Blum came over and greeted us with a nod.

When we took our seats I looked up at the central screen. Aerial imagery fed in. Voice communication intercepts could be heard. Multi-spectral systems painted signatures across the images of various indicators the experts could interpret.

Willy started the conversation. "What the fuck are we looking at?"

"Best I can tell they're showin' us all the data they're collectin'. I have no idea what some of what they're showing us means."

"Good, didn't want to think I was the only moron here."

I glanced over at Willy, but didn't want to keep this line of insult going.

Alene didn't comment. When the video started she seemed enthralled.

The bus pulled up to the main gate. The driver apparently shot the guard and stepped off the bus. A moment later the infra-red showed the heat of an explosion that consumed the bus. We saw the heat signatures of cartel gunmen, including the bus driver who casually walked away. The gunmen took positions to provide overlapping fire.

The Army had a security problem with the way the barracks had been designed. Shoot anyone who tries to respond. Wait until the Army brings in the heavy equipment to free the troops and then disappear into the country side so the Army can never find you. The problem wasn't how many *sicarios* the Army killed but how easily the cartels could stymie the Army security. I needed time in the simulator to get ready for a live mission. I was getting impatient and probably showed more than I wanted to. Alene looked at me with a question in her eyes.

We watched the scenario play out. "Each one of them might be the guys delivering weapons and drugs to the fuckin' lettuce pickers who live down the street." Willy said. "You know I invited them over for beers an' burgers in my back yard when they first moved in? They reciprocated just once with enchiladas… but at my place. At the time I didn't think twice 'bout only one visit. But now their actions make sense. They didn't want a Dallas cop comin' near 'em."

Everyone was silent as the Army made an attempt to break out and take on the cartel gunmen. They weren't successful and pulled back.

"I'm tryin' to remember what they said they did for a livin', even though I know now everything they said was all bullshit. Professionals of some kind. Pool cleaners, or janitorial services? No that wasn't it. Something about a restaurant. He made the food and she cooked the books? I should have known better than to believe 'em. Their enchiladas tasted like shit. My daughter, maybe five then, wouldn't eat one. I did, but ugh."

Alene looked at me as if she wanted some explanation of Willy's comments. "We need to get over to UTEP, I'll fill you in later." I said. As I stood, I noticed the scene on the screen. A helicopter appeared, equipped with a Gatling gun. The airship began to strafe the area where the cartel members were concealed. Some were flushed out and ran, only to fall to the stream of bullets coming from the aerial guardian. Others stayed put. "Small arms. Guys on the ground are shooting back." Willy observed.

"What kind of bird is that?" I asked Blum.

"Huey." He didn't take his eyes from the screen.

"Don't they have anything more modern?" Willy seemed incredulous.

"You're talking Mexico here, not Saudi Arabia."

"I thought we were givin' 'em billions to fight the cartels," I said.

"We are. But they choose how they're going to spend the money."

Willy nodded. "So what the fuck, man? I mean why aren't we just lending them what they need? Didn't Roosevelt do that in the big one? I seem to remember a program called Lend Lease. Isn't that how it worked? We couldn't sell what the Russians and Brits needed before we joined the war because they didn't have any money. So we gave them what they needed under Lend Lease."

I was in awe of Willy's knowledge. Willy caught my look. "History Channel. Wouldn't want you to think I read a book."

"Sometimes you truly amaze me." I responded.

"Well, don't get used to it."

The room went silent. A rocket plume showed in the infra-red, the rapidly accelerating weapon reached into the sky. The rocket collided with the 'copter just before the explosion blocked nearly all visibility. Finally the image emerged of the burning Huey. We saw the slowly rotating blade. The Huey plunged to the ground with the crew.

"Holy shit." Willy gave words to what everyone must have been feeling.

"TOW missile?" I asked.

"Looked like a FIM 92 Stinger to me." Blum observed, "Shoulder-fired. Man portable. More advanced than TOW. Some say Stingers turned the tide and drove the Russians out of Afghanistan."

The infra-red showed the burning carcass of the bird. The cartel *sicarios* surrounded the crash, probably to make sure the crew was dead. The soldiers in the barracks had stopped moving. They probably understood the significance of what just happened. I knew the stakes had been raised. The Mexican Army would have to respond in kind

"How are the cartels getting advanced weapons?" I asked. "Surely we aren't selling to them. If the weapon truly was a Stinger, the US was selling to someone who in turn is reselling or providing to the cartels. But who? Why?"

Willy got us to refocus. "So when we gonna kick their ass?"

"Won't happen unless they come north," Blum answered.

"They're already here." Willy responded angrily. "In my fuckin' neighborhood. Probably yours too, if you stopped to look around." Willy stood. "I guess it's time to climb back into your torture chamber an' see if me an' Carr, here, can figure out a way to kick their collective butts."

Take No Prisoners

Juan Dominguez sat in an old pickup truck across from the downtown exit ramp from the airport highway into Monterrey. He was enjoying the expressions on people's faces as they drove by. His men had left hours ago, in the middle of the night, but their handiwork hung from the overpass about a hundred yards away. Thirteen bodies. All were dead before they were hung for the citizens of this fair city to see. He was sending a message and a challenge to the Juarez *sicarios*: Zetas take no prisoners. Dominguez particularly liked the fact that none of the bodies wore shoes and the right hand had been painted red. The display wasn't intended to be subtle. From the looks on the faces of the locals driving by, he felt confident the take no prisoners message wasn't being lost.

The *Policia* arrived. Only one car at first. Dominguez saw the driver talking on his cell phone. Was he calling headquarters or warning someone? With the locals he could never be sure which, but in this town he expected more likely to be the latter. The driver angled his vehicle to cut off the through traffic wishing to pass under the overpass. He turned on his lights but didn't get out of the vehicle.

About ten minutes later five more cars arrived. Two cars rerouted the traffic and the other officers got up on ladders to cut the bodies down. Dominguez enjoyed how gingerly the *Policia* handled the bodies. He would have just cut the rope and let them fall. Certainly wouldn't hurt them. But then Dominguez never expected he'd be called upon to cut down bodies.

His cell rang. *Fucking Castillo,* he thought. *Wants to know why he wasn't told in advance. Shit.*

"Yes?"

"Understand you're having fun this morning."

"Doesn't get much better."

"Really?" Castillo wasn't happy.

"You watching this?"

"Just a report on television. They won't show anything." Castillo waited.

"Why you care about this one? Nothing unusual."

"I said little bites." Castillo was feeling challenged. *Time to step back.*

"Thirteen is a little bite, when you're dealing in thousands of *sicarios*."

"You're forcing Guzman to respond in kind. We want to stay below the radar, remember? We want to weaken him first."

"I expect we'll get a bunch of cross overs. Guys who want to work with people who have balls."

"Back off." The threat was clear.

"Done." Dominguez had to capitulate or he'd be the next one hanging from an overpass.

"Have you found the money to make our payment?"

Dominguez had an answer, finally. "I'm ramping up production in Monterrey. Had to commit to increase the raw material inventory, but that's done now too."

"What are you doing about the FBI agent?"

This topic surprised Dominguez. He was getting sloppy and needed to anticipate better. "The Messenger has the situation well in hand."

"I heard the agent disappeared."

"We found him quickly enough."

"I want him done tonight. And by done I mean dead, or do I have to spell out dead for you?" Dominguez wasn't ready, but he'd have to do something now.

"That can be arranged, but why tonight?"

"I don't like to wait -- for anything. He was supposed be dead weeks ago."

"You underestimate the value of the messages we've sent."

"They're not the fucking messages I wanted sent. You do him tonight or don't bother coming back." Ultimatums. Castillo was feeling more threatened than Dominguez had thought.

Positioning for Castillo's job was going to be much harder now. He knew those whose support he needed would be watching. If Castillo sent the message that everyone should back away to let things cool off everyone would know Dominguez had been responsible for the thirteen bodies rather than Castillo. Exactly what he wanted people to think. He'd wait for the message and then decide his next move. In the meantime he had to do something about that FBI agent before Castillo gave the killing to whom? Probably Herbiberto. Bringing anyone else in would ruin his plans. *But how to thread the needle?*

Anyone Else

Willy rode to UTEP with Blum. I drove Alene to the airport for her noon flight.

"Do you really think you can be ready?" She asked as we drove.

"No choice."

"What else do you need, besides more time?" She seemed afraid to ask.

I glanced at her out of the corner of my eye. She looked at me expectantly. "I need you to believe in me. If you give up, there isn't anyone else."

"Professionally or personally?"

Her question caught me unprepared and I answered without thinking, "Either."

I pulled up in front of the terminal. I helped her with her compact bag. She travelled light. I thought she was more like me than I realized. Alene smiled at me, but I couldn't tell if her smile was of affection or apprehension. I surmised the latter, but maybe just because of my own apprehension about many things.

"Come see me when you get back. We have a number of things to chat about."

I watched her all the way into the terminal, feeling a little sad. Once inside she glanced back at me before going to the ticket counter. My feelings for her were growing and I needed to be careful since too many things didn't add up.

Teachers' Pet

Back at the simulator lab, I suited up and joined Willy who was talking with a short wiry man, wearing a black T-shirt and khaki pants. Muscles bulged everywhere. The tattoo on his left arm sent shudders through me. A skull dripped blood from an empty eye socket and a crack ran from front to back. I looked into the man's eyes. I didn't see anything resembling empathy.

"Zed." The man said, shaking my hand.

While I rubbed the circulation back into my hand, Zed said. "I met Dr. Tom, the guy who created this here machine. Brilliant. Knows absolutely everything about virtualizing anything. But he never killed a man. He never fought for his life. He never nearly died because he made a mistake in a battle. I like to say I'm Dr. Tom's alter ego. I never virtualized nothing. I never want to. But I've done all those other things. I'm here to make you better, using his genius."

"Who is this guy?" Willy asked.

Blum responded casually, "The guy who's going to save your ass when the shit comes down, 'cause he'll have made sure you don't fuck up."

"Is this a test?"

Blum didn't respond, but Zed did, getting right into Willy's face, "The opposition is the only one who gives tests. I don't need to test you, 'cause you don't listen and learn, Pedro will give you a test you'll never pass. And I don't need to waste my time on a dead man, who just don't know it yet."

Willy didn't back off. "If you're such hot shit, why aren't you out there killin' rather than wastin' your time with us dead men?"

Zed closed what was left of the tiny space between them, "Because I follow orders and my CG sent me here to see if I could make a difference."

"CG?" Willy asked.

"Commanding General US Special Operations Command."

Willy blinked twice before responding, "He somebody important?" Willy knew the answer. Zed knew he knew.

I felt sure Zed would as soon kill a man as shake his hand. He'd already shaken both Willy's and mine. I put my hand on Willy's shoulder and gently pulled him back.

"What the fuck?" Willy asked, stepping back.

"Think about your kids. What can Zed teach you that'll help you protect 'em?" Willy acknowledged my point. I felt relieved the macho spraying fest had finally ended.

"Get scaled in," Zed instructed. "We're using silenced Sig Sauers. You need at least four extra magazines. The stuff you did yesterday was standoff fighting. We're going to close the distance today. Tomorrow will be up close."

His progression didn't make sense to me. "How do we close the distance if we're battling virtual humans?"

"Tomorrow we'll have people in with you, marked as Opfor."

"Opfor?" Willy asked.

"Opposing Forces. Although we'll look virtual when you attack us, we're real. This is to see if you've learned how to defeat someone who's as much interested in living as you are, when only one of you will."

"So you're only gonna teach us to kill? What are we supposed to do when we don't need to kill 'em?" I asked.

Blum came part way out on the floor. "Very observant. Yes, we're segmenting your training so you only have to worry about one thing at a time. But believe me, before you're done, you'll be making the kill or no kill decision in a nanosecond, 'cause most of the time, that's all you'll have."

Willy jabbed me. "What are you? Teacher's pet?"

"You're both qualified on the handgun, so we don't need to orient you on the weapon. Get scaled in. I'll run you through the first scenario." Zed turned his back on us and moved out onto the floor of the simulator.

Implied Rules

After gaining proficiency at close range with a silenced Sig Sauer, we moved on to what Zed called the up close and personal. He showed us techniques to render a man helpless or dead. We practiced his techniques in slow motion, not immersed, but on each other. We watched as Zed and Barry, the instructor from the previous day put metal collars around their necks and donned Kevlar vests. The knives Zed handed us had blades that wouldn't cut butter. Still the collars and vests were to make sure we did no permanent damage.

Willy and I immersed. We found ourselves in a Mexican village. Using the hand signals we'd learned the day before, we split up and came around a virtual building from different sides. I peeked around the corner. Two guards faced away from us, talking in low voices. Willy and I couldn't see each other. We had to hope the other would take down his subject at about the same time. In theory, if one struck immediately before the other, the second guard should be distracted. In theory.

I came up on my man. Barry. I said a prayer for Willy and attacked, bringing the knife across the guard's wind pipe. I lowered him to the ground. Zed turned to see what had happened.

Willy attacked, jamming his knife into Zed's chest only to have Zed deflect it with his hand. Zed raised his Sig Sauer to Willy's forehead and slowly pulled the trigger. "Willy's dead."

I felt bad for Willy. Zed had pretty much humiliated him. At the beginning of the next scenario, Willy took Zed down with his silenced handgun almost as soon as the exercise began. I had to work a little harder to bring down Barry. We got into a wrestling match for the knife before I finally swept his legs from under him and brought him down, with me on top and the knife up under his throat.

Each scenario got harder. Willy ended up with Zed, who found a way to defeat him every time.

Finally I switched with Willy and faced Zed. Willy defeated Barry after a short struggle. Zed and I continued to study each other, both waiting, looking for an opening. While I hadn't tried any of my methods on Zed, I felt sure he'd been observing me. What could I use to defeat someone who'd survived hundreds of hand-to-hand battles?

I switched my knife from my left hand to my right as if getting ready to throw it at Zed. I heard the report of Willy's handgun. Zed flinched as electricity shocked him, registering the lethality of Willy's shot. Zed looked over at Willy who fired a second shot from his Sig Sauer. Zed flinched from the second shock.

Zed raised his 3D goggles. "'bout god-damn time you figured out you're a team," he told Willy before turning to me, "You let Willy exhaust himself trying to figure me out, but you never once helped him. Why not?"

"Implied rules."

"Last time I ever want to hear anything about rules. There are no rules, gentlemen. This is life and death. If you don't make the right decision the first time, you die. You take out your target first. I don't care if the second target's an old woman, you take her out, even if that means you're wasting lead."

"Why would I ever want to take out an old woman?" Willy asked.

"I lost some close friends to grandmas with explosive vests. You never assume on a battlefield. If they're in range to hurt, you waste the mother."

"Why are you so warped?" Willy asked.

Zed pulled off his black T-shirt revealing scars all over his torso. "This is why. I've been dead a dozen times. Only because my combat brothers saved my ass am I here talking to you. I've lost three quarters of my men because I couldn't get them out alive. Maybe I'm warped. But it's because bad guys out there made me what I am."

Colonel Blum stepped out onto the floor again. "Zed's one of our most decorated combat veterans. You need to listen to him. The men you may find yourselves facing are just like those who almost killed him many times."

I had to say something but was at a loss for words.

Zed wanted to get us moving. "Well ladies, I think we have cartel minions to kill before we sleep. So now that we're all on the same team, you ready?"

Secure Communications

When I took a break from the exercises, I picked up my cell phone. Alene left a message. "You need to call in at your earliest."

I placed the call.

"Oliviera."

"Bob Smith checkin' in."

She hesitated, as if she didn't realize who was calling her, "Your friend in El Paso?" I continued.

She sounded shaky and not focused. "Do you recollect your recent vacation?"

"Like yesterday, 'cause it was."

"Well, it turned out unexpectedly. You need to return." I listened carefully, she was pulling herself back together.

"That have priority?"

"The family needs a bit of time. So finish what you're doing tomorrow."

Alarm bells rang. "How does this side trip fit in with our week to prepare?"

"You're the face down there. Sorry."

Damn. No time. "Remember the garden spot."

"I trust you've learned the lessons and won't make the same

mistakes."

Something had changed since yesterday, but what? "So no relief on when?"

"Sorry."

"Is someone setting us up to fail?"

"You said you'd find a way."

"But that was with a week."

"That was before you knew it was a whole week." She had me there.

Something about the mission continued to bother me, so I decided to ask a question that might give me a clue. "Why me?"

She hesitated just long enough to convey her discomfort. "We went through the reasons when I offered you the job."

"We talked, but I can't help but think there's more going on here than you're telling me. You said you needed me to be completely frank with you, but I need you to be the same if we're going to succeed."

"I'll tell you in person. Make sure you stop here on your way through. We need to maintain secure comms."

The Bridges of El Paso

Even though it was Willy's turn to drive back to the hotel, after the day in the simulator he was too tired and handed the keys to me. The moon bathed the flat El Paso landscape with pale light, only leaving lurking shadows. Willy sat beside me with his eyes closed. Zed had worked us hard. I could scarcely believe a virtual workout could be so physically demanding. But the aches I felt confirmed how much I'd worked.

Our performance improved, even more than the day before. Our progress had been good, but nowhere near good enough to be ready for Alene's deadline. But Willy and I were becoming effective together in a way Lon and I never were.

From behind the wheel of the rental, the flashback to the Dallas garage gripped me and I began to sweat. I felt the shots knock me down. I pushed the scene out of my mind and reengaged the road ahead. The images didn't appear during the exercises anymore, but came over me when I rested. The memory simply wouldn't go away. Through everything I'd never had flashbacks before. Day dream memories, yes, but never a memory that overrode what I was doing.

I came to a long bridge on the road to the hotel.

The memories reminded me I was in bonus time. I should be dead. The events had been out of my control. Some would consider what had happened to be my fate, others luck. I felt responsible I'd led the gunmen to the precinct in the first place. Cops died because of me. I owed them big time.

A black Suburban in front of me on the bridge slowed. I checked my rear view mirrors to see if I could get around the vehicle, only to see another black Suburban pull up beside me. Bells began ringing in my head and not the good kind.

"Willy."

He was asleep. I checked the rear view mirror again. Headlights appeared right behind me, although I couldn't make out the vehicle. Probably another Suburban. Were these the same people who came after me in Dallas? I had to assume yes.

I punched Willy's left arm. "Willy, we got company."

"We there yet?" he asked still half asleep.

I felt the bump of the vehicle from behind. Willy felt the bump too. He turned.

"What the fuck?"

We were out on the bridge, boxed in. I knew whoever was in those vehicles could kill us both. I tried to evaluate the alternatives in a split second. And then I remembered Sergeant Adams, who hit the brakes to save my life.

I did the same.

I cut the wheel sharply to the right, causing the rental to slide rather than roll straight forward. The car's tail bumped against the outside Suburban. The right front went into the railing along the bridge.

I floored the gas pedal. The back wheels burned rubber against the pavement.

We came to what must have been a weak spot in the railing.

With a sudden lurch forward the Honda sailed over the side of the old bridge.

"Holy shit …" was all Willy could get out before the Honda

landed ...hard, on the dry river bed, throwing us around the cabin and rattling our teeth. I wasn't sure how the Honda would handle the impact. But I kept the gas pedal floored. We had forward movement.

The Honda picked up speed. The faster I drove the more dust rose to obscure our departure. But I knew we weren't safe yet.

Bullets pierced the vehicle.

I zig zagged across the river bed, trying to elude the shooters, guessing they only had limited range assault rifles.

"God-damn." Willy exclaimed, grasping his right side.

I feared the worst. "You okay?"

"A flesh wound. And you know I got plenty of flesh."

I breathed easier. I judged we were at maximum range of the assault weapons.

A place where I could get up the river bank loomed ahead. I spun the wheel to do a 360 and create a dust cloud, which we drove through to cross up the bank.

Once on the streets I wove through the neighborhood randomly.

"Okay Willy. What's the verdict on the wound?"

"Hurts like shit, but think I'll live.

"There's an Army hospital here. William Beaumont Medical Center."

"Not an option."

I started to search for a civilian hospital in a mostly Army town.

Easing the Pressure

Dominguez listened to Castillo on his cell phone. He was in his tiny Matamoras apartment, one of thirteen he kept in different cities. The description of the hit on the bridge had pleased Castillo, at first.

"What do you mean you think he was killed?"

"They haven't found the body yet, but they put so many bullets into his car he couldn't possibly have survived."

"Find the car and bring me his head."

Castillo gave Dominguez the opening he was looking for. "I delivered your message and I want to deliver another."

"At least you're asking permission." Dominguez noted the sarcasm.

"Thirteen heads in a bag. Ciudad Juarez."

"No." Dominguez expected the response.

"Then Guadalajara. We need to show we're not just focused on one family. The Sinaloa need to show us more respect. They've been pushing us around in the Baja."

"Cabo was their territory. We're trying to push them out."

"We have a beachhead. Things were going well, but they're coming at us now. Getting dicey whether we'll be able to hold our ground." Dominguez waited now. He knew Castillo would want to think about his request. He'd focus on the downside. What would Dominguez gain by thirteen heads in a bag? He had to get back in line as the loyal lieutenant or he'd be gone.

"What if he's not?" Castillo asked.

"Not what?"

"Dead." Castillo exploded

"Oh." Dominguez had hoped Castillo had moved on from the FBI Agent.

"You drop his head on my desk and then you can deliver your bag of heads in Ciudad Juarez."

Dominguez noted he said Ciudad Juarez rather than Guadalajara. Something was going on there, but what? He had a more immediate problem since Enrique called and said he hadn't found the car. At least he knew Castillo hadn't given the job to Herbiberto… yet. Dominguez needed to call the Messenger.

In Their Sights

I dropped Willy at the emergency room at Providence Memorial Hospital, just off West University, then went to hide the car so we wouldn't have any unwelcome visitors while Willy got treated. A young physician removed a NATO issue bullet and put in stitches. The wound was minor. I wondered how I was going to tell Alene about the attack. I didn't see any way we could be as ready as I'd want to be for her mission in a week. We had one day left in the simulator, but Willy was out of commission. I had to go see Alene and then head to Mexico City on the kidnapping.

When the orderly pushed Willy out in the wheelchair I was taken aback. His wound must have been worse than I thought. Then I remembered the wheelchair was for insurance purposes. Doctors didn't want someone walking out, only to faint and fall.

"Doc says I should be good to go if I can just avoid quick movements that might pull a stitch." Willy said. "You ever see me make a quick move? I mean like nothing to worry about there."

"We'll see how it goes."

I was surprised at how few questions we got at the hospital once we showed our law enforcement credentials. I thought there'd be a hundred forms to fill out telling the hospital everything including the sex of the bullet taken from Willy's side.

I'd decided to change cars at the airport rental agency and was now driving a black Ford Fusion. The bullet holes in the other car raised a bunch of questions. My Federal identification did the trick once more. I only filled out an accident report. I thought the events were no accident. I convinced the rental agency to give me a new car when I agreed to pay for the damage. To my amazement, the agency took my credit card even though the cost exceeded my limit by more than ten thousand dollars. Guess they figured the US government would pay.

We checked in to a new hotel about 2:30 am, got about two hours of sleep and arrived at UTEP a little before six. Zed had already suited up to immerse. He glanced at us. "What happened?"

"Seems somebody's not happy we're here." I observed.

"Fuckers tried to do us on a bridge." Willy added.

Zed nodded. "I was afraid something would happen."

"Why?" I asked.

Zed apparently felt compelled to respond. "There's more to the story than we've been telling you," he admitted. "Some contingency planning is going on to destabilize the cartels, especially the Zetas."

"I'm in." Willy volunteered. I'd expected something was in the works, but destabilizing the cartels wasn't something the Justice Department could be directly involved with.

"Better listen before you sign up." Zed said.

"If you're the best of the best black ops guys, why would you want two civilians along?" I asked.

"The operation we're working can't be led by the Army. If it were then the US would be taking military action against a sovereign nation."

"Bullshit. We're doing all kinds of things in other people's countries all the time." Bells were ringing in my head. His answers didn't add up. Did the preparation tie in with the mission Alene just told me about? The preparations had to have been in the works longer than either Alene or Zed were telling us.

"Congress won't let us do black ops in North America. Besides Mexico officially has a law enforcement issue, not a military insurgency."

I folded my arms across my chest. "You're tellin' me we're supposed to go in and do what you normally do, because the President won't let you do it?" The whole situation just couldn't get any more fucked up.

Zed nodded.

"But there're only two of us. You need what? Fifty or a hundred of us trained and working together? You can't expect we can do what you do after two or three days in a simulator. What are you thinkin'?"

Zed sighed, "We realize we could never adequately prepare you to do what we do in a week or even a year. And we don't have a year or even a week. The operations have to be led by law enforcement. But not everyone on the op has to be a law enforcement type. If some military advisors are along to keep you out of trouble, it's still civilian. And civilian ops will go down much better than either the Army or CIA coming into Mexico to help them deal with the cartels."

I shook my head in disgust. "So we're your cover. You don't really expect us to do anything other than keep out of the way. Don't get killed while your team does its thing." I barely concealed my anger.

Zed was uncomfortable, "In my opinion you can lead the team into Mexico, with the full knowledge and support of the Mexican government, to ..."

"Bullshit, Zed. The Mexican government's a lot of people. A whole bunch of 'em are on the payroll of the cartels. So if the government knows, we're all dead before we get there." I held my ground. I wanted the truth.

Zed tried to stare me down, but broke the stare first, "You're right. Only the President of Mexico's aware of this mission. He'll stand up if necessary to back our presence. That was all the reassurance the President needed to authorize the effort."

"Into the valley of death rode the six hundred."

He ignored me. "We're professionals. We've been studying the Zetas. You've been a part of those data gathering exercises."

"So that's why Alene sent me down here, to watch and do nothing." Pieces started falling into place. She sent me to El Paso to get my finger prints all over the preparation. But why keep me in the dark? Why not simply come out and tell me what she had in mind? Was any of what I had started feeling for her and I thought I saw in her real?

"What does Alene Oliviera know?"

Zed hesitated a moment, apparently unsure how to answer. "She authorized your participation but probably wanted to protect you."

"Protect me!" I lost it, "Protect me from what? Everything that once was important to me is gone." Then stopped, horrified. "Do the cartels know? Is your little deal here why they've been tryin' to kill me for the last month?"

Zed's "We don't know what they may or may not know," sounded lame to me.

"Well you just cleared up one big fuckin' mystery.'

I closed my eyes. Images flooded my consciousness: Bill's body with the two bullet holes; Tom Strickland taking a sniper's bullet in the head; the bombing of my apartment house and the innocent people I pulled from the ruins; hearing Janice before I found her body; the gunman in the van squeezing off the shots that struck me in the chest.

Anger welled. "This operation better be worth what I've lost."

And then I realized, "You're manipulating me again, aren't you?"

Zed neither acknowledged nor denied the accusation.

I started walking toward the door, "I'm out."

I burst through the door into the oppressive Texas heat and walked toward the black car in the parking lot. As I got closer, I realized all four tires were flat. I looked around. At 7 a.m. not many people were moving about on a university campus

I thought about Alene. I had to believe she'd set me up. I didn't want to believe she would or could. She'd lured me here with the promise of a chance to rehabilitate myself and maybe even a chance to continue my career. But she didn't expect me to survive any more than I did now. God damn. Were all of the feelings I started having for her part of her plan? Disarm me emotionally so I wouldn't respond? Go on giving her the benefit of the doubt so I wouldn't see what she was doing to me? Just let her continue shoving in the knife? Did she know more about the attacks on my family than she'd told me? I pushed the anger aside and listened for the bells in my head. They weren't ringing. *Why?*

I turned around and as I came back in I found Willy and Zed suited up and preparing to scale in. Both looked at me with surprise. I crossed the room with purposeful step and put on my gear. "I forgot." I said. "I'm already a dead man."

Joint Resolutions

A cab took me to Bryan Tower back in Dallas. The dock area proved the best entrance, wanting to make sure no one saw me. I felt the full beard that now covered most of my face, but remained thin on my chin where I'd skinned my face in the apartment blast. The beard wasn't fully grown in yet, but clearly changed the way I looked. No one would recognize me. I hadn't had a beard since college so none of my pictures featured a beard.

I went to find Nick. He was hard at work at his computer. He looked up when I approached.

"The person you're interested in must have a high level sponsor."

"How do you know?"

"He's not in their personnel system, he's used at least four different names while employed there and somehow he continues to collect paychecks and get promoted. He's now a Captain and appears to be using the name of Antonio Morales."

I froze at the name, wondering if it could be the Captain I'd met in Mexico City. "Where's he posted?"

"Not sure but he won the Olympic bronze in the bi-athlon.

I thought it curious a killer would surface in the Olympics. "Any indications of who his sponsor might be?" I wanted to try to understand what I was dealing with.

"Footprints seem to lead to the Director of the Federal

Investigations Agency. Currently a gentleman by the name of Fernando Garcia Cardoza. Indications are that Garcia probably came to his current position with outside help."

"From what you're seein' is he runnin' the show or just a conduit for others?"

"Again, have to interpret, so take this with a grain or two of salt. As I see it, Garcia's not the guy in charge. Looks to me like he makes a nice living and probably doesn't have a lot of stress in his life. While he has a good resume on the website, doesn't seem to support his current responsibilities."

"What does your Federale Intel buddy, Alondra, have to say about him?"

"She could never go there."

"Understood." Nick had fallen for his opposite number with the Federales, a gorgeous woman as smart as they came. But outside her formal duties she wouldn't give Nick the time of day. Still Nick clung to the belief she would come around.

I remained uncomfortable with Nick's assessment, "So our friend has friends of his own in high places."

"I'd say that's a definite."

I nodded, but still had no idea how to find Dad or Bill and Janice's killers.

I walked back to Alene's office. I wondered what had happened to Dad. Why hadn't his captors tried to contact me? Maybe they had and just couldn't reach me because of changing phones and moving all the time. But someone found me in El Paso. Dad's captors could get a message to me if they wanted to. I just didn't understand why there'd been no news of Dad if indeed he were still alive.

Alene returned so I went to her office. Alene looked up as I appeared in her doorway. "You remember our discussion about not shading information?"

Alene smiled at me. "Yes. Why?"

"My new best friends from the Army confirmed some of the things you told me at dinner have been in the works for some time."

"Tell me more," she said.

"If you don't know then someone's lyin' to me."

Alene was cautious. "I think you need to be a little more explicit."

"I have this fact pattern. Even though I'm the Ops Director you send me to the border to watch the cartels. Then you send me to Mexico City to assist in a kidnapping believed to have been perpetrated by one of the cartels. You send me to El Paso to train in a state-of-the-art virtual simulator. Now what do you think I should make of all these facts when someone tells me I'm supposed to be leadin' a mission that seems to make those trips all look like preparation? Particularly since they clearly predated the gun issue with ATF?"

"I need a little more information since many things are going on simultaneously. You may be reading connections into independent events."

"Maybe so, but it doesn't feel like things are independent."

Alene listened patiently. "I understand things have been a little trying …"

"Tryin'? Are you shittin' me? Somebody's tryin' to kill me. And that person also wants to wipe out anyone who ever knew me.

Doesn't quite live up to your billin'."

"This may take more than a minute." she began again, motioning me toward a chair, rising and shutting the door.

"It's okay. I've been sittin' a lot recently."

"That's not the report I've been getting. Sounds like you and Graves have been working your asses off. Blum has pushed you as far as he possibly could," she said.

"That mean you're not bringing in Nick to replace me?" I was still unsure of where I stood with Blum and Alene.

She frowned, realizing she'd become transparent. "Blum admitted he was wrong about you."

She began slowly, trying to put the story together as she went. "You know when you were selected for the Rapid Response Team, you had more skeptics than supporters."

I waited in silence, wanting her to get to the point.

"Politically the President can't set up a team such as ours to deal directly with the cartels since they're a Mexican issue. So he authorized the team to gather information and prepare for the day when the cartel violence spills across the border. A rapid response team was what you were told. Response has to be the public perception."

"But?"

"But the problem is we can't trust the Mexican government with the Intel we obtain on the cartels. Every time we give the government information the source ends up dead. The President needed a means of providing Intel so Mexican officials can conduct missions to take down the cartels but without any indications of the sources and without time for the cartels to prepare. Our mission's to assist the Mexican government in containing and destroying the cartels without our presence and involvement becoming evident."

"Do I fit some profile of the perfect fuck up? One who just might seem credible enough to lure the cartels, but not smart enough to get out of the way before being rolled over by the cartel steam roller? Or worse yet get caught in a cross fire between our non-existent troops on the ground and the cartel *sicarios*? I just want to know how you thought the situation was all going to end, at least in your perfect world."

"It all ends with the Mexicans defeating the cartels using our information."

"You told me we'd be operating on this side of the border like with the Garden Spot. Are you telling me we were always planning to go over and embed in their teams?"

She nodded reluctantly.

"Does anyone else out there know?"

"No. Well, yes. Eric Holder, the attorney general, was directed to implement the action. Wilbur Washington needed to know as the department lawyer and John Thomas as the Deputy Attorney General for Ops. "

"Then how'd the cartel know to zero in on me and not you or anyone else?"

Alene wrestled with the question, "I don't know. If there's a leak I need to shut it down. If they've got someone on the inside, which I think likely, I've got to remove him or her. I've been doing everything I can think of, and Eric's helping me."

"Well you can add Blum and Zed. They're settin' up the op. Maybe others too."

"I only know who knows within the Justice Department"

"Well, what official do you have?"

"A single memo."

"So the maverick FBI agent went off and did something the President could deny knowin' about in advance."

She looked down before answering, trying to decide what specifically she should or shouldn't say.

"The President of Mexico's supposedly aware we're preparin' to do something." I challenged her silence.

She looked right at me, "I can confirm their Ambassador's discussed options with their President."

"Puts a big fat hole through the whole deniability argument, don't you think?"

"Only if the Mexicans acknowledge it, which I doubt."

"I appreciate your candor, but either you know more than you're tellin' me, or there's a whole 'nother dimension neither of us are seein'."

Alene pondered my observation, maybe thinking about whether ATF or DEA were working angles on our efforts we were unaware of. I really don't know.

"I know you're just doin' your job, followin' instructions and all. I'm sure you don't wanna disappoint the President, particularly on something so sensitive. But, you know, it would've been a whole lot easier on me if I'd a known what you all were doin'."

Alene shook her head "We simply couldn't take the risk, since so many things weren't set. Premature disclosure would have compromised everything we were doing."

"Into the Valley of Death rode the Six Hundred." I responded angrily.

Alene hesitated a moment, "Your father's alive," she revealed, "I wasn't supposed to tell you."

I froze. It felt as if a razor blade had just slashed open an unhealed wound. "How do you know?"

"We have assets in the country. One spotted him. Confirmed his identity with a picture we received after his body wasn't found in the debris of the fire."

"What can you tell me?" I said, holding my breath.

"Zetas apparently moved him from one safe house to another. He was walking. No visible signs of ill treatment. Unfortunately we couldn't follow and don't know where they took him next."

"So we know the Zetas have him." I asked and she nodded. "I hear this big but…"

"He looked pale and thin. Don't know what he looked like before," she said.

"I haven't seen him in a while."

Alene nodded. I wondered if she knew I hadn't seen Dad since the funeral. She studied my face as if she felt everything I felt. *But how could she?*

The Line

The next day Willy and I flew to Mexico City and met Captain Morales at Federales headquarters. The low rise ancient building was surrounded by a tall masonry wall topped with concertina wire. Barriers had been erected in the street to control traffic in and out. The barriers were intended to prevent bombers from getting close to plant explosives. The Federales were one of the points of attack against the cartels. Their siege mentality was clearly evident, just trying to get into their headquarters.

When I saw Captain Morales I wondered if he held Dad? Was he the one who murdered Bill and Janice? The Captain looked quizzical when I came in with Willy. "You've changed your appearance," he noted as we shook hands.

"It's a new rule. With tight budgets we don't have enough men so they ask us to change our appearance once a month so the bad guys will think there are more of us."

The Captain thought I was serious. "We should consider such an approach as well." He seemed to weigh the option for a moment. "I'm glad you returned to help us with the tragic end of this kidnapping."

"I'm sad for the reason of my return, but happy I can assist in your investigation. Do you have any clues we didn't discuss last time?"

The young Captain led us to a work up board. The Federales had a chronology of the kidnapping and subsequent discovery of the body. Graphic pictures of the young woman's severed head resting upon the pile of her former body were posted. I wondered if the pictures served as a reminder of what was at stake or as a warning of what would happen to any Federales who too vigorously pursued the case.

Morales quickly walked us through the major events and clues, of which there were very few. The review was mostly for Willy as I already knew just about everything he cited, except one … no one notified the Federales about where to find Sonja Arroyo after she wasn't released at the park immediately after the money was transferred. A passerby walking her dog called in the discovery of her mutilated body.

"What help can we provide?" I asked.

"Any satellite imagery you have of the area where her body was recovered for the preceding twenty four hours. Any signals intercepts you have."

"Doubt they would say her full name on a telephone call." I observed. "Did she have a nickname or some other name people used to refer to her that would have identified her?"

Morales hesitated. "I think her parents had a nickname for her. I will ask Sergeant Sanchez."

"What about a reward for information?" Willy inquired.

"Rewards are seldom effective in Mexico. Nonetheless her parents have offered one million US dollars. People are afraid. Generally people think security can't be provided. Witnesses fear their families will suffer. I'm sure someone saw something. But fear keeps many things from ever reaching us."

"Who do you think's behind the kidnapping? Just a gut. Not looking for hard evidence." Willy asked.

"A cartel. But which one? I can't say. Any one of them could have a motive. Each has butchered people. Until now all drew a line at rich civilians. The cartel leaders are businessmen, of sorts. The cartels have had the run of the country for a very long time; only the President has changed the game. Whoever's behind the kidnapping and murder wants to punish the President and his government for their pursuit."

"You gave a nice summary of what and why, but not who." I pushed back.

"You're correct. I can't separate the cartels. All have the same goal. Each wants to own the drug trade. Each wants to become incredibly rich. So who stepped over the line? I don't understand enough to know who'd do so first."

I suspected he was going to use us to give him information he could sell to each of the cartels. What we found out about them and shared with him. Very entrepreneurial.

"If you could tell us who was more likely, you know, prioritize the cartels, we might come up with something more quickly."

Captain Morales shrugged.

"Since you can't we'll see what we can find."

"Thank you. I must insist it's the only way."

"Understood. I'll make the call from the Embassy if one of your men could give us a ride over?"

"Sergeant Sanchez." The Captain called.

Confirmation

On the way to the Embassy, I sat in the front seat next to the iPod-wearing Sergeant Sanchez. "You have a former Olympic biathlete in the department."

"Captain Morales." Sanchez responded.

I felt my heart beating at a furious rate. The blood rushed from my head. Captain Morales had handled the bullet casings used at the Triple C. He knew who killed Bill and Janice. He probably knew where Dad was. I needed to tread lightly.

Did Captain Morales know who I was? He didn't act like he did. But was the kidnapping a convenient way of luring me to Mexico? Was the end game that I'd simply disappear before the mission began? Was Alene aware of what was going on? Was she involved? Had I been set up again? Or maybe the cartels were simply watching me to see when the rest of the team would appear. Whatever the case, I felt more exposed than I wanted to be.

I saw the gray Embassy building just ahead on Paseo de la Reforma. "Please let us off by the Sheraton Maria Isabel and we'll walk up."

"Do you want me to return for you?"

"When we get the information Captain Morales requested."

I studied the statue of the Angel of Independence in the traffic circle. I wondered if anything could ever lead to independence from the cartel violence for the Mexican people.

Nothing and Everything

From the Embassy conference room I put through a scrambled call to Alene. "The Zetas?" greeted me.

"Don't know yet. Was hopin' you'd tell me."

"I see the usual imagery and signals Intel requests. What else do they need?"

"At the moment that's all. Get the impression there may be a reason for the mañana attitude."

"And that is?"

"I suspect the investigation's bein' done by some of the people responsible."

"I hope you've documented your suspicions because they can't go forward without indisputable evidence."

"If I told you the person responsible for the investigation could be linked to the murders at the Triple C would that be sufficient?"

A long silence hung between us. Her response was cautious and quiet. "Depends on the evidence."

"A shell casing with his fingerprint."

"Haven't seen a shell casing in the evidentiary inventory."

I heard her realize evidence had been found but not turned in. She wasn't pleased, but unsure how to deal with me in my apparent noncompliance with procedure. "You need to go back and check the log."

"Why do I get the impression something was withheld?"

"Check the inventory," was all I'd give her. I knew Nick submitted the casing after the fingerprint was lifted and the analysis conducted. But I couldn't tell Alene I'd withheld the evidence to give me a head start. Nick would also put his analysis into the log and file. I wasn't sure he'd done so yet.

"Okay, I'll play along, particularly in light of our conversation yesterday. Hypothetically let's suppose the evidence is there. What's the course of action?"

"Glad to hear this is now my op and I can determine what we go after and how we execute it."

"Hold on. This is all hypothetical." I could tell she didn't want to go along with my head long rush to find the Triple C killers. But frankly I no longer cared about playing her game, if in fact she was playing a game with me. Alene had little choice but to work with me.

"If this is a law enforcement assist to the Mexican government, then I'm the nominal leader. I plan to carry out a mission that'll achieve our primary objectives, for both countries. And that means we will disrupt the Zetas."

"You don't …"

"I'm sure I won't strike terror into the heart of the Zetas, at least not by myself. But what I think we will do is to serve notice the party's over. No matter how much the Zetas up the stakes, they'll not win the next round of encounters. We won't let them."

"And how do you back up those words, mister FBI agent?" She was struggling with how to deal with me. I wasn't going to make it easy for her.

"We execute a surprise mission, because there are no leaks beforehand, and we show law enforcement can prevail."

"I can't..."

"You know what an epiphany is?"

She didn't respond.

"Well our friends south of the border made sure I had one. You see I'm already dead. They killed me in the precinct motor pool. So every day has been a bonus day for me. And I don't expect I'll be comin' home from this little deal. The Zetas evidently know too much about me. I won't escape them. But at least I'll make them pay and disrupt their cozy existence."

Silence from Alene. "You realize the attitude you just expressed would disqualify you from even participating in the upcoming mission," she said at last.

Alene didn't take the bait I gave her about not coming back. I wanted to know how she felt about me, but she went down the supervisor path. Her response told me all I needed to know. "Fully. But I also know you're in a bit of a box. You don't want to go back to the President and tell him the man you recommended is a psychopath. Worse yet he'll likely never come back from the mission. You should just let me go, and never come back. Then your report is simply 'Agent Carr attempted to execute the mission as directed, however, he was unable to survive a vicious counter attack. Agent Carr represents the spirit of the Bureau. He did all he could, personally, to ensure the success of the mission.' Did you take down my summary? Will save you time, later."

"Despite what you think I'll buy your dinner when you return."

Maybe she did care about me more than she'd been communicating. "Do I get to select the wine?"

As I hung up, Willy asked, "What was that all about?"

"Nothing and everything. Like every call I make back."

I felt drained. I needed hours to sleep before I had miles to travel. The finger print had now been entered into the case file. I'd raised the print to the awareness level of Alene. So my options would soon be limited. How was I going to take care of the business before me? How would I gain Dad's freedom? How would I be able to provide for Dad once I did gain his freedom if he were still alive? I couldn't provide a room in an apartment for him if I was moving myself every few days to avoid Zeta assassins.

I thought the Triple C would always be there. I thought Bill would always provide for Dad. I'd be free to live the life of an FBI agent. Now I saw my life would change radically no matter what the outcome. And the worst thing was I couldn't clearly see which of the various outcomes before me would most likely prevail.

"I need your help."

"About god-damn time you remembered I was here."

"How do we make sure we never have to deal with the cartels in your neighborhood again?"

"Simple. Kill them all."

"You know, Willy, while I may agree with your suggestion, I doubt seriously you and I, and even Zed and Colonel Blum are gonna kill them all."

Willy looked more serious than I'd ever seen him. "I know. I've been thinkin' 'bout that a lot. As long as the money flows they'll be somewhere in my neighborhood. Maybe not next door. Maybe over on a side street. But they'll still be there. They'll be somewhere along the route to school my kids take every day. So we gotta find a way to make it unprofitable for them to be there."

I knew Willy was right about the drugs not disappearing any time soon, no matter how many cartel minions we killed or imprisoned.

"God-damn. The problem isn't the kids, or their parents. It's not the producers or the pushers. It's the fuckin' law. What else creates the artificial value of all this shit? Only way I can see to end the violence is to make the drugs legal, you know? If the value drops 'cause you can buy narcotics at the corner drug store, cartels can't make any money and pushers got nothin' to sell. You think they can stay in business?"

"You and I can't change the law." I responded.

"Shit, I know that. But you asked me. The law's the answer. Everythin' else we're tryin' to do is all bullshit. You know the situation as well as I do. Unfortunately we don't have any leaders left in this here country, so we're stuck with this insane situation."

Willy pulled inward reflecting on something he wouldn't share, but then he concluded. "So stop bullshittin' me and let's figure out how we kill sicarios and dealers as quickly as we can. That's our only choice."

I thought about what Willy said for a long time. I knew he was right. Since the real solution lay with Congress, I knew our only option had to be a law enforcement and military option. I recognized the cartels had probably gone down the same logic a decade before. The cartels decided the American people would never let their elected officials fundamentally change the nature of the game.

The more I thought about the situation I realized I had no influence at all. I was a cog in the killing machine and I better damn well get on with killing before they struck again.

Near Real-Time

The final mission rehearsal took place the next day in El Paso. Willy and I had flown from Mexico City, but went through Dallas. By the time we were dressed and ready, Colonel Blum appeared with two guests: Alene and a middle-aged bearded man, stocky build like the power lifters in the Olympics. Zed recognized him, "Afternoon, Dr. Tom. What brings you here?"

The bearded man shook hands with Zed, "Got a little present for you Command Sergeant Major. A virtual staircase. "

Dr. Tom was followed by someone he referred to as Randy, who had graying hair in a ponytail and wore clogs. Definitely not prior military. They took up positions behind the computer desk.

I went over and stood next to Alene. She whispered. "I need you to show me you're ready."

"A little late don't you think?"

She demurred then looked into my eyes. I gave her an appreciative look. She smiled back, but I could tell she was still trying to resolve how to deal with me.

"I promised you I'd find a way to make this work."

"That was before you accused me of not being straight with you."

I leaned closer, "Things still don't add up. There's more going on than I can see and don't want to get blind-sided … again."

"Understandable, but while you're trying to figure out life, I've got a mission to run and you're the central figure in it. If you're not a hundred percent in I've got to know. Right now I don't think you are."

"I'd be a hundred percent if I trusted you, and right now I don't know if I can."

She took a half step back to look at me, surprised at my remark, a question on her face "What are you trying to tell me?"

"I can't say more without crossing a line between us. If you're feelin' even a little of what I am you won't have any more questions."

Randy, the engineer, called, "Soup's on."

Alene looked as if she were trying to read my mind as Willy and I entered the scenario, which was a market place next to a building we were to search for cartel sicarios, weapons and drugs.

I saw a man walking away with a cell phone to his ear, so I ran after him, took the cell phone from him. I motioned for Willy to look for a back or side entrance to the house. Willy found a window on the side. He went in. I circled around to the back. I found another window and entered.

Once inside, I moved through the dim light into a hallway. I cleared one room at a time, as I had been taught, peeking around a corner to get a first look without making myself a target. Soon Willy and I had the whole first floor cleared without firing a shot. Now came the stairway, always the most dangerous place in a building. The opposition could either train fire down on us, or simply drop a grenade. There's no place to hide in a stairwell.

I visualized what I thought I'd encounter. I thought through how to make sure I didn't expose myself. The stairwell appeared to be the only way up. So we had no alternative. The opposing force knew there was only one way up as well.

I had my weapon up, checked all the way up to the top of the stairwell.

Nothing.

I placed one foot into the stairwell, and then started the nerve wracking climb up, one step at a time, sweeping my muzzle across every possible place someone could be hiding. I slowly came around the first turn. Still nothing, so I moved a little quicker. I checked over my shoulder to make sure Willy followed, covering my back.

I came to the second turn in the stairwell and faced a door. I kept my finger on the trigger, ensured my safety was off. I had a second magazine tucked into my breast pocket in case I went through the first magazine, even though I'd been trained to take no more than two shots at a time. *No full automatic. Make sure every shot counts. Don't just fire to fill the air with lead. Know the target. Make sure it's a target that has intentions toward you or one of your team.* I knew there'd be civilians in this space. In the real world I'd need to protect them at the same time I took down the bad guys.

At the top of the stairs, I checked to make sure Willy and I weren't exposed. No signs of anyone. Did we enter the wrong house? No. I knew this was the safe house. I wondered if the cartel abandoned, or, worse, booby trapped the house.

I studied the door handle thinking. *No opposition in an identified safe house. Booby traps possible. Would they use remote detonation? Would they wire something to a door, just like the one in front of me?* I had to go through the door; there was no other way in. And that sent off the bells in my head.

I motioned for Willy to move to my right so he could see into the room as soon as the door opened.

I reached for the knob and slowly began to turn.

I felt the mechanism clear.

Over my shoulder I checked to make sure Willy was ready.

The door came open slowly, Willy leaned forward to see in...

... the noise of the explosion deafened me ...

... threw me back into the stair well on my back...

... to the landing below.

I felt all four of the sensors on my body activate simultaneously. I didn't survive.

My scene turned red, but I was still able to see Willy enter the room. I heard several shots.

Willy came back into the stairwell. "We got the bad guys, but you bought it."

I pushed up my 3D goggles, "How do we clear without sacrificing one of us?" I asked Zed. I noticed Alene was gone. I puzzled on her leaving so suddenly. Was something up?

Zed responded. "You did everything right for a quick clear. But booby traps are everywhere. You have to make a judgment about how best to handle the situation. In this case your only alternative was to wait the bad guys out."

But I was trying to understand why Alene didn't stay at least until the scenario was over. Had something come up? Would she come back and brief us? Curious.

The Unexpected

The sun set about two hours before. Dominguez watched his team advance toward the villa just outside La Perla, south east of the city of Chihuahua. He paid a lot of money to set up tonight's little visit, but he was confident. Guzman was home tonight. Dominguez had five different people confirm the man's travel plans. Five. Castillo wouldn't be able to fault him for the planning.

His assault team would be met at the delivery entrance by the kitchen and told where to find Guzman. After tonight the Zetas would be the undisputed leaders of the Mexican cartels. And he was the master mind, even though Castillo would get all the credit. But then he could afford to be generous tonight because he expected Castillo would only be able to celebrate for a short time.

The assault team was small, only seven men; heavily armed, with silenced weapons and wearing bullet proof vests. He believed in the old saying, trust but verify. Dominguez trusted his contact inside; a cousin. Blood always carried more weight than someone who just worked for you, no matter how big the check.

Dominguez checked his watch. His plot would be over in a few minutes. He just needed the confirmation his men got Guzman and any of his lieutenants who'd be with him. Dominguez wanted to know specifically who was there. He gave pictures of some of the men he expected to find with Guzman to the team, but expected they wouldn't be able to tell him specifically which ones they killed because they'd want to get out of there as quickly as possible.

The assault team reached the delivery gate. Dominguez's cousin appeared and let them in. Only he closed the gate behind them.

Dominguez didn't like the closure of the gate. He would have preferred to have the gate remain open. Why'd this concern him? Was something wrong or was he just being paranoid? Maybe his cousin was being careful. Maybe his cousin wanted to ensure someone else didn't find the gate open and send up a signal. He had to hope his cousin had everything covered. He'd know in a few minutes.

The short burst of gunfire from within the Villa startled Dominguez. His assault team carried silenced weapons. The plan was to go in stealth, execute the key players and get back out without drawing in the guards. The unsilenced gunfire meant something didn't go as planned. He watched for them to make their way back out the gate.

When no one came out after fifteen minutes, Dominguez realized no one would. He cautiously made his way back to the waiting truck.

Turning Tables

Twenty-four hours later Ruben Castillo looked out a window, worried. A lace curtain hung between him and the street just beyond. He and Juan Dominguez were in a darkened warehouse, one of many in this suburb of Ciudad Victoria. The bright moonlight through the window illuminated the room. He held a Sig Sauer 9 mm handgun with a laser scope sight in one hand. His other arm was bandaged. Blood stains were prevalent over much of his formerly white suit. His hair was askew and the dirt on his face hid cuts and bruises.

"Guzman's sicarios didn't follow us here, so relax." Dominguez lit a cigarette with his trembling hand. One arm was in a sling even though he held a similar Sig Sauer handgun. He had a large bandage on his left cheek. On balance Dominguez looked worse than Castillo, but seemed calmer.

"How the fuck do you know?" Castillo was still trying to understand what had happened after they launched the surprise strike on the Juarez leadership.

"You pay me to know. When Guzman discovered what we were doing he positioned his own team to come after you. He was just evening the score."

"Why didn't you anticipate he'd come after me? Guzman's *sicarios* killed everyone we sent in after him and nearly everyone protecting me. And you're reassuring me? I'm lucky to be alive."

"I thought Guzman would be dead. Besides I've already dealt with the traitors who told Guzman we were coming. They're deep in already forgotten desert graves. You don't have to worry about them."

"How did you find them so quickly?"

"I compartmented the hit. Only five people knew including us."

"So which one sold me out?" Castillo wasn't going to settle for the half answer.

"Doesn't matter. They're all dead, buried and forgotten."

"I want their families done too. Tonight. Make it happen. Got to send a message. This can't stand."

"Herbiberto's got the list."

Castillo didn't like the way Dominguez seemed to be saying he had everything under control when he didn't think so. "Do I have to worry about you?"

"What do you mean?"

"You used to have everything all figured out. I never had to worry about my safety. But now? I won't be able to lift the fucking toilet seat without wondering if it'll trigger a bomb."

Dominguez shook his head in dismissal but didn't respond.

"So how did they know we were coming?"

"As I keep telling you. Enough money buys anything you want. Apparently Guzman found the number."

"What the fuck am I supposed to do? Just let them shop Wal-Mart for someone who'll sell me out? If you can't protect me what good are you?"

Castillo shoved papers and a lamp off of a nearby table. He stepped into Dominguez's face. "You're a worthless piece of shit. Your buddy Hernandez-Anjul isn't the Messenger of old, who killed whoever we said. He still hasn't carried out one simple order, which was to kill that fucking FBI agent. And you don't make him. I paid a lot of money to our friend in the White House to find out who the Agent was. He killed my brother in the Dallas safe house two years ago. Shot him in the head. No mercy. No chance to recover." Castillo relived the whole affair in his mind, feeling the loss of his brother and remembering the cries of anguish from his mother.

Dominguez didn't respond.

Castillo's anger lessen as he refocused. "Not enough bites, big or small." Castillo regretted letting Dominguez push him before he was ready.

"We had evidence they were coming after us." Dominguez reminded Castillo.

Castillo exploded. "Because of the thirteen you hung. We had to act before they did. Why didn't you tell me you hung Guzman's son?"

"He was illegitimate. No one thought Guzman cared about him. He was just doing retail in a Mexico City neighborhood."

Castillo moved back to the window and looked out. "Okay. Next order. I want Guzman dead. I mean really dead, this time. I want him done in public. I want people to see him die over and over again on television. You should use that fucker the Messenger, but he's not reliable. Who else you got? I still can't believe you let the Messenger grow a brain. He should just fucking do what he's told. We're probably sitting here as a result of Guzman thinking I'm weak. Can't even finish off one fucking FBI agent."

"Go sit down. You make me nervous. You might accidently shoot yourself."

Castillo wasn't about to let Dominguez get away with giving him an order. He pushed closer, holding the handgun to his lieutenant's temple. "You let me down. Guzman could have killed me."

Dominguez didn't move; just stared at Castillo. After a moment he calmly said, "You think I'm the problem then just go ahead and pull the God damn trigger." Dominguez returned his gaze to the shadowy outside world beyond the lace curtains.

Castillo pulled the trigger knowing the safety was still on, but he wanted to send a message.

Dominguez glanced at him, snatched the weapon and tossed it into a chair.

Castillo put his hand on Dominguez's shoulder. "Okay. Guzman thinks he won this round. But he has no idea what we're capable of doing to him. So I want you to lay a trap. We need to do this elegantly. I want people to say after Guzman's dead that Castillo's an artist. He didn't just kill the fucker, he desecrated him."

"I'll take care of Guzman in my own way," came across low, but non-threatening.

"No. You'll listen to me and do it my way." Castillo was thinking about special toys he might get help him demonstrate the Zeta's power to the world. A dirty bomb, maybe? "All of Mexico ... no, all-of-the world needs to understand the Zetas rule. I remember that movie. Braveheart. At the end they cut up Wallace and displayed the pieces in different cities. Guzman can be Wallace. In the end we'll cut him up and display the parts of his dead body in different cities as a warning to anyone who might even think about trying to kill me."

"Just like the Arroyo woman?"

Castillo had expressed his unhappiness with the way Sonja Arroyo was handled. It was another fuck up by the Messenger. He would have ordered Dominguez to kill the Messenger, except Dominguez swore by the guy. Castillo wondered what was going on between the Messenger and Dominguez.

"I think I know a direct path to Guzman." Dominguez

informed Castillo, catching him by surprise.

"Yeah? I approve any hit on Guzman. Like I said we've got to desecrate him."

Dominguez was no longer listening.

Marching Orders

Sitting in Eric's DC office Alene was tired. Shuttling back and forth between Dallas and the District was sapping her strength. She thought Eric would let her hold most meetings by Telcon. They'd talked about daily calls as the primary means of communications before she got her apartment in Dallas. Eric's schedule was crowded and the daily calls had been reduced to twice weekly. Now he was less comfortable with the arrangement. The result was long nights on airplanes so she could attend more meetings in person.

The President wanted a report. The ATF gun running was continuing to make the news. Eric might be called to testify before Congress about what he knew. But the ATF situation wasn't her's. So why was Eric making it her problem?

"You need to brief the President about your progress, to put some good news before him. I'm not happy about how long your preparations are taking and need you to advance the mission. I don't care if you have to lead it yourself. You're in charge. Handpicked by the President. He expects you to get the Intel into the hands of the Mexicans without compromising the sources."

Alene heard the anxiety in Eric's voice. She wondered what was causing him to be so agitated. She had to make him understand the possible consequences of his demands. "As I said, we're moving too fast and for the wrong reasons. My team's only had about a week to learn what to do and how to conduct a mission."

"Can't help it. We didn't pick the time the press discovered the ATF had been running guns across the border to try to trace who was buying them."

"I understand. But just listen for a moment. You don't want another situation like the south Texas gun exchange the team broke up. Too many were killed. We didn't know what to expect and the cartel was more prepared for us than we realized."

Eric went to his large window and looked across the square outside. Alene hadn't seen the Attorney General this tense before. There must be more to come out. Apparently something wouldn't be favorable to either Eric or possibly the President himself. She'd have to keep what she didn't know in mind.

"I hear you." Eric said. "It's never a good day when we lose good people. But what's the story with your Ops Director, what's his name?"

"Carr."

"Right. Is he working out or do you need to replace him?"

Alene's antenna went up. She hadn't expected this question. Eric must have heard something, only she couldn't imagine what. "I couldn't ask for anyone better."

"Why am I getting bills for shot up rental cars and tires?"

She was surprised the bills got all the way to Eric, but bureaucracies like to gossip too. She had to be careful how she phrased her response. "I think his name's been passed along to someone on the other side. He seems to be a target."

Eric dropped his head as if he just heard another piece of information he didn't want. He talked more to himself than to her, "Walter's being investigated."

"Josephson? For what?" Alene was incredulous.

"Selling information. Apparently including about what you're doing."

"But why?" She couldn't believe Walter Josephson would do such a thing. She liked and respected him.

"He's been having money problems. Seems his wife's been living beyond their means, expecting he's going to get a big corporate job when he leaves office."

"He's not coming back if the President's re-elected?"

"No. He's already told the President of his intentions to leave."

She didn't know that since there'd been no announcement. "Do you believe the accusation?"

"We were alerted his bank was going to foreclose and he suddenly came up with enough to pay off his mortgage. He was behind on his credit cards to the tune of nearly a hundred thousand dollars. Paid them off as well. Apparently Walter wanted to bury the money so his wife wouldn't go through it. I feel sorry for him." Alene heard a sadness in Eric's voice. He'd worked closely with Walter as the President's Chief of Staff and she knew the President and Eric had immense respect for him.

Alene tried to comprehend the news. "Why didn't Walter just leave early and take the corporate job rather than waiting?"

"Don't know. We can only surmise someone approached him with a deal he couldn't refuse."

"So you think Walter sold information to one of the cartels?"

"The money came through a Dallas firm. Montezuma Produce and Chinese Laundry. We suspect they have ties to the Zetas, but no proof."

She understood the investigators hadn't put all the pieces of the puzzle together. The Administration handlers were trying to understand how big a scandal they had on their hands and when it would make the papers. She understood why Eric was so tense. "When are you going to confront him?"

"When the audit team finishes up. Probably next week. Do you understand why we have to put some good news on the man's desk?"

Alene nodded, still shocked about Walter. She wondered how she'd have to change things if the Zetas or one of the other cartels knew what she and the team were about to do. Then she realized that Walter may have identified Jim to the cartels. If he had, Jim was right about being a target. If Walter had it also meant everything they were about to do would be much harder. She needed some time to think through the implications and plan out a course of action. Another sleepless night on the return flight to Dallas.

The Plan

Alene looked exhausted when she came into the conference room at the El Paso Intel Fusion Center. Her eyes were puffy and somehow even her clothes weren't as neatly pressed as usual. She wasn't a makeup person. She didn't need much and deliberately downplayed her appearance. Normally Alene seemed to radiate. I couldn't take my eyes off her. But today she didn't radiate anything except a perception of fog between herself and the rest of the world.

"You okay?" I asked when she saw me and came over.

"Last Flight back from DC and first out from DFW makes for a very short night."

"What can I do to help you this morning?"

"Coffee?"

"You don't drink coffee." I reminded her.

"I'm making an exception." Her emphasis on 'exception' alerted me to a new determination in her voice, despite her exhaustion. I wondered what happened in her meeting with Eric. I expected we'd learn the answer shortly.

Alene was about to start the meeting when I returned with the coffee. Since she normally didn't drink coffee, I had no idea how she took it and expected she probably didn't either. I was right. She took a sip, made a face and then added one cream. Another sip and a half packet of sugar. Apparently she now knew what worked for her.

"Thanks."

"Anything else I can do for you?"

"Make this mission a success and things will get better for everyone." The coffee was having the desired effect of helping her concentrate. She moved behind the podium. "Gentlemen, please take your seats."

Willy, Colonel Blum, Zed and John McDonald, the graying Texas Ranger who was head of the Texas Intel Fusion Center, responded to her request.

"Our preparation time's over. We have to see if the virtual preparation has helped us. Can we embed in Mexican Army teams to provide just in time Intel that helps them succeed against the Zetas?"

Willy spoke up, "What changed?"

Alene reluctantly answered. "The political situation."

"Here or there?" Willy pushed.

"Both. Everything we're doing's linked. What happens there affects what happens here and vice versa."

Alene just looked so tired, I wanted to help her get through this meeting. "Do we have a plan for getting started?"

"Yes. First mission's tonight. The Intel will come into Jim. He will put together the plan. The Mexican Army will have troops and transport waiting for us outside Nuevo Laredo at Midnight. You'll give the brief once airborne."

"Not an ideal way to conduct a mission, Ma'am." Zed this time.

"I understand your concerns, Command Sergeant Major, but we couldn't get the Intel release any other way. You'll split up in the transport and brief the leads once airborne. The Mexicans will be under radio silence. You'll need to stay close to their commander on the ground to help, but this is and will be a Mexican operation. We aren't there officially. And if our presence comes out, we're only advisors. We have to maintain advisory status."

She looked at me in a way that told me I had to maintain control of the American force and myself during the mission. I couldn't let things get out of control or our whole group might get shut down. The President, the Attorney General and the Mexican government were watching. Everyone wanted to know if what we were attempting could work. I wanted to know too. But I also wanted to find Dad and have my revenge.

"When do I get the Intel?" I asked.

Alene slid a sealed envelope across the table to me. I opened it and quickly read.

The Deadly Maze

Two a.m., I stifled a yawn. Willy and I were dressed in gray camouflage uniforms. We wore night vision goggles pushed up on the top of our helmets. The body armor bulked us up. I held an M-4 assault rifle and sat in the back of a black MH-47G Chinook helicopter with the rest of the assault team. We were flying low over the outskirts of Monterrey, Mexico. Another Chinook followed. We were the lead team. I thought it ironic my Mexican Army counterpart, Major Ricardo Guerrera -- Ronald the Warrior – was designated the mission lead. I didn't know if the fact that his rank, lower than Colonel Blum's, was intentional, but Blum acted as if he didn't notice the slight. Guerrera was the liaison and intelligence officer, but the Mexican Army put him in charge. Unusual. Colonel Blum and his team were officially with us to advise Willy and me. We were the ones to ensure the mission succeeded, with no definition of success apparent. And officially we weren't here.

I had a sense this mission wouldn't go as we hoped. We didn't discuss its location or nature with our Mexican counterparts until we were airborne. The pilots weren't given an exact location, only told to fly to Torreon. We'd give them the last leg once we arrived. Colonel Blum briefed Major Guerrera. Zed, in the other helicopter, provided the same brief to his counterpart, Sergeant First Class Herrera. Delaying the information exchange in this way prevented anyone feeding information to the cartels to give them accurate information about what we were about to do. But still, I just didn't like the situation or the target.

I knew everyone expected heavy resistance. But at 2:30 in the morning we hoped most of the Zetas would be asleep. We expected the factory workers would be toiling through the night.

Usually the local Federales would arrest and shut down crystal meth production. But the intelligence the US provided and the locals verified showed this particular factory was more than just another production site. Most crystal meth factories were small and produced small quantities. This one was much larger-scale, with shipping docks where the raw materials came in and finished goods were loaded on tractor trailers. The crystal meth was shipped to distribution points, both in Mexico and the US. This was big time. Lots of money flowing through. Lots of cash available for bribes, to buy raw materials and to keep the factory workers happy.

I poked Willy who seemed to have zoned out, "You awake?"

"Past my fucking bed time. Why is it these gonzo guys all think the middle of the night's the time to catch the bad guys in their beds?"

"Because whimps like you are asleep. Middle of the night gives the element of surprise. I suppose you'd of just driven up, knocked on the door and asked if they'd mind if you arrested them and stuck them in a federal prison for the rest of their lives?"

"Sounds better to me than roustin' 'em like this."

"C'mon. You'll be back in your hotel room fast asleep before dawn."

Willy tried to scratch an itch, but through everything he wore he couldn't. "Fuck. I must be allergic to body armor."

The helicopter started to descend. I leaned forward to look out the now open door. In the moonlight I saw the factory buildings below. With partial cloud cover the night seemed darker than usual. A good thing for the operation, Blum had explained to me.

As we got closer I saw our target building. And then the 'copter's forward movement stopped. Blum was up on his feet, throwing fast ropes out the door. His troops literally flew to the ropes and disappeared downward. Willy and I followed the men in front of us. In a moment we were sliding down. I wound my feet around the rope to slow as I approached the ground, then stepped quickly away before Willy came down on top of me. I picked up Zed, who'd been in the second 'copter. He motioned us to follow. In a moment both Willy and I were standing with Zed, Major Guerrera, and, only a moment later, Colonel Blum.

Zed used the hand signals he taught us. We took up our rehearsed positions, pulling the night vision goggles over our eyes so we could see more clearly. I felt for the three magazines of ammunition I carried. I wanted to make sure I could reload quickly.

The Zetas had apparently pulled their guards inside as we arrived. None engaged us. I knew many of the Zetas had been Special Forces operators for the Mexican military. They were well trained, could recognize threats well, and had probably rehearsed the defense of this building hundreds of times. So they had the advantage. They knew every inch of the place. The assault team and I had only a sketchy understanding of how the factory was laid out from a former employee now serving time. The information was old. Many surprises surely awaited us. A large number of preset shooting lanes favoring the Zetas would greet us.

I'd been on the ground less than a minute when the breaches occurred. We entered simultaneously at all possible entry points. Shots were fired from within. Zed signaled to his men to enter. He followed them, with us right behind him.

I found myself in a narrow corridor. I had to step over one body wearing a Mexican Army badge to follow Zed onto the factory floor. Here I found tables and an array of equipment. I knew some of the DEA guys I worked with on the Task Force could tell me exactly how this laboratory worked. I didn't think I needed, or particularly wanted to know the details.

Factory workers were everywhere. Some held their hands up

over their heads; others crouched, trying to make themselves smaller targets. A few wearing earphones still worked, ignoring the men with weapons drawn around them. And then the room seemed to fill with gunshots. I took a round into my body armor. The impact threw me backwards. I flashed back to the motor pool at the Dallas police station. But I cut the flashback short, rolled over, and tried to identify where the shots were coming from.

"Into the corridors!" Zed screamed as I saw the flashes of shots coming from very small holes in the walls. I thought of the shoot holes in the walls I'd seen in Rothenburg, Germany, erected in the late 1200s. This factory space seemed to be just as impregnable from the side I was on. We needed to get to the other side of the walls. We could only take them out from there.

Willy crouched low. He returned fire, drawing the attention of the men behind what I expected were fortified walls. The Zetas had planned for an attack. They knew how the drill would go.

I aimed at the first small window I identified. Tap, tap. I drew fire to make sure Willy got out. He went flying onto the floor before me, having taken one or more bullets into his back plate armor.

"Fuck!" was all I heard. I grabbed my friend and quickly dragged him toward the door, taking a round in my armor for the trouble.

In the corridor I watched bullets pass through the wall board over my head. Together we crawled away until I didn't see any bullets coming through.

"You okay?" I nearly had to shout to be heard over the gunfire.

"Fuck me, yeah. What kind of hell hole is this?"

"Stay down. I think Zed went this way."

I crawled along the corridor. An explosion was followed by

another and still more came from around the building. The level of gunfire and explosions rose rapidly for several minutes and then tailed off into brief exchanges.

When we got down the hallway I found a booth-like structure attached to the interior wall. The doorway was open and what was left of a man could be seen slumped against a wall. An AK-47 lay on the floor next to him. Apparently we were using grenades to take out the shooters. I now understood the explosions I'd heard. But we hadn't brought enough grenades to take out all of the men.

We went past several of the shooter rooms and turned a corner. Bullets greeted us. I pushed Willy against the wall. The wall afforded no protection, so I pushed him onto the floor, coming down next to him. I saw down the hallway with my night vision goggles. The flashes from the barrel of the shooter's weapon located him.

I returned fire.

This time I saw the gunman fall into the corridor and lie still. His lack of movement didn't make me feel safe. I fired at places on the body that shouldn't be armor plated. Only then I stepped into the hallway.

Willy followed, "Anybody I know?"

"A gentleman from Jersey?" I replied.

"Hey. I resemble that."

We approached the shooter cage. As we got close, I fired multiple shots at the lock, reached for the door and held my weapon ready to fire with my other hand. As the door swung open, a shooter inside opened fire, his AK-47 set at full automatic. He emptied a clip at us, catching Willy in his chest armor with multiple shots. The impact of the bullets knocked Willy to the ground, but I took the shooter out with a head shot at close range.

No pulse, dilated eyes.

I knelt down over Willy.

"What are ya gonna do, kiss me?" Willy said. I helped him to his feet.

We came upon a room where the Zetas apparently slept. The room was littered with bodies. Most were next to a weapon, but none were alive as far as I could see.

"Fuck me," Willy exclaimed. He followed me into the room. We went through into the next space. Here we found the armory. The locals had enough weapons for hundreds of men. The number of weapons confirmed we were up against a large force. Two of the assault team guarded the space to make sure the Zetas couldn't resupply.

Willy and I passed through into a different corridor, seeing bullet holes through the plaster board. The holes pierced the outside metal walls as well. The shooting had finally stopped. In a moment we entered what must have been the office. Here we found their computer system. Apparently the cartel kept computer records. I knew they'd be very helpful to the Mexican Army in prosecuting whoever they were able to bring in. But part of my responsibility was to download the files. I needed to return with them so our analysts could glean as much as possible.

The computer was evidently processing a report. I removed the external hard drive I brought in my back pack, plugged the drive in and started copying the entire directory. Willy stood guard over me, watching both entrances. Colonel Blum approached, gave the signal to Willy as a friendly. "This what you hoped to find?"

I recognized the voice so didn't look up, "We should learn something."

"Unless they change everything again, knowing we took this site down." Willy pointed out.

"Appears to be a standalone system. But I think we may find a dial up number. Maybe we'll be able to locate the main site and overload it to bring it down." I explained.

"Blind them so they can't see what's going on?" Blum asked.

"From a business side, yeah. But we don't want to destroy their system. We'll want to look through their files at some point."

"It's amazing what you guys can do."

"Nick's the amazing one, not me." I concluded.

"Speaking of the Wizard, did you ever talk to him about whatever it was he was chasing after you about?" Willy asked.

I looked up, unsure. "When was this?"

"Yesterday. Called me because he said you'd apparently changed phones again."

I wondered. The Task Force had given me several phones. I could have been using the wrong one without realizing. "So what'd he want?"

"Said he had some new information on 'the Messenger'. What's that all about?"

I hesitated before answering. "Someone I've been trying to locate."

"What's his name?" Willy asked.

"Miguel Hernandez Anjel, also known as Antonio Morales"

Colonel Blum followed our conversation with more than mild interest.

"Ain't that your asshole buddy from Mexico City?" Willy asked.

"This an internal affair?" Blum asked.

"Why?" I watched the Colonel carefully.

"Miguel Hernandez Anjel's one of our assets."

I froze. The man responsible for killing my brother and kidnapping my father worked for us? I didn't know what to think, but before I got angry I needed to understand what Blum knew. I looked at the computer to ensure the files were still copying, and then stood up to face the Colonel, "What do you mean, asset?"

"We pay him for certain information."

The file copying concluded. I couldn't believe we were paying a murderer for information and he was probably using whatever he learned from us to carry out his killings. I disconnected the external drive and returned it to my back pack.

"Why are you interested in him?" Blum continued.

"A shell casing. His fingerprints are on it. Found in the remains of a ranch house that burned to the ground with three bodies in it near Waco, Texas."

Willy looked at me astonished.

"Who was in that house?" Blum asked.

"My brother and his wife."

"Holy shit, and you've been hanging out with that scumbag?" Willy exclaimed.

"Yeah, well…."

"No wonder you been so fuckin' jumpy the whole time we were down there."

Blum saw where the conversation was going, "We got an op to

finish up. You got everything you need? It's time to let the Mexican Army have access."

Willy piped up as if Blum's comment reconnected a thought for him. "He's a Federale, you know."

"Who is?" Blum asked.

"This guy we been talking about. Hernandez or Morales. Seems to be connected. Wouldn't be surprised he knows all about this deal we're doing here."

Blum nodded now understanding the implications. He looked at his watch, "We got transport outside burning fuel at a fast rate. We need to go, now."

Zed appeared at the door. "You need to come see. Found their stockpile of pseudoephedrine, the controlled ingredient in crystal meth. Edmiston, our Intel guy tells me it's got to be worth several billions of dollars. Yes. Billions, like with a B. No wonder they had this place fortified the way they did."

Four Mexican Army enlisted men in camouflage uniforms came into the room to dismantle the computer.

We stepped aside and followed Zed towards the warehouse. We weren't far down the corridor when the room behind us exploded.

Adjustments

The message came in on Castillo's cell within an hour. Dominguez and Castillo were riding together in a black Volkswagen Phaeton. The car was like a limo inside, but didn't look like one outside. The misleading appearance explained why Castillo preferred the VW to his Mercedes, although Angel was his driver for both.

The message was cryptic, "Monterrey went off line?" Castillo asked not understanding at first. "I know you can't tell me on the phone, but what the fuck do you mean?"

Castillo listened for only a moment and put his cell away. "We need to go back." Angel turned the car around.

Castillo didn't say anything more, apparently thinking through the implications. "How much we paying your guy to tell us what we need to know?"

"Which guy and about what?" Dominguez wasn't walking into anything blind.

"Your Federale, the Messenger. He's supposed to tell us when something's going down that involves us, right?" Castillo phrased the question very carefully.

Dominguez phrased his response as carefully, "We pay him a hundred and twenty thousand pesos a month."

"Well, he's not worth ten pesos."

Dominguez changed tactics. "We can pay him only for specific information."

"I think we'll just kill him instead."

Dominguez was surprised the conversation didn't go like so many others. He also knew Castillo didn't like the Messenger. He wasn't one of Castillo's guys, since Dominguez had recruited him. The failure to kill the FBI agent was probably in the background here. "Okay. Mind telling me why?"

"He just cost me nearly ninety billion pesos. That's billion, not million."

Dominguez had purchased the Monterrey inventory to ramp up production so they could make their scheduled payment. He was able to piece together what had probably happened. "What do we know?"

"Alvaro was cryptic because we don't know who's listening."

"Thought you had a new phone."

"I do, but that doesn't seem to stop someone from tapping into my calls."

Dominguez didn't want to play the game with Castillo. "So Alvaro said Monterrey went off line. Does that mean the phone lines went down, the computer glitched, or is someone taking the system down for some reason?"

"Alvaro wouldn't call about an IT problem."

"He didn't say anything more?"

"Said it went off line in the middle of a report. He called everyone who should have been there. One of them should have answered. No one did."

"So for the time being, all you know for sure is Monterrey went off line." Dominguez tried to keep Castillo focused on facts. He wanted to keep him from declaring war when he was still licking his wounds from the attack on Guzman.

"Alvaro was in a panic. He's not someone who would get that way for nothing."

" Who would have taken us down?"

"That's what I want to know. Had to be the government. You know how much we're spending on security in Monterrey alone? Twelve million pesos a year. Not even Guzman would have been crazy enough to try to go after us in Monterrey."

"Somebody on the inside?" Dominguez asked to keep Castillo from jumping to conclusions.

"Who? The operations are all family. Had to be to keep everyone loyal. Just too much cash and pseudoephedine to put in the hands of strangers."

"Everyone happy with what you're paying?"

Castillo was contemptuous of Dominguez' question. "Reward for information? Nobody there was going to get off the gravy train. I mean what would the government have paid? A few thousand pesos? Would have to be millions to make taking the chance worthwhile. If the Army came up with a big reward we'd have known. Wouldn't we?"

Dominguez had to consider the question. He had multiple sources who would have alerted him if a big reward were posted. They would have notified him if the Army were launching a raid against them. So how could someone have pulled off a take down on what he thought to be their most secure site? "I don't think there was a reward. But just supposing there was, you can be sure whoever turned us in won't live to collect it."

"See. Even you aren't sure. We got to find out how this happened. Who was involved? Why Monterrey? Is the President trying to send us a message? If they got our pseudoephedrine, how do we get it back? Ninety billion pesos is a lot of fucking money. I'm not going to just roll over and let someone pick my pocket. You need to get it back. I don't care if they're storing it in the fucking Presidential Palace. You find a way."

Dominguez nodded, "Ninety Billion," as his mind worked overtime.

"If the site is down, we have to get back into production immediately. The only way we can is with our raw materials. We were trying to corner the supply so Juarez couldn't ship. If we can't supply our customers, they'll start buying from Juarez. We can't let that happen. "

"We just saw how money got us into Guzman's compound. I'm not discounting someone took a bribe and left a door open. If a small well-armed group had gotten inside and knew where to go, they might have been able to take it off line. You think it was probably the government, but I'm not convinced."

"Run it down. We should know when we get back. If it's on television news we'll know all we need to know about who. If not, then your little exercise about finding out which cartel might be needed. You're thinking Juarez, not Sinaloa?" Castillo opened a different window.

"Could a been Sinaloa. As you said, the other cartels watched us go after Guzman, they could a thought now was the time to strike. Everyone's jockeying for position because they see the old agreements are collapsing."

"Particularly if the Army's coming after us." Castillo was going back to where he started.

"So if it was the Army, and we didn't get any warning, how could they pull it off?" Dominguez couldn't reconcile why no one had warned them.

Castillo confirmed what Dominguez wondered, "If it was the Army I'll have to have a conversation with my guy at the White House. He should be able to confirm if they were involved." His tone turned nasty, "And if I find out that fucking FBI agent was, I'll have your balls on my desk along with the Messenger's head."

Dad

We were going right back at them the next night. I put together the plan and we began walk-throughs in the sim. Willy and I finished with Zed about five o'clock. We'd identified a lot of unknowns and potential problems. The sim time was intended to make sure we had an approach to address each area. Zed came up with several good ideas and Willy and I were able to execute them quickly.

Getting on the same page with Willy and Zed was important. I felt good that we'd be able to respond appropriately, but I didn't feel as good about the mission itself. So the strike had to be quick, dropped in from the air. We had to bring everything we needed with us. We devised a plan requiring twice as many men. The Mexican Army wasn't happy with our request for four MH-47s, four Apaches and one hundred and forty troops to meet us in Reynoso at midnight. They'd asked about how much fuel they'd need. I was concerned information might be relayed about our mission to someone we didn't want to know. We needed to disguise its nature as much as we could. I told the Mexican Army they needed full tanks as we had multiple missions on the docket and wouldn't make a final decision about which one or ones until we met at midnight. If the message I sent was relayed, it would diffuse the preparations at the other end since no one would know for sure where we'd strike.

Alene came by to see me. "Are we ready?"

"You watched our preparations. How'd we look?"

"I'm just glad I don't have to watch when you're doing a real mission." There seemed to be something behind her statement I couldn't quite grasp.

"That bad?"

She didn't answer my question. "What can go wrong?"

"We have twice the people to carry, much further to go, a more difficult target to secure and an unknown set of defenses. Other than that, it's a piece of cake."

"How are you feeling about it?" She wanted to get at something and for some reason didn't want to come right out and ask me.

"I'm feeling better about you."

"What do you mean?"

"You look a lot more rested than yesterday morning. Nothing like a win to get people back in line behind you."

She nodded, "Took off a lot of pressure. On both sides."

"Your strategy worked. We conducted the most successful raid on the Zetas, ever. And only because no one could leak what we were doing."

"Now that we've gotten one under our belt, I need you to do it all again. And tomorrow as well."

I almost censored my response, but then didn't to watch where the cards fell, "How about one at a time? We need to establish a battle rhythm, and not just between you and me."

She didn't respond right away. "We only have one win. I need you to stay focused. This isn't a short term deal. I need you ..." she hesitated, searching for the right words. I was hoping she'd stop there, but she didn't. "I need you to up your game each time we go out. It won't get any easier."

"To answer your original question, I'm uncomfortable. My

discomfort has both a good and a bad side. If I'm uncomfortable I'll be twice as focused to make sure everything goes right. The bad side is I think a lot more can go wrong tonight than can go right. I have to react at the first signs of the unexpected, and keep everyone focused."

"More important, you have to come back."

I hesitated, initially hoping she was saying what I wanted her to say, but then another thought occurred to me. "You're thinking about our little conversation about ending things."

She nodded.

"I'm not so blind as to think I can walk through a river of bullets without one hitting me. A lot of people will be trying to make sure I don't come back tonight. When I talked with you last week, I knew a lot of people wanted me dead. I thought you were on the list. I still think you know things you haven't told me."

"Just come back and then we can work through your concerns."

"It took me a long time not to see Lexie every time I look at you. But now I'm learning things about you."

"Like?"

"Discovering you like milk and half a sugar with your coffee, because you don't really drink it."

She finally smiled. But then my cell phone rang.

"Hello, Jim?"

"Yes."

"This is Jan, Alene's administrator."

"She's right here, just a minute." I started to hand the phone to

Alene.

"Jim? Wait a second. I have a call for you. Came in on your line here. Says he's your father."

My heart stopped as did my breathing, "Put him through." Had he been released? Was it really him? Or were the Zetas trying to send a message to me? "Dad??"

"Jim?"

Only one word, but I'd heard him say it so many times the nuances echoed through my mind. He sounded weaker than I remembered; tired maybe. "Yes, Dad."

Alene watched my reactions carefully, but respectfully.

"I'm not free to talk."

I had trouble getting my voice to work, "That's okay."

"I have a loaded handgun pointed at my head. I've been told to tell you these men will kill me and you, unless you step away. Go back to your old job and let the Mexicans solve their own problems."

"Would you have me step away after they killed Bill and Janice?"

"Bill and ... ??"

"They killed them, Dad. And burned the house to the ground. Everything you built is gone."

"I didn't know." He sounded shaken.

"I can't step away until you're back with me, and Bill and Janice's killers are in jail or dead."

"Dead would be better." And he was gone.

I had Dad's blessing to follow the path I'd chosen. Clearly not what his captors had wanted or expected to be the result of the call. Alene looked at me. "Your father's okay?"

I had to refocus on Alene and not say what I was thinking. "For the moment, but they still have him." Dad was alive! But for how long? I simply didn't know how much time I had, nor how I'd find him, but I would .... somehow.

Swinging for the Fences

I'd checked with Lon who affirmed the Zetas chose Ciudad Victoria to be their stronghold. I thought the choice curious, Ciudad Victoria is the capital city of the state of Tamaulipas. The cartel probably had every major political official on their payroll.

Corrupt politicians complicated the mission. I couldn't rely on the locals to assist. If anything, we should expect the locals to be outright hostile to us coming in. If we took down the Zetas they'd lose bribes representing a significant part of their income. Quite possibly the local officials might end up in prison with the Zetas who survived the raid.

I checked my watch. Three-thirty in the morning. This time four MH-47 helicopters carried one hundred and forty Mexican soldiers along with Special Operators from both Mexico and the US. The helicopters also carried the US Law Enforcement officials consisting of Willy and me. As with the last raid, I obtained the most up to date intelligence: where the Zetas were, and what kind of protection they had in place.

Several agents tried to penetrate the Zetas, but had disappeared. Several shipments of weapons destined for Ciudad Victoria had been intercepted at the border, though for every shipment we seized, probably ten or more got through. The Zetas were armed with the latest weapons, we could be sure.

So again, I went into the lion's den. Only this time, there would be many more lions. The Zetas would be more dug in than at the Monterrey factory. I expected them to be focused on destroying our whole team. The Zetas wanted to send a message to the Mexican and

US governments. They'd stand up to anything we sent their way.

Flying behind the four Chinooks were two Apache helicopter gunships. They were intended to take out any barriers the team couldn't penetrate from the ground. Two more Apaches were stationed within ten minutes to provide additional backup if needed. Anything closer would have made obvious an Op was in work.

As last time, Colonel Blum briefed Major Guerrera once airborne. I knew Zed was doing the same with Sergeant First Class Herrera in the trailing 'copter.

Willy and I were seated next to each other, "Blum mentioned he expects the defending cartel sicarios will be going for headshots." I said. "So keep your head down."

"Headshots? That's good. Means I'll never know what hit me." Willy remarked.

"Means you need to do the same."

"Next thing you'll be telling me is to wait 'til I see the god-damn whites of their eyes. Who the hell are you? John Paul fucking Jones?"

Willy back to his usual level of profanity helped me relax. When he went silent Willy wasn't up for the mission. He couldn't multi-task when he was trying to work through something. I knew we were getting close now. We'd be going into the fray real quick.

I heard the high pitch sound of the blades change. We were slowing and beginning the descent. The target villa our Intel bubbas had identified as Castillo's home was in the center of the city. Of course his home was the largest on the street, but surrounded by lots of other families. Blum had explained Castillo had made a deliberate choice. He wanted to make an attack on him involve innocent women and children. Castillo wanted to make sure we couldn't determine which men were cartel members, and which were innocent. He sought any opportunity to make the attacking force hesitate. Any hesitation gave the defenders another instant of advantage. Any advantage in the special operations world generally spelled the difference between life and death.

Colonel Blum motioned to us to get ready. Just like in Monterrey we wanted to maintain air cover and not give the defenders a stationary target to attack. All four Chinooks would drop in their forces simultaneously at the four intersections around the villa, and then back off.

Colonel Blum moved to the other end of the door. I soon had the rope in my hands. My first view of Ciudad Victoria presented itself as I went out the door. The Apaches moved into position over the Villa. The first sounds were of the .50 cal machine guns on the Apaches as they fired. Their targets were men on the roof of the villa.

I unwound at the bottom and stepped back just as Willy hit the ground. As we turned toward Zed the Special Operator who'd been sitting on the other side of Willy hit the ground and followed us as well.

Zed wasn't waiting for anyone this time. He advanced toward the target villa, keeping low and close to the buildings. I ran to catch up. Willy did his best but had fallen behind. In a moment, lights started coming on in the houses around us. I expected gunshots any moment. But the only sound disturbing the night came from the helicopters and the occasional machine gun fire from the Apaches. No one came into the street.

As we reached the villa, I recognized the door from the simulation. As I turned to look for Willy, what sounded like a hundred engines started up all at once around me.

Garage doors flung open. Armored buggies launched into the street from nearly every house. Each one had three shooters; one in the passenger seat and two in the back facing the rear. The sound seemed like *Cinco de Mayo*, with the fireworks engulfing us.

I took a hit into my armor plate from behind, which threw me to the ground behind Zed. Cutting the expected flashback, I got into a crouch with my back to Zed. The two of us lay down suppressing fire at the vehicles around us. Aim, two shots. Aim, two shots. Aim, two shots. Willy finally joined us and the cadence of our shots. Aim, two shots. Aim, two shots. Aim, two shots.

I went for the drivers first to disable the vehicles. The drivers were wearing armor, and kept hunched down -- difficult to hit. I slowed down my shooting, took better aim for the head and found success.

"Head shots. We got body armor." I called out.

Willy took out the shooters as soon as the vehicle ran off the street.

The other troops had formed up to provide cover for each other. All were starting to have success against the hundred or more armored buggies rushing at us from all directions.

I caught sight of windows opening on the upper floors of the houses all around us. "Look up. We got more company."

I raised my M-4 and took out each person I found, one at a time. My M-4 was equipped with the M-203 grenade launcher. I saw what looked to be a machine gun in one of the windows and launched a grenade. No one would be joining the battle from there any time soon.

One of the buggies targeted us. The front armor made it hard to find the driver. I launched another grenade, dropping it into the back seat. The explosion took out all four passengers at once. Only the now dead driver didn't hit the brakes. The vehicle kept coming right at us.

"Gotta move!" I yelled, pressing back hard against Zed and pushing Willy away. I scrambled to my feet. The vehicle ran over the spot where we'd been only a moment before and crashed into the villa behind us. I rose up enough to check the driver and shooters. Dead. My movement caught the attention of another shooter. I felt a round hit my armor and ricochet off, piercing my left ear lobe. The bullet knocked off my helmet. The heat of the round scorched the side of my face. I didn't have time to scan the area for the shooter.

Willy did. A single shot removed the threat. I put my helmet back in place.

Zed, Willy, and I backed into each other again. We crouched down to minimize our profile and picked up locating and eliminating shooters.

The momentum shifted. A hand carried missile was launched. The sound caught everyone's attention. One of the two Apaches exploded. The other gunship made a frantic sweep in an effort to escape. Another missile was fired. The first Apache crashed into a building a block away, setting it on fire.

The second Apache came down hard on the street. I saw the crew scramble out alive. But we still didn't know where the missiles were coming from. The MH47s hovered not far away. We'd lost our air cover and had no idea what to expect.

The Mexican Army spread out to check out where other missiles might be. One defender stepped to the front of an open garage door with a shouldered TOW launcher. He was cut down by shooters from several different locations before he could launch.

I turned back to the buggies. They continued to attack us and I got back into the rhythm. Tap, tap.

The battle raged on for more than a half hour. But finally the last buggy was taken out of commission. The shooters were all dead. Not one surrendered. I scanned the third floor windows.

"No targets!"

Zed made hand signals to the squad and fire team leaders. We advanced again toward the house.

"You think they know we're here, yet?" Willy whispered.

"Doubt it." I whispered back. Zed ignored our irreverence. He set the teams for the breech. I was to follow two of Zed's men. Willy came up behind me. Zed raised his hand with all five fingers up, and then counted down until he clenched his fist. All teams hit the breech together. I didn't have time to think. At the last moment I remembered to change my clip so I'd have thirty rounds inside.

Two Special Operators blew the door. One peeked inside, got a visual and then entered. I had my M-4 ready. I followed the men into what was apparently the kitchen. I saw coffee cups. I could smell the coffee brewing. No sign of anyone, but they'd been here just a few minutes before. We did a quick clear of the rooms on the first floor, not finding anyone. I followed Zed's hand signals and we moved into position at the base of the stairwell. I'd known the stairwell would be the most dangerous part of the mission. I dreaded what we had to do next, but the stairs probably lay between us and Castillo.

Willy and I took the front and back cover positions, meaning we'd be watching for any shooters who might appear on the upper floors. In this case we had to cover two floors.

"No movement." I said just loud enough for the team to hear.

"Check." Willy responded.

A Mexican Special Operator started up the stairs with his weapon up. I saw movement from the third floor. "Shooter." I called. Two shots and I took him out. The shooter fell over the railing, landing on the first level next to me. I put another round through the man's head, just to be sure he wouldn't resurrect and kill one of us.

The Special Operator raced to the top of the stairs just as a dozen or more shooters came to the railing on the third floor. Willy and I held our positions. We targeted in each shooter, taking two shots at each. We dropped them one at a time. Some came over the railing and others fell back. Those who fell back were problematic for us. We couldn't be sure if they were dead, wounded or just resting and ready to come at us again.

The other two Special Operators contributed to the return fire. Both Willy and I took rounds into our armor plate. We were able to recover quickly and continue to take down the shooters.

I replaced my clip, knowing I only had one more.

A grenade dropped to the floor near me. Without thinking I stepped forward and kicked it like a soccer ball into the kitchen. The grenade exploded only a second later, but the kitchen walls contained most of the shrapnel. I brought my weapon up to sight, not having time to consider what I'd just done.

Movement on the third level. Not early enough for me to lock on the target. I waited. Quiet settled over us, even though I knew people all through the house were searching for the leader of the Zetas.

Another grenade came down the stairwell. "Grenade," I yelled and dove away. I figured the Zeta held the grenade longer to eliminate the chance to kick it.

The grenade actually exploded before hitting the ground with a bright flash but no shrapnel. We were lucky. Had it been a regular grenade we would have been dead. My ears were ringing and the explosion made my head ache, but I was still alive.

I brought up my M-4 and pumped two M203 grenades onto the third floor then moved to the other side of the stairwell and pumped off two more.

I saw a man slump against the stairwell railing. I fired a single shot into the back of his head.

Willy and the other special operator took positions of cover on the stairwell. We saw no more movement. I started up the stairs, scanning in every direction. On the second level I joined the Mexican Special Operator. Willy slowly came up to join us. The US Special Operators stayed on the first floor to cover the stair well as we cleared the rooms on the second floor. We were on the bedroom level. We went through each room, one at a time.

No one.

We gathered again at the stairwell, provided cover for the Mexican to make the trip to the third level. No resistance. We followed him up, single file, continuing to provide cover.

When all three of us reached the landing, one of the Mexican Special Operators went to a closed door to the right. He turned the knob, just as I yelled, "No!"

He pulled the door open just a few inches before a blast threw him back, killing him instantly. As the smoke cleared we pushed into the empty room.

Crossing the hallway, another Mexican Special Operator moved to the left of the door and reached over to open it. He turned the knob and pushed the door open. Nothing. He peeked around into a single blast to the face, killing him instantly.

The Zeta guard moved his aim to me, but wasn't fast enough. I placed two shots into the center of his forehead.

The guard fell backward revealing four others. They fired simultaneously.

Willy and I dove to the opposite sides of the doorway, taking hits in our armor. I was too close to use the grenade launcher.

I took a flash bang grenade from my vest, pulled the pin and slowly rolled it into the room.

The grenade exploded, stunning the occupants.

We were in through the door, taking their weapons away before they could see again. We kept them covered.

I discovered a tall craggy-faced man cowering at the far end of the room. He wasn't Ruben Castillo, but realized from the defenders set around him, he must be someone important. He rubbed his eyes from the flash bang, apparently unharmed.

I hit the push to talk button dangling from my chest. "Secure here. We have someone, but not our objective. Third floor. Could use some help."

Within a couple of minutes we had more help than we needed. Colonel Blum and Major Guerrera came into the room together. Neither could confirm the identity of our prisoner, but Guerrera led him, handcuffed, out of the room.

Colonel Blum inspected us. I had blood and burn marks on my face and the missing piece of my left earlobe. I was dazed from the explosions, the mad rush of the assault and exhausted from the street battle. I was trying to understand whether we'd accomplished anything since Castillo wasn't here. We'd tipped our hand and not walked away with the prize. Alene would be disappointed in me. I wasn't looking forward to telling her I'd failed. I didn't know when we'd get another clear shot at the top guy. We'd not disrupted the Zetas the way we intended. But tomorrow would be another chance to get things back on track.

"Looks like you could use a little attention. Glad you kept your head down."

I noticed a bandage around his left bicep. "Looks like you didn't escape."

"I'll recover." Blum shrugged off my observation then brought us back to reality. "We were never here, so we better catch our ride before someone decides to ask some questions.

Failure

Alene wasn't in the mood for excuses until she saw Jim's missing ear lobe and the burn mark on his face. Then she softened. "You okay?"

"Richochet. Just didn't get out of the way fast enough." Jim answered.

Alene remembered the mission briefing. "I thought Blum told you to keep your head down."

"He did."

"But you weren't listening. Or were you just trying to be the hero and do it all yourself? You've got a team around you. You don't need to be leading the charge. You don't need to be the one who takes Castillo down personally. You just need to be there when it happens."

She was angry at Jim. Not because he didn't get Castillo, but because he hadn't been able to escape without injury. All the warnings were there that he was going to do things his way. Be reckless to take down the cartel if that was what it took. If this had been the audition he would have flunked and Alene would have moved on to the next guy on the list. Or would she have?

She needed results and fast. Would the next guy have been able to prepare in a week as Willy and Jim had? Would the next guy have taken down billions in Pseudoephedrine? Would she give up where the team was because she was afraid Jim would get himself killed trying to get revenge and bring his father home? The team hadn't scored the coup she or they wanted in Ciudad Victoria, but the team had further disrupted the Zetas. The team had someone important, but hadn't been able to figure out who he was as yet. The buggy drivers had taken out six of our men, and one-hundred and two Mexican soldiers. But when the sun came up the Mexican Army counted over four hundred and forty bodies of others who had lost their lives that night. Alene wished she knew if they had all been cartel or if her team had truly killed innocent bystanders? The Zetas had set it up so it would be impossible for the invaders to tell which were which. The adverse publicity would fall to the Mexican Army since the team wasn't there, at least officially. But she was never sure when the media would get wind of things. She dreaded seeing articles about how the Mexican Army was suddenly being more effective in the war against the cartels. Such a story would cause people to start asking questions she and the President weren't ready to answer.

"What's the plan for tonight?" Jim asked.

"Did you hear what I said?" She wasn't going to let him sidestep.

"Assume I've heard and will comply unless I tell you differently."

Alene dug in. "No. We're not going to work that way. I told you right up front you have to follow my direction or you're off the team. Now what's it going to be?"

Jim looked at her expressionlessly until she looked away. She knew Jim knew what was bothering her. And now she'd have to give him some room to maneuver. "What's the plan for tonight?"

She wouldn't look into his eyes, "The Intel hasn't been released by Washington. They're reviewing what went wrong last night."

"That the official estimate? Something went wrong because we didn't take Castillo down?" Jim asked as if surprised, although she could see he was thinking he shouldn't be.

"Not yet. But most likely." She sounded discouraged.

Jim decided he needed to cheer her up. "So when can we finish that discussion from yesterday that got cut short?"

"Your father."

"The one before that."

She thought back, "The one about needing you …"

Jim cut her off before she could say more. "Yes, that one."

"…to up the stakes?" She remembered.

Jim hesitated then asked, "Am I?"

"What? Upping the stakes? Yes."

"No, taking my game up correspondingly to what you need? Am I fulfilling your expectations? Am I what you want?"

"In an Ops Director? You're the best I've ever had. Why?" She didn't go where Jim seemed to want her to go. She couldn't.

"You're the best Director I've ever worked for."

"The way you describe Bud I'm not sure if that's a compliment." She laughed.

"It's a compliment. I don't give them often or freely so please take it."

Her face lit up and she relaxed, finally. "When I was in high school I dated the captain of the football team."

"Were you a cheerleader?"

"No, captain of the debate and chess teams. Anyway, I went out with this guy for a month, or something like that, and then it finally hit me."

"What?" Jim asked, apparently surprised she was talking about herself which she rarely did with anyone. She was surprised too that she was telling him embarrassing things about herself.

"He never complimented me. I had a GPA twice his, had been accepted to Harvard on a major scholarship, and had done it all on my own. And yet I wasn't consequential because he was the football player."

"What's he doing now?" Jim asked her.

"Selling cars for his father's dealership. Probably own it someday, but that's all he was ever going to be after playing football in college. He was never going to go pro, too small and he just didn't have the arm. But he was the one who walked on water because he played football."

"Are you comparing me to him?"

She was surprised by his question, "Yeah, I think so. You've given me the benefit of the doubt since the first day. You've paid me a compliment, actually your eyes have paid me a lot of compliments. You seem to appreciate me in a good way. That's important in a relationship."

"Having a relationship with you is important to me."

She couldn't take it the next step, so she didn't respond.

Upping the Stakes

Alene called Eric at seven p.m. mountain time, knowing it was nine p.m. Eastern. She also knew he'd been at work since six a.m. Eastern. The call from Jim's father was still bothering her. When she'd read the reports about his being kidnapped the situation was somehow all abstract. What happened didn't really touch her personally. Just another case like all the others the Justice Department handled every day. Having watched Jim talk with his father and realizing it was like her talking with hers, knowing Jim's father was in the hands of killers, the situation sudden became very real. And very personal.

Her call was scrambled using a device that fit neatly over the mouthpiece of the hotel phone. Had to be a land line. Too easy to intercept cellular.

"Yes, Eric, that's the intent. We want to create instability and chaos in the Zetas. Two nights in a row should have them off balance so we can come back tomorrow night."

"How many nights can you keep this pace up?"

"I don't know. I expect Jim will tell me when we've pushed as far as we can."

"Jim? That Carr?"

"Yes, my Ops Director. He's done a great job even though we didn't get Castillo, and he has tomorrow night well planned and rehearsed."

"He goes in with them?"

"Yes. Senior person on the ground if that ever becomes an issue."

"The President's grateful to you and your team for the action you took. You helped the Mexican Army set records for seized merchandise and materials. But we're holding on tomorrow's mission. We want to take a look at why you didn't achieve your objective before you keep pressing. Besides, your team must be exhausted after two nights in a row."

Alene was disappointed with the judgment against her plan, but she knew Eric was right about how tired the team must be. She could see it in Jim's eyes and Willy seemed to shuffle more than normal. She changed the subject to answer a question she had, "The Intel hadn't identified the amount of pseudoephedrine we found."

"Seems Carr's been able to pull rabbits out of his hat. Did the same thing on that cocaine deal a while back."

"Jim works exceedingly hard to identify situations having the biggest potential impact on the bad guys. He recommended both of those targets, and both proved important beyond our expectations in disrupting cartel operations and hitting them in the pocketbook."

"Is that why they're working so hard to take him out?"

Alene had to seriously consider Eric's comment. Would the Zetas up their game if they realized Jim was behind the Monterrey and Ciudad Victoria operations? Why'd the Zetas have his father call now? Had they already figured out Jim's role?

"I don't know. Could be."

"You heard what happened to the pseudoephedrine?"

"No." She wondered why she hadn't been briefed.

"You ever heard of Juan Dominguez?"

"Castillo's reputed deputy?"

"Yes. Well he intercepted the truckers who were hauling it from the Monterrey site. Trucks have disappeared along with the drivers."

"How do you know Dominguez was involved?"

"One of our street sources in Mexico City. Confirmed Dominguez paid the hijackers in cash."

"How credible's the source?"

"He was one of the hijackers."

"He know where they took the drugs?"

"Unfortunately no. The Zetas switched drivers. Had one who did the snatch and another who did the delivery. Typical of Dominguez."

"So no one has the whole story."

Alene was beginning to wonder if all her team was doing to help the Mexicans was worthwhile? After billions worth of pseudoephedrine were seized, the cartel was able to simply hijack it back. What was the use? The idea was to make the drug trade uneconomical for the cartels. The current approach wasn't working. Even when the rules were changed, the cartels simply took back what was confiscated from them. "So at the end of the day, our massive bust had very little effect."

"On the contrary. You shut down a major source of meth amphetamines coming into the US. As a result, millions of dollars of drug sales aren't going on today."

"But they'll be back in production tomorrow and selling again on Thursday. Who are we kidding here, Eric?" She was starting to understand Jim's comments about whether what they were doing was worth the lives and cost.

"Can't worry about unintended consequences, Alene. We need to disrupt and keep the Zetas off balance so they can't do the basics like producing and distributing drugs. We have to make it unprofitable, untenable and infeasible for them to stay in business. That's the only way we win."

"If they'd destroyed that pseudoephedrine, I'd feel a whole lot better about accomplishing what we'd set out to do. But with them taking it back just because we didn't think through security amazes me."

"Oh, we did think through security. Our recommendation was destroy in place."

"What does that tell you? Someone on the inside's pulling the strings."

Eric changed the topic. "We can only focus on those things in our control. You're doing great. Just pace yourself."

She thought about the leak in the President's office. "Sure. Tell me about Walter."

"Josephson? What's to tell?" She knew from his reaction Eric didn't want to discuss Walter.

"That's what I'm asking you. Have we indicted him?"

"About to."

"Clear evidence then?"

"Yes. He was selling information."

"About what I'm doing in Mexico?"

Eric hesitated, "I have to be careful here. We have recorded a verified call from a prominent cartel leader this week."

"And what did this cartel leader want to know?"

"Whether your team was involved in the Monterrey raid."

Alene couldn't understand why Walter would pass along information on her ops when there were so many more important things that would have been much more damaging and much more valuable. "Anything else?"

"Whether your Ops Director was involved."

Alene hesitated. She'd been looking for the leak that had caused Jim to be targeted. She'd hoped Walter wasn't in the middle. "By name?"

"Yes, by name."

Alene hung her head. The leak was much worse than she'd thought. Someone had found a sympathetic ear so close to the President. She'd never be able to explain what had happened to Jim. "And was the call from the same cartel?"

"Yes."

Alene finally understood all Jim had said was true. He wanted her to believe him, support him. He wanted more, clearly more of a relationship, but she just didn't know if she could go there with him. She wanted to; she needed to. But fear that he might not come back from a mission she sent him on kept pulling her back. Hope was fleeting.

Necessity

Juan Dominguez ate a steak. He only ate steak when he was planning to kill someone. Across from him at an otherwise empty table for four in a Monterrey club called The Blue Moon was Ruben Castillo, who ate salmon. Castillo wasn't going to kill anyone .... himself. Two days had passed since the raid on Castillo's home in Tamaulipas and they couldn't go home yet.

"What do you think the indictment of Walter Josephson means?"

Castillo finished chewing before answering. "Nothing. They can't trace anything back to us. Josephson wrote out the information he gave us and mailed the only copy, which I have. The money went through the laundry in Dallas."

"So why'd the Justice Department indict Josephson? He's the God damn President's Chief of Staff?"

"You think we were the only ones Josephson was selling information to?"

Dominguez shook his head -- a stupid assumption. "Explains why we didn't get any warning."

Castillo smiled, "Guess he had other things on his mind. Like jail."

Dominguez wanted to reset the discussion on his terms, "Maybe so, but the Army captured Juan Carlos and as your CFO he has all the financial records."

"Had access. I shut that down. Juan Carlos won't talk and they'll never figure out who he is without evidence."

Dominguez had to push back so he'd establish his value to Castillo.

"I think you're overly confident. We don't know what the Army knows and without our ears in the White House, it's going to be harder to find out."

"This is where your friend the Messenger can redeem himself. He has those contacts with the American Army. I know he's been feeding them bullshit. Now's the time for him to get real information for us."

"Done. But that's not going to be enough. We need to make an immediate statement. We know the Americans were there, and…."

"And the fucking FBI agent was right in the middle of it. If I'd had his head on my desk like I told you, we'd be eating at home and not in this shit hole." Dominguez walked right into his anger. He had to recover and there wasn't much time. Dominguez had an idea. He wasn't ready, but he had no choice.

"I've been thinking…"

"I don't pay you to think, I pay you to kill and make me money."

Dominguez waited out Castillo's anger. "Look at history. When things got tough the Americans left Viet Nam. If we up the stakes public opinion will turn and their media will ask, why are they fighting us?"

"The American public doesn't even know their government's involved."

"Exactly. We need to embarrass the government. Expose

them."

Castillo didn't respond immediately, which Dominguez saw as a good thing. He was considering what Dominguez had to say, which sometimes he didn't do.

"What do you have in mind?" opened the door for Dominguez.

The Fire Storm

A week later Willy and I had returned to Dallas to plan the now delayed third raid. Since we didn't get Castillo, Washington asked for a strategy review.

At three-thirty seven p.m. a white Chevy van pulled up in front of Bryan Tower on Olive Street in the heart of downtown Dallas. Seven men led by Juan Dominguez exited the van and removed large packages from the rear. Each moved towards the entrance at a leisurely pace. Each glanced up at the forty-five story building. The van driver moved across the street to back into a space in the short term parking in front of the parking garage. The van's motor continued running.

The lobby guard addressed the seven men as they approached his desk, "Can I help you gentlemen?"

Dominguez answered in nearly flawless English, "We have a scheduled meeting."

"With whom?" the guard demanded. It was the last thing he'd ever say. A bullet pierced his brain from a silenced 9 mm Glock pistol. Dominguez moved the guard out of sight and took his badge and key card. The monitors showed multiple locations around the building including the foyer outside the Rapid Reaction Force offices. Dominguez disabled the camera. One of his men went to the elevator and pushed the call button. The others removed the wrappings over their AK-47s. By the time the elevator arrived, all of them had their weapons checked and chambered.

All seven boarded the elevator together. Dominguez pushed the button for 44 and didn't say a word during the assent. The mission had been practiced multiple times. Dominguez knew exactly how much time he had to get in and get out and when to meet the driver who'd be at the front door.

When the elevator door opened, the assaulters quickly approached the entrance. Dominguez used the guard's key card. He pulled the door open and stood aside so his team could enter. The team set up their firing positions in two columns, moving to the right and left of the corridor into the outer office space. Alene's office was immediately to the left of the entrance. Her administrator, Jan, controlled access into the back rooms. She became the second casualty of the raid. But before she died, she pushed the alarm.

The Task Force members closest to the doors moved into defensive positions. The short corridor into the back rooms provided no protection. Both of the lead assaulters opened fire on agents, killing them instantly, but went down quickly from return handgun fire. Those behind used them as shields while setting up automatic fire. The intruders filled the room with bullets.

Willy and I made our way to the weapons cabinet, unlocked it, rammed a magazine into each M-4 and chambered a round. We passed each weapon along to the rest of the team still in the bull pen. Willy and I took the last weapons from the cabinet and stuffed several extra magazines into our belts. We moved in opposite directions without having to say a word.

All of the remaining assaulters except Dominguez moved into the bull pen. They took up positions to pick off my team mates one at a time. Our side now began to return fire in a coordinated fashion. I felt wind rushing through the room. The windows had been the first casualties. Papers and smoke flew. The smell of cordite aroused me. I knew I'd returned to battle. I knew I could die at any moment. I also knew everyone else on the team would die if Willy and I didn't do our jobs. The team counted on us to set up a cross fire.

I lay on my stomach and inched towards the corridor leading

to the elevator foyer. I had to get behind the assault team. Willy worked his way around from the other side to also get behind the assaulters.

The distance wasn't far, but the wind and the smoke made it hard to hear or see. The last thing I wanted to do was shoot one of our guys. So I had to positively ID each and every person I fired at.

I didn't know how many came in, didn't know where they were but expected to find intruders on both sides. My first shot would give away my position and I would have to pull back. I thought through my options as I crawled to a point close to the corridor.

The scene was worse than I imagined. Bodies on the floor. Not a single window intact. Four gunmen, shooting at anything moving. By some miracle the active intruders I could see were all to my right with the exit and two downed men to my left. I took a look to the left but couldn't see anyone else. That didn't mean no one was there. The four men to my right were shooting two-shot bursts, just as I'd been taught.

I raised my weapon and took out the closest gunman from behind with a shot to the back of the head. The other three turned and fired on me. The intruders now knew they'd been flanked. They needed to find cover. One rolled a smoke grenade towards me, but after it exploded, the wind sucked the smoke out of the building. In a moment I could see the gunmen again. I took out the closest man with a single shot.

The other two turned their fire on me. Willy reached his position on the other side. He touched off a few rounds, wounding one, but didn't put him down. This sent the two remaining gunmen scurrying for cover from another direction. The intruders had identified their adversaries. They divided their sectors of responsibility. Each fired a few shots into the bull pen and then a few shots towards Willy and then me.

More fire came from the bull pen. Each of the assaulters tossed smoke grenades into the room. Again the smoke was sucked out. A flash-bang grenade exploded, momentarily blinding anyone who hadn't closed his eyes. I'd seen the assaulter toss the grenade. As I opened my eyes, the two remaining intruders were on the move towards the corridor, their weapons firing a continuous stream at both Willy and me.

I rolled to my left to avoid the bullets, came up and fired a single shot which felled the man closest to me. The other turned from Willy to see if his partner was okay. Willy double tapped. The last assaulter went down.

I called out, "Are we clear?"

"Clear at this end." Nick responded.

We stood. The wind howling through the space made it hard to hear. I noticed Willy favoring his left arm. He was bleeding. He apparently took a round. My instinct was to check on Willy, but I knew I had to check on the assaulters first.

I inspected the first man I'd shot. He wouldn't be getting up again. I looked at the next man I'd taken down. The back of the man's head showed two neat holes. I'd blown away most of his face. Not much threat from him either.

A movement behind me and I turned in time to see a young man step out into the hallway from the reception area. From a handgun he fired a silenced shot that left a burning sensation in my left thigh, pushed me back into the wall. He let the exterior door close behind him. Willy reacted first, moving quickly into the short corridor.

I took only one step to follow....

The explosion knocked me off my feet ....

.... and the whole room went black.

Death of a Cop

After the raid on Castillo's Ciudad Victoria villa he refused to go back. Instead Dominguez went to meet him at Castillo's apartment across the street from the Angel Inn in Mexico City. The Angel Inn was famous as the place where Mexican politicians did business. Power lunches, power dinners, and power meetings in between. The Angel Inn was the place to see and be seen, if one were trying to climb the political ladders in a country with a single term limit.

Castillo couldn't meet publicly with those whose political careers he'd helped along the way. Those Castillo decided he wanted to meet with in person came by the apartment before or after a meeting at the Angel Inn. The apartment wasn't a secret. The government officials coming there from time-to-time made Dominguez nervous. He only went when absolutely necessary. Dominguez had thought on more than one occasion he'd sell off the apartment when he replaced Castillo.

Dominguez arrived before sunrise. He knew his picture was out in enough places now so he could no longer move freely. While the Zetas still had cover from the politicians, he knew lower level people would benefit greatly from taking him out. The benefit might be in the form of a payment from one of the rival cartels, or satisfaction at revenge for a family member or friend whom Los Zetas had eliminated for one reason or another. He had enemies he wouldn't recognize so he became more cautious.

Castillo was a late riser, so Dominguez went to the den. He brought his iPad and read the news reports of the Dallas Massacre, as it was being labeled. Dominguez thought the description suitable, although he realized the massacre went both ways since he lost all six men he took in with him. He was unhappy he'd been forced to kill the

FBI agent, because now he would have to find another to implement his grand plan.

Dominguez found it curious the newspapers didn't list the victims, indicating the families hadn't been notified. He'd hoped to put the evidence in front of Castillo showing the FBI man was dead. Apparently he wasn't going to be able to do so today. At some point the police would release the names. Then Castillo would have the evidence.

About ten Castillo, still in a bathrobe and looking sleepy, entered the den and sat down in his favorite chair. "I got you a thirty day extension on the payment. They understood, but no further excuses. Don't disappoint me."

"We should be able to cover the payment by then." Dominguez calculated.

Castillo's voice changed. "Where is it?"

"It?"

"The head. I told you I wanted his head on my desk. The coffee table would do, but I don't see it."

Dominguez knew Castillo would never be happy, but he hadn't thought him to be serious about the head. "I didn't have time to go back in once the bomb went off."

"You should have made time."

"It wasn't like being in Mexico City. The fire rescue was only a few blocks away. They arrived as we drove away. If I'd gone back in, I never would have gotten out."

"Why do you continue to do everything I ask of you except this one thing?"

"He's dead. I identified him, shot him and blew up the place. He was the closest to the bomb when it went off. You have your revenge or satisfaction or whatever it is you want. We have more important things to talk about today than whether I delivered the head of an FBI man to you."

"There you go again, making assumptions. How do you know we have more important things to talk about? I decide what we talk about, not you. I decide what's important. Not you. This FBI agent is important to me. His head on my desk is important to me. I don't care if you have to go dig up his grave and sever it in the grave yard. But I want that head."

Dominguez regretted killing the agent. It had ruined his perfect plan, but he'd find another. He had to keep reminding himself as long as Castillo survived his freedom was limited. And the limits on his freedom gave even more urgency to his developing plans beyond the one that had involved the agent.

"You'll have the head. As soon as they bury him I'll retrieve it for you."

Castillo nodded at the iPad. "You going to show me his name in the newspapers?"

Dominguez shook his head. "Haven't notified the next of kin yet."

"Let me see."

Dominguez handed the iPad to Castillo. Castillo scanned the article, looked at the picture of the offices after the explosion and handed the iPad back to Dominguez.

"You apparently failed to leave a calling card."

"Calling card?"

"The article doesn't say anything about who was responsible. Just said the police and federal agencies were cooperating in their investigation."

Dominguez was incredulous. "You wanted me to leave a calling card?"

Castillo enjoyed himself. "Your plan was to force their government to admit to what they're doing in Mexico. The government can decide what they want the newspapers to say. They can speculate that US gangs, or militia, or terrorists were behind the attack and there'd be no tie to Mexico. I think you failed in your basic mission."

"When the newspapers start digging in why someone would attack that office it will come out what they're trying to do."

"Again, an assumption you can't support."

"The task force knows it was us."

"Do they? From what the article said you killed so many of them I'm not sure any survived. You may have put them on the defensive; you've done so right along. But you just don't close the door. Instead the Americans send others against us. You haven't won a victory here. We have to be more prepared than before for US involvement."

"We can handle them."

Castillo shook his head. "Shows how little you understand the Americans. I spent four years going to their Yale University. I used my time to study them. They won't back off until public opinion turns against their efforts. That's why your failure to leave an unmistakable calling card is so important."

Dominguez had to counter Castillo. Then an idea came to him. "We can run an editorial in our newspaper in Laredo exposing the American actions."

Castillo raised his eyebrows. "A good idea for a change. Make it happen. Any way the newspaper can get other papers to run similar stories or editorials?"

"They have some kind of network or something where they reprint each other's editorials. I'll make sure the Laredo guys push."

"I want you to write the story, but I want to see it before you publish."

Dominguez was feeling better. He'd turned the corner with Castillo, at least in this meeting. But the next meeting would be a different story. He was hanging on, but each day was getting tougher and tougher to stay in Castillo's good graces. "Have it to you before I leave today."

"Needs to have a lot of facts. That's what seems to get people's attention."

"I'll work the facts with the guys in Laredo. They have access to databases and other sources of information."

"And I want his head on my desk."

Dominguez swallowed. "You'll have it."

"When?"

Two Weeks Later

Back in the Saddle

I'd been knocked out in the explosion at Bryan Tower. Guess I'd been thrown against the wall. I'd had almost continuous headaches since. My left leg wound also slowed me down, but I was more determined than ever to pursue the rest of the Hispanic gentlemen to the source and make them pay. Willy was still in the hospital with a severe concussion. He was closer to the door when the bomb went off.

The facilities people found us a new place to hang out in only a day. The Los Colinas temporary offices for the Rapid Reaction Force were actually nicer than the ones we had at Bryan Tower. I heard they'd been used by a Fortune 500 company that had consolidated offices somewhere else. So the rich woods, marble floor and heavy duty internet infrastructure were all an upgrade. The fact I didn't have to pay for parking turned out to be an unexpected plus of being in the suburbs. The office was a lot closer to the airport. And since I spent a fair amount of time on airplanes, I saw the location as another plus.

I wandered about a bit before finding my office. Someone put a piece of paper on the door with my name. Whoever was in charge of seating had the decency to not put out name tags of those who'd died in the attack at the tower. So I found a lot more empty desks than there were people. With Willy still in the hospital, his was empty.

I found Alene in her new office. She'd been in Washington on the day of the attack at Bryan Tower, but had been by the hospital to see Willy and the others who'd sustained injuries. She'd also been attending funerals for the many who died, as had I. Jan's funeral was the hardest for her; they'd become close in the few weeks they'd worked together. Jan had three small children and a husband who seemed lost.

"Everyone I've talked to said you and Willy kept the situation from being a lot worse," she said.

I shrugged, "How are you doing?"

"How do you keep people from getting killed in this business?" I heard the helplessness in her voice.

"You don't." I answered. "People do their jobs. It's the other people who kill us, and that's why we're here. To try to ensure as few people are killed as possible."

She looked down. "I don't know if I can do this job anymore."

"Why? You didn't send those men to kill us."

"You don't think the attack was because of the Ciudad Victoria raid?"

The question occurred to me but I didn't want her to think her decision was responsible for so many deaths. "No one knew we were there. So why would you put them together?" I sat down in a chair across from her desk.

"They knew." She admitted in a very soft voice.

"How?" The bells went off in the back of my head. She was apparently going to tell me something she didn't admit to last time we talked. I was beginning to feel like a rotating door, wanting to get closer to her and help her one minute and angry the next.

"Don't you watch the news? Walter Josephson."

I didn't know what she was talking about. I never watched television.

"He was indicted for selling information."

I had to ask since I didn't have a clue. "Who's Walter Josephson?"

"The President's Chief of Staff. It's a huge scandal." She seemed surprised I didn't know.

"He sold me out?" I couldn't believe the betrayal had been at such a high level. I figured someone well down the food chain was responsible. "Why?"

"Money," was all she'd say. "They're still questioning him and he isn't being overly cooperative." She'd been betrayed by someone she admired. The door was swinging again, apparently for her too.

Trying to put my anger aside, realizing whatever happened wasn't part of the plan and not something she could've prevented, I asked. "How do we recover?"

"I honestly don't know." The helplessness was evident.

"At least we've plugged one hole. You should have a pretty good idea what the Zetas know based on what you've briefed to the President."

She nodded. I watched her rally. The deaths of those on her team had hit her hard.

I continued, "We pick up the plan where we left off. Go after heroin next and then cocaine, just as we discussed. Chip away at them until they simply aren't viable."

"But won't someone else step in? Pick up the slack and supply the market?"

She had me, but I had to show her we could do something important now. "You may be right ..."

"Am right." She responded authoritatively.

I realized I'd failed to lift her spirits, so I changed tact. "Why do Harvard grads always have to be right?" I smiled.

"Even if we aren't, we'll never admit it to a Yale grad." The sparkle slowly returned to her eyes along with the suggestion of a grin.

"I had this one professor who used to say that Yale grads could afford to let Harvard grads be right once in a while because in the afterlife we'd be vindicated."

"Theology professor?" she asked.

I shook my head, "Economics."

She laughed out loud.

"I've heard the President likes to say that we can only change the things that are within our control." I said. "Suggest we start there."

"How exactly?"

"We have to find out who we took into custody in Ciudad Victoria."

"Claims he was just a neighbor. A businessman who stopped by to chat and was taken upstairs for protection when the shooting started."

I smiled at her. "At three in the morning. What do you think?"

"It's bullshit. But I don't know how we convince him to talk."

I winked at her, "Put that penny in my jar."

Arrival of Boy Wonder

I went to see Nick. He was surfing the web when I approached. I dropped into the chair next to him.

"How's the Wizard this fine bright morning in Los Colinas, Texas, wherever the hell that is?"

"It's on the way to the airport." Nick responded, subdued.

I studied Nick. Something seemed different. The easy smile had disappeared. The joke didn't come as the first response. The eyes were haunted by something. I had a pretty good idea what. Having seen the same bodies of friends and colleagues Nick had seen two weeks before; having withstood the same attack; having taken shots from those who were trying to kill me; having been thrown across the room by the C-4 bomb set by the assault team.

I knew Nick understood he now came up on the radar of some very nasty people. Knowing someone wanted to kill you was never pleasant. It became even more unpleasant knowing those who had him in their sights had succeeded in eliminating most of the rest of the team.

"Hear you want to be an agent." I said.

"Are you kidding? After what happened, all I want is to be an agent. Screw all this analytical stuff. I just want to kick some ass."

"Really?" His response wasn't unexpected, but somehow didn't fit the impression I had of Nick as a guy who lived to solve problems, not kick butt.

"Okay. Maybe I'm being selfish, but I don't want to have to

rely on anyone else to protect me. If I'm out there with you and I get killed trying to take them out, okay, that's one thing. But not if I have to sit back here in an office and wait for them to come in through the door again like what happened last week." Nick looked away before continuing. "If you and Willy hadn't stood up, I probably would've been one of the body bags the coroner took out the front door."

I thought back to my first traumatic experiences. I couldn't share them with Nick, because officially they never took place. "You having nightmares?" I asked as softly as I could.

Nick stared at me, evidently trying to decide what to say.

"It's really okay if you are. In fact, I'd be worried if you weren't."

Nick looked uncomfortable, "Yeah."

"I'm still dealing with another incident where I should have been killed, except for one man who died to make sure I wasn't. And that's made the situation even worse."

Nick looked at me differently, "Didn't know."

"I'm on borrowed time. I'll tell you about it sometime over a beer. Just want you to know it's all right to have those dreams. People can help you with them."

He seemed relieved. The smile, while not as free as before at least made a partial reappearance.

"Hey! I wanted to show you what I've found so far."

"The Wizard's back to work?" I teased him.

"Never stopped." Nick brought back a web page he'd been working on. "Here it is. A report from the Mexican Federales about three men they picked up in connection with cartel activity nearly three years ago. Before things really got out of hand."

"Who are they?" I wondered if any would mean anything to me.

"Arturro Vega, Juan Dominguez and Luis Herrera."

"Herrera. The Sergeant for the Mexican Special Forces was named Herrera."

"I'll look into him. The problem with all these guys is no one ever heard of them."

I listened to what Nick tried to tell me, "So who do you think they are?"

"My guess? Up and comers. I found a reference to Herrera. He was wounded in a shootout with the police and hasn't been seen publicly since. He could be in the Army now as a plant. Would've thought he'd be an officer, though. Vega's been referred to in several articles I've come across, but he's like a guy with no finger prints. He seems to always be around all the action, but no one ever finds him."

"What about the third guy?" I came back.

"Dominguez? He's the most interesting one of the three. He never seems to be anywhere very long. Seems like he deliberately moves around a lot. Like a rotational assignment in the Bureau. My guess is he got to know almost everyone and probably did a lot of favors for guys along the way."

Nick surprised me by seeing a parallel to the bureau.

"Dominguez is the reputed number two to Castillo. He have an angel somewhere?" I asked.

Nick hesitated, "I know he's reputed, so I did a little more research on him than on the others. Was able to find a cell phone."

"Can your Intel lady friend help you? Alondra?"

Nick pulled inward for a moment. Apparently she was still an open wound. He shook his head "Didn't think I could ask for that, yet. She's still real wary of us."

"You sound discouraged."

""Well, you've seen her. I mean, I just can't get her out of my mind."

I'd been down this road before. "And she doesn't seem to know you exist."

"Well, yeah. How'd you know?"

I didn't want to tell him about Lexie Jones and the near disasters I had before she finally gave me a chance. "Some things never change. But my advice is: don't give up hope. Things have a way of comin' around if they're meant to."

"What are you saying?"

"Sometimes folks have a habit of tryin' too hard. If they stop tryin' and just be themselves, the real you comes across. And if the real you connects you're better off."

Nick smiled. "This the voice of experience?"

"Let me just say I've tried both ways and had much more success as a smart ass than as a death defying cop."

I watched Nick consider my advice. He seemed to remember something .... "Oh, by the way. Did I tell you I got Dominguez's cell phone records?"

"Yes."

"I found an interesting link. He called someone who could be your friend Morales or Hernandez-Anjul."

Nick had my attention.

Pushing the Envelope

Castillo and Dominguez walked toward the waiting car. They were about to conduct a meeting of the Zeta leaders. The venue was in Saltillo, northwest of Monterrey, but not anywhere people would be looking for them. The meeting was in the home of one of Dominguez's lieutenants. His wife and children were out at her parents. The Zetas had the whole house, small as it was, all to themselves.

Dominguez felt he'd regained some ground in the losing battle to keep Castillo happy by making the half-billion dollar payment a week early. But Castillo was cranky and went right after him about the FBI Agent again. "I don't agree. We should back off. You're obsessed with this FBI guy and he's nothing."

"If he were nothing we'd be having this meeting in Victoria as we always have, not in Saltillo."

"He's not the reason. He's only one man."

"But he's always in the middle of everything. What does the Messenger say?"

"He counsels patience. This agent will make a mistake and we'll be all over him. You'll have his head. It's only a matter of time."

"Too much time. You had him. Blew up the whole fucking building and he walked out. I'm not willing to wait for him to be careless. He's clearly not. You need to finish. You've never failed. I still can't believe he walked out of that office building."

"I know, I shot him, too." Dominguez knew he'd deliberately shot to wound.

"No points for style, my friend. Dead is dead and this agent isn't yet dead."

Dominguez hung his head. He knew he deserved this dressing down, but at the same time he was actually glad the agent hadn't died. Dominguez knew if what he expected would happen, did, all the harassment from Castillo would be worthwhile. But he couldn't tell Castillo. The leader of the Zetas would never go for his plan. Too risky, he'd assess. While Dominguez was doing everything he could to finish the assignment, he hoped it wouldn't end as Castillo wanted, but the way he hoped instead. Dominguez wanted the bigger statement. Castillo wouldn't approve. So Dominguez had to keep everything close and hope Castillo gave him the room he needed to maneuver. If he succeeded there was no question who'd replace Castillo.

"You want to make a statement."

Dominguez felt like Castillo was reading his mind. "Yes, we need to keep our foot on their throat."

"You need to find Luis. He has something he's been trying to get me to use."

Dominguez was surprised. Luis Rodriguez was one of their all-time explosives experts. What could he possibly have to fascinate Castillo? "I thought Luis retired."

"You know how the old guys are. They go spend money somewhere for a few years. And they get bored. Want to get back into the action. Luis started tinkering and he came up with something. He showed his device to me a while back. You know, he came up with one of those things you say wow, this is really something. But it comes down to where would I use it?"

Dominguez wasn't sure if he was being set up. Luis was as ruthless as they came. The meeting could be a trap to get Dominguez out by himself and he'd run into a shotgun blast to the face. He couldn't trust Castillo. Luis should be a harmless old man. But a visit wouldn't be safe. "Where's he living these days?"

"Same old house in Reynoso. Nobody'd ever try to arrest him. He must have his place rigged to explode if someone sneezes wrong. But this time leave a calling card."

Why would Castillo tell him how dangerous the place was if he were trying to get him to go? Didn't make sense. He'd have to go tomorrow. Castillo wasn't going to let the FBI agent sit much longer. All of a sudden Dominguez would find himself out of the loop and someone else would take the agent out. And then Dominguez would be out as well. He hoped the Messenger was right on the timing, but he'd have to move on the Luis meeting anyway, just to survive.

First Conversation

Alene returned from Washington. I called to ask if we could have dinner. I wanted time with her, but I wanted the time off the record and not in her office. She agreed and we met at Nonna Restaurant, in Dallas just off Lemon Avenue at Lomo Alto.

Nonna's was a hole in the wall, with seats for only about fifty. The restaurant was regarded by many people I knew as one of the best Italian places in Dallas. So we took an early time and table in the back corner where we could talk.

Alene came directly from the office, but I saw her differently, not as my supervisor, but as someone more central to my life. When I ordered a bottle of Jacopo Biondi Santi, an Italian red, Alene expressed her surprise. Maybe I had learned something about wine. Was I gaining credibility as someone who could be more than another work associate?

"So if I can learn something about wines, can you learn from the past?"

"What do you mean?" She was guarded and her smile disappeared.

"Willy and I were talkin' the other day."

"That's probably not a good thing," she teased.

"Yeah, well .... he said something I've been thinkin' about a lot."

She hesitated, "Go on."

"The Mexican violence won't end as long as drugs are illegal in the US."

"A statement of opinion. Nothing to do with history." she observed.

"No matter how many cartel leaders we take out or the Mexican government takes out, there's a long list of others ready to step in. You remarked on the Zeta situation. Dominguez seems poised to take over if anything happens to Castillo. The reason's simple. There's just too much money on the table. You can send me out on a new mission every day for the rest of my life. I can kill or capture another cartel leader each week. And the violence still won't end. Even if I shut down a whole cartel, another will step in and take over their distribution. The situation's like a hydra with so many heads it simply can't be killed."

"You're frustrated."

The first course came. The waiter served and left. "We're throwing spears at different heads when we should be trying to starve the beast. Now this is where the history comes in. Think back to prohibition."

"I've heard that argument a hundred times. It's not the same," she protested.

"Wait. Gangs controlled the alcohol trade in the US. When we legalized booze again, their whole infrastructure fell apart. The violence stopped because the profits went away. The situation's exactly the same."

"I disagree. The 1920s was a different era. Different issues, different politics. You take the same actions today you'd get a different result."

"Maybe, but if we take the money out by making drugs legal, but regulated, the economics change."

"The economics you learned from your Yale Professor who still thinks Yale grads will be right when they get to heaven?"

She was having fun with me, but wasn't just dismissing my arguments.

"He was only one of many professors I had. But my guess is your Harvard professors taught the same cause and effect principles."

"They did, but none ever used the drug trade as an example of how things would turn out in the end."

"Guess they expected you to be able to figure that part out on your own."

She nodded. "So humor me and tell me how you think this could work?"

"You have to buy drugs at pharmacies. Purchase marijuana and certain low dose narcotics over the counter but with an age minimum. Require a prescription for those with more serious effects. At the same time you create civil penalties where others are endangered by the possible consequences of your use."

"Just like alcohol. Would you have treatment programs to help people rather than putting abusers in jail?"

"Would avoid introducing casual users to a wider range of illegal activity."

"I've heard the same argument from the marijuana people forever."

"People are going to use no matter what the government does, just like with alcohol. So why not regulate the trade? Let the government collect fees from legitimate businesses rather than permit the cartels to make exorbitant profits to fund lawlessness while we drain our treasury trying to stop them."

"You're saying the drug dilemma seems just like the oil situation. We buy oil at high prices from those who use the profits to undermine our government."

"Exactly."

She thought about the discussion then responded. "You just argued to push ahead with our strategy to take down the Zetas. Have you changed your mind?"

"No. The Zeta strategy's the short term focus, but it's not a solution. The short term strategy doesn't solve the problem."

"We're in the law enforcement business. You're talking about changing the law. Congress would never vote for what you're suggesting."

"At Yale they taught us to look at history for answers to current issues. Few situations have never been faced before. Always a different set of circumstances you have to adjust for, but the basis is generally the same."

"Harvard taught history too." She was pulling my chain, but I refused to take the bait. "So this is where the history comes in?" she smiled again.

"We had a time in our past when the country was even more divided on another issue. Had been for decades and we changed the law."

"I just don't see Congress acting on your suggestion."

I struggled but finally got out what was hard for me to say. "Remember what you said to me just before the raid where Lexie died?"

Alene looked at me, apparently knowing how hard it was for me to go there. She shook her head, embarrassed she couldn't remember.

"You said we have to adapt, because if only one side does, the side that adapts will win every time. I've never forgotten."

"I don't see what you want me to see."

"If what we're doing isn't working, maybe it's time to adapt."

"What do you have in mind?"

Silent Movie

The next day, Nick and I sat next to each other on the American Airlines flight from Dallas to El Paso. The strategy review was over and Alene was under pressure for another quick success. We talked about what we could do that would have the biggest impact and settled in on a raid against the west coast heroin traffic route. With Willy still in the hospital, she sent us off to conduct that mission even though Nick had never been in the simulator.

"What was the deal with the telescope at Bryan tower? What was it pointed at? You sat near it." I asked, having returned to thinking about the attack on us.

"The telescope? Jack Ruby's Carousel club."

"Supposed to be a reminder that sometimes our enemies are amongst us?"

"Something like that. I never got the whole story. It all predated me."

Nick was fidgety and talkative, probably anxious about going out on a mission. "Why do you always sit so far forward? It's supposed to be smoother if you ride over the wings or in the tail." Nick complained.

"I like it up here. We don't have to wait forever to get off."

"You in a hurry or something?"

I didn't respond.

Nick shrugged. "Did Alene give you any insight into what

we're supposed to be doing down here?" He asked.

I didn't want to discuss on a plane so, "We get the mission briefing package here."

"How can you operate in a perpetual vacuum?" Nick seemed to be gaining new found respect for the deployed agents.

"Astronauts do it all the time. Why should we be any different?"

"Astronauts have a lot of protective gear between them and the vacuum."

"We have our wits. What else do we need?"

Nick had no answer. So he looked out the window as we made our final approach into El Paso. Since we were on the left side of the aircraft we had an unobstructed view of Mexico as we came in. I wondered what Nick might be thinking about the vast flat and arid land just on the other side of the Rio Grande. I thought about someone named Juan Dominguez, who'd probably had a whole bunch of conversations with the man responsible for the death of my brother and sister-in-law and probably knew where I'd find Dad. Dominguez was out there somewhere. He might be in Ciudad Juarez, within walking distance of where Nick and I were going to be. He could be in Mexico City having lunch with the President of Mexico. He could be out in the middle of nowhere killing yet another family.

I planned to find a way to ensure Mister Dominguez ceased to exist.

I asked Nick to do a search of the law enforcement databases in the US to see if this particular gentleman came up anywhere. He was thought to be the second in command of the Zetas. Too bad he hadn't been in Ciudad Victoria when we raided Ruben Castillo's villa. I might have been able to save myself a lot of trouble.

The plane touched down. "Marines." I mumbled.

Nick turned to look at me, "What?"

"Marines."

"What about them?" Nick seemed confused.

"We have an ex-Marine pilot."

"How do you know?"

"The way he landed. Air Force pilots are used to landing with reasonable runways so they come in nice and smooth. Navy pilots mostly land on carriers. So they fly above the ground and then figure out how to drop on the deck in just a few feet but at relatively high speeds. Their landing's always hard because they're ready to go full power, pull up and come around again. Marines have all these short and vertical landing planes. So they come in real slow, hang there a while and let the plane drop in. That's what this guy did."

"Didn't know you had such keen powers of observation." Nick gathered his stuff.

I moved into the aisle as soon as we heard the tone. Nick remained seated. I pulled down our overnight bags from the overhead, tucked in my shirt and checked my cellphone for messages and email. The door opened. I moved up to follow the first class passengers off the plane. Nick came out right behind me. Together we started up the jet bridge towards the terminal building.

Nick moved in front of me, but turned to say something.

A massive explosion erupted from the bowels of the aircraft …

… Lifted the plane off the ground and tore it apart.

The explosion threw us forward, and away from the aircraft.

We lay on the jet bridge for a good two minutes before either of us responded. I felt the intense heat, rose first, dazed. Blood ran down my face. Everything unfolded as if it were a silent movie. Then I realized I couldn't hear.

I helped Nick to his feet. Flames roared out of what was left of the aircraft. I couldn't imagine that anyone still on board could get off alive.

As I pointed Nick towards the terminal, airline personnel rushed down the remains of the jet bridge to see what could be done. Nick and I helped other passengers to their feet, assuming they couldn't hear either.

Everyone seemed to be dazed. The silent movie continued. People who'd been waiting to board the plane came back toward the now missing terminal windows. They stood far enough back to avoid the heat from the burning wreckage. I watched Nick try to say something. I shrugged. He removed an iPad he kept notes on from his backpack. I watched as he typed out, 'Bryan Tower?'

I shrugged, not wanting Nick to feel guilty or thinking he might have been the cause of innocent people dying on the plane. I didn't want Nick to think about such a link even though I felt guilty as hell.

A medic approached me. He looked at the blood on my face. Someone from the airline came up and spoke to me in the silent movie constituting my world. The medic wanted me to come with him, but I thought I said, "Take care of the others first." Ringing in my ears suddenly overwhelmed the silence.

Castillo

Dominguez didn't like being summoned to see Castillo. Nearly every time this happened he ended up being verbally whipped for one failure or another, even when he'd actually been successful. *Was Castillo losing it? Had he really changed as much as it seemed from when they were inseparable sicarios in Mexico City? What had it been? Maybe five years.* Once Dominguez liked being with Castillo, talking about how they'd do things differently when they got to the top, but now he hated spending time with him. Maybe he hated it because Castillo no longer discussed how to do things. Now Castillo told him what to do, when to do it and how to do it. Their relationship was nothing like it'd been. Castillo was in charge and Dominguez went along to do what Castillo wanted.

Why'd it have to get this way? Dominguez knew he and Castillo saw the world the same way. They'd learned success came from being more ruthless than anyone else. So how'd the split occur? Would he have been plotting if Castillo had treated him the same way he did five years ago? Dominguez told himself no, but he knew he would have been. He and Castillo were alike. If the roles were reversed he'd probably be making life hell for his subordinates. He wouldn't trust anyone and would micromanage them just like Castillo was micromanaging him. So why was he so resentful?

Dominguez skipped up the steps to Castillo's Monterrey house. This one was out in the country. Nothing around this house for a mile in any direction. Castillo wanted to make sure he'd have warning if the Army came at him again. And he'd installed defenses as sophisticated as he could obtain from anywhere in the world. Dominguez knew Castillo was particularly fond of Israeli technology. Most of the sensors around the property were of Israeli manufacture.

The weapons were mostly American, mainly because it was easier to get them and ammunition was readily available. TOW missiles were set up to take down any assault teams, whether airborne or on the ground. He also had an array of Russian made RPGs for closer engagement with armor and vehicles.

Castillo was taking no chances on a repeat assault. The guards were all family. No mercenaries, no *sicarios* from the cities. He trained his guards well, he paid them well, and he armed them with whatever they asked for. He sent them and their whole families on vacations out of Mexico as a reward. Castillo's uncle was the head of his body guard. Castillo sent his cousins to universities to learn how to run the Zetas like a business and how to invest the money he was making. The idea was to ensure the family would have a perpetual fortune to draw upon even after his time as the Zeta leader.

Dominguez knew their relationship had changed irreparably. He might still be the number two in the cartel now, but Castillo training his cousins to run the cartel was a clear indication he'd never rise to the top. Castillo was trying to take the Zetas private, in a sense. Transfer responsibility and authority to his family members. While the transfer would take time, Dominguez had already seen the signs of trusted allies being replaced. In this business replaced meant dead.

Dominguez entered the kitchen carrying a leather bag. The kitchen was where Castillo liked to have his meetings. His mother lived in this house and she cooked for him whenever he came.

"Madre Castillo." Dominguez gave her the kiss and hug he was permitted as the best friend of her son. She brought over the pastries and black Turkish coffee she knew he liked.

"Ruben. I brought you the bag I carry everywhere now. Soon it will contain the head you wish." Dominguez held up the leather satchel.

Castillo laughed. "Very good. I like that you're taking my request seriously."

"He can't elude us much longer. Each time we're closer."

"It's good to see you're trying. A whole fucking airplane this time. How many have died for this one man? One hundred and sixty-one on the airplane? Fifty-three at his office. Six at the police station in Dallas. Five at his apartment complex. Three at his ranch. The numbers are getting bigger. That's a help. Either you'll get him or kill half the people in Dallas trying."

"Did you like the calling card?" Dominguez asked knowing this had to be a key topic they'd discuss. Get it out on the table early and see where things were.

"Only CNN carried your call to the local station. The others referred to it, but didn't play it." The glass was always half full with Castillo. "The editorial was good. How many other newspapers have picked it up?"

"Twelve so far. I expect it'll go to national media next week."

"That's good." Castillo responded, but didn't sound focused.

"We're back in full production at the new Meth factory. We moved it to Torreon in an industrial park near the airport. Transportation costs are higher than Monterrey, but we actually have lower labor and security costs."

"We need to reclaim the market share we lost while we were out of production. We're going to need to build another. Been thinking the next one should go to Guadalajara. Know just the place."

Something was wrong. "Guadalajara? How are you going to manage the Sinaloa?"

"I worked an agreement with them. I pay to build and equip the plant. They operate it. We split the production."

"You trust them?" Dominguez couldn't believe Castillo was

sleeping with the Sinaloa. Castillo would never have gone that far without consulting him in the past.

"As much as I trust you."

Dominguez didn't like the implication. "You declare a truce?"

"I'm building bridges to a new future. One where our interests align and the violence ends."

Dominguez thought about the implications. Castillo was moving toward an accommodation with the Sinaloa, against the Juarez. Would the Juarez cartel join with the Gulf cartel to put pressure on their backside? If he were the leader he'd be doing a similar deal with the Gulf cartel to at least keep them neutral. This was a dangerous development. He needed more time to think through the implications. But he needed to sound like he was on board. "Probably don't need quite the capacity we put into Torreon if you're going to split up the distribution." He floated out there to see if Castillo was following his own instincts.

Castillo seemed to be getting bored with the discussion. "No, I want it to be the same capacity. If we lose one or the other plant I want to be able to shift production between them. Need to make sure we don't lose market share like we did."

"Makes sense." Dominguez was reading Castillo's body language. Not good. Dominguez decided to let Castillo get to whatever was on his mind.

Herbiberto, Castillo's sharpshooter, appeared at the kitchen door. Herbiberto's presence could only mean Castillo intended to have him killed. Herbiberto went to Madre Castillo. Same kiss, same hug. That had never happened before. Castillo had made his choice and Dominguez was out, only Mama Castillo hadn't been told. Herbiberto came to the table and sat down with them. Madre Castillo brought him a cup of tea.

Herbiberto'd never been invited to their meetings before. He may have been a first tier lieutenant to Castillo, but only by taking out someone Castillo was unhappy with. He was muscle, not management.

"I invited Herbiberto to sit with us." Castillo began.

Dominguez nodded, shook hands. "Herbiberto."

"Normally when someone fails me twice I'd just tell Herbiberto to kill him. But I'm not going to do that to you. Haven't done that to you. You've failed how many times now?"

Dominguez shrugged.

"I have to ask myself, why is my most reliable lieutenant unable to kill this FBI man? Mama tells me I'm probably asking too much of you. I should ease your burden and let you focus on killing since that's what you normally do so well."

Dominguez glanced at Castillo's mother who was cooking rabbit for lunch.

"So you won't have to worry about the Guadalajara meth factory, or the Torreon factory or the Laredo newspaper or any of the other things you've been working. When you walk out of here you have only one thing you're responsible for. Bringing back the head in your bag."

Now all that had gone before was apparently over. He was going to complete the job he'd been given and then be dispatched. Nothing more, nothing less. He had to move quickly or Herbiberto just might decide to take him out and do the FBI agent job himself to gain favor with Castillo.

"Herbiberto's now doing my operations?" Dominguez asked, knowing that if the answer was yes, then he had his proof since Herbiberto had never done operations.

Castillo turned to his mother, "See Mama. You were right. Juan would understand, you said. He's your one true friend. He'll follow whatever you decide." Castillo turned back to Dominguez.

Reality settled over Dominguez. Castillo would have him killed when he delivered the head of the FBI agent. "Guess there's only one thing to do."

"That's right. Only one thing." Castillo nodded to Herbiberto.

Dominguez, knew Herbiberto would be his shadow until he delivered the bag to Castillo. When he did, Herbiberto would put a bullet in his.

Skirmish

A week later Barak Obama sat in a chair cross wise to the facing couches in the Oval Office. Nate Williams, the new Chief of Staff sat silently on the opposite couch taking notes. Alene and I sat across from Nate. We chatted about my experiences in Mexico. The President was particularly interested in how I captured the man who turned out to be the Zetas' money man. More precisely he wanted to know how I got him to talk. His role explained why the Zetas fought so hard to keep him from falling into our hands. Probably also explained why they came at us at Bryan Tower. I told him about Willy and how discovering Zetas in his neighborhood had shaken the unflappable Dallas Detective.

The President changed direction, "Your point paper provides a lot of specifics to support your suggested course of action. The fact that California spends almost twice as much on prisons as it does on the UC system surprised me. The fact is we spend nearly eight times as much incarcerating someone as we do educating them at the University level. Our priorities are all wrong, I'll grant you."

I glanced at Alene. She wasn't smiling even though he was saying what we wanted to hear. "Sir, when you examine numbers against populations, we have almost seven times as many people in prison today as any other nation in the world. In 1980 we were about average. What happened? It's because kids want to get high the way their parents do, only their choice isn't alcohol."

Obama's expression didn't change, but his tone of voice did. "I hear you, but I don't see how anything can be done given the priorities of Congress." The regret was unmistakable.

I shifted in my seat, not only because of the pain I experienced sitting, but because I knew I was about to make a recommendation to the President of the United States. "Sir, the professors at Yale made sure I spent a lot of time readin' history before I became an Agent. They pointed out a fella to me. Said he had an opportunity to make a transformative decision. His name was Abraham Lincoln. I'm sure you've heard of him."

Obama smiled.

"Sir, he was fightin' a war to settle a major difference of opinion among our people. Those who were about to lose that skirmish were none too happy. He had the courage to change the laws underpinnin' nearly every major debate in the country. He made the changes through a proclamation, realizin' a polarized Congress would never catch up to the people. He didn't check polls or rely on the advice of so called experts. He simply did what he deep down inside believed to be the right thing for all Americans. At the time his decision had to be incredibly difficult. But he put the good of the nation above politics. In the end people judge his presidency more for the Emancipation Proclamation than for winnin' the Civil War."

"Are you suggesting I need to do something as transformative?"

"You have a chance to change the economics of the illegal drug trade. A lot of smart folks agree a change of direction is needed. Look at who signed off on the report of the Global Commission on Drug Policy. A former Secretary of State, A former Fed Chairman and the former Presidents of Brazil and Mexico. All the drugs we're talkin' 'bout were legal in our country much longer than they've been illegal. Go back to prohibition and look at how we returned alcohol to a legal status. We penalized those who endangered others through their behavior when under the influence. Make it illegal for those who waste their lives dependent on drugs to receive welfare or other social support. I think you can come up with a model that works, sir. We've shown as a society we can manage alcohol. These cartels are just our generation's version of the prohibition gangsters. But the cartels have lots more destructive weapons and gobs more money. You decriminalize drugs; that changes the economics fueling the violence. We get back a safer country to our south. You empty out our jails and pour the savings into education. The change gives people a chance for treatment, particularly for truly addictive drugs, and hope for a better life in the form of higher education."

"You're talking the economic impact here, but what about Mexico? Such a change would disrupt their whole economy."

"Who benefits?" I asked, and I watched Barak Obama try to answer my question. "Not the people. It's the cartel leaders and the criminal elements they employ. Let the cartels produce the narcotics if they chose, but sell them legally with legal profit margins. Make the jobs honest jobs contributing to a healthy economy, not ones based on death and violence.

The President looked to Alene, "Do you agree with Agent Carr?"

"I think we have to help Mexico. If we continue to wait we'll have cartel violence in our streets you or your successor will have to deal with."

"So you don't think supporting the Mexican authorities will permit them to eventually get this all under control?" Obama looked directly at me.

"Sir, I can't give you an official assessment. But my personal observation is that as long as incredible amounts of money fuel the drug trade, no matter how many people are arrested or killed, someone will step into the void to meet the demand."

The President looked straight at me as if to ask another question, but was then distracted as Genevieve, his assistant, poked her head into his office, "Mister President, the Attorney General is here to brief you on the shooting of Senator Aldrich."

The President nodded, then returned to me, "Believe me when I say I want to find a way to end the violence. But for now, what you both are doing is the best hope for our nation." He rose, stretched and shook Alene's and then my hand.

He moved off to his desk as Genevieve escorted us from the Oval office. Alene offered a weak smile as we carried our disappointment with us. I just caught a fragment of Nate Williams' comment to the President as the door shut behind us, "…you have to think about…."

In the outer office, I stopped for just a moment in front of Eric Holder, the Attorney General. "Sir, FBI Agent Jim Carr."

"Yes, I recognize you. How are you recovering from your injuries?"

"I'll be fine, sir."

Genevieve called, "He's ready for you now, Mr. Attorney General."

Holder wasn't finished with me. "Stop by so we can have a chat before you head back. My assistant will open a spot for you."

I shook his hand and found his grip strong, even though I saw the exhaustion in his eyes. "Thank you, sir."

I followed Alene out wondering how she saw the meeting. Once out in the hallway I looked at her until she glanced at me. "What?" she said.

"Your assessment?"

Alene wouldn't look at me as she responded. "He listened."

"You regret taking a position that wasn't aligned with your job?"

She stopped and turned into me, angry. "That was my job … and yours, God damn it. We have to disrupt now and try to force change. But we also have to raise possible alternative futures. That's our job. Nobody else is going to do it. A lot of scenarios are discussed before any one gets traction. I don't think either of us think this one will lead anywhere, even though it's the right answer. But we had to try. We had to step forward and raise the question. What else are we going to do to solve this long term?"

"Are you angry at me for convincing you to do this?"

"No, I'm angry I didn't write a better paper."

The First Supper

Alene changed for dinner. She was transformed in a way I'd never imagined. She was the beautiful woman I'd tried hard not to see when we were working together. The silky black dress was plain, but clung to her. Simple eye liner made her emerald eyes stand out Cleopatra-like. Her perfume stirred those memories I shut down. I realized I wouldn't be able to work for her much longer because I wanted more than a work relationship.

Ceiba was on 14th Street, NW, within walking distance from Alene's apartment. The restaurant served contemporary Latin American cuisine. She told me she wanted me to experience some of the good things about Latin America so I didn't think it was all drug factories and cartel murder rampages. We were taken to our table in the back. I couldn't stop looking at her. She obviously noticed but said nothing.

Small talk and ordering filled the first few minutes, but then I had to say something about the meeting with the President. "You did a great job." I began.

She shook her head.

"No, really. I thought the report was thorough and complete. We have to recognize I have no credibility. The meeting probably would have gone better if I'd not been with you. I'm still damaged goods in more ways than one."

She reached across the table, put her hand on mine and it was like an electric shock pulsed through my body. "I understand. I lost someone too and went through a period much like what you're coming out of now."

Her words seemed to change everything. "Would you tell me about it?"

She hesitated, looking inward. "Bob was an Intel officer in the Swat Valley. On his fifth tour. From what they tell me, he walked into a booby trap trying to get his guys out of a targeted building."

The story was all too familiar. I'd seen more than my share of such incidents.

"You also wore his cologne. That's why I had to ask you to change yours. I like your new cologne, by the way. And then you used his name as your pseudonym when you called me."

She'd been reacting to me the same way I'd been reacting to her, for many of the same reasons. And I hadn't put it together.

But then she went off in a totally unexpected direction. "Do you remember the sim exercise when you opened the booby-trapped door and the bomb killed you?"

I remembered and nodded.

"I had to leave. I couldn't watch you die like Bob. Even if it was a simulation."

I was surprised she admitted her reaction. She seemed to get her emotions back under control. "I think I have a pretty good idea of what's going on."

I didn't think so. "Have you been with anyone since?"

She shook her head.

"Neither have I. I've already thought about you more than any other woman in the last two years. I've not let myself feel anything since; and yet ..."

She placed her hands in her lap, looking down.

"We've been having much the same feelings and denying them in much the same way." I said.

She looked up at me. "I'm not Lexie."

"And I'm not Bob."

She shook her head. "But what you're suggesting's impossible …"

"I understand we can't have a relationship while I report to you. But I'm not in a hurry. I need you to know how I feel. What I'm looking for. And how hard it is for me to see you every day knowing I just have to wait."

Alene looked at me differently. Her eyes left mine for a brief moment and then she said, "I don't know if I'm ready yet either, so maybe slow is good."

Another Dinner

Two days later back in Dallas I received a call on my cell phone from a male voice I didn't recognize. "Meet me at the Clyde Warren Park, near the stage at seven p.m. tonight. I have important information about your father. But come alone. If you're followed you'll never see me."

The line was dead. I didn't even have a chance to ask if he had the right number. So the time had come. Was this the trap I'd been expecting since Dad disappeared from the Triple C? Sure smelled like it. But was Dad dead or alive? That question had recurred to me every day since the brief conversation with him. I can't tell you how many times I'd imagined finding his dismembered body like the young Arroyo woman, piled up neatly with the head atop the pile. And yet somehow I resolutely believed he was alive. Wouldn't I feel his absence if he'd died? Wouldn't I know somehow? I didn't, for a minute, think they'd take me to him. The purpose of this meeting was something else. Why now, after all the attempts they'd made to kill me? Why this way? Why not a sniper shot through a window given that was Morales' specialty? Then I realized a call to a cell that had only recently been assigned indicated the task force had been penetrated much more deeply than I cared to admit.

I should have reported the call to Alene and sought her guidance on a coordinated response. But I chose not to. If the call were real, whoever was on the other end had demonstrated a detailed understanding of how we operated. If I told Alene, she'd have the backup in place and snipers on the roof waiting to take down the snitch. My intuition told me, as I played the call over and over, whoever called was real and Alene's preparations would scare him away.

A little later I went to see Nick. We made some arrangements that would bail me out if I got into trouble. Nick loved setting up the technology support and agreed to monitor things for me without asking questions or telling anyone.

The Clyde Warren Park was in downtown Dallas, built over the Woodall Rodgers Expressway. The park served to link the uptown and downtown parts of the city on the edge of the arts district. Performance halls, art museums, playhouses and a plethora of shops, offices and residences lined the area. It was a magnet for people during the day, but not so much in the evening when my mystery caller wished to meet. The dinner guests would be flocking to the restaurants, but the office workers would have already abandoned the area. The residents would be home for their evening meal. Enough traffic to hide in, but not enough to impede an escape. Whoever planned this meeting had studied the area and chosen well where and when to meet.

I arrived about ten minutes early. From the playground a short distance away I watched the stage to see who came. I watched the kids on the rope jungle gyms and running through the water sprays. Not many kids this time of night, but enough to make my appearance there not seem out of place.

I felt the man behind me more than saw him. Maybe it had something to do with the round piece of metal suddenly pushed up against my back. "You don't follow directions very well."

"It's not seven yet." I responded, thinking about spinning away from the weapon and disarming the man, but realizing I'd trapped myself. I couldn't take the chance the gun would go off with children around. Someone might get hurt or killed by such an action. I also had to go along if I wanted to know what happened to Dad. "You said you have information for me?"

"Yes, but another place will be better suited." I tried to place the voice, but it wasn't the same as on the phone. He touched my right shoulder to let me know I needed to walk in that direction. We were headed toward the park entrance on Harwood Avenue. As we walked toward the stage, which was just beyond the exit to the street I looked to see if my new found friend had some of his own there waiting to join us. I couldn't see anyone who looked out of place. Mostly young couples, a few with children.

When we turned left onto the access road, a black BMW sedan, just like thousands of others in this German car crazy city, pulled up. I was encouraged to get in the back seat. The doors locked immediately. My new friend went around and got in next to the driver. We drove south out of the city on Interstate 35, leaving behind the Wizard's support systems. I was on my own, now.

"So what's this information you planned to share?" I asked to start the conversation.

"I need to introduce you to some important people. They'll share what you need to know," the passenger, whose face I could only see in profile, responded. And that was the last thing he said until we arrived in San Antonio three and a half hours later.

The compound was smallish for what I expected. With the land, stone fence, house and security I doubt the owner had more than a million dollars in the place. Maybe that was the point. The owner didn't want to be conspicuous. We entered through the gate and were greeted by two security guards carrying automatic weapons. Looked like modified AK-47s, but I don't think I'd ever seen them modified in quite the same way before. The short stock and Picatinny rail meant they weren't concerned about accuracy, only how much lead and explosives they could fling at someone as quickly as possible.

We were waved on to the house. I looked for other security forces, but found just the two. I didn't trust that to be an accurate judgment, but hoped to prevail if I had to fight my way out of here, which I was beginning to think was more than just a possibility.

The car came to a stop at the front door and both the driver and my new friend came around to my side. They frisked for weapons as I emerged from the vehicle. Of course I had my 9mm Glock, which they helped themselves to. I was surprised the search stopped there. I expected they'd go for the cavity and whole nine yards. If they were just going to kill me, the drive all the way to San Antonio didn't make sense.

Entering the marbled foyer with a grand staircase rising towards the heavens, I found not a stick of furniture, painting or carpet within sight. Apparently the house was a property in transition, probably rented for thirty days and then sold to someone else. Perfect place to ensure you couldn't be traced. When you finally tracked it down, someone else lived here.

The gun in my back nudged me toward the kitchen.

Standing behind a massive preparation area in the center of the kitchen was the diminutive Juan Dominguez. I recognized him from the picture Nick had shown me of the three up-and-comers in the cartel world. He stood, drinking a glass of red wine from a single bottle on the dusty counter. I looked at the label. L.A. Ditto, Nebbiolo from Valle de Guadalupe in Baja, California. Not something you'd easily find in San Antonio.

To his left was a rough looking man with curly black hair who was observing the whole thing. His body odor told me the white collar was new to him. He didn't seem to be directly involved. The bulge under his jacket told me he was armed. He reminded me of how Alene had acted when I led the cocaine bust nearly three years ago. Watching, no, observing. I could think of at least three different roles Mr. Bulge could possibly be playing. But which one? The answer might be important.

I had a flash of a man backing into the hallway of Bryan Tower right after he'd shot me. So Juan Dominguez was there. He'd led the attack himself. Apparently I'd moved up on the priority list. Never thought they'd have someone at the top trying to kill me personally. What was going on here? Why was I suddenly so important for the Zetas to spend this much time trying to kill me? Why hadn't they done so in the park? Why bring me down here for a face-to-face?

I nodded to the two men.

"Agent Carr. We have much to talk about. I hope you can stay for dinner, as my guest of course."

"Only if you'll let me choose the wine."

My remark caught Dominguez off guard, but he recovered, "Of course. The wine. I would offer you a glass, however, we only have just the one." He gathered his thoughts and continued. "You've been miraculously lucky."

"Some would say skillful, but I'm sure none in this room." I responded.

"No, I wouldn't expect anyone here to describe you that way." Dominguez came around from behind the preparation counter carrying his glass of wine.

"You have some information you'd like to share?" I bluffed that I was taking him at his word.

"I'm going to introduce you to someone who is most eager to meet you. He's come a long way to do just that." Sounded like Dominguez was savoring the occasion.

"Anyone I know?"

"You've never met, but your lives have been intertwined for years."

His description of intertwined lives confused me. I couldn't imagine who he was talking about since Morales had only been on the scene for a few months. What was their plan? What did they expect to happen tonight? And why tonight? Were we getting too close? Did the attack on Ciudad Victoria change the whole equation? They had Dad call to warn me off. They must know I was still engaged. What was their end game?

Shushi Zushi seemed a strange place to have a dinner meeting, but it was going on Midnight and no customers remained. In fact, I thought the sign said they'd closed at eleven. We walked down the empty row of booths with large pictures of oriental gardens hung on the wall. Spare decoration, lots of wood, chrome and a ceramic floor. Not a sushi maven, it wasn't my taste. The man sitting at the back corner table with a briefcase atop was indeed the man whose picture Alene had shown us before we went into Ciudad Victoria. I couldn't imagine how our lives had been intertwined as Dominguez had characterized us. Castillo had brought me here for a reason. What was it? To kill me personally seemed to be the only explanation, but why a sushi place? Why San Antonio? He'd been trying to have me killed for a long time. A huge effort. Even had Dominguez personally involved. With all that, why was I standing here now, face-to-face?

Dominguez encouraged me to sit directly across the table from Castillo, but I didn't. Castillo glanced up at Dominguez and nodded without explanation. "So you are FBI Agent Carr?"

I nodded, imitating him, although I'm sure he didn't notice.

"Do you know why you're here?"

"You have information you wish to share with me," I responded, more focused on where everyone else was in the room than on Castillo. My heart rate increased noticeably. All the body language said I wouldn't be leaving here alive. But I still didn't know why Castillo wanted me dead. The observer came up right behind me.

"Did you know we share the same alma mater?" Castillo asked.

I couldn't imagine Castillo at Yale, but tried to remember if I'd ever met him. Came up blank. "If you're looking for the secret handshake I could have saved you the expense of bringing me down here."

He smiled. "No. They didn't want me in their secret societies. I was just a smart poor boy from Ciudad Victoria."

"Who took a non-traditional route to the top." I noted since he was making it seem we were peers, which I knew we were not.

Castillo reflected on my comment for a moment and his expression changed. He removed an antique looking silver Colt six shooter from the brief case sitting on the table and set it before him. "You studied history, so maybe you recognize this weapon."

"Only the type, used after the Civil War."

"It's the weapon Pat Garrett used to kill Billy the Kid."

Castillo was still treating me like a classmate. It didn't make sense to me, given the body language of everyone else continued to send out a strong message that I wasn't going anywhere alive. "Impressive."

"And symbolic. The Kid was an embarrassment to Garrett, who'd been his friend. When the Kid became a problem, Garrett solved it personally. You've become an embarrassment to me."

I was finally about to get the answer I'd spent many a sleepless night trying to answer: why? There was also no question where this little dinner conversation was going. I could wait to learn why or try to prevent Castillo's plan from succeeding. I had no time to make a decision as it was clear I'd be dead shortly after Castillo revealed the mystery.

"You going to release my father?"

Castillo laughed silently. That was all I needed to know.

My leftward spin into the observer enabled me to reach into his jacket.

I grabbed his pistol, flicking off the safety as I pulled it out.

A single shot into his chest and I turned back toward my right and Castillo who now had the Colt up, but not yet aimed.

Tap, Tap. Two shots in the forehead. Castillo fell over backwards. *Two shots just like Bill and Janice.* I turned into the observer to shield me from the others.

I knew I had the advantage of confusion. Castillo was clearly dead. The rest of the men were there to protect him. Since they'd failed and no one was in charge I banked on them being hesitant about how to respond. I had to hold up the observer now, feeling bullets enter his body.

I turned my living shield just enough to see the driver, two shots and he went down.

Another shot hit the observer and the force pushed me back.

I had to redouble the effort to hold up the observer as I had his whole weight to support now. I couldn't let that distract me. I needed him to be my shield or it was over as I was still outnumbered two to one.

Dominguez and my friend from the park were probably maneuvering to get multiple angles on me. I couldn't allow them to succeed.

My new friend from the park moved to partially obscure himself behind a column. He fired the rest of his clip into the now dead weight observer.

I turned slightly and shot twice. The park gunman went down as well.

One more.

I looked around but Dominguez was gone.

Gunmen were probably waiting for me outside. Probably more than one. I eased the observer down and went to the bar, finding a phone and calling 911.

"This is FBI Agent James Carr. I'm at Sushi Zushi. There's been a shooting here. Four men down."

"FBI Agent Carr?"

"Yes."

"We just got a call about you. Said you were shot. Police and emergency responders are on their way."

"Tell the police there may still be shooters in the area and to approach with caution. And alert the Medical Examiner as I don't think any of these gentlemen are going to the emergency room."

The first responders and police all arrived about five minutes later. A small crowd had gathered outside, but no indication of more shooters. I thought it curious others hadn't come to rescue Castillo, but had called 911. Why'd they report I'd been shot? They'd lured me with Dad. I wouldn't get any information now and had to assume since Castillo intended to kill me I wouldn't have gotten any if I'd waited. I rationalized taking action that prevented me from finding Dad, feeling guilty I'd done so.

Setting aside my disappointment, I still didn't know what intersection I had with Castillo or why he wanted to kill me personally. I was an embarrassment. What did that mean? I wondered if bringing me here was a setup of the Zeta leader? Was that why I'd been spared through so many attempts on my life? Had Dominguez planned to use me to become the top Zeta? Where did the Messenger and Dominguez intersect? Did the Messenger work for Dominguez? Was Dominguez the guy behind everything that had happened to me? What did that mean? Would the threat to my life end now that Dominguez had what he wanted? Would Dad be released? Would life go back to normal?

But then another thought occurred. Dominguez didn't hang around to kill me when he had the chance. Nor did he have others ready to take me out. What would happen next? I feared things had just gone from bad to worse.

The Target

Dominguez walked down the hallway of the Federale building in Mexico City. He knew where to find Antonio Morales' office, having been there many times before. He was wearing a prosthetic nose that changed the shape of his face. And the identification he showed as he entered the building identified him as Luis Morales. He told the security guard he was the captain's cousin from Monterrey.

Morales wasn't in his office. Dominguez tried to decide if he should wait or call him on his cell when he saw the tall captain coming his way. Morales saw Dominguez, nodded and sped up his pace.

"Welcome cousin. What can I do for you today?" Morales greeted him.

Dominguez shook his hand. The Captain ushered Dominguez into his office and closed the door behind them.

"Congratulations," Morales began but Dominguez cut him off.

"We need to talk about the President."

"You got my note?"

Dominguez nodded, but was impatient to know what Morales knew.

"My sources say next week." Morales confirmed.

"Where?"

"Not Washington. That's actually good for us."

"Do you know where if not Washington?"

"My sources confirm the meeting between the presidents will take place along the border, but the exact location's still being negotiated." Dominguez's antenna went up because Morales wouldn't give him at least the probable places being discussed.

"What else did your sources say?" Dominguez was curious about what Morales wasn't telling him.

"My sources say Los Zetas will break up into several factions without Castillo. They don't think you have the support to keep it the way it was."

Dominguez had heard the same rumors repeated by his lieutenants. "Los Zetas wasn't the way it was. Castillo was changing everything."

"Including you, I heard."

There could be only one source who would know of Castillo's plans. "Herbiberto?"

Morales nodded, "Said you were out and soon to be dead."

Dominguez grimaced with the thought he'd been right about Castillo's intentions. Another piece of evidence confirming he had to act when he did. He hated to have to kill someone as talented with a rifle as Herbiberto, but the only way to get control of Los Zetas was to eliminate the loyalists to the old leader. Setting it up so the FBI agent killed him was a pure delight for Dominguez. Better to cut out the cancer in the beginning and build with a new foundation. He'd already taken the first steps. His meeting with Morales was another in building the new foundation. If their plan worked, Dominguez would be solid as the leader of the Zetas. No one would challenge someone who had the reach he intended to display. And no one would mistake Dominguez's role.

"Did Herbiberto tell you who else was moving up?"

Morales nodded, "As a matter of fact he said a number of things of interest. He was trying to figure out what we were doing. Why I hadn't been able to kill the FBI Agent. I made him believe the Agent was practically superman."

"You were always smarter than Castillo gave you credit for."

Morales wasn't interested in faint praise from a dead man. "Castillo wasn't as smart as he thought either. We can work through Herbiberto's short list pretty quickly. I already have my men locating them and assigned to take them down."

"Is this the service I pay taxes for?"

Morales raised his eyebrows, "You pay taxes?"

"No." Dominguez laughed. "What else do I need to know from your conversation with Herbiberto?"

"He said Castillo told you to kill me."

"Yeah, when you failed to kill the FBI agent."

Morales seemed puzzled, "Did you tell Castillo of our little plan for the agent?"

"Of course not. Castillo was all low risk. He was afraid of the big opportunity. Never would've approved going ahead."

"You should be pleased things were delayed from what I first thought would happen." Morales tested the waters.

"You know I wasn't happy. Castillo kept forcing me to take actions I didn't want to. Thought we'd blown the plan at least twice, but somehow everything worked out."

"You created quite a reaction going into their headquarters in the US and then taking out an airplane."

A perfect segue, Dominguez thought. Almost like Morales was reading his mind. "I need people who think boldly. What I really wanted to talk about is giving you a bigger role."

"I like what I do."

Morales seemed curious, but apparently wanted to establish whatever he did would be on his terms, Dominguez thought. "And you're very good at what you do, but you're also a big picture thinker."

"I like to think so."

Dominguez was encouraged. "Are you willing to give up all this?" He gestured to the small office. "For about ten times what you're making now?"

Morales shook his head. "You disappoint me. Only ten times? Sinaloa offered me twenty."

"Sinaloa's desperate because they need to stop Los Zetas from taking over their distribution and their customers in the US."

"I could help them."

Dominguez smiled, "Of course you could. And on the other hand, you could be running their entire territory and operations if you join me. As soon as we take them out I'll need someone to manage the western operations. Don't you still have your house in Guadalajara?"

"Yes, I do. But a guy's got to eat and ten times just doesn't make it worth my while."

"After you do the President we can talk money again. Seems we already agreed to ten times just for one bullet. I'm talking ten times every year as a base and a percentage of what we do together."

Morales smiled. "Glad to see you were listening. What kind of percentage are you talking? Need to keep the Sinaloa informed of counter offers."

Dominguez shrugged. "You're not listening. We can talk money again after you do the President. In the meantime you decide you like what the Sinaloa are offering without knowing mine, that's your choice. But you go over you'll be on the top of my hit list."

"Would've been disappointed if I weren't."

McKelligan Canyon

Public reports of Castillo's death were only that Federal agents had killed the Zeta leader in a shootout. No other details were offered. The media made a big deal out of the lack of specifics, but the Justice Department claimed that release of such information would jeopardize other ongoing operations.

I'd called Dan, Bill and Janice's son, to tell him the man responsible for his parent's death was dead, but the real killer was still out there. Dan was not consoled. I told him the journey wasn't over, that I had the name of someone who'd been there and was pursuing him. Dan asked about his grandfather and I could only say I didn't know. It was a hard call and I struggled more than once.

Alene looked at me across her desk. She looked more rested and relaxed than I'd seen her in a very long time. "Eric wants to know why we made the Mexicans spend all that money to send the Army into Ciudad Victoria if you were just going to shoot him at a San Antonio restaurant."

She was upset with me for not following procedure, and I hoped angry that I'd risked getting killed. "So, can we can get back to work?" I responded

"I'm sorry you didn't find your father, and I'm angry you didn't tell me about the call. You still don't trust me do you?"

I couldn't respond to three different messages so I responded to none. "Willy doesn't think he has revenge for his former partner Strickland, doesn't feel safe in his own neighborhood and I think the Bryan Tower massacre has weighed even heavier on him. I want to get him back in the saddle."

She repaid me with, "Did you see the news from Guadalajara? Seems the police found a bag containing thirteen heads in a park. The heads were of Sinaloa cartel *sicarios,* one of whom was a nephew of the reputed cartel head. The talk on the news is about who delivered justice? But behind the scenes the talk is which cartel threw down the gauntlet."

"Dominguez asserting himself?"

"Maybe. It looks like the stakes are being raised."

"We need to move quickly, before Los Zetas works through the changes."

"What happened to slow?" she asked. I understood the double meaning.

"If we're going to have a future, I have to resolve the past."

"That why you went with them, knowing you'd probably not come back? Not telling me what you were doing? I can't stand the thought of having you not come back."

"Do you want me to quit? Now?"

Her eyes were tearing. She looked at me then slowly shook her head.

I got Willy on the next flight with me to El Paso. Willy was as white as a sheet as we approached to land, but the landing was uneventful. I wouldn't look back as we went up the jet bridge, seeing the burned out aircaft just down the row. But nothing happened. When we arrived at the UTEP lab, Colonel Blum and Zed were talking over a map.

"McDonald deliver the Intel package?" I asked as I approached them.

"We have an urgent reassignment. The President of Mexico just handed us a gift. He's coming to the US for a meeting with the US President." Zed began.

"Why is that a gift?" I asked

Zed answered, "Because they're meeting at the McKelligan Canyon Amphitheatre."

I drew a blank.

Colonel Blum responded, "They're meeting about ten miles from here. Dr. Tom's virtualizing the whole area for us now."

Someone must have known about the planned meeting. I thought Walter Josephson would have known. And if Josephson knew the Zetas must have known. The bells in my head were deafening.

"So how do we convince the Secret Service guys to let us play ball?" Zed asked.

"Tell them we have the whole area modeled and they can play 'what if' to their hearts content, but they should include us. In the meantime, we need to start working through the mission scenarios. We need to understand every possible way the Zetas can attack."

"What if it's not a sniper? What if they go with a bomb in a truck, or a UAV with a missile, or who knows what?" I started free associating. I was afraid Morales wouldn't appear. My heart rate was up. Was the Mexican President the target Dominguez and Hernandez-Anjel had been after all along? I had to slow things down.

"We work through all scenarios. We come up with a plan to respond to each one." Blum concluded.

I called Alene on a scrambled line.

"You see who's coming to El Paso?"

"Eric just informed me. Asked if we could provide support to the Secret Service."

"You coming over to help us?"

"Not initially. President asked for a new brief for his discussions with his Mexican counterpart. I'll be there when the President comes in, but only to back up Eric on policy discussions. The two presidents are having a private session. What I'm getting is the President wants to discuss our approach in detail. The Monterrey effort is still seen as a success on both sides of the border. Both presidents want to find a way to expand the model."

"Will I get to see you?"

"Not until afterwards; and maybe not then." I wasn't excited I may have to wait to see her until I got back to Dallas. "If the presidents agree on expanded joint operations it will delay what we discussed."

I hadn't considered success getting between Alene and me. "I miss you." There I said it.

"It won't be long, now." What was she trying to say? That she didn't miss me? That our mission op tempo might be drastically increased and I'd see a whole lot less of her? The call unsettled me.

After my call to Alene I suited up and scaled in. Soon Willy and I found ourselves scouting out sniper positions. We tried to decide where we'd need to place ourselves to counter a sniper at each location. We looked for positions where a low flying UAV could be intercepted. We placed vans with explosives at varying locations. We determined the blast radius of different types of explosives. We set up cordons to ensure if anything did get through it'd be far enough from the two presidents to prevent injury.

The rest of the day consisted of ops to deal with attacks on the convoys from and to the airport. We modeled the entire route, identified the points of greatest vulnerability. Finally we placed markers where and how to isolate the threats.

The Secret Service arrived about six in the evening. Two junior agents came over to review our analysis. After only a brief overview the agents called their team leader and four more senior guys came over.

The agents scaled in and walked through the entire protective plan Blum, Zed, Willy and I devised. They had different ideas of how to handle some of the vulnerable points; they made several suggestions of better approaches to securing the route in and out. Secret Service didn't respond to the UAV defenses, leaving flying threats to the military to deal with, although the agents wanted to comment on the final plans before signing off.

At about ten, two of the agents joined us at Riccardo's restaurant on Montana Drive for dinner. The Secret Service guys seemed to relax realizing the FBI and Army simply wanted to help since we had advanced planning capability with models of the areas we created for the Virtual Immersion system.

When I told them about Captain Morales, his background, and how we suspected he'd be sent to kill the President of Mexico at this event, their demeanor changed. Could the US President also be a target? A dual assassination?

Gone Missing

The news media from both the US and Mexico arrived early. Their mobile studios set up to carry the live broadcast of the joint presidential news conference to both countries. The event was billed as a major address by both presidents. However every news outlet wanted to know why no background briefings were scheduled. The various analysts kept guessing what could be of such importance that Felipe Calderon, President of Mexico, would join Barak Obama somewhere other than in Washington? The speculation focused on long expected changes to the North American Free Trade Agreement. Teams from both countries had been working on the changes for over a year. But why not Washington? No explanation was forthcoming.

The two presidents seemed ready to announce the agreement. Apparently the timing would give the Obama administration a chance to put the changes into effect before the next US President came in if he were not re-elected. A new President would want to put a different spin on implementation of the changes.

I walked among the network control vans, tried to understand how their locations changed Dr. Tom's analysis. While Dr. Tom's team had modeled everything for the Virtual Immersion system, the sizes and shapes of the vans didn't always match what Dr. Tom modeled. The differences could open up new shooting lanes we hadn't anticipated. So Dr. Tom and his team made new measurements and adjustments.

I watched as the massive wingspan of what I thought was Air Force One first came into view, making the approach into the El Paso International Airport. I couldn't understand the aerodynamics of such a massive device or how it was able to fly. And yet on the approach to the main runway, Air Force One seemed to just hang in the air. The aircraft slowly descended until gently touching down, sending up a small dust cloud from the multiple landing gears shouldering so much weight.

Two identical aircraft were already on the ground next to a remote hanger space. I realized any of them could have been the presidential aircraft.

The Secret Service advised me the protocol was to have the US President land first so he could welcome his Mexican counterpart. They'd then proceed together in one bulletproof car. The presidential limo would be surrounded by a fleet of up armored Chevy Tahoes. Each one contained an undisclosed number of weapons to handle any emergency along the way. I remembered the up armored GMC Denalis at the garden spot when Strickland was killed. I thought about the Suburbans that tried to box me and Willy in on the bridge here. Neither were pleasant thoughts.

"One president down and one to go." I noted

"You better get your gear on." Willy suggested. "The games will begin and you'll be sitting back here watching the whole mess, while us heroes gotta go save the fucking day… again."

Willy and I went to the security office set up in a nearby pavilion. As we crossed the parking lot I looked at all of the vehicles already there and wondered if they'd all been screened for explosives. Screening was a Secret Service job. I knew a bunch of the Secret Service guys from counterfeiting work on which I'd cooperated. I didn't know any of the presidential detail. And these guys absolutely had no sense of humor. A couple of times at dinner I'd started down a path with Willy and seen the looks. So I just backed off and let whatever I'd started to say just hang there.

I picked up a Chay Tac .408 caliber Sniper rifle bringing back a flood of memories I didn't want to revisit. Donning a tactical vest, I loaded up with extra bullets for the Chay Tac, and a flash bang, a smoke and a regular grenade. I just had a bad feeling. No matter how much weaponry I brought with me, I expected it wouldn't be enough or the right ones.

Willy wasn't about to schlep a whole bunch of extra weight. He carried only an M4, slung over his left shoulder, but resting in front of him. We attached our security detail IDs to our molle vests and moved out of the security room to take up our positions checking people into the site. The guards all had a picture of Captain Morales, the same picture Nick had found on the Internet and hardly worth using. So Willy and I, who had both met Captain Morales, were assigned to the gates to check everyone in. I pulled about a dozen men of Hispanic backgrounds aside to put them through secondary screening. They weren't Morales, but they were worth a second look because of an unwillingness to look us in the eye or answer a question crisply. Each one cleared the secondary and was admitted into the Amphitheater grounds to take up their position in support of the event.

By four o'clock everyone had checked in. An hour remained before the televised news conference. The Secret Service closed the gates and sealed the area. The only party yet to arrive was the limo with the two presidents and the escort. They'd show thirty minutes before the broadcast.

I walked through the network news mobile control rooms. As I passed one of the trailers a short graying man came out. "Hey, are you security?"

I nodded. "How can I help?"

My name's John Libretto. I'm the senior news director here. One of our mobile cameras is missing. Don't know if someone picked one up by mistake, but it's kinda hard to think they wouldn't have noticed our peacock plastered all over the case."

"How many cameras like that do you have here?"

"Three. With one missing we're kinda screwed. It really limits our ability to cover the speech properly."

I tried to understand the implications. "I'll see what I can do for you, sir."

"Need it back pronto and ask for me, John Libretto."

"Got it."

I turned towards Willy. "What do you think? Are the cameramen the threat or is Morales trying to distract us from him?"

"The weasel wants the glory. He ain't countin' on these cameraman fuckers. Probably just a distraction so he can get a clean shot."

The Bluff

While Willy informed the Secret Service of the camera issue, I went to the Univision trailer and I knocked on the door. A young guy poked his head out.

"Can I see your Senior Director?"

The young man nodded. In a moment a silver haired man with dark complexion came to the door. "May I help you?"

I showed him my security badges. "We were informed one of the other networks is missing one of their broadcast cameras. Just checking to make sure you have yours."

The man gave me a curt nod. "Yes, we are accounted for."

I started to turn, but stopped, "Do you know for sure the cameramen are the ones you sent out?"

"My cameras are all up, I can't see the cameraman, I can only tell him what I want him to do."

"So he has an earpiece, but he can't talk to you?"

"There's no reason to. We see what he's sending in and tell him what we want him to photograph."

I looked at my watch and realized I didn't have enough time to work through all of the broadcast teams. Even if I tried, apparently they didn't know for sure who was running their cameras.

I raised the younger of the two Secret Service agents I had dinner with the night before, told him about the missing cameras, and informed him Univision had no idea who was manning theirs. I speculated Morales could be somewhere in or near the building, waiting in the background to take the first shot before his compatriots finished business if needed in the panic response. The agent listened but seemed distracted. He said he'd handle the problem. *Thanks very much but this is Secret Service business.*

I couldn't just stand by. I knew Miguel Hernandez Anjel wouldn't go to a predictable spot. He'd seek a target of opportunity, some place we'd overlook. Some place we'd discount. But where?

I knew I had to get up on a platform to see a path to the stage. I was sure Miguel Hernandez Anjel wanted witnesses to his brilliance. Therefore he intended to take down the President of Mexico before a live television audience. The shot would be taken when the Mexican President would be on the stage. So I went to the stage, even though it was now restricted. The Secret Service wouldn't let me enter. I called Dr. Tom.

"Can you immerse and go up on the stage? Need to find any places with a clear shot path to the Mexican President's podium?"

"Just so happens one of my guys is in right now. I'll ask him."

I listened to the muffled exchange. Dr. Tom came back on, "You have the close in stuff, the lighting cat walks and all. How far back you want to go?"

"A mile or two."

I heard Dr. Tom talking to his guy. After a few minutes he came back on. "The roof of the main building of the William Beaumont Army Hospital has the best line of sight."

"Not the obvious places. Something you'd say no way at first look. But if you thought about it… maybe…"

I waited for what seemed forever. I heard a muffled discussion between Dr. Tom and his guy in the system. Finally Dr. Tom came back on the phone. "He says there's this bluff in the Franklin Mountains State Park. Probably out of range. But you said maybe..."

"How far?"

"More than a mile. Maybe a mile and a half."

"Thanks." I knew he'd identified the kind of challenge Hernandez-Anjel would relish. Send a message to the world with a shot only he could make.

I was on the phone to the Secret Service. "Need a lift up to the park. There's a bluff with a tough shot, but one we need to check out."

The response came back, "We checked it already. Beyond range and not a threat. But the Medevac could probably get you up there fastest, if you want to take a second look." sounded like the compromise they arrived at, "But you'd have to go now. We can't get you back because the bird has to be here when the President's in the building."

"Let's go."

As I raced over to the helipad, I called Willy and met him.

The Fair Exchange

Expecting a close range exchange, I gave my Chay-Tac and grenades to Willy in exchange for his M-4 before climbing out. I watched the Medevac with Willy lift off. I surveyed the area with the scope on the M4. I kept advancing on the place where Dr. Tom had directed me. I checked my watch. I had no more than fifteen minutes before the events would begin.

I heard through my radio headphones they'd rounded up most of the cameramen. John Libretto identified the missing camera and unknown cameraman. Secret Service took the mystery cameraman into custody finding a plastic single shot handgun on him. The interrogation started immediately. The faux cameraman slashed his wrists with a hidden razor blade. He was taken to the same hospital where Willy had his bullet removed what seemed a lifetime ago. The Secret Service didn't learn anything of value.

Catching a glint of metal, I turned to my left. After studying the terrain I made out the figure of a man. He was lying prone, focused at the McKelligan Canyon Amphitheater. The man was under trees making it hard to locate him from the air. I used the brush as much as possible for cover. I soon found myself very close to the target, all without apparently attracting his attention. I saw him sighting in on a point nearly two miles away.

I took a single step to close the gap, breaking a branch. "I've been expecting you, Agent Carr."

Since Hernandez-Anjul knew I was there, I stood up. Keeping the Mexican in my cross hairs, I approached.

"We have your cameramen."

I noticed Hernandez-Anjul had an earpiece in one ear, "Correction, you have one of my camera men. You think you have me. But you'd be mistaken ... on both counts."

I approached within ten feet of the sniper, continuing to keep him in the sights of my weapon.

Miguel Hernandez Anjel turned to look back at me. "We did a lot of research on you when we learned you were the one. I think I know you better than my own cousin, who I grew up with."

"Then you know you're dead."

"Or you are dead. After all, we could have killed you, how many times?"

"As I could have killed you knowing you killed my brother and sister in law."

A warped smile appeared on Hernandez-Anjul's face, "Ah, but there's one small problem. You see, I didn't kill your brother or sister in law. That honor goes to the man standing behind you with a handgun pointed at your head."

I ignored his comment, "So why were your finger prints on the shell casing if you weren't there?"

"Because I loaded the magazines for my team. Yes, they were my team, but I wasn't there. I'm a marksman. Not many can make the shots I do. Particularly not at the distances I shoot. But your family ranch? Your family wasn't a job for a sniper. It was a job for men like Arturo Sanchez. He's ready to finish the job you didn't let him complete in Waco. So he has a big incentive to finish you today. You're a thorn in his side and a blemish on his otherwise perfect record of kills. A record approaching your own."

"I'm done with killing people at a distance. That's not me anymore." I responded harshly, not willing to be dragged back into my years in the Army. I'd been trying to put my past behind me ever since leaving the Special Forces.

"I see you regret your skill at killing. But you're so good."

I kept Hernandez-Anjul in my sights. I didn't flinch when I heard a twig break from a step behind me, verifying someone was indeed there. My mind raced trying to take this situation to the logical conclusion. "I take you out, he'll never hit the target. He doesn't have your talent." I bluffed hoping I understood the situation.

"No, I don't. But you do. Over two hundred verified sniper kills on your record while with the Army Special Forces. Very impressive. " Sergeant Sanchez responded from behind me. However, I still didn't waver in my cover of Hernandez-Anjul.

"You see, we've already won. Sergeant Sanchez will kill you in a moment. I will then shoot the President of the Mexican States with this weapon, very much like the one you used for so many years. We'll ensure your fingerprints are in the correct place. Then we call in your Secret Service to come claim your body. The Federales will have killed the assassin of our President. At the same time we'll have ensured your government doesn't intervene in Mexican internal affairs. Not after a US federal agent was killed assassinating the President of Mexico. The event will create as much suspicion in my country of your government as the Iranians and the whole Muslim world has had since you orchestrated the Shah's return."

The whole plot was now before me. Hernandez Anjul never intended to kill me, only set me up so I'd obsessively pursue him here. How could I turn the situation around now? "You're a man of science, Hernandez-Anjul. Sanchez pulls his trigger. Sound travels faster than a bullet, so I react to the sound, killing you, because I'm way too close to miss a head shot at this range. So you've failed your mission. Your President lives, Sanchez fires a missing shot and no one cares. What then other than you and I are both dead?"

Hernandez-Anjul looked at his watch. "It's time. We'll see who's right."

The silence hung as I waited, knowing the two presidents had probably arrived at the amphitheater below and they'd soon move to the microphones where they'd be exposed to the assassin's bullets.

I heard Sergeant Sanchez grunt and fall.

I didn't flinch, keeping Hernandez-Anjul in my sight. He was decidedly unhappy about what he saw. A wave of relief came over me. I had to steel myself not to relax. I mustn't provide an opening. The confrontation and test of wills wasn't even close to being over yet.

"Detective Graves took the shot from the roof of the Walter Beaumont Army Medical Center. Now we have a new set of choices. I can either shoot you, and claim I stopped you just before you took the shot; or we wait until the chopper comes back for us. I turn you over to our interrogators and life goes on."

Hernandez-Anjul kept watching Sanchez as if waiting for him to get up and finish me off. But I knew that wouldn't happen. Willy was an Expert on sniper weapons.

Hernandez-Anjul must have been calculating the odds of avoiding a sniper he couldn't see. A sniper who'd just killed his ace. "There's one other scenario. A fair exchange. Your father for me."

I couldn't open that door. I hadn't dealt with any of my feelings. Not with any of them. Dr. Graham had told me only putting to rest the events at the Triple C could start the process of healing. But not now.

"You can talk with him." Hernandez-Anjul offered.

I watched Hernandez-Anjul speed dial, but reached forward and took his phone. I waited until someone answered and clicked off, recording the last answered number.

Hernandez-Anjul watched me with anger and apprehension. "Your father's now a dead man." He threatened, but somehow his threat rang hollow. Or maybe I just didn't want to believe I'd just caused Dad's death. I needed to decide what to do with Hernandez-Anjul.

"I'm still a little unhappy with you about a bunch of things. Like you sending your boys out to kill me in the Dallas precinct house. Sending them to kill my brother and his wife, and burn down the home I grew up in. I got the idea we'd never be friends. I'm not too happy you took a bunch of shots at me, stole my car and loaded it up with explosives that brought down my apartment house. The explosion killed some of my friends and neighbors and put me and a whole bunch of other folks out on the street. Fire bombin' my hotel wasn't exactly a friendly gesture either. The attempt to kill me on the hotel and bridge here? I could have done without. So you see, I'm not really too eager to let all these events slide."

"What if I give you an invaluable piece of information?" He sounded calculated.

"Like what?"

"Information that will change your presidential election."

"What do I care about elections?" I tried to make the response as casual as possible, but he seemed to gather hope anyway.

"You let me go and I'll give you information that'll let you name your price to the next president of your country. Any price. You could be the Attorney General."

Attorney General was an easy one for me to field, although I couldn't seem to get my heart rate back down. "Met him recently. Doesn't seem to be having much fun."

Hernandez-Anjul seemed incredulous, but maybe he was just getting desperate knowing Willy had him in his sights. "You can have anything you want."

"I can't get my brother or his wife back. Despite your little show I believe my father's dead as well. I won't rebuild my childhood home. Just doesn't make sense to me now. Sure I can buy another old Porsche, but I don't need your information to buy a car. I already got another apartment so no biggie there. Shooting at me? Don't think your information will keep anyone from shooting at me. Seems to be just a fact of life these days. So what does this information get me?"

Morales played his ultimate card. "Alene Oliviera."

I froze.

I was just beginning to think I might be able to finally deal with my feelings. I couldn't put Alene there with Lexie and Bill and Janice and Mom and probably Dad. My mind raced.

I felt my finger tighten on the trigger.

"We both know what she means to you."

The blood drained from my head making me dizzy for a moment. I did my best not to let Hernandez-Anjul see my reaction. Apparently Willy was right about how transparent I am. "Tell me."

Hernandez-Anjul regarded me for a long moment. Then he responded, "You're a man of honor. You'll be obligated to let me go."

I didn't respond one way or the other. He became more desperate.

"One of your presidential candidates has received over $40 million dollars from companies all over your country. If you trace their ownership, they have a common parent: the Montezuma Produce and Chinese Laundry Company in Dallas."

I hesitated as I heard the click in my mind, remembering the name of the company we'd staked out the night of the Dallas precinct shootings when it seemed my life had changed forever. I couldn't show I remembered. "Why should anyone care about contributions?" I wondered aloud.

"The Zetas pay for all the fruit and vegetables Montezuma buys in Mexico, but they generate fake invoices. Montezuma pays for nothing. Then the produce company transfers the excess profits on selling the fruit and vegetables to the laundries as additional paid in capital. Montezuma owns ten thousand laundries across the US. The laundries make campaign donations of about $4,000 each on average, with the capital contributions from the parent company. Laundered money, quite literally."

"So illegal drug sales are behind the contributions?"

"No. The Zeta money comes through their sponsor. A certain Middle Eastern nation who put them into business in the first place and still calls the shots. The Zetas' sponsor provides all of their advanced weapons, helps them recruit certain *sicarios,* and plans their strategy. The money flows through a maze of companies.

"Why would a Middle East country get involved in Mexico?"

"Shows how little you understand. Think about it. Those small oil rich Kingdoms are ruled by families. The Arab Spring showed the people aren't really too happy with their arrangement. Iran threatens daily across the Persian Gulf. The Muslim Brotherhood seems ascendant. Al Queda's trying to change the rules and the rulers. At least one Kingdom's hedging its bets in case Iran or their people decide they want a change."

"So how do you know all of this?" I tried to sound like I didn't believe him, but the link to Montezuma made too much sense. Beyond the Montezuma link I didn't know.

"The Zetas did their best to hide their relationship. But the dollars are so large and pass through so many hands. Eventually the money shows itself when the Arabs are concerned maybe not all the money they think they're entitled to is getting back."

Then the flaw in his logic became clear. "And of course if I took this story to anyone, you'd be long gone. So I have no one to verify anything. If I took you in, you'd never repeat any of what you just told me. The Zetas would kill you in prison because they couldn't afford to let you say another word to anyone. So why should I care?"

"Because you're a man of honor. Now you owe me."

My primary thought was of Alene. How do I protect her from Hernandez-Anjul and the men he commanded? But then I realized he'd never tell me what I needed to know to protect her. I had to decide. But I needed one more key piece of information. "Why's Juan Dominguez trying to kill me?"

"Dominguez? You really don't know?" Hernandez-Anjul seemed genuinely surprised. "You disappoint."

"Why's he want me dead?"

"Castillo wanted you dead because you killed his brother."

"When did I kill his brother?" I had no idea.

"The big cocaine bust, as we called it. Dallas what, nearly three years ago."

I thought back but couldn't place which one I'd killed that could have been his brother. Why'd we missed that link?

"Dominguez had the idea to lay the blame on you for killing our president. You and your family were just supposed to be dead because Castillo wanted you that way. Dominguez made you collateral damage to his rise within the Zetas. Your killing Castillo wasn't in the original plan, but Dominguez couldn't resist when Castillo backed him into a corner. And now killing our president will show anyone who'd oppose Dominguez that he can bend the US to his will. Who'd dare take him on? He's much more ambitious and dangerous than Castillo."

I still couldn't figure out which one had been Castillo's brother. Had to set the thought aside. Couldn't think about it now. I thought about his explanation and description of Dominguez. I didn't know what I needed to do about him. Would he continue to pursue me if I survived? Did he know about Alene? If Hernandez-Anjul did, I had to assume Dominguez did as well.

Hernandez-Anjul interrupted my thoughts, "Your Colonel Blum has learned much of value from me, over the years." He was trying to build a case.

I'd been trained by the FBI to take prisoners and learn whatever they might reveal. Only information prevented bad things. I had to prevent the bad guys from succeeding. Hernandez –Anjul was no exception. He possessed a great deal of information we didn't. If he cooperated the information would be a major blow to more than just the Zetas. My duty was to take him in.

But he'd introduced Alene into the equation. He'd work with Dominguez to harm Alene, Dad and my sister Tess, even from prison. He and Dominguez started the scorched family vendetta. I could never be sure of Alene's safety just as I still had no idea if Dad were really alive. And then there was Dan, who counted on me to avenge his parents. My Special Forces training taught me to kill with no regrets.

I couldn't kill him as much as I wanted to. But I couldn't let him live either.

I watched Hernandez-Anjul, hoping he'd make it easy on me by trying to kill me, try to escape, do anything to force me or Willy to act. Maybe he understood my predicament.

I had to choose between revenge and keeping those I loved safe or doing my duty. "This has to end right now." I probably wished more than commanded

Whether a conscious decision or not, I can't tell you. I heard the rifle discharge the single shot. But I know the weapon didn't fire itself. I had an impossible decision to make. Protecting Alene, Tess and maybe Dad won out.

The Proclamation

Alene watched the Presidential broadcast live from the green room where actors waited before their performances at the McKelligan Canyon Ampitheater. She arrived with Eric Holder and the President on Air Force One. She and Eric had been waiting in the green room for the broadcast to conclude. The closed door meetings were scheduled to take place there in just a few minutes.

She knew Jim and Willy were in El Paso, cooperating with the Secret Service but she had no knowledge of the events only a short distance away. She listened to President Obama first announce he and the President of Mexico would sign an amendment to the North American Free Trade Agreement. That didn't get her attention as the amendment was expected and discussed ad nauseum in the press.

But then he went on, "Based on historical precedents I'm making a proclamation today, backed by a series of Executive Orders resulting in a substantial change in our criminal laws. We have known for quite some time the US is the major market for illegal drugs in the Western Hemisphere. We're the reason why drug trafficking has grown in Mexico, and we illegally supply the weapons enabling the spiraling violence our neighbors to the south have experienced."

The President's statement caught Alene's attention and she thought of the meeting in his office with Jim. Had they had any impact on his decision? Why was he doing this now? Eric hadn't said a word about any of what he was announcing. It hadn't gone through the usual policy reviews, she knew for a fact.

"In our private talks, *El Presidente* and I have come to the conclusion the United States must help restore the rule of law in his country. And as I was recently reminded, the drugs we're discussing have been unlawful for much less time than they were legal in the history of our nation. If we change the economics of the drug trade, those who cause the violence won't survive. An associate recently labeled the cause as an arbitrary legal classification. He pointed out to me that if we change the classification we change America for the better. We face up to the kind of society we are. We realign freedom with responsibility. If parents and individuals have the responsibility rather than government the rest of us must hold everyone accountable.

"President Lincoln ended an earlier debate that raged for decades in just this manner. President Monroe addressed hemisphere security with a similar approach, issuing a doctrine much earlier in our history. As your President, I'm obligated to and must do what's right for America, for our neighbors in Mexico and to ensure the security of our hemisphere. The issue of drug illegality is bigger than one individual, even a president. The issue's the foundation for a society that reflects the strong spirit, and desire to engender freedom and prosperity for all.

"For these reasons I proclaim the citizens of our great nation will no longer be subject to prosecution for using certain drugs; the production and importation of such drugs will be regulated by the Federal government; the drugs will be available through properly licensed commercial establishments; our Food and Drug Administration will inspect the supplies and ensure they meet standards we shall set.

"I will enact Executive Orders establishing penalties for operating motor vehicles or machinery under the influence of any of the newly decriminalized drugs. We will also mandate the use of any of these drugs above certain strengths shall require the supervision of a physician and individuals dependent upon these drugs won't be eligible for Federal or state benefits.

"Further I'll sign executive orders making a Federal crime, punishable by a mandatory federal prison sentence, for anyone or any corporation transferring assault or military grade weapons of any kind, internationally without a State Department permit.

"I'm taking these actions now to stop the cycle of violence, help re-establish the rule of law in our neighboring country, begin the process of returning individual responsibility to the American people, and realign our resources to stress prevention and treatment over incarceration. I also hope we can rebalance our spending on education and our prison systems so our focus is on building a society of opportunity." Barak Obama turned to the man at his left.

"I will now ask the President Calderon of Mexico for his comments on these actions. He will also describe how we will work together to coordinate the implementation of these changes to our laws."

Alene called Jim's last known number trembling with excitement.

Reaction

Dominguez watched the broadcast from McKelligan Canyon with his newly installed leaders of the Zetas at his new ranch south of Matamoros. He'd been busy purging all of Castillo's other lieutenants. His plan was simple. He'd told each of his people who they'd replace as long as they killed the man they were replacing. All of the former lieutenants were now dead and Dominguez's team was in place. The strike had been quick. Had to be. He needed to prevent Castillo's people from organizing and deciding to pick someone else.

"Felipe. When was the Messenger supposed to take the shot?" Dominguez asked. Felipe was now head of Dominguez's security organization and sat across the room.

"He said when the President took the podium to respond to the US President."

"Isn't he taking the podium now?"

"Appears to be what he's doing."

"Why hasn't the Messenger taken the shot?"

"I don't know." Felipe answered as if afraid he'd be blamed.

Everyone watched the Mexican President's brief remarks and return the podium to President Obama.

"No shot." Dominguez voiced his anger. "What the fuck is going on? The Messenger takes those shots. He makes those shots. No one else can, but he does. So what happened?"

Felipe spoke up, "Shall I call him?"

"No. Wait 'til they've left the stage. He may've had to change his plans."

Everyone went quiet as they watched concluding remarks from President Obama. The cameras remained on as the two presidents left the stage to go to a private meeting. The US Ambassador to Mexico and the Mexican Ambassador to the US trailed the two presidents from the stage and were apparently joining the meeting about to commence.

Carlos, Dominguez's Mexico City lead spoke up. "Juan. What does it mean for us that Obama's changing the drug laws? Can he do that?"

"I don't know. Why didn't we know he was going to make changes?"

"Probably because Josephson, your White House source, is in jail." Carlos pointed out.

"But changes like this don't happen overnight. The changes must've been discussed before the FBI arrested him. Find out what you can. We need to know what they're doing." Dominguez directed Carlos.

"Got it."

"Who do we have in Washington now?" Dominguez knew but wanted to see how his team responded.

"Josephson was at the top, but he's gone. We got a few guys in Justice. Lower level. Don't know what they'll know, but I'm sure they'll get pulled in on the changes their president wants to make."

"We need to know fast. Can't let the other cartels get ahead of us in responding."

"Was Castillo meeting with the Sinaloa about these changes? Did he know?" Carlos asked.

"Don't think so. Castillo was trying to make an alliance against Guzman and the Juarez boys. He was petrified they'd come back after him after the Army raid on Ciudad Victoria."

Felipe spoke up, "From what I heard he had a right to be scared. Guzman's mounting something against us. Trying to hold onto the Meth routes we had to give up when the Army took down the Monterrey plant. Trying to take over more of the cocaine as well. He's still ranting about how we tried to kill him from what I hear."

"They've left the stage. No shot." Carlos noted.

"Felipe. Call the Messenger now. Find out why he didn't take the shot and then kill him. We're not going to get another opportunity. I can't accept failure when the stakes are this high."

Dominguez was sending a message to his whole team. Everyone would be held to the same standard. Failure wasn't acceptable. Dominguez was already well on his way to being more intolerant of failure than Castillo. The transformation was complete.

Second Conversation

I sat next to the two bodies. I'd called in and was waiting until the presidents left to get a pick up. I'd called Dan to tell him that the man who killed his parents was now also dead. Dan had only said 'Hello' and nothing more.

Hernandez-Anjul's cell rang. The number had a Mexican prefix. I waited for the call to go to voice mail. I wondered if this was Dominguez? I'd have answered, but I wanted to wait for the next discussion to come after I knew Dad's fate.

My cell rang. I checked and saw Alene's number. "Did you hear the President?"

"No, sorry, I've been a bit busy."

"He quoted you."

"What?" I couldn't believe what she just said.

"Proclamation. Decriminalizing certain narcotics."

I gazed over at McKelligan Canyon Amphitheater. I knew the President was still there. "When I had my one-on-one with Eric, he asked how our briefing to the President went. I wonder." I mused aloud. "Can we do dinner tonight?"

"What happened to slow?"

"I don't want to wait any more. I've waited my whole life to start a life."

She hesitated, but then decided. "If you do, one of us will have to leave the team."

"Bud's been after me to come back so he can get promoted."

"You said he'd be a disaster." She was playing with me now.

"Not as much as another day not being able to tell you how much I love you."

Night Lights

Alene and I took the late flight into Dallas Ft. Worth Airport. We were both tired and took a cab to her apartment.

"You coming in?" She asked as I offered her overnight bag.

"So much for slow."

She responded with a coy smile. I carried in both our bags.

Once inside the door, she threw her arms around my neck as our lips met with an almost electric shock. Her lips were soft and tender, slightly parted, inviting…..

I didn't want the kiss to end, but she didn't want to stand in the doorway either. She backed away, took my hand and led me into the apartment.

But now I felt her gentle pressure on my hand and finally realized she was here, we were both here.

Her one bedroom apartment on the eleventh floor overlooked the American Airlines Center in downtown Dallas. I saw the airport lights in the distance but in the darkness I couldn't see much else.

"The office should be over there." I pointed in a direction and she came right into me, holding me tighter than I could remember ever being held.

She leaned her head back waiting for me to kiss her. Our lips met eagerly and this time her slightly open mouth was greedy for me. I can't tell you how long the kiss lasted, nor can I tell you who broke off first.

I looked into her eyes and tried not to think of Lexie, but the feelings and emotions were so raw I needed a moment to get myself back into the present. I think I saw recognition in her reaction to me. Maybe she thought about her Intel officer who died in The Swat Valley. Maybe we were both dealing with all of the feelings we had denied to ourselves these past months while we worked together.

A short kiss and she pulled away, kicking off her shoes as she went toward her kitchen. "What kind of wine?"

"I'll trust your judgment."

"Why don't you trust my judgment at work?"

I came up beside her, put my arm around her and looked at the bottles in a small wine rack on her countertop. She had a half dozen bottles, none of which I recognized.

She selected one. "You'll find a corkscrew in the drawer next to the sink."

The bottle was a Purple Angel Carmenere from Montes in Chile. I did my manly thing, fought with the cork.

Pouring the wine into two glasses she produced from a cabinet, we then returned to the living room. As we were about to sit upon her couch I noticed a well-worn book upon her coffee table. The Kama Sutra. I was uncomfortable knowing she probably had a wider range of experience than I did. I leaned down and opened up to a certain page. "Haven't seen this since I was in college, the first time."

She laughed, "Ever try splitting of the bamboo?"

I shook my head, "Been a while since I had time to read."

She closed the book. "Thought we could get started by just

talking.

The evening was getting harder by the minute. "Easy for you to say. I'm not much for talkin'."

She kissed me again and talking became unnecessary.

We sat upon the couch overlooking the city lights. "To us." I said. She snuggled into me and I held her, looking out at the night time lights and wondering if this could be how the rest of my life would play out.

The Last Chance

Nick delivered as usual. He was able to trace the phone number Hernandez-Anjel called just before I killed him. He had a name from the phone company and location using GPS coordinates showing a street address in Saltillo, Mexico when the phone was used.

A tiny UAV flew over the address, capturing imagery of the building and those around on a quiet street. Dr. Tom modeled the street and house. By noon Zed led a small group of us through the most probable scenarios we could expect.

By afternoon an undercover Mexican Navy special operator wandered through the neighborhood, getting a first-hand lay of the land. In the Mexican military the need for the highly trained special operators had grown to the point they employed their version of the US Navy Seals to help in the war against the cartels.

Saltillo lay so far inland few from the area ever thought of a naval career. The chosen person was an exception. He grew up in town. He'd been a soccer star on the high school team. He told folks he'd come home and joined the family business with his brothers selling building repairs like roofing jobs, putting up new siding, installing concrete walks, kitchen remodels, interior painting and so forth.

He got inside some of the surrounding buildings and memorized the layouts. Some of the owners let him take pictures to provide an estimate. He went to the building in question; but no one answered the door. He didn't expect to get lucky. But having been inside several houses on the street by six p.m., he made a pretty educated guess as to what we'd find inside.

Several hours later Alene saw me off at Ft. Bliss. Willy stood with his back to us to give us privacy as the MH-47 loaded.

"Just another step in the long road." She tried to lower my expectations.

"If he's there I'll bring him back."

"Don't get careless. I need you to come back as you are."

I shook my head, "You need me to come back ready to move on."

As much as I wanted closure, I didn't expect to come back with all the answers I needed. I kept telling myself Dad was probably dead. This mission was probably just running down the last warm clue we'd have for a very long time with the demise of Hernandez-Anjul. I also thought that Dominguez may have intervened, killed or moved Dad and set up an ambush for me. Just hard to know how it would play.

Alene kissed my cheek, squeezed my arm and watched me board the helicopter.

Saltillo

By one a.m. no lights illuminated the street.

I'd been unusually quiet. I made no jokes, no observations and asked no questions. Everyone around me must have understood what I felt. We quietly moved into position for the raid. The team was intuitive about what would be needed to succeed.

What I felt preparing for the mission I'd envisioned as I left the Triple C so many weeks before has been lost to me. Waiting to go in was just so hard. I felt the wall around my heart taking abuse from inside. But I wouldn't open the door. Couldn't open the door. Not yet.

I knew that the men in the house might know Captain Morales had dropped off their grid. No one had heard from him in at least a couple of days. I could only hope they didn't know he intended to assassinate the Mexican President. They would be well aware he failed if they did.

I thought Dad might be in the building, unless his captors had orders to move him after the failed assassination. To say the least, I wasn't confident I'd walk out of Saltillo with anything more than another riddle to solve.

Major Guerrera gave the hand signal to put his team into action. We breached simultaneously through front and back doors and two windows. I followed Zed in through the back door, expecting the *sicarios* would want to get out the back.

I wasn't disappointed. Three men practically ran into our arms, realized they had no chance to escape, dropped their weapons and raised their hands over their heads.

A brief exchange of gunfire was heard from the front of the house. I realized some of the shots were coming from upstairs. The occupants of the house must have been engaged at the stairwell.

Guerrera's Special Operators took the prisoners out the back door.

Zed led the way to the center of the house with Willy following directly behind. I hung back covering the rear in case someone decided to come in behind us. When we reached the stairwell we found four of Guerrera's men exchanging gunfire with someone up on the second level.

I cleared each room on one side of the first floor. Willy took the other.

Zed joined Guerrera's men. In only a moment the gunfire ended.

As I came back into the hallway I heard the pounding of boots as the Special Operators started up the stairs.

And then I heard the yell, "Grenade!"

I dove backwards into the kitchen just before the explosion. I avoided most but not all of the shrapnel. I felt myself peppered in my buttocks, legs and arms.

By the time I was back up on my feet I saw two Mexican Army dead at the foot of the stairwell. Zed came back into the hall and rushed up the stairs, laying down short bursts of suppression fire.

He was at the top of the stairs before anyone else started up. I heard him call out, "Stairwell clear! Get your asses up here!"

I approached the stairwell cautiously, checked the third level above Zed, saw no movement. I took the stairs two at a time.

On the next level, I found the two Zeta *sicarios* Zed had taken out on his way up, lying on each side of the stairs.

I checked to make sure they were dead. I then covered Zed. We went room to room, covering each other, clearing each and checking for any sign of Dad.

Nothing I found gave me any indication Dad might be or had been there.

We found clothing and stuff the cartel members kept like magazines and iPod players, a whole lot of ammunition and backup weapons.

Coming out after clearing the last room, Willy and Colonel Blum covered the stairwell to the third floor along with Major Guerrera and three others.

I gave them a hand motion to stay put and took the stairs, again, two at a time.

This was the end of the line for me.

If Dad wasn't here and none of the men we took prisoner could give me any more information, then I had to assume he was indeed dead. The realization weighed heavily on me. I told myself ever since his one call they'd probably killed him. But I didn't believe he was dead. My rationalizations had been a means of coping. But I'd never given up the hope I'd find him alive and rescue him. And now I realized I'd finally have to abandon hope. I'd need to find a way of moving on with whatever remained of my life.

I had my M-4 up and ready to shoot as I broached the top of the stairs.

Checking 360 degrees around, I found only three rooms.

I went to the room to my left.

The door wasn't latched. I pushed it open a tad…

No response.

I pushed the door wide open with my left hand. My right hand supported the M-4 with my finger on the trigger.

I found a bare room, without any furniture, window curtains or anything on the walls or floor.

No other doors, like for a closet or entrance to a bathroom.

I realized the center room must be the bathroom serving two bedrooms. Coming back into the hallway I cautiously pushed open the middle room door and confirmed my suspicions.

After stepping inside, I checked the shower to make sure no one hid there. I checked the linen closet and found it also bare. The room appeared as if nothing had been stored and seldom, if ever used.

My expectations fell again. I doubted I'd find anything in the other bedroom; but went through the motions anyway.

I pushed the final room door open just a tad; saw this room had been used.

Slowly pushing the door open the rest of the way, I saw a mattress on the floor in a corner under the window. I saw someone lying on the mattress with his back to me, but couldn't tell who.

Approaching cautiously as I came closer I saw Dad.

My first thought was to go to him, but then the bells Zed and Colonel Blum had worked so hard to install in my head started ringing.

I checked around the room.

This room had a closet. The door was closed. I advanced as quietly as I could, wearing combat boots on a bare hard wood floor.

I touched the handle.

The door burst open and two .45 caliber slugs exploded into my chest armor from about two feet away.

The impact of the bullets threw me backwards across the room.

Dazed, I brought up my M-4, triggered two shots just as another .45 caliber bullet painfully slammed into my body armor on my left shoulder near my face.

The man in the closet slumped over.

Colonel Blum entered in a crouch. He put two bullets into the head of the man hiding in the closet. Blum crossed the room, visually checked the dead man and did a final visual scan to make sure the room was secure.

He then approached me and extended a hand to help me up. I waived him off and crawled over to the mattress.

I touched Dad's shoulder very gently, "Dad? It's Jim."

He didn't move. "Dad??"

I removed my helmet and gloves and felt my father's carotid artery.

I looked up at Blum with tears streaming down my face. I said in a voice so raw I didn't recognize it as mine, "He's alive."

Sun Rise

Dad suffered from malnutrition and dehydration, but was up and on his feet again in about a week. He insisted on moving to his grandson Dan's two bedroom apartment in Fort Worth, even though I heard all the bells in my head telling me not to let him. He won out telling me nothing scared him anymore. Just the same we have Sunday dinner together every week.

I asked to return to the FBI Dallas office and my request was granted with deep regret. Soon after my return the Dallas office was deemed to be ready for a new Special Agent in Charge. Bud was promoted as I anticipated. What I didn't expect was that I was put in charge as his replacement. I guess someone got the brilliant idea that if I was in the office filing reports and talking all day with the guys in the head shed I couldn't very well be out killin' the bad guys. Now since killin' the bad guys was what I thought they wanted me to do, I was mystified by their logic and not for the first time.

Alene kept her job as the Rapid Reaction Force lead, since she had foiled the plot against both presidents; at least that was how it was officially classified. I wasn't about to make anyone think differently since it meant Alene probably had lifetime tenure. I was all for helping her stay in government as long as she wanted to. Although I wasn't crazy about her new Ops director, Josh Washburne, a hot shit golden boy from Washington, who'd never killed anyone, personally. I tried to warn her. She said something about having used up all the good will she had on me and she needed to make the guys back in the district think she was a team player. I didn't buy that argument and tried to get her to look at Mike Garrido. She pointed out that Mike had no political pull. She needed someone who had respect back in the district.

She'd never told me about how difficult it had been to keep everyone in line when no one thought I could pull off the assignment. She's an amazing woman and I'm just beginning to appreciate her.

I gave up my apartment since hers was nicer. We bought a wine rack that held twelve bottles. We're going to consume a lot more wine between us than she had alone. Something about those night lights and the altitude make me appreciate her particular attributes even more than when they were inaccessible to me. Maybe seeing her as I had that first night in that same apartment freed up the inhibitions I'd imposed on myself. Maybe she relaxed hers as well. Whatever it is, I've come to appreciate her in a way I could never have imagined. Now that has happened, I'm happier than I've been since another green eyed temptress first stole my heart and made life worth living. But that was before events spun my world out of its predictable orbit. Even now I wonder about Juan Dominguez and when he'll pop back up and change everything for me once more.

After a month of missing persons, bank robberies, counter terrorism and our new life I came home to find Alene waiting for me with a Montes Purple Angel. "What's this?"

"The President asked me to stay on for his second term."

Just as a night months before, the wine was great, she was phenomenal, but she still hadn't convinced me to try to 'split the bamboo'

About the Author

dhtreichler toured the global garden spots as a defense contractor executive for fifteen years. His assignments covered intelligence, training and battlefield systems integrating state of the art technology to keep Americans safe. During this time he authored seven novels exploring the role of increasingly sophisticated technology in transforming our lives and how men and women establish relationships in a mediated world.

Keep up with all of dhtreichler's latest work and essays at www.dhtreichler.com.

Also by dhtreichler

The Ghost in the Machine: a novel

Life After

The Tragic Flaw

Succession

The End Game

I Believe in You

Rik's

The Illustrated Bearmas Reader – Ralph's Ordeals

The First Bearmas

38028151R00234

Made in the USA
Middletown, DE
09 March 2019